OUTSTANDING PRAISE FOR KLEMPNER AND...

P9-BYV-185

"In the form of a crackling thriller, *Felony Murder* explores the murky areas of right and wrong when the cops become a law unto themselves. The perfect antidote to the glittery world of the O. J. Simpson case, it takes you through the tawdry, real-life criminal justice system where you cannot tell the cops from the crooks."
— William Kunstler and Ronald L. Kuby, Attorneys-at-Law

"For four years now you've been hearing that every new legal thriller is just like John Grisham. Well, Klempner does write just like Grisham. St. Martin's should sell this first novel with a money-back guarantee."
— *Kirkus Reviews*

"Joe Klempner has made good use of his background both as an investigator and a criminal defense attorney—but it's his skill as a storyteller that makes this a book you can't put down. He's got a winner here."
— The Hon. Edwin Torres, State Supreme Court Justice and author of *Carlito's Way*

"Klempner is not only a good writer, he teaches you things about the courts and the criminal justice system you'll find nowhere else."
— Robert Leuci, author of *Fence Jumpers*

"An enjoyable, deliberately unsteady ride with just enough twists, turns, bumps and potholes to keep the reader interested, focused and clinging to the pages that will reveal the solution at the final destination."
— *New York Law Journal*

"This first novel will provide plenty of fun for conspiracy thriller fans."
— *Ellery Queen Magazine*

FELONY MURDER

JOSEPH T. KLEMPNER

St. Martin's Paperbacks

NOTE: If you purchased this book without a cover you should be aware that this book is stolen property. It was reported as "unsold and destroyed" to the publisher, and neither the author nor the publisher has received any payment for this "stripped book."

FELONY MURDER

Copyright © 1995 by Joseph T. Klempner.

All rights reserved. No part of this book may be used or reproduced in any manner whatsoever without written permission except in the case of brief quotations embodied in critical articles or reviews. For information address St. Martin's Press, 175 Fifth Avenue, New York, N.Y. 10010.

Library of Congress Catalog Card Number: 95-21087

ISBN: 0-312-96037-9

Printed in the United States of America

St. Martin's Press hardcover edition/September 1995
St. Martin's Paperbacks edition/September 1996

10 9 8 7 6 5 4 3 2 1

To Alan, who is with me still.

ACKNOWLEDGMENTS

Many thanks to Larry Denson for his toxicological expertise; to Mike Wittman for long hours of printing assistance; to Seth Rothman for getting the manuscript read; to my agent, Bob Diforio, and my editor, Ruth Cavin, for their loyalty and support; to my three children, Wendy, Ron, and Tracy, for their early encouragement; to the various judges, lawyers, and other court personnel who have permitted me to borrow their lives and populate these pages with them; and to my wife, Sandy, for rekindling my fire to write after many years.

FELONY MURDER

A person is guilty of murder ... when ... he commits or attempts to commit robbery, burglary, kidnapping, arson, rape in the first degree, sodomy in the first degree, sexual abuse in the first degree, aggravated sexual abuse, escape in the first degree, or escape in the second degree, and, in the course of and in furtherance of such crime or of immediate flight therefrom, he ... causes the death of a person.

New York Penal Law
Section 125.25(3)

ONE

Joey Spadafino is cold. Cold and wet. He huddles in the doorway and shifts his weight from one foot to the other, trying to wriggle his toes inside his shoes to keep them from becoming numb. His breath sends the snowflakes scattering from in front of his face as they pick up the lights of Bleecker Street.

It's not the coldest night he has spent on the street, but it's already the worst. Unlike rain, which Joey has found comes pretty much straight down and allows you to get out of by taking refuge in a doorway, snow blows sideways. In fact, it now seems to Joey that the snow sometimes blows up, like it's coming from underneath the street. And it's not a dry snow that you can shake off you. It's these big, wet flakes that seem to be made out of melting ice, that make your clothing wet as soon as they land on you and soak the soles of your shoes.

Joey has no watch, but he knows it's well after midnight. He slept for an hour or so earlier, but he's afraid to fall asleep again. He's heard stories of people on the street freezing to death in their sleep 'cause they got cold and wet and stopped moving, and got found dead the next morning. So he keeps moving his feet, keeps wriggling his toes, concentrates on making it through the night.

Joey thinks about lighting another cigarette. He scored two dollars from a lady walking a dog early in the evening, when the snow was just starting. She'd asked him didn't he have a place to go to get out of the snow, and he'd said no, he was afraid of the shelters, which was true, and she'd reached into her purse and taken out two dollars, which she'd handed to him. He'd thought about snatching the purse and taking off with it, but he hadn't done it, hadn't had the nerve. He had thanked her instead. It was a big dog she was walking, anyway.

He'd taken the two dollars and bought a pack of cigarettes. He'd figured the cigarettes would get him through the night better than a slice of pizza would have. They'd last longer, they'd occupy him more. But by now he's smoked half the pack, and his mouth tastes like a goddamn ashtray, and his stomach's empty, and he wishes he had the slice of pizza.

The meeting had broken up at 0230. If you could call it a meeting. The Police Commissioner, his two deputies, Pacelli and Childress, and Chief Inspector Haber, who headed up Internal Affairs. They had sat in the corner table at Chandler's, gradually substituting good whiskey for mediocre food, and talking about the old days. It had been Pacelli's idea that they meet, the First Dep saying they needed to talk about restructuring the patrol force in the wake of another round of anticipated budget cuts. But talk had soon turned to the days when a cop could be a cop instead of a public relations expert, and how respect for the uniform was a thing of the past, and how overconcern for minorities was destroying morale. The last was a somewhat delicate topic, since the PC himself was black, and the meeting had broken up shortly thereafter, to a glass-draining toast to the days when dinosaurs patrolled the streets.

The brass had split up outside, shaking hands and slapping backs under the streetlamps in the gusting snow. Santana, the PC's chauffeur, had the motor running in the Department auto, and it was warm inside, too warm.

"Turn the heat down, willya?" the PC said, sitting down next to his driver. He refused to ride in the back.

"Yessir," said Santana, reaching forward and fumbling with a dial on the dashboard. But if he did anything about it, it didn't seem to help. The PC reached to loosen his tie, but it was already undone. He felt like he might vomit. Had he drunk that much? Was he getting the flu, like so many of his men? He tried to crack his window open, but the automatic control seemed to respond to his commands too quickly. Unable to stop it at opening just a bit, he settled for leaving it half open, with snowflakes blowing into the car and over him.

"Home, sir?"

"Yes, home," the PC said.

Santana drove carefully through Midtown, down to the Village, toward the Bleecker Street townhouse. He slowed for the red lights before taking them, skidding slightly each time he accelerated again. The snow seemed trapped in the beam of the headlights. They were about to take the turn onto Bleecker when the PC said, "Pull over. I'll get out here and walk the block. I can use the air."

"You sure, sir?"

"Yes, I'm sure."

Santana pulled to the curb. The PC thanked him for the ride and stepped out into the snow, slamming the door behind him. Santana waited and watched the PC turn up his collar and begin the walk across Bleecker Street. Then he pulled away from the curb and continued down Seventh Avenue.

At the moment he first notices the man whose death will so profoundly affect his own life, Joey Spadafino is playing a game with himself, attempting to keep warm. He's trying to think of the hottest place he's ever been. Not just like Rockaway Beach in August, when the sand gets so hot in the afternoon it can burn the soles of your feet, but places like that elevator in the Polo Grounds Projects Joey had got stuck in between floors for an hour and a half, or the place behind the big boiler in P.S. 6 where he and Chico used to get high.

When he sees the man walking toward the doorway where he's huddled, Joey's first thought is that the guy's drunk. A black man, taller than Joey and heavier. But old, must be sixty. Well dressed, an expensive-looking overcoat. And totally wasted. Walking with his head down, weaving back and forth. Every several steps he seems to sort of misjudge the height of the pavement, so his foot strikes it before he thinks it's going to, and each time he's got to correct himself and find his rhythm all over again.

Joey looks up and down the block. Empty. The falling snow acts like an early-warning system. The flakes would light up from the headlights of a car pulling into the block, even before the headlights themselves come into view. Nothing.

In seconds the man's going to pass by him. If he wants to, Joey can take this guy off easy. He holds his breath, feels his pulse pound in his chest. He raises himself up slightly on the balls of his feet, becomes taller, more menacing. The guy's fifteen feet away, ten feet, five. . . .

Janet Killian had just put her baby daughter down in her crib following what was supposed to have been her two o'clock feeding, although it was actually more like two-thirty. While she sometimes envied those mothers whose babies slept through the night from the moment they came home from the hospital, the truth was she kind of liked nursing Nicole in the quiet darkness of the early morning. It was perhaps their closest time together. Janet Killian was a single mother, a working single mother, and quiet time with her daughter was a precious commodity, even if it was a commodity that came at the price of sleeping through the night.

She pulled the blanket over the baby's shoulders, felt the warmth of the tiny back, already rising and falling in the regular breathing of sleep. She walked to the window to see if it was still snowing.

Drawing the curtain back, Janet watched the flakes blowing by, catching the streetlight. The sidewalk had turned white, although the snow had a slushy look to it, rather than the powdery appearance of her Midwestern memories. Then, across the street, something commanded her attention. A man, kneeling, bent over something in the snow. She squinted to see better, cupped her hands around her face to shield off any light from within the apartment. The something, she realized, was another person, another man, lying on his side on the pavement. And the first man was now going through the fallen man's pockets.

"Hey," Janet said, but in keeping her voice quiet so as not to wake her baby, it came out as little more than a whisper against the window glass. She reached for the phone, heard a dial tone, hesitated, then forced herself to dial 911. She continued to watch the man going through the other man's pockets, now taking something, now holding it up to the light.

"Emergency Operator Twenty-three," a woman's voice was saying. "May I help you?"

"Yes," said Janet. "I'm watching a crime" was all she could think of.

"What sort of crime, ma'am?"

"A robbery, I guess, a mugging."

"Where is this occurring, ma'am?"

"Right across the street," said Janet. "Across from Seventy-seven Bleecker Street."

"What are the cross streets, ma'am?"

"What?" Janet did not understand. The first man had stood up now. It looked like he was standing on the fallen man, or straddling him.

"Seventy-seven Bleecker Street, ma'am," the woman's voice was saying. "What streets is that between?"

"Oh," said Janet. "Sixth and Seventh."

"Sixth and Seventh," the woman repeated. "Ma'am, I'm going to ask you to hold on a moment. What's your phone number, in case we get disconnected?"

But Janet was now staring into the face of the standing man, who was looking directly up at her. She lowered the phone to her side, hearing "Ma'am? Ma'am? Ma'am?" continuing to come from it. She could see that he was a white man, and young. She could see him look away from her window, to what must be another window. Now he stepped back from the fallen man, looked down at him, and backed away farther.

"Ma'am? Ma'am?" The voice was still coming from the phone at her side. The young man started walking toward the corner, slowly at first, then faster. . . .

"Hey, get away from him!" Joey's suddenly aware of a man's voice somewhere above him, aware of lights coming from windows in the building behind him. And across the street a woman in a window is staring at him.

"Shit," Joey says. He looks at the wad of bills held together in a money clip, thinks of dropping the money, pockets it instead. Fighting the impulse to run, he starts walking toward Seventh Avenue, muttering "Shit, shit, shit, shit" over and over.

When he seems to be getting no closer to the corner, he breaks into a jog, concentrating on not losing his footing on the snow. At the corner, he turns uptown, dropping back into a fast walk. But there are cars, and the oncoming headlights light up the front of his body. He turns around, begins walking downtown, hears the first siren off in the distance. Tries to concentrate on what he's got here, tries to think. Fingers the wad of bills in his pocket, feels the money clip, slips it off, and palms it in his pocket.

The siren's getting louder. Joey cocks his head, trying to locate it. Thinks at first it's coming from his right, then from downtown, from in front of him. He considers turning around again, but is afraid to.

At the corner, he walks close by a wire trash can and drops the money clip in. An alley appears on his right, and he turns into it. But a noise from the blackness startles him, and he's back on Seventh with the siren getting louder. He breaks into a jog again, a run. . . .

TWO

A glance in his calendar book reminded Dean Abernathy that today was the day he was supposed to call the Assigned Counsel Office to see if they had any assigned cases they wanted him to handle. They had called him Friday after he'd already left for the day, and left a message on his answering machine. The cases didn't pay much, since the hourly rates he had to bill for at the end of each case were so low, but private criminal cases were hard to come by in these times. Besides, it was better to be busy than to sit around.

Still, it was only nine o'clock Monday morning, and there might not be anyone in the Assigned Counsel Office yet. So Dean assembled the files he would need in court that morning and reviewed each one before putting them in his briefcase. Run-of-the-mill stuff. A "buy and bust" drug sale to an undercover cop, where they had caught the defendant five minutes later with "stash" (more drugs packaged identically to those sold) and "cash" (the prerecorded money the undercover cop had used to buy the drugs). A DWI for whom Dean would try to get a reduced plea, from Intoxicated to Impaired, so he could at least get a provisional license to drive to and from his job. A guy who had thrown a plate at his girlfriend because she rejected the dinner he cooked for her and instead fed it to their dog. Dean snapped the briefcase shut and put on his scarf and coat. It had snowed last night, and the walk to court would be a cold one.

On a chance, he dialed the number of the Assigned Counsel Office. It rang three times. He would give it four.

"Assigned Counsel," said a woman's voice.

"Hi, this is Dean Abernathy. Someone called me late Friday about taking a couple of cases, and I'm returning the call."

"What panel are you on?"

"Felony," Dean answered.

"Let me see," she said. Then, "No, nothing at the moment. They must have found somebody to take those."

"No problem," Dean said.

"You're not on the Homicide Panel, are you?"

"Yes, I am." The Homicide Panel was made up of the most experienced criminal defense lawyers who took court-appointed cases. It paid no more than the other panels, but membership on it carried a bit of prestige, a rare commodity indeed in the Criminal Court Building.

"Well, Judge Mogel just called from AR-1. He's going to need someone this morning on the Wilson murder. Are you interested?"

"Wilson murder?" Dean was embarrassed to say he didn't know who Wilson was or what the Wilson murder was.

"Don't you listen to the news?"

"I guess not." The truth was, Dean confined his radio listening to the weather and the traffic. Television was for sports and movies. In court, he'd read the *Times* folded behind the lid of his open briefcase in order to catch up on the news.

"Police Commissioner Wilson was murdered. Died during a mugging."

"Wow," said Dean, slowly and stupidly.

"Do you want it?"

Reflexively, "Yeah, sure."

"Okay," she said. "I don't have a docket number yet, but the defendant's name is Joseph Spadafino, S-P-A-D-A-F-I-N-O. He's twenty-eight, and he's being arraigned this morning in AR-1."

"Very good," said Dean, having no idea yet if it was very good or not, still digesting the fact that the Police Commissioner had been killed. "Thanks." He hung up the phone, took a blank manila file folder from a box, and wrote the name JOSEPH SPADAFINO on it. He added it to the files in his briefcase and headed for court.

One Hundred Centre Street, the Criminal Court Building. If our prisons are terrible places because we want them to be, thought Dean Abernathy as he entered the revolving door, then our courthouses are designed to be almost as bad, a sort of preview of coming attractions. Poorly lit, filthy, noisy, overcrowded, smoke-infested, too cold in the winter, too hot in the summer. It was as if they were kept that way intentionally, to prepare the defendants and their families alike for what the next step, prison, would be like, to soften the shock of what lay in store.

He flashed his attorney ID at the court officer, who permitted Dean to bypass the line at the metal detector. He wound his way through defendants, police officers, jurors, court personnel, and others to the rear of the first-floor lobby, to the felony arraignment part known as AR-1. He pushed his way through the double doors and saw that Judge Mogel was already on the bench, waiting for cases to be called.

Murray Mogel's chronic poor health made him look older than his sixty-six years. To most, he was a cynical, sarcastic man who had little patience for prosecutors or defense lawyers. To Dean, who had known Mogel since the days they had both been Legal Aid lawyers, Mogel was indeed cynical and sarcastic. But his cynicism was even-handed: he disbelieved police officers with the same disdain that he disbelieved defendants, with the result, as most defense attorneys knew, that he was a good judge to waive a jury in front of and take one's chances with. Not that that mattered today, when Mogel, as the arraignment judge, would simply be setting bail and an adjourned date on defendants making their first appearance in court since their arrests. And in Dean's case, in the case of the *People of the State of New York v. Joseph Spadafino*, there would be no bail, since there seldom was in murder cases.

"Come up, Mr. Abernathy." Judge Mogel had spotted Dean and, characteristically, did not wait for Dean to ask to approach the bench. Dean unhooked the chain that separated the audience portion of the courtroom from the well, where the participants stood, and walked up to the bench.

"Good morning, Judge."

"Hello, Dean." Judge Mogel extended his hand, and Dean shook it. It was thin and cold from the circulatory problems that came with a bad heart. "I hear you've been assigned to the Wilson case."

Dean nodded, not missing the nuance that the case, in which the deceased was a well-known public figure and the defendant an unknown citizen, had taken on the name of the victim.

"Well, the papers aren't ready yet, but your client's inside." Judge Mogel waved vaguely in the direction of the door to the holding pen, which contained prisoners waiting for their arraignments. "Talk to him and let me know if you have any objection to the TV cameras. They've made a request for a pool camera." This time Judge Mogel waved toward the far side of the courtroom.

Dean turned and saw a dozen or so people huddled in groups of three and four. They were unmistakably press: technicians with headsets and wires and rolls of duct tape; well-dressed men and women who fussed with their hair or neckties. Dean now recalled seeing an *Eyewitness News* van parked on the sidewalk outside, its antenna expanded to full height. This was the show today.

"Who's handling it for the DA's Office?" he asked.

"Walter Bingham. Good man," Judge Mogel added. "Know him?"

"Yeah, he's okay." Walter Bingham was one of the senior trial assistants in the New York County District Attorney's Office. He was pleasant enough, easy to talk to, and a pretty fair seat-of-the-pants lawyer whose good looks and imposing height didn't hurt him, and who had a nice way with a jury. If Dean had any reservations about Bingham, it concerned his somewhat narrow view of what information a prosecutor was required to share with the defense. More than once, Dean recalled, Bingham had been slow to turn over some document or reveal some small bit of evidence that contradicted his theory of proof.

Dean stepped back from the bench, left the well area, and walked to the front row of seats reserved for lawyers and police officers. He folded his coat, put it on one of the empty seats. There was no such thing as a coatrack here. He placed his inexpensive briefcase on top of his coat, leaving it unlatched so that if someone reached over from the second row to try to steal his coat, the briefcase would fall to the floor, spilling its contents and serving as an alarm. This was Criminal Court, after all: there were criminals around.

Dean took out his Department of Corrections pass and headed to the holding pen. He was stopped in his tracks by Mike Pearl, the veteran courthouse reporter from the *Post.*

"I hear you're representing Spadafino," said Pearl.

"I guess so," Dean said.

"Anything you can tell me about him? You know, criminal record, family, personal stuff. Anything."

"Mike, I haven't even met the guy yet. You know as much as I do."

"I hear he's got a prior robbery."

"You see," Dean said, "you know *more* than I do."

Dean found Joseph Spadafino sitting alone in the farthest pen, the one usually reserved for prisoners the corrections officers kept segregated from the main bullpen of adult males. At various times of the day or night it was used for females, youths, homos (Corrections' stubbornly archaic term for gays and transvestites), and "obsos" (mentally disturbed prisoners who needed special observation). And celebrities, high-profile prisoners whose notoriety required extra precautions. Joseph Spadafino was a celebrity.

"Mr. Spadafino?"

"Yeah."

"My name is Dean Abernathy, and I'm the lawyer who's going to be representing you. Hang on to this." Dean handed him a business card. The prisoner studied it, then read from it.

"Ab-er-ath—"

"Abernathy. Call me Dean. That's easier. What do they call you?"

"Joey."

"Okay, Joey, nice to meet you." Dean extended his hand, and the two men shook. Dean figured shaking hands with inmates cost him four colds a year. In the age of AIDS, hepatitis B, and drug-resistant strains of TB, it was a practice most of his colleagues had abandoned. But Dean would be damned if he was going to start off an interview by creating more distance between himself and his client. There was enough to begin with.

He looked at Joey Spadafino. Small, several inches shorter than Dean's own five-eleven. Skinny, no more than 135 pounds. Handsome once, probably, but it looked like his features had sort of given way somewhere along the line. A nose that had been broken more than once. Curly brown hair that looked dull and dirty. A fair share of scars, scabs, cuts, and bruises, some old, some fresh. Bloodshot eyes peering out from dark sockets, suggesting he had been awake for a good forty-eight hours. And a faint but decidedly putrid smell that seemed to come in alternating waves of unwashed body odor, stale cigarette smoke, and something else Dean could not quite identify.

Nice overall impression.

"Excuse me, Counselor," came a voice from behind Dean, who turned to see a uniformed court officer at the door. "The papers have come up. This is your copy." He handed Dean a folded set of papers. Dean thanked him, and he left.

"Okay, this is good," Dean said to Joey, "we can go over these and see what they're saying.

"This yellow cover means you're being charged with a felony. You know what that is—a crime that you could get state time for, more than a year. This," Dean said, turning to the first page of the stapled packet, "is the complaint. The important part of it says"— his eyes scanned over the legalese and focused on the charges and factual allegations—"that, according to Detective Zysmanski of the Manhattan South Homicide Division, this morning, at approximately two-forty A.M. in front of Seventy-six Bleecker Street, you committed the crimes of murder in the second degree, robbery in the second degree, and robbery in the third degree, under the following circumstances: Zysmanski is informed by persons whose name and addresses are known to the District Attorney that, by means of physical force or threat, you removed personal property and United States currency from Edward Wilson, and that during the commission of the crime or the immediate flight therefrom, Edward Wilson, who was not a perpetrator, died. And it says," Dean added, "that you made statements."

"I didn't kill anybody, Mr. Aba—"

"Dean. And I know that. At least I know they're not even saying that you did. What they're saying is that you were robbing him, and he happened to die of a heart attack while you were robbing him."

"That's different," Joey said.

"Well, it is and it isn't," Dean said, smiling in what he hoped was a kind way, even if the lesson was about to be a cruel one. "But first, this business about the statements. What did you tell them?"

"I told them what happened, that I took his money, yeah, but I didn't hurt him or nuthin'. I mean he was drunk, real drunk. He just kinda fell down. So I took his money. But I didn' *kill* him, I didn' *murder* him!"

"Who'd you tell this to?"

"Jesus, everybody who asked me. Lissen, I ain't got nuthin' to hide here. I took the fuckin' money. But I didn' *kill* nobody, they know that." Joey held his hands out, palms upward.

"Who's everybody, Joey? Who did you tell? Uniform guys? Detectives?"

"Detectives, yeah. Lots of 'em."

"Did they give you your rights?"

"No. Yeah. I dunno. Later, yeah."

Dean suppressed a smile at the multiple-choice answer, asked instead, "Later, did a tall guy from the DA's Office show up?"

"Yeah. Guy with a mustache." That would be Bingham.

"Did they videotape it?"

"Yeah."

"Okay," Dean took a deep breath. "You want the bad news or the bad news?"

"All's I got is bad news." Joey looked down at his shoes. Dean's eyes followed. The laces had been removed as a precaution.

"I'm afraid so. First, of course, the guy was the Police Commissioner. Second is the felony murder rule. We'll be talking about that a lot, but basically what it says is that if I'm committing a certain felony, and the victim dies during it for any reason—heart attack, accident, runs into a car, shoots himself trying to defend himself, gets shot by a cop, *whatever*—I'm guilty of murder."

"That's not fair."

"Life isn't always fair," Dean said, without wondering if the rule was fair or not. "It's the rule." Then, "We'll be in front of the judge in a few minutes. All that will happen is he's going to remand you—there won't be any bail set—and give us a date next week. They'll be presenting the case to the grand jury, which is going to indict you. The next time we come to court it'll be upstairs, in Supreme Court, where we'll plead not guilty. In the meantime, I'll be investigating the case, trying to find out as much as I can. If you like, I can have you brought over before next week, so we can sit down together and talk more. Would you like that?"

Joey nodded mechanically.

"Okay. In the meantime, there's a couple of things I want you to do. Number one, most important, *keep your mouth shut.* You've done enough talking already. This is a big case. There's a lot of guys in here would like nothing better than to hear you say something about the case, then drop a dime on you to help themselves. So *nothing.* Understand?"

Another nod.

"Next, can you read and write?" It was a precaution Dean had adopted after an embarrassed defendant had reluctantly admitted to being illiterate only after Dean had pressed him repeatedly to write down his account of his arrest. The illiteracy had in turn undermined the credibility of the arresting officer, who had claimed that the defendant had read a confession written out by the officer before signing his name to it. But Dean had almost missed it.

"Yeah," said Joey.

"Well, get hold of some paper and a pencil, and in the next day or two, write down everything that happened. That day before the incident, the incident itself, the arrest, everything that happened at the precinct, everything until you met me. Can you do that?"

"Yeah."

"I want as much detail as possible. It's just for us, for the next time we meet, before you start forgetting things. Don't lose it. Don't show it to anybody but me. Okay?"

"Yeah." Joey probably had not been very good with homework assignments in school, Dean decided, so he would not hold his breath. But it was worth a try. Sometimes little details remembered shortly after an arrest became pivotal months later at trial.

"Next thing," Dean said, "the television people are out there. They've asked the judge for permission to have a camera in the courtroom. He has to let them. The best I can do is to strike a deal so that nothing prejudicial gets said in front of the cameras, like your record. Okay?"

A nod.

"Do you have any people?" Dean asked. "Anybody out there you want me to try to get in touch with for you?"

"Yeah. No, not really." Multiple choice again. "I got a mother and a sister somewhere. But I been on the street. I've sorta lost contact, you know what I mean." It was not a question.

"On the street, like homeless?"

"Yeah."

"How bad is your sheet?" Dean turned in the packet of papers to the computer printout of the defendant's criminal record. It was several pages long.

"Not that bad," said Joey. Dean had once asked a fortyish prostitute the same question and got the same answer. Her printout had showed 122 arrests in the past five years.

"Been upstate?"

"One time." Joey nodded. "Two to four for a sale."

It was Dean's turn to nod. A sale meant drugs. Two to four years was a sentence reserved for second felony offenders. So Joey Spadafino had at least two prior felony convictions behind him, no family to speak of, no home. He had admitted on videotape to robbing the victim and, thanks to the felony murder rule, had thereby admitted to murdering him. And the victim just happened to be the very popular Police Commissioner of the City of New York. Not bad for starters.

Back in the courtroom it had become standing room only. Police brass, beefed-up court security, more press, and the just plain curious had come to see who had mugged the Police Commissioner and caused his death. Dean spotted Walter Bingham, the Assistant District Attorney who had taken the videotaped statement from Joey and who would be prosecuting him. As Dean neared him, he saw Bingham had not shaved.

"Hello, Walter," Dean said. "Looks like you spent the night at the precinct."

"Yeah, thanks to your client. How've you been, Dean?"

"Okay."

"Mr. Abernathy, Mr. Bingham, please step up," Judge Mogel was calling from the bench. As they approached, the courtroom hushed as spectators strained to hear what would be said.

"I've got this application from NBC, joined in by the other networks and a bunch of local stations," said Judge Mogel, quietly enough to frustrate all but the lip-readers in the audience. "If it were up to me, I'd tell them to go to hell, but the Court of Appeals says that absent good cause they're allowed to televise this. I don't want a circus, so I've already told them they'll be allowed one pool camera, and they'll all have to work off that. Any objection, Dean?"

"No objection, Judge, if we can have a couple of ground rules."

"Such as?"

"Such as, number one, no mention of the defendant's record. I'm not asking for bail."

"That's fair. What else?"

"No mention of any statements. I intend to oppose any coverage of a Huntley hearing, if we ever get that far." A Huntley hearing was an inquiry into, among other things, whether the police had warned a suspect of his constitutional rights before questioning him.

"Judge," protested Bingham, "I've got to serve statement notice. I'm required to do it on the record."

"Fine, you'll do it," said Mogel. "You'll say, 'The People serve notice pursuant to CPL 170.10.' Nothing else. As to what the statements were, you'll provide them to Mr. Abernathy in writing, within the fifteen-day statutory period. Anything else?"

"No," Dean said.

"No," said Bingham.

"All right, it'll take them a while to set up the camera. Come back in twenty minutes."

Dean spent the twenty minutes prying information out of Walter Bingham and dodging reporters. He didn't like trying his cases in the media, even on the rare occasion when he had a case in which the media was interested. Besides, today he really had nothing to say to them that could help his client.

From Bingham he learned that Joey Spadafino had admitted the robbery to several detectives during the hours following his arrest, but had hedged by the time Bingham took the Q&A, the videotaped question-and-answer session. Dean asked Bingham when he could get a copy of the video.

"Are you going to have him testify before the grand jury?" Bingham wanted to know first.

"No," said Dean, "I think he's helped you enough already."

"Next week" was Bingham's answer. What it meant was that he was playing it close to the vest. He was required to give the defense a copy of the video, but he would wait until the grand jury had heard the evidence and voted its indictment before turning it over. That way, in case the defendant chose the somewhat unusual step of testifying before the grand jury, he would have to do so without first seeing—or having his lawyer see—what he had said during the Q&A. Dean had mixed feelings about the rule. On the one hand, it did serve to prevent a defendant from tailoring his testimony to what he had said earlier. But it sure felt like walking through a mine field without it.

The arraignment was a nonhappening insofar as it brought no drama, no surprises, and no substantive developments in the case whatsoever. None of that prevented the media from treating it like a major news event. Commissioner Wilson had been a popular figure, a black man who had come out of the squalor of Brooklyn's Bedford-Stuyvesant section. Born Deshawn African Wilson to a single mother, orphaned at six, raised by a nearly blind grandmother who had somehow managed to keep him and his three sisters fed, clothed, and in school, he had entered the Police Academy at eighteen with the borrowed birth certificate of an older cousin, Edward Lee Wilson. Though he had confessed the ruse after making sergeant at the age of twenty-eight, it had cost him his first and middle names and he was stuck for life with the less mellifluous "Edward Lee." Twice seriously wounded in the line of duty, Wilson had earned a string of decorations exceeded only by the legendary Mario Biaggi. Unlike Biaggi, however, he had simultaneously retained a reputation as a scrupulously honest cop and a commander of absolute moral integrity. As he rose through the ranks to captain, deputy inspector, and eventually Chief of Patrol, that reputation had brought him national recognition. Three years ago the Mayor had named him Commissioner, bypassing several whites and other blacks who outranked him in both title and years in the Department.

As Commissioner, Edward Wilson had been innovative and popular. A champion of the uniformed force that had spawned him, he put more men back on the street, where he felt they belonged. He streamlined paperwork, brought the Department into the computer age, and hired civilian employees to perform many of the clerical tasks that police officers had traditionally spent so much time doing so poorly. He was a fierce advocate of minorities within the ranks, and he defined minorities as women, blacks, Latinos, Asians, gays, and any other group of one or more who chose to wear beards, mustaches, sideburns, ponytails, earrings, garlic cloves, or anything else that their hearts desired. But as tolerant as he was of what he termed these "superficial distinctions," he gave no quarter in two areas: corruption and brutality. Under him, the New York Police Department had regained its stature as a worldwide model, and Edward Wilson had himself become a familiar face on national magazine covers and Sunday-morning panel discussions. There had even been talk of a run for the Governor's mansion, should Mario Cuomo ever decide to hang up his spikes. That thought, if indeed Wilson entertained it, had apparently been put on hold a year ago, when a heart attack that sidelined him for six weeks raised concerns about his long-term health.

Watching himself on the ten o'clock news that evening, Dean Abernathy was secretly pleased at his sudden fame. He had said virtually nothing at the arraignment itself. The camera had focused on Joey Spadafino being led in front of the bench, on Judge Mogel's ordering him held without bail pending action by the grand jury, and on Walter Bingham's announcement that the presentation would begin that very afternoon; back to Spadafino, looking small and lost as he stood bracketed between Dean and a large uniformed court officer. Then Dean on the courthouse steps, staring directly and sincerely into the camera and stating that, while he could not yet comment on the facts, the public could be sure that "there's more than meets the eye here." Whatever that meant, Dean laughed to himself, clicking the channel selector back to the Knicks-Pistons game in time to see Patrick Ewing miss a free throw. The score appeared, superimposed over Ewing's face dripping sweat as he concentrated on his second free throw.

DETROIT	68
NEW YORK	60

"Shit," said Dean, clicking off the set. He got up and went to the kitchen. An inventory of the refrigerator revealed a pitcher containing either apple juice or iced tea, he couldn't remember which. Something scary in a Chinese food container. Six clementines: Dean generally succumbed to the Korean grocer, who in this case had marked them six for ninety-nine cents, but he made a point of maintaining the illusion of free will by rejecting the penny change. A bruised tomato. Two carrots that would either require a peeler—which Dean had temporarily misplaced—or taste like earth.

Dean closed the refrigerator door and tried the freezer. Much better. A box that promised pizza made on French bread. A package of tender, tiny peas. Several plastic containers of mysterious leftovers. A number of foil-wrapped objects of different shapes and sizes, none suggesting food. He settled on the French bread pizza.

Rejecting the microwave his brother Alan had bought him after watching Dean go through a pack of matches trying to light his oven without sacrificing body parts, Dean deftly lit the flame on the second try. He had learned to hold the match with something other than his fingers—a pair of pliers worked best, though tonight he could not locate them and settled for an old roach clip left over from his marijuana days.

Dean lived alone, partly by choice, partly by virtue of the fact that Elna Terjesen, his onetime roommate and sometimes bedmate, had six months earlier left him a note one evening in place of her self and her worldly belongings. He still had the note.

Dear Dean,
I cannot compeat for your attention with your work any longer. I know you are "on trial," as you call it. But when you get home at midnight, as you have every night this week, and then ignore me, it is too much. I have kneads too.
I wish you a good life.

Elna

It was just as well, thought Dean. Who wants a girlfriend with kneads, anyway? Dean walked back into the living room, settled into the overstuffed chair that had over the years taken on the shape of his own body, and clicked the game back on in time to see Joe Dumars hit from three-point range.

| DETROIT | 77 |
| NEW YORK | 62 |

He clicked the game off again and picked up his copy of the *Times*, which he hadn't had a chance to read during the day.

POLICE COMMISSIONER WILSON DIES DURING A MUGGING ATTEMPT

Wilson Is Apparent Heart Attack Victim

Suspect, 28, Is Arrested

Police Commissioner Edward Wilson collapsed and died early Sunday morning during a mugging attempt in front of his Bleecker Street townhouse in Greenwich Village.

A 28-year-old ex-convict, Joseph Spadafino, was being held by the police and was expected to be charged with murder. It was not immediately clear whether the suspect would also be charged with robbery or attempted robbery.

Commissioner Wilson, 62, had been the most decorated black patrolman in the history of the Department. He had risen through the ranks to the position of Chief of Patrol before being appointed Commissioner by the Mayor three years ago.

Had Heart Condition

Last January, Commissioner Wilson suffered what was described at the time as a "minor" heart attack. He missed six and a half weeks while recuperating, and was given a clean bill of health by his physicians.

Sources close to the Commissioner's office confirmed that Mr. Wilson had been feeling "under the weather" for the past several days. (Continued on page B1)

When Dean looked for the continuation of the article, he recalled that he had used Section B as his tablecloth at lunchtime, and it had ended up being thrown out because it smelled of tunafish.

Dean clicked the television back on. A red pickup truck muscled its way up rocks on an impossible incline as a male chorus sang about the Heartbeat of America. He clicked off the sound and pinched the bridge of his nose, allowing his eyes to close for the first time since five-thirty in the morning.

In his dream, he was back in college, hitting jump shot after jump shot, from the corner, from the top of the keyhole, from half-court. They put Joe Dumars on him, then Isiah Thomas. Dennis Rodman stepped up to triple-team him, but he continued to hit. With the clock winding down, he dribbled through the entire defense, then took a last-second, off-balance jumper from three-quarter court. The buzzer sounded with Dean falling out of bounds, into the adoring crowd, the ball in midair, arcing perfectly, inevitably toward the basket. The buzzer continued, but in a high, piercing whine that brought Dean up out of his dream, out of his sleep, to the sound of his smoke detector and the unmistakable smell of burned pizza.

Joey's first night back on Rikers Island makes him feel like he's reliving a bad dream. By the time the bus arrives at C-93, he's so exhausted that he can barely stand up. Someone says it's 1:30 A.M. If that's so, Joey has been awake for close to forty-eight hours. During that time he's been allowed one sandwich, consisting of two pieces of white bread and one slab of bologna, sliced thick, which caused him to gag and almost throw up, and five containers of watery coffee. He's managed to bum three and a half cigarettes from other inmates, and a Wintogreen Life Saver from a CO. It's the combination of the cigarettes and bologna he can taste, however; the Life Saver lost out long ago.

As tired as Joey is, he knows he's got to stay alert, has to keep his guard up. He's small, which sometimes can actually be good—he isn't regarded as a threat, or as somebody whose intimidation will earn sudden respect for another inmate. But at the same time, being small makes him an easy target, and he can't afford to seem like a pussy or a pushover on top of that.

So when the driver sets the emergency brake and the CO up front tells them to get up and move out, Joey's the first one up, yanking at the handcuffs that join him and a Puerto Rican whose clothes smell like beer and marijuana.

As their turn comes, they file off the bus. It's cold in the courtyard, and there's snow on the ground, something Joey couldn't see through the steamy windows of the bus. He fights to keep from shivering. Inside C-93, Joey and the Puerto Rican are uncuffed for the first time in three hours. Joey rubs his wrists; they're sore and red, and his skin is broken in two places.

"Gonzalez! Mobley! Richardson! Spadafino!" A black corrections officer shouting names off cards directs Joey and three other inmates through another gate and leads them into a room without furniture. "Strip down," he tells them. "Stop when you get to skin."

That Joey's been through this routine a dozen times before makes it no less humiliating. He removes his clothes and, since there's no place else to put them, sets them in a pile on the concrete floor. He feels puny, pale, and unmasculine.

He's made to raise his arms for the CO so that his armpits can be checked as well as his hair, his mouth, his scrotum, and the soles of his feet. Then, while the CO goes through the clothing piles on the floor, an Indian or Pakistani-looking man in a white lab coat, who looks like a doctor but probably isn't, comes into the room carrying a pen-sized flashlight and snapping a rubber glove on one hand. Joey takes his turn bending over and spreading his cheeks. This is done in front of the corrections officer, the Indian, and the other three inmates. He closes his eyes and grits his teeth as a finger enters and probes his rectum painfully.

Welcome back to the Rock.

THREE

The following afternoon Dean got a call from Walter Bingham.

"How're you doing, Dean?"

"Okay. What's up, Walter? My client kill anyone else?"

"No, not that I know of," said Bingham. "I just wanted to let you know that I'll be finishing up the grand jury presentation tomorrow, and I want to make sure you don't want him to testify."

"Yeah, I'm sure. But thanks for checking." Dean could not decide if Bingham was truly being thoughtful or really wanted Spadafino to testify so he could have another crack at him. But Spadafino had already implicated himself to Bingham in the videotaped Q&A, so Dean decided to give Bingham the benefit of the doubt on this one.

"Listen," Dean said, "I'd really like to get the Q&A. And the statements he made to the detectives. I'm not putting him into the grand jury, Walter. I'll put it in writing if you want."

"You could always withdraw it."

"Give me a fucking break, Walter."

"All right," said Bingham finally. "Get me a blank tape and I'll make you a copy."

God forbid the District Attorney's Office should spring for the three dollars a blank tape cost, Dean said to himself, particularly when they bought them by the case and probably paid fifty cents apiece for them. No matter, Dean wanted to see the Q&A.

So Dean took a slight detour from his office on Broadway, walking up to Canal Street. There Senegalese street peddlers sold what could pass for Louis Vuitton handbags, car stereo shops offered tape decks only slightly scratched from being pried out of dashboards the night before, and Chinese merchants displayed trays of watches bearing names like Rolex, Movado, and Piaget for under ten dollars. The odors of fresh fish, skewered meats, and incense filled the winter air, and the sounds were a blend of accents and dialects imploring the passersby to "Check it out, man, check it out" . . . "Three dolla, three dolla" . . . "Swetta, swetta, swetta." A Puerto Rican three-card monte player dealt his cards on an inverted carton, dutifully paying off his shill, while his lookout scanned the street for the po-lice. A black man displayed a single gold-colored chain in his palm, his furtive look meant to convey that it was both genuine and hot, and that the price was very negotiable. Dean bought one low-quality blank videotape at a stand run by a Korean woman who grumbled impatiently as she scribbled out the receipt Dean requested.

At the District Attorney's Office on the seventh floor of the Criminal Court Building, Walter Bingham was signed out to the grand jury, no doubt presenting evidence in the case of the *People of the State of New York v. Joseph Spadafino.* He had, however, left a manila envelope with Dean's name on it and a note inside.

> Dean:
> This is the statement Spadafino made to Det. Rasmussen of Manhattan South Homicide.
> Leave me a tape and I'll have a copy of the Q&A made for you. It should be ready for you to pick up tomorrow morning.
> Walter

Annoyed that he would have to wait another day for the Q&A, but consoled with the written statement, Dean left the tape for Bingham and headed back to his office to see just how badly his client had incriminated himself.

Pretty badly, it turned out.

STATEMENT OF JOSEPH SPADAFINO TAKEN AT MANHATTAN SOUTH HOMICIDE OFFICE. PRESENT ARE MR. SPADAFINO, DETECTIVE RICHARD RASMUSSEN, AND DETECTIVE DOMINICK MOGAVERO. INTERVIEW COMMENCES AT 0445 HOURS.

I, Joseph Spadafino, having first waived my Miranda rights, do voluntarily make the following statement of my own free will,

Detectives sure do have a way with the English language, thought Dean.

Early this morning, at approximately 2:00 to 2:30 A.M., I was in the vicinity of Bleecker Street in Greenwich Village, lower Manhattan. I was in a doorway, trying to keep out of the snow. I had been there several hours and was very cold. I am homeless and I had no place to go.

So far, so good.

At the above time and place I observed a black male approach in my direction. I noticed that there was nobody else on the block at the time. I thought that the black male would make a perfect target for a robbery, in that he did not appear to be paying attention to his surroundings.

Oops.

I considered robbing the black male. I could see that he was well dressed. He was wearing an expensive-looking coat.

I did not hit the black male at any time. I did not cut him or hurt him in any way. I did take the black male's money and a metal money clip that was holding the money. I did this while the black male was lying on the sidewalk.

Shit.

It was never my intention to harm the black male in any way. I only wanted his money, because I was cold and hungry.

END OF PAGE 1 OF 2 PAGES. SIGNED

Joseph A. Spadafino

STATEMENT OF JOSEPH SPADAFINO (CONTINUED)

When the black man came alongside me, I jumped out and yelled, "Freeze, motherfucker!" as loud as I could. Then I told him to give me his money. The black man suddenly grabbed his chest and fell down. That is when I took his money and his money clip.

After I took the money I heard voices and saw people in the building across the street. I threw the money clip away. I put the money in my pocket. I walked away. When I heard sirens I began to run and got caught after a chase.

The money I had on me when I was apprehended was the money I took from the black man.

This statement has been read to me by Det. Rasmussen and it is true.

INTERVIEW CONCLUDES AT 0525. END OF PAGE 2 OF 2 PAGES. SIGNED

Joseph A. Spadafino

So much for Joey Spadafino. A perfect felony murder confession, Dean said to himself. As was so often the case in felony murders, the suspect, anxious to distance himself from the homicide, readily admits the underlying felony while insisting—often quite truthfully—that he never intended to kill the victim. But the very admission of the underlying felony is his undoing, since his guilt of that felony, now fully acknowledged, makes him equally and automatically guilty of murder for the death that occurred during it.

Dean reread the statement. It was all there: the intent to rob, the demand for money, the actual taking. That added up to a robbery. A third-degree robbery, to be sure, since there was no weapon and no accomplice. But a robbery of any sort would do. Add a death during the commission—even if it was never intended, even if it was the sudden giving out of the heart of a man with a known heart condition—and you had a classic felony murder.

And in that instant, Dean could predict the future for Joey Spadafino with absolute clarity. Given the notoriety of the case, the popularity of the victim, and the overwhelming evidence against his client, there would be no plea bargaining for this defendant, not even in New York County, the plea-bargaining capital of the Western world. Joey Spadafino would end up pleading guilty to felony murder. His sentence would be life imprisonment, with a minimum of somewhere between fifteen to twenty-five years.

Dean felt suddenly very tired. He recognized the familiar tide of depression that seemed to well up and engulf him so often in this business. Why should he be upset about a two-bit punk who had caused the death of a good, innocent man? And in realizing that he should not be, he realized too that his depression was not only for Joey Spadafino, it was for Dean Abernathy. For he knew already that he would lose this case, that he would be powerless, that Walter Bingham would beat him, that there would not be one fucking thing he could do about it.

FOUR

Funeral services for Commissioner Wilson were held the following day. If an Inspector's funeral is an impressive display, drawing the top brass in the Department and a supporting cast of hundreds of uniformed officers, a funeral for the Police Commissioner himself is an awesome spectacle. Because police officers work in what essentially breaks down to eight-hour shifts, at any given moment for every officer on duty, there are two others off duty. And on this cold and overcast day in February, it seemed that every off-duty cop in the city joined the hundreds officially assigned to the ceremony, having put on his or her dress blues and white gloves and queued up on the frozen ground of Woodlawn Cemetery in the Bronx, where Deshawn African Wilson was to be laid to rest. A dark blue sea made up of literally thousands of uniformed personnel, most on their own time, assembled to pay their respects. Every senior officer, from the rank of lieutenant on up through captains, precinct commanders, inspectors, and deputy chiefs, turned out in the gold braids and bars that distinguished their uniforms from those of the rank and file.

The Mayor attended, joined up front by the Governor and the Vice President of the United States. Two United States Senators, six congressional representatives, and a justice of the

Supreme Court were amid the hundreds of dignitaries assembled. Among those to address the crowd were the Mayor, the Reverend Jesse Jackson, and the slain Commissioner's son, Dwight Wilson, himself a sergeant in the Thirtieth Precinct. A twenty-one-gun salute marked the lowering of an American flag and the presentation of the colors to the Commissioner's widow, a tall, unveiled woman who somehow managed to maintain her composure and dignity throughout. A final benediction, intoned by His Holiness John Cardinal O'Connor, ended with a prayer for divine mercy on the poor, misguided soul who had cut short the life and career of a true soldier of God.

The same day that last respects were being paid to Edward Wilson in Woodlawn Cemetery, Dean Abernathy picked up his copy of the videotape from Walter Bingham at the District Attorney's Office. This time, Bingham was in.

"Get your indictment yet?" Dean asked him.

"You know I can't tell you that." Technically, Bingham was right. The grand jury, by laws the origins of which can be traced back to the days of the Inquisition, operates in secret. A group of ordinary citizens—twenty-three at full strength, with a quorum of at least sixteen required to vote—are drawn from the same rolls as those that provide trial (or "petit") jurors. They serve for set terms, typically a month, meeting in regular half-day sessions, either mornings or afternoons. They sit in a room designed like a small amphitheater, filling seats that radiate out from the front of the room, where a witness sits behind a wooden table. No judge presides in the grand jury room. The prosecutor, an Assistant District Attorney such as Walter Bingham, stands at a podium at the rear of the room, from where he questions the witness. The law bestows upon him the quasi-judicial duty of legal adviser to the grand jurors. But in reality, he is there to present witnesses and seek indictments against criminal defendants accused of felony charges.

Typically, the grand jury hears only those witnesses whom the prosecutor chooses to present, those civilian victims and police officers or detectives with testimony bearing on the guilt of the accused. Occasionally—but only occasionally—a defendant will waive his right to silence and, accompanied by his lawyer (whose role is limited to sitting silently and ceremoniously beside his client at the table), tell the jurors his side of the story in narrative fashion. Thereafter the prosecutor is free to cross-examine the defendant, and the grand jurors can themselves suggest additional questions for him to put to the defendant. But the right of the defendant, and his lawyer, to be present is limited to that portion of the proceedings during which the defendant himself is testifying; it does not extend to permit their presence during the testimony of other witnesses, whether hostile or friendly, who precede or follow the defendant. Throughout the process, a court reporter seated at a stenotype machine records every word. An interpreter is provided if the witness needs one. No one else is permitted in the room.

After hearing the witnesses, the grand jurors consider the case they have heard. Generally it is a bare-bones, no-frills presentation: the prosecutor, with no defense lawyer to cross-examine the witnesses or call witnesses of his own, has given the grand jury only as much as they need to hear. Knowing that if the case ultimately goes to trial the defense will then be entitled to pierce the veil of secrecy and obtain the transcribed testimony of those witnesses who have appeared before the grand jury, the prosecutor avoids questioning his witnesses in detail; instead he elicits from them a sort of shorthand summary of the events. It is invariably enough.

At the conclusion of the testimony, the prosecutor tells the grand jury what crimes he would like them to consider charging the defendant with and explains any rules of law peculiar to those crimes.

Voting not on the much more difficult issue of whether the defendant's guilt has been established beyond a reasonable doubt (a standard reserved for trials), but only whether they are satisfied that "probable cause" has been demonstrated that a crime has been committed and that it is the defendant who committed it, the grand jurors need not reach a unanimous verdict (a requirement again unique to the trial courtroom). Instead, a bare majority of their number is all that is required to vote an indictment, a piece of paper formally accusing the defendant of those crimes for which he will be held over for trial in Supreme Court.

It has been said, and often repeated, that a grand jury will indict a ham sandwich if asked to do so. The truth of the statement has hardly been undermined by the fact that the source of the quote, the chief judge of New York's highest tribunal, the Court of Appeals, ultimately found himself indicted by a grand jury, possibly even feeling a bit like a ham sandwich.

"Come on, Walter," prodded Dean. "Stop being such a hardass. Did you get your indictment yet?"

"Well," said Bingham, "let's just say there were no surprises."

The surprise came when Dean watched the videotape that night.

Dean did not have a VCR. Actually, he had one, but he had somehow managed to break it trying to figure out how to record a Giants-Redskins game one Sunday afternoon when he had to be at a wedding reception for a friend from college days. First the timer had stumped him. Whatever he did, it continued to flash "12:00" in green numbers. Then the VCR worked, but he lost the reception on his TV screen, which turned a snowy gray, accompanied by a whooshing noise that replaced the audio. Late for the wedding and frustrated at his mechanical ineptitude, Dean had finally ripped a wire out of the back of the VCR. His TV picture had been restored and the whooshing noise had vanished, but his VCR was history.

So Dean had needed to be resourceful. With his copy of the Spadafino Q&A in his hand, he went through his address book, going alphabetically through names of candidates who might have VCRs that actually worked.

Of the various Abernathys that monopolized the first page, only Dean's sister Tillie seemed a possibility, but that meant traveling to far-off New Jersey. Dean's parents were out of the question: his mother lived in fear of electromagnetic fields and refused to use any appliance more sophisticated than a toaster. She made an exception for a black-and-white television set to watch her daytime soaps, but kept it on a foam rubber pad to avoid static buildup.

Joanne Bushfield had a VCR, if Dean remembered correctly, but seeing her would mean listening while she filled Dean in on all the events of her life in the four months since they had last spoken. And that thought struck Dean as about as appealing as reading a four-month stack of the New York Times classified ads sections in a single sitting.

Herb Carson had two VCRs. He knew how to make copies of movies he rented. But Herb had a penchant for cigars and tended to favor those that smelled the worst and lasted the longest, and he liked to save them, half smoked, in ashtrays scattered throughout the apartment.

Arlette Franks had a VCR, for certain, because she was into amateur pornography. While Dean was dating her, she had suggested renting a videocamera and taping their lovemaking. All Dean could imagine was turning on *Eyewitness Video* or some such program one night and being confronted with the two of them going at it on her dining room table.

Penelope James had a VCR, too. But she was an Assistant District Attorney herself, and watching the tape with her struck Dean as somehow unseemly.

Vinnie Mastrangelo probably had a VCR, but Vinnie had moved and Dean didn't have his new number.

Hotwire Harry Reynolds no doubt had a dozen VCRs. Although Dean didn't make it a practice to keep clients' names in his address book, he'd made an exception in Harry's case. Dean had represented Hotwire Harry some years back on a charge of violating Federal Communications Commission laws. It seemed Hotwire Harry, an electronics whiz, had figured out a way to have his long-distance phone calls billed to any number he chose. But Hotwire Harry couldn't resist the irony of choosing the Internal Revenue Service as his victim, and had managed to get caught. Dean had got him off with a fine and a warning, and Harry, out of gratitude, had ever since showered Dean with a steady stream of well-intended but seldom used gifts. These included a state-of-the-art radar detector (which Dean never used, his Jeep being all but incapable of exceeding posted speed limits), an unblockable caller-ID contraption for a telephone (dutifully buried in the back of Dean's bottom desk drawer, since such devices were still strictly illegal in New York State), a "hot" cable box for Dean's TV (which Dean resorted to only in the event of a true video emergency, such as a Giants or Knicks game being blacked out on normal channels), and a variable-speed, self-lubricating vibrator with interchangeable "warheads" (Dean had yet to find to a suitable companion he dared even *show* that one to). No doubt about it: any of Hotwire Harry's VCRs would turn out to be illegal, stolen, or worse. Dean decided to continue his search through his address book.

Elna Terjesen had a VCR she had bought from a fellow flight attendant, who in turn had a boyfriend with access to all sorts of electronic equipment that was forever falling off trucks and going for a fraction of list price. But Dean hadn't heard from Elna since she'd walked out of his life and set off in pursuit of her own kneads.

In the end, just before getting to the XYZ page, he called Mark Wexler, a fellow defense attorney who at various times had been Dean's rock-climbing partner, sailing navigator, and marijuana connection during his smoking days. Which meant, of course, that they were forced to smoke a joint and a half between them for old times' sake before even starting the tape.

> BINGHAM: Hello, Mr. Spadafino. My name is Walter Bingham and I'm an assistant district attorney. I know you've already met these two gentlemen, but for the record they are Detective Richard Rasmussen and Detective Dominick Mogavero of Manhattan South Homicide. You've spoken with them already, right?

The camera panned to the two detectives, then settled back on Joey Spadafino. He sat alone behind a gray metal table. He looked tired and somewhat lost.

> SPADAFINO: Yeah, right.
> BINGHAM: Okay, before we start, I'm going to ask you certain questions about your Constitutional rights.
> SPADAFINO: They already did that.
> BINGHAM: I know, but I'm going to do it again. First, you have the right to remain silent. Do you understand?

Spadafino nodded, looking down at the table.

BINGHAM: I'd prefer you to answer out loud. You don't have to, but I'd prefer it if you would, so I can be sure you understand me.

SPADAFINO: Okay.

BINGHAM: You have the right to remain silent. Do you understand?

SPADAFINO: Yes.

BINGHAM: Anything you say may be used against you. Do you understand?

SPADAFINO: Yes.

BINGHAM: You have the right to have an attorney present at this and every other stage of the proceedings. Do you understand?

SPADAFINO: Yes.

BINGHAM: If you cannot afford an attorney, the court will provide one for you, free of charge. Do you understand?

SPADAFINO: Yes.

BINGHAM: Knowing all this, do you wish to voluntarily answer my questions?

SPADAFINO: Yes.

So much for the Miranda rights. Bingham had covered them perfectly, and whatever followed would stand up in court.

BINGHAM: Okay. As you know, Mr. Spadafino, I'm investigating an incident that took place on Bleecker Street, in front of Seventy-six Bleecker Street, at approximately two-thirty this morning. Were you there at that time?

SPADAFINO: Yeah.

BINGHAM: What were you doing there?

SPADAFINO: Nuthin'. Trying to keep dry.

BINGHAM: How long had you been there before this thing happened?

SPADAFINO: I dunno. Coupla hours, I guess.

BINGHAM: Did there come a time when you saw the deceased?

SPADAFINO: Huh?

BINGHAM: The guy who died.

SPADAFINO: Yeah.

BINGHAM: Where was he when you first saw him?

SPADAFINO: Comin' down the block.

BINGHAM: What was he doing?

SPADAFINO: Walkin', he was walkin'.

BINGHAM: Was there anyone else around?

SPADAFINO: No.

BINGHAM: What did you think when you first saw him?

SPADAFINO: Honestly, at first I thought about askin' him for some money, you know, some change. Then I saw he looked drunk. So I did think about takin' him off. I admit that, I did think about that.

BINGHAM: What do you mean by "taking him off"?

SPADAFINO: You know, robbin' him.

BINGHAM: Did you have a weapon of any sort?

SPADAFINO: No.

BINGHAM: How were you going to rob him?

SPADAFINO: Jus rob him. Act bad. You know.

BINGHAM: And did you do that?

SPADAFINO: No.

BINGHAM: No?

SPADAFINO: No, I didn't.

Dean moved forward to the edge of his chair, as surprised by the answer as Walter Bingham had obviously been. But here was Joey Spadafino, the same Joey Spadafino who a half hour earlier had signed a written statement admitting the robbery, now backing off from it. Dean listened intently as Bingham pursued the point.

BINGHAM: Are you sure?

SPADAFINO: Sure, I'm sure. I was the one who was there.

BINGHAM: Well, Joey—okay to call you Joey?

SPADAFINO: Yeah.

BINGHAM: Well, Joey, you told the detectives here that you did rob him.

SPADAFINO: I told them the guy fell down, and that's when I robbed his money. That's exactly what I told them.

There it was again. Part of the problem was that Joey, the homeless ex-con, didn't know the legal definition of robbery. But Dean, the lawyer, did. In order to rob someone, you had to use physical force against your victim, or at least place him in fear; if all you did was take money from someone—say a guy lying on the sidewalk—it was only larceny. And though larceny was a crime, it wasn't one of those crimes that made a death that occurred during its commission a felony murder. While the distinction was a meaningless one to Joey Spadafino, it certainly hadn't been lost on Rasmussen and Mogavero.

RASMUSSEN: You told us you demanded his money, and that's when he fell down. Right, Joey?

SPADAFINO: No.

RASMUSSEN: That's what you said, Joey.

MOGAVERO: That's what you said.

SPADAFINO: You guys are confusin' me.

BINGHAM: You want to take a break, Joey? You want some coffee?

SPADAFINO: No, no. I'm okay. Listen, I didn't kill the guy. I didn't touch the guy. I swear to God. He fuckin' *fell*. You gotta believe me.

BINGHAM: But you did take his money, right?

SPADAFINO: Yeah, I took his money.

BINGHAM: And at some point you were going to rob him?

SPADAFINO: Yeah. No. I thought about it. To be perfickly honest, yeah, I thought about it. At some point.

BINGHAM: And you did take his money?

SPADAFINO: Yeah.

BINGHAM: What else did you take? Anything else?

SPADAFINO: No. Yeah. I mean there was this metal thing holdin' his money. So I guess you could say I took that, too.

BINGHAM: It's not what I say. It's what you say. Did you take that, too?

SPADAFINO: Yeah. It was attached to the money.

BINGHAM: Now, the money you had on you when you were arrested, Joey. Was that the money you took from the man?

SPADAFINO: Yeah.

BINGHAM: How about the metal thing? Did you have that on you when you got caught?

SPADAFNO: No.

BINGHAM: Why not? What did you do with it?

SPADAFINO: I trew it away.

BINGHAM: You threw it away?

SPADAFINO: Yeah.

BINGHAM: Why?

SPADAFINO: I ain't stupid. I figure I get caught with that, that ties me to the guy.

BINGHAM: But you kept the money?

SPADAFINO: Money's money.

BINGHAM: You remember where you threw the metal thing?

SPADAFINO: Yeah, I remember. Inna trash can on Seventh, a block downtown.

BINGHAM: Seventh Avenue?

SPADAFINO: Yeah.

BINGHAM: Which side of Seventh Avenue?

SPADAFINO: The same side.

BINGHAM: Okay, Joey, just a few more questions. Have these detectives treated you all right?

SPADAFINO: Yeah.

BINGHAM: Nobody's beaten you or threatened you?

SPADAFINO: No.

BINGHAM: All right. That concludes the interview. The time is six forty-eight A.M.

The tape went blank. Dean leaned over, stopped the tape, then pressed the rewind button. He had some mechanical aptitude after all. He looked over to Mark Wexler for a comment on the tape, but Mark had his head down, already busy rolling another joint.

"So what do you think?" Dean asked.

"I think you better smoke this. You're going to need it."

FIVE

In the case of the *People of the State of New York v. Joseph Spadafino,* that Friday was One Eighty Eighty Day. This day derived its name from Section 180.80 of the New York State Criminal Procedure Law, which decreed that a defendant charged with a felony had a right to be released from custody six days from the moment of his arrest, no matter how long his record was or how serious the charge against him, unless the prosecution had obtained a grand jury indictment or was prepared to establish probable cause at a preliminary hearing. Since preliminary hearings, unlike grand jury presentations, were conducted in public with the defendant and his attorney present throughout and permitted to cross-examine the prosecution's witnesses, the District Attorney's Office virtually never resorted to them. Instead, they sought and obtained indictments whenever possible, and invariably consented to the release of those defendants they were unable to indict. Because they were not about to consent to the release of the murderer of Police Commissioner Wilson, they had obtained an indictment against Spadafino with two days to spare and were prepared to announce that fact on One Eighty Eighty Day to the court and the rest of the world.

The media again turned out in droves for what Dean Abernathy knew would be another nonevent. But turn out they did, to zoom their pool camera in on the drawn, dejected face of Joseph Spadafino as he stood before the Part F—for felony—judge and heard Walter Bingham announce that the grand jury had voted a true bill, meaning an indictment, against Spadafino for the charge of murder in the second degree. A date was selected and the case adjourned two weeks for the defendant's first appearance in Supreme Court, where felonies were dealt with once an indictment had been filed.

Dean said hardly a word during the proceedings, which were over in two minutes, and afterward only Mike Pearl of the *Post* bothered to stop him and ask him for a comment. Dean declined. The truth was, he had nothing to say.

With Joey Spadafino lodged at Rikers Island, not the easiest place to get out to, Dean decided to take advantage of his client's presence in court by going upstairs to meet with him again after the adjournment. They sat across from each other in a closet-sized cubicle, separated by a wire mesh that made looking at the other person a difficult exercise in visual concentration. Dean found his eyes continually drawn to the details of the mesh, the way a film director might shift the focus of a camera from background to foreground, leaving Joey in the distance, reduced to a featureless, watery blur.

Dean explained the significance, as well as the lack of significance, of the court appearance they had just been through. He described in some detail what lay ahead. Although Joey was no stranger to the criminal justice system and had actually done time upstate for a minor drug sale, he struck Dean as somewhat naive in his understanding of the process, a naïveté that surprised Dean but posed no problem. He far preferred it over the arrogance of the jailhouse-lawyer type intent on impressing his attorney with his own experience and legal skills.

"So how are they treating you, Joey?" Dean asked.

"Okay, I guess."

"Did you ever get a chance to write out what happened that night?"

"Yeah." Joey reached into the back of his jeans and fished out a worn sheet of paper, folded into a pocket-sized wad and covered with penciled words. "I'm not much of a writer," he said as he extended it through the slot under the wire mesh. Dean took it and unfolded it. The writing was large and primitive. He felt as though he were reviewing the composition of an eight-year-old. At the top was a title:

HOW I CAM TO GET A RESTED
BY J SPADAFINO

Dean decided to postpone reading it. He forced himself to focus on Joey's face through the mesh.

"This is terrific," he said. "I'd like to take it and go over it thoroughly, okay?"

"Yeah, okay. I don't spell too good."

"I don't care, neither do I," said Dean.

They shook hands by pressing palms, fingers extended upward, against the mesh that separated them.

HOW I CAM TO BE A RESTED
BY J SPADAFINO

The nite I got a rested it was snowing and I had no plays to go so I was stay in a door on bleakr st I was very cold and hunger to I almos die of the hypodermia I seen the guy walk tword me At first I think a bout robing him but then I chainge my mine All if a suden the guy grab his cheast and fall down I didden push him or eny thin When hes on the ground I wen threw his pokets and founded the money then peeple saw me so I left There was a mettle thing holding the money I threw it in a gabage can then I got caut by the police

At the stashun house they fingerpaint me and take my picsure and aks me alot of qeustins I tole them the sam is I tole you I didden push the guy or tuch him or nothin honist I didden euin saye eny thin to him Then they bring me to cort and I met you I took the money but I sware I neur did nothin els THE END.

Sine *Joseph Spadafino*

Dean read the story over and over until finally he could get through it without the distraction of the infantile printing, the misspellings, and the utter absence of grammar. Joey Spadafino was saying that not only had he not touched his victim until the man fell, he had never even *said* anything to him. In other words, he was now denying the robbery as well as the murder, just as he had denied it in the videotaped Q&A with Walter Bingham. The same robbery he had admitted earlier in his signed statement to the detectives. Well, Dean smiled, Joey might be stupid, but he wasn't crazy. At least he'd figured out somewhere along the line what felony murder was all about. Too bad for him he had figured it out so late.

That afternoon Walter Bingham called Dean to tell him that the autopsy performed on Edward Wilson had been completed.

"I don't have the written report yet," he said. "That usually takes a couple of weeks. But I spoke to the ME this morning." The ME was the Medical Examiner. "He confirms that it was a heart attack."

"Too bad," said Dean. "We were pinning our hopes on suicide." It was a bad joke, as well as a tasteless one, and as soon as he had said it Dean was sorry. "You'll send me a copy of the report when you get it?"

"Sure thing," said Bingham.

"By the way," said Dean, "I watched the Q&A. Shame on you for not getting him to admit the robbery."

"Yeah, I must be slipping. I checked with Rasmussen. Apparently after your client signed the confession they explained the significance of it to him."

"That by admitting the robbery he buys the murder?"

"Yeah. So, naturally, by the time I get him, he's wised up and not admitting the robbery anymore."

"Smarter than most of my clients," said Dean.

"Not smart enough," said Bingham.

Out of court as well as in court, prosecutors love to have the last word, thought Dean. But he didn't say anything. He was wondering if Bingham's explanation made sense and whether it adequately explained the change in Joey Spadafino's story. It did make sense, Dean had to admit. He was less certain about the answer to the second question.

Lawyers who went into the office on weekends were mercenary, workaholic fools who had no outside interests, Dean Abernathy had long ago proclaimed. He himself was anything but mercenary and had a stack of unpaid bills and a checkbook full of almost as much red ink as black to attest to the fact. He was a workaholic only on those occasions when he was on trial; at all other times he was master of the early-afternoon getaway. And when it came to outside interests, Dean was second to none. He sailed, he scuba dived, he rock climbed, he biked, he visited the dinosaurs at the Museum of Natural History, he read, he skied—

He skied.

The weekend gradually came into focus: Dean and a beautiful companion of the female persuasion gliding down the slopes of Vermont, sipping hot rum concoctions by the fireside, making passionate love under a down-filled comforter as the snow fell gently outside in the New England night. . . .

Only thing was, Dean had never been much when it came to making plans ahead of time. No matter; it was Friday night and, as the saying went, there was no time like the present. Surely the list of eager candidates waiting hopefully by their phones would run into the dozens. He walked to the bathroom, faced his rugged good looks in the mirror, lifting his chin ever so slightly to accentuate its strength. "Yes," he said with self-assurance, fighting off a vague sense of déjà vu that he had seen Ted Danson play this role once in a *Cheers* rerun.

He dialed Joanne Bushfield's number. She could be boring, but then again she had certain indisputable strengths, and as Dean listened to the phone ringing, he didn't doubt for a moment that those strengths would be made to order for the weekend he had in mind. But the phone continued to ring.

He dialed Arlette Franks, the aspiring amateur pornography star, having no idea whether she skied or not, but dismissing the fact as secondary. Anyone could be a snow bunny and sit in the lodge, after all. Dean had once tried unsuccessfully to pick up a gorgeous blonde with crutches and her leg in a cast by the fire at Killington, only to hear later that the crutches and cast were nothing but props. But Arlette's answering machine was the best Dean could do. At the beep, he hung up.

He dismissed Penny James, the Assistant District Attorney, as too serious for a whole weekend.

He toyed with the idea of calling Elna Terjesen but finally convinced himself that, even if she was "stateside," as she liked to call it, there was no way that the Sweetheart of Swissair would be sitting around on a Friday night without plans for the weekend.

Down to Jennifer West. Dean realized that his social life had slowed to a crawl these last six months. He silently made a pact with whatever god happened to be on duty that, if only Jennifer would answer, he would strive to get out more and meet people.

The phone answered on the second ring. Dean cleared his throat.

"The number you have dialed, 496-2212, has been changed at the customer's request to an unlisted number," said the voice of a female robot. "The number 496-2212 has been changed—"

The drive to the Rikers Island jail was not that bad on a Saturday morning. Dean had detoured by his office to pick up the Spadafino file. He wanted to have his copy of Joey's signed statement to the detectives so he could confront Joey with it. He wasted no time.

"Joey, I noticed when they were videotaping you, you told the DA that the detectives hadn't beaten you or mistreated you in any way. Remember?"

"Yeah," Joey nodded.

"Was that true?"

"Yeah."

"They didn't threaten you?"

"No."

"They didn't make you sign the statement?"

"No."

"So why did you sign it?"

"I figgered it'd help me," said Joey.

And Dean could understand that, of course. It was the old felony murder trap, the suspect figuring that in being honest and admitting the felony that he *had* committed, while denying the killing he had never intended or even—in his mind—caused, the police would recognize and reward the truth, and he would be spared the far more serious murder charge.

"You now understand that it doesn't work that way?"

"I guess so," said Joey.

"Well, you understand that if you were robbing the guy and he got a heart attack and died, it's murder."

"Yeah." Joey nodded. "You splained that to me."

"So did the detectives, I understand."

"Say what?"

"The detectives. They 'splained that' to you, too," Dean heard himself say, and was immediately sorry that he had made fun of his uneducated client. He recognized those old companions, Frustration and Anger, as they circled around him, already picking up the scent of defeat.

"No, you was the first," said Joey in a small voice.

Dean sat for a while. He had heard Joey's words but was somehow unable to process them, to digest them. The protective shell that had formed around him prevented him from reacting to them. He sensed vaguely that they meant something, had some significance, but he felt powerless to decode the message.

So he said, "What?"

"You was the first to eggsplain it to me."

Dean smiled at Joey's attempt to correct his pronunciation. But he knew he had to press on.

"So why did you change your story?" he said.

"I didn't," Joey said. "I didn't change nuthin'."

"Joey, by the time you spoke with the DA on the videotape, you were denying the robbery. You changed your story. You said you never told the guy to give you his money."

"I never *did*. Honest." And the way Joey's eyes met Dean's, it was hard not to believe him.

"So why the fuck did you tell the detectives you did? Why did you tell them you said, 'Freeze, motherfucker'? Why did you tell them you told him to give you his money? And why did you sign this goddamn statement?" He threw the two-page document in front of Joey Spadafino, whose mouth hung open in puzzlement.

Joey bent over the statement. His lips formed silent words as his eyes moved laboriously back and forth, working their way down the first page. He got to the bottom of the first page and nodded. Dean could not tell if the nod signified agreement with the written words or triumph at having completed a page.

Joey folded over the first page and began the same slow process with the second. He stopped. His brow knitted up and his eyes narrowed into a squint. The back-and-forth movement of his eyes grew exaggerated to the point where his whole head swung from left to right, right to left, in denial. Still he read the words.

Finally he looked up. "I didn't say these things" was all he said.

"Did you sign the statement?" Dean asked.

"Yeah."

"Are those signatures yours?"

"Yeah," said Joey, looking at the bottom of both pages. "Yeah, that's my handwriting."

It struck Dean that in Joey Spadafino's uncomplicated world, maybe there was no contradiction, maybe all of those things could indeed be true: he hadn't told Wilson to freeze or demanded his money, and he hadn't told the detectives that he had; yet he had signed the statement in which he had admitted precisely those acts, and the two signatures were his. And now an expectant Joey was looking straight at Dean, waiting for an explanation as to where things had gone wrong.

"Can you really read, Joey?" Dean said gently.

"Yeah, I can read." Annoyed.

"Read to me."

Joey bent over the document. Dean pointed to where the narrative continued on the second page.

"When . . . the . . . black man . . . came . . ."

"Okay," said Dean. He was aware of a splitting headache. "Tell me what's in here that *isn't* true. Tell me what part of this you *didn't* tell the detectives."

Dean had to look away as Joey repeated his reading exercise. He could hear sibilant sounds as Joey formed words.

It was some minutes before Joey spoke. "It's all true but this part: 'When the black man came . . . alongside me . . . I jumped out and . . . yelled . . . "Freeze, motherfucker!" . . . as loud as I . . . could. Then I . . . told him to give me his money.' I couldna told them that, cause that didden happen. You gotta believe me, Dean."

Dean did not. But then again, Dean was having a hard time believing Joey on any part of this one.

At C-93, Joey Spadafino's having a hard time, too. He thought he might be welcomed as something of a hero, a celebrity. After all, he's here on a murder charge, and that fact alone provides him a certain amount of status. Furthermore, the guy he's charged with murdering was the fucking Police Commissioner, the number-one cop in the whole city. That, he figured, should be worth something.

It turns out he figured wrong. For one thing, the Commissioner was "a brother," he keeps hearing from the black inmates, and offing a black cop isn't quite the same as offing a white cop, they've let him know. For another, Joey's found himself, for the first time, on B Block. B Block is a secure unit within a maximum-security jail. It's reserved for inmates with bails of $100,000 or higher, or, as in Joey's case, with no bail at all. This means it's full of guys charged with murder, multiple armed robberies, and A-1 drug felonies. In spite of that, a lot of them have never been upstate before, so they really haven't learned how to do time yet, how to settle in.

For security reasons, nobody on B Block's allowed to work. A job would require them to leave the Block and move around within the walls, and they're prohibited from doing that. The result is that you've got seventy-five guys, all nervous and frustrated while they wait for trial, with nothing but time on their hands. They eat, sleep, watch TV, and they fight. They fight over what channel to watch, who gets to use the phone first, whether one in-

mate "dissed" another by "eyeballing" him, or who gets an un-claimed container of milk. Joey's witnessed a stabbing over a radio being played too loud.

Many of the inmates have weapons. They're generally home-made: a piece of bedspring, a sharpened fork or spoon, a razor blade embedded in a block of wood. The radio stabbing was done with the handle of a toothbrush that had been filed down to a stiletto point. It was good enough to puncture its victim's liver.

Joey hasn't had to fight yet, but already he's come close. Be-cause he arrived with his shoes ruined by the rain and snow, he was given a pair of sneakers by a social worker. The sneakers were second-hand, but the truth is they looked pretty new. They weren't a brand name, like Nike or Adidas or anything, so Joey figured they'd be okay. To make sure, he scuffed them up pretty good before taking a chance on wearing them.

The first afternoon he's wearing them, he's stopped on his way to lunch by two Dominicans. "Nice shoes, man," says one, an ugly guy with a "telephone," a scar that runs from his earlobe to the corner of his mouth. Then he speaks in Spanish to his friend, a tall, dark-skinned guy with a bad eye, who spits a lot and stares at Joey with his one good eye while the other eye kind of rolls around in its socket. Joey says, "Thank you." At that mo-ment two older inmates, white guys, walk by. Joey cuts between the Dominicans and runs to catch up to the white guys. They turn to look at him like he's crazy, but meanwhile he's gotten away from the Dominicans. As he continues down the hall, he hears from behind him, "Watch your back, maricon." Joey doesn't speak Spanish, but he understands maricon. It means "faggot."

Joey knows it would be easy enough to give up the sneakers. Problem is, you give up your sneakers and they want your socks. Give up your socks and they want your shirt. Before you know it, you're standing there with no pants on.

Joey's thought about asking to be put in protective custody. The thing is, it's sort of like the sneakers: once you go into PC, you got to stay there, 'cause everyone figures you for a snitch, whether you are or not. It seems everything you do in here has got consequences. So Joey'll try to make it out in Population. At the same time, he watches his back and has taken to carrying a sharpened length of coat hanger on his way to meals.

SIX

The media assembled again on Joseph Spadafino's next court date. Unlike the first two, this appearance had the promise of some substance. Having been indicted, Spadafino had had his case transferred from Criminal Court to Supreme Court. In New York County, that transfer meant going to a higher court in the most literal sense, from the first floor to the eleventh. There, in one of three "up front" parts, a defendant is arraigned on the indictment, for the first time entering a formal plea of guilty or not guilty. There his lawyer is provided a copy of the indictment containing the various charges the grand jury has voted. Accompanying the indictment is a Voluntary Disclosure Form in which the District Attorney's Office has supplied certain particulars as to post-arrest statements attributed to the defendant, physical evidence recovered from him, identifications made of him, and the like. And there his lawyer often makes an application for a reduction in bail or, in a case such as Spadafino's, for the initial setting of bail.

The presiding judge in Part 70 was Brenda Soloff. She was even-tempered, businesslike, and generally regarded as fair. She presided over no trials, and the Spadafino case would come before her only this once. She would take the defendant's plea, consider a bail application if one was made, and send the case on to a trial judge, supposedly picked at random, with whom the case would remain thereafter.

Aware of all this, Dean Abernathy knew he had a decision to make. He could ask Justice Soloff for bail, or he could wait, gambling that the trial judge might be a better bet. If Dean went with Soloff, he could expect to be stuck with her ruling, since the trial judge would probably adhere to it.

Dean decided to take his chances with Soloff, not so much because he regarded her as good on bail, but more because he knew that a high-visibility murder case such as Spadafino's would be treated as an exception. In place of the usual procedure, in which a clerk literally pulled the name of a trial judge at random out of a drum, the administrative judge would designate the trial judge, making the selection from a short list of tough, veteran judges accustomed to dealing with major trials. Invariably strong on keeping control of their courtrooms, generally knowledgeable in the law, and sometimes even-handed during trial, such judges were seldom liberal when it came to bail.

Dean had other reasons to make his bail application now. Even if Justice Soloff might decide to set bail, she would set it somewhere up in the fifty-thousand- to one-hundred-thousand-dollar range, and of course there was no one to put up any bail for Joey, let alone those kind of numbers. But Walter Bingham's ego would compel him to make a full argument against bail being set at all, particularly with the media in attendance. So Dean had registered no objection to the presence of the television camera, and even let slip to Ralph Penza of Channel 4 that he would be asking for bail for the defendant.

"Joseph Spadafino," read the clerk, "you have been charged by the grand jury with murder in the second degree and other crimes. How do you plead, guilty or not guilty?"

"Not guilty," said Joey.

"Would Your Honor hear me on the question of bail?" Dean asked. "There's been no previous application."

"Certainly," said Justice Soloff.

"First, while it's true that the defendant does have a prior record, his only convictions are for drug crimes. He's never before been even arrested for robbery or anything to do with violence. Second, while this incident ended in a terrible tragedy, I'm told by Mr. Bingham that the cause of death has been determined to have been a coronary, and not the result of any force or blow administered by the defendant. But for Commissioner Wilson's bad heart and my client's bad luck, all we'd have here would be a simple third-degree robbery, a Class D felony. And finally, if I understand the prosecution's case, it hinges largely upon a statement that the police claim my client made, which is contradicted by a videotaped statement he made to Mr. Bingham less than an hour later."

Justice Soloff looked up from her examination of a computer printout of the defendant's criminal history. "Mr. Bingham?"

"Yes, Your Honor. Mr. Abernathy has omitted a few things," Bingham began, standing well off to one side so that he could simultaneously face the judge and be profiled by the camera. "As to Mr. Spadafino's record, he has two felony convictions and five other arrests, not counting this one. As to the cause of Commissioner Wilson's death, that's totally irrelevant: the indictment charges felony murder. And the felony, if Mr. Abernathy will look at the indictment, is *first*-degree robbery, not third-degree. As to the strength of the People's case, it's absolutely overwhelming. We have much more than the defendant's confession. We have two eyewitnesses," Bingham revealed, taking the bait, "one of whom saw the entire incident. We have the money taken from the deceased and recovered from the defendant. We have a money clip, unique in design, recovered from a trash can precisely where the defendant told us he discarded it. We've even matched the brand and number of cigarette butts found at the crime-scene doorway with the half-empty pack of cigarettes the defendant had at the time of the arrest. There were eleven butts, and there were eleven cigarettes missing from the pack. And we've recovered a weapon from the defendant, a knife, which fits the description of the knife used in the robbery, according to one of our witnesses. If that's not a strong case, I don't know what is."

"All right," said Justice Soloff. Unlike Bingham, she didn't raise her voice for the camera. "I'm satisfied that this appears to be a strong case. It's a serious case, notwithstanding the immediate cause of death, which isn't relevant. And the defendant seems to be homeless, with no immediate family or roots in the community. I'm not going to set bail." Then, "The case is assigned to Judge Rothwax, Part Fifty-six, and adjourned to the twenty-third of this month."

*   *   *

Back at his office, Dean tried to digest what he had heard in court. Bingham had sprung several surprises. The indictment itself had contained the first, and Dean now read it in full for the first time.

SUPREME COURT OF THE STATE OF NEW YORK
COUNTY OF NEW YORK

--x

THE PEOPLE OF THE STATE OF NEW YORK :

                        :

               -v-   : INDICTMENT

                        :

JOSEPH SPADAFINO,   :

               Defendant.   :

--x

THE GRAND JURY OF THE COUNTY OF NEW YORK, by this indictment, accuse the defendant of the crime of MURDER IN THE SECOND DEGREE, in violation of Penal Law Section 125.25(3), committed as follows:

The defendant, in the County of New York, on or about January 31 of this year, engaged in the commission of the crime of robbery, and in the course of such crime, and in the furtherance thereof, and of the immediate flight therefrom, caused the death of Edward Wilson, not a participant in the crime.

SECOND COUNT:

AND THE GRAND JURY AFORESAID, by this indictment, further accuse the defendant of the crime of ROBBERY IN THE FIRST DEGREE, in violation of Penal Law Section 160.15(3), an armed felony, committed as follows:

The defendant, in the County of New York, on or about January 31 of this year, forcibly stole property from Edward Wilson, and in the course of the commission of the crime and in the immediate flight therefrom, used or threatened the immediate use of a dangerous instrument, to wit, a knife.

THIRD COUNT:

AND THE GRAND JURY AFORESAID, by this indictment, further accuse the defendant of the crime of CRIMINAL POSSESSION OF A WEAPON IN THE THIRD DEGREE, in violation of Penal Law Section 265.02(1), an armed felony, committed as follows:

The defendant, in the County of New York, on or about January 31 of this year, possessed a dangerous knife with intent to use the same unlawfully against another.

ROBERT M. MORGENTHAU
District Attorney

Attached to the indictment was another piece of paper, an Information filed by the District Attorney alleging that Joseph Spadafino had previously been convicted of a crime. That fact served to elevate the possession of the knife, otherwise a misdemeanor, to the status of a felony. By not permitting the inclusion of the allegation in the indictment, the court protected the defendant's right to have his case tried by a jury unaware of his prior record. Only if he took the stand to testify in his own defense would his record be revealed, and even then the jury would be instructed to consider it only in weighing his credibility as a witness.

For Dean, the shocker had been the first-degree robbery. Unlike second- or third-degree robbery, first-degree robbery required the use or threatened use of a weapon. It was clear from the wording of the indictment that the grand jury had been satisfied that the defendant had not only possessed a knife, but had somehow used it during the robbery of Edward Wilson.

Dean reviewed the notes he had scribbled during Bingham's

argument against bail. Two eyewitnesses . . . one had seen the entire incident . . . money recovered from the defendant . . . a "unique" money clip recovered from the trash precisely where the defendant said he had thrown it . . . the match between the cigarette pack and the butts found at the crime scene . . . the knife recovered from the defendant matching the description of the knife seen by a witness.

Where had this knife come from? Dean had heard nothing about it from Joey. It hadn't been mentioned in the signed statement made for the detectives. Bingham hadn't asked about it during the videotaped Q&A. There had been no word of it in Joey's written narrative prepared for Dean. And now it had come out of left field at the bail argument.

Except, Dean realized, the grand jury had heard about it two weeks ago. And they couldn't have learned of it through Joey's statements, because none of his statements mentioned a knife. That meant they had heard the testimony of an eyewitness, one close enough to see—and later be able to describe—a knife used by Joey Spadafino during the course of the robbery.

Dean turned to the Voluntary Disclosure Form Bingham had supplied him at the arraignment. He compared the time of the crime with the time of arrest and noted that they were a mere six minutes apart. The location of the arrest was just as bad, less than three blocks away. There were references to the signed statement and the videotaped Q&A. Dean turned the page.

PEOPLE v. JOSEPH SPADAFINO
VOLUNTARY DISCLOSURE FORM

PHYSICAL EVIDENCE VOUCHERED

From Defendant:

1. $288.15 United States currency
2. One pack of Kool cigarettes containing nine cigarettes
3. One folding pocketknife with blue handle
4. One dark blue jacket
5. One blue wool cap
6. Two packs of matches

<u>From Crime Scene:</u>

7. Eleven cigarette butts, "Kool"
8. Thirteen used matches

<u>Other:</u>

9. One gold money clip with NYPD shield "#1"

There was the knife again, recovered from Joey. Dean could only imagine what other bits of information his client had neglected to tell him. Well, at least he knew about the weapon now, as well as the eyewitnesses, the cigarettes, and the money clip. The strategy of drawing Walter Bingham out with the bail application had proved successful. But the small victory had been a Pyrrhic one, completely eclipsed by the gravity of what Dean had learned. Bingham had been right, and Justice Soloff had been kind in characterizing the prosecution's case as strong. It wasn't strong. It wasn't overwhelming.

It was an absolute, goddamn lock.

The day's mail brought a telephone bill for $311.15, of which $209.38 was past due and had to be paid the day before yesterday or Dean's phone service would be disconnected; a bank statement showing a balance of $88.56, of which $1.20 was "available"; the fingerprint cards of a defendant whose case Dean had got dismissed last year; an L.L. Bean catalog; several envelopes bearing postage less than 32 cents (which meant they went directly into the trash, unopened); and the autopsy report on Edward Wilson.

AUTOPSY

Case No. M-237758

Approximate Age: 62   Approximate Weight: 205 lbs.

Height: 73"

Identified by: Garth Wilson   Residence:
Stenographer: Mary Singletary   Residence: 145 E. 92 St.
New York, NY

AUTOPSY PERFORMED BY DR. VAN DEN BERG, DEPUTY MEDICAL EXAMINER IN THE PRESENCE OF DRS. ABDULLAH, DE CICCO, PULASKI and SINGH.

I hereby certify that I HANS VAN DEN BERG have performed an autopsy on the body of EDWARD WILSON at Manhattan Mortuary on the 1st day of February 30 hours after the death, and said autopsy revealed

EXTERNAL EXAMINATION:

The body is that of a 6'1", 205 lb. black male appearing slightly younger than the reported age of 62 years. Rigor mortis is present in the cool body, and liver mortis is faint, dorsal, and purple. The scalp hair is gray, 1" in length. The irides are brown. Natural teeth are present in the upper and lower jaw. The torso is unremarkable.

INTERNAL EXAMINATION:
The viscera are in their normal anatomical locations. The appendix has been surgically removed many years ago.

Dean had no interest in Wilson's appendectomy. He scanned down the page until he came to what he was looking for.

CARDIOVASCULAR SYSTEM:

The heart is somewhat enlarged and weighs approximately 550 grams. There is evidence of scarring to the cardiac muscle, both past and recent. There is a massive and clearly lethal subendocardial hemorrage in the left ventricular outflow track, extending to the area of the myocardium.

The remainder of the systems appeared normal. Dean skipped down to the bottom of the fourth and final page.

DIAGNOSES:

1. MASSIVE CORONARY OCCLUSION.

2. CIRCULATORY SYSTEM COLLAPSE.

OPINION:

CAUSE OF DEATH:
    HEART ATTACK, SUSTAINED DURING ROB-
    BERY.

MANNER OF DEATH:
    HOMICIDE.

                        Hans Van den Berg, M.D.
                        Deputy Medical Examiner.

SEVEN

A letter from Joey Spadafino arrived on Wednesday.

An envelope from a prisoner looks like no other mail. To begin with, it is almost always addressed in pencil, the occasional exception being the archaic, uneven type of an old Remington or Smith-Corona portable. The upper left-hand corner contains a return address, whether a street, a road, or a post office box—but never the name of an institution. (One prison in upstate New York actually goes by the name of "Drawer B," followed by a box number and a zip code.) The city or town generally bears a pleasant, bucolic name, such as Green Haven or Great Meadow. Sing Sing becomes Ossining; Clinton Prison turns into Dannemora. The biggest concession to incarceration might be the letters "C.F.," initials meaningless to the general public but signifying to those familiar with the system that the sender is a resident of a correctional facility.

The writer's name will more often than not be preceded by a "Mr." as a statement to the recipient—or perhaps a reminder to the writer himself—that within those walls resides an individual still worthy of title and stature, and hence respect. For immediately following his name comes the reminder, the designation by which he is better known behind those walls: his inmate number.

And, thereafter, some briefer combination of letters and numbers informs the knowledgeable reader of the prisoner's unit, tier, or section within the institution. Hence, in this case:

Mr. Joseph Spadafino A-2335628

1616 Hazen Street U-4E

East Elmhurst, N.Y. 11370

In the center of the envelope Dean's name and address was carefully printed, and the absence of spelling mistakes strongly suggested that Joey had copied the information painstakingly from the business card Dean had provided him.

Finally, prominently penciled on the envelope, in much the same fashion as the average citizen might note "First Class Mail" or "Personal and Confidential" on correspondence intended for a friend, a loved one, or a business associate, were the words "LEGAL MAIL," a loud and clear warning to those in authority that within this crudely ciphered exterior lay all the majesty of a constitutionally protected communication between attorney and client.

Dear Mr. Dean

Why are they sayin I robed the man I tole you I took his money but thats all I neuer robed him I neuer pult out my nife This is the Gods honist trueth Why wood they say those things And a nother thing I neuer tole the D'ts that I rob the man They must of forgered page 2 of my statemint Please Please Please help me I haue no body but you

I am not the best person but I am not a rober.

Your client and friend

Joey

Dean read the letter three times. He stapled the envelope to it.

Why was it that nobody, not even the Joey Spadafinos of the world, faced with absolutely indisputable proof of their guilt, could ever simply admit that they had in fact committed the crime?

He tossed the letter in the file.

The light snow that fell Thursday night was enough to persuade Dean to play hooky the following day.

Dean was a single practitioner. He liked it that way. He had no boss or partner to answer to. Every piece of paper that bore his name, from the simplest *pro forma* motion to the most lengthy and complicated appellate brief, was his work. His clients knew that he, and not some associate or paralegal, would be the one handling their cases. He answered his own phone, opened his own mail, and when able to, paid his own bills.

There were drawbacks, to be sure, of going it alone. Income was highly irregular and totally unpredictable. The single criminal law practitioner forever finds himself in a state of either feast or famine. A cluster of new cases can fill his pocket with cash and make him feel like a millionaire one day; a month later he finds himself wondering if he'll ever earn another dime. When he first put his nameplate on his door, Dean had bought a ledger to keep track of his receipts on a monthly basis. The very first month he recorded that he had taken in just over $12,000. Multiplying it out, Dean had giddily projected that his income for the year should be $145,000.

He didn't see another penny for three months.

There were schedule conflicts as well. Trials, particularly lengthy ones, and court appearances outside his "home court" of Manhattan occasionally meant calling on others to help out, so Dean had forged loose arrangements with several colleagues, whereby they covered for one another in pinches. His closest colleague was his officemate Gerry Leighton, whom Dean regarded highly enough to entrust with his clients' cases when Dean himself was away or otherwise unavailable. Furthermore, over the ten years he had been practicing, Dean had earned a good reputation with the judges he appeared before on a regular basis, and they knew his rare absences from court were unavoidable, so they tended to cut him a little slack.

The best part was that, except for his court schedule, Dean's time was his own. By habit, he woke early, was often in his office before seven, biking the five miles in good weather, taking the subway in bad, or driving his Jeep when the spirit moved him. He found the early-morning hours at the office his most productive time, before his suitemates were there to come into his room for advice, stamps, or conversation and before the telephone began to ring. Even if caught up with his work, Dean would still arrive early. Dressed in the jeans, sweatshirt, and sneakers he commuted in, he would spread *The New York Times* out on his desk. The business section he sacrificed for orange peel, a piece or two of fruit being the only food Dean would eat until dinner. Then, his feet propped up on his desk, he would devour the remaining sections. Sports would be first if the Knicks or Giants had won the evening or day before; otherwise he might skip that section. Then he would work his way to the metropolitan news, the national, and—if time permitted—the international, with news about which Dean usually felt rather remote and powerless to do anything, and often chose to ignore altogether.

By nine o'clock it was time to change into one of several suits Dean kept in his office, put on a shirt and tie, and substitute a pair of loafers for his sneakers. By twenty after he was on his way to court, a seven-minute walk. Dean liked to be the first lawyer there. He trained his "out" clients, those who had been released on bail or their own recognizance, to arrive as early as he did. And the court officers who manned the various courtrooms knew Dean's penchant for punctuality, and brought his "in" clients to court early whenever possible.

When not on trial, Dean would generally have two or three cases on each day in court for pre-trial appearances of one sort or another. Starting early, he could often complete them by midmorning. Then, back at his desk: more paperwork, phone calls, reviewing the following day's work, and preparation for future trials.

By early afternoon, Dean had often had enough of his office, and one or two o'clock invariably found him back in jeans and sweatshirt. Those who had become accustomed to his routine knew better than to try to reach him at his office after three.

Dean's goal was to make two days out of one: the first he spent at work, the second he indulged himself. In nice weather he was up on the roof of his apartment building by midafternoon, with a book and a Thermos of iced tea. He had several writing projects he was working on: an introduction to rock climbing, a novel about a sailing adventure, and a book of poems (though so far he hadn't had the nerve to disclose his poetry writing to anyone). In winter he would build a fire in the blackened fireplace of his tiny living room. He was something of a purist about the fireplace, and refused to use either the Duraflames so popular with city dwellers or the prepackaged firewood sold by the neighborhood Korean grocer. Instead, he retrieved his chainsaw, sledgehammer, and wedges from the basement storage area and lugged them upstate, cutting and splitting logs until his Jeep struggled heavily on its old leaf springs during the ride home. He would read or write in front of his fire, often sleeping in front of it on colder nights.

The routine worked well as long as Dean was not in the midst of a trial. When he was, the transformation was total: he worked virtually around the clock, his involvement with the case leaving him additional time only for enough food and sleep to survive. He immersed himself in the trial, he obsessed. He invariably went into court better prepared than his adversary, and he used that advantage to free him to concentrate on the subtleties of the trial: the psychology of preconditioning the jurors even as they were being selected, the packaging of his client as believable and sympathetic, and the preparation of his summation, which he began to construct long before the first witness took the stand. All this effort was sometimes not enough, but Dean, ever the sports fan, kept mental track of his own won-and-lost record well enough to know that he got a far higher percentage of acquittals than any other lawyer he knew.

No trial consumed Dean now, however. The following day, with no court appearances scheduled, cried out for his attention, and the snow beckoned. He would go skiing.

First light found Dean Abernathy on the New York State Thruway, two hours north of the city. Hunter Mountain was not Vermont, and though it could be a dreadful place when swarming with skiers on weekends, it was a good enough spot during the week. And if no blond or raven-haired beauty was available to share Dean's fantasy of a New England weekend, he would settle for some fresh air and exercise by himself.

The snow had left only an inch or so downstate, but as Dean exited the Thruway and headed west from Kingston, he found the ground well covered, and even the trees displayed their overnight catch of powder. The sun rose behind Dean, reflecting brightly in the rearview mirror and casting the square shadow of the Jeep onto the pavement in front of him. He turned down the heater to acclimate himself to the cold. He thought momentarily of Joey Spadafino, then fought hard to chase notions of work from his head. This was his day off. He was going skiing. The case could wait till tomorrow.

But try as Dean might, Joey's letter kept coming back to him. Why was Joey so insistent in trying to persuade Dean that he had not robbed Commissioner Wilson, even to the point of making the absurd claim that the detectives had forged his signature on the second page of his statement? Hadn't Dean taken the trouble to show Joey the statement, and hadn't Joey recognized and identified his own signature at the bottom of each page? Why was he recanting now?

And the answer seemed painfully obvious to Dean: Joey had grasped the gravity of his early statement to the detectives. Whether he had learned this soon after from them, as Walter Bingham had suggested, or over the days that followed from Dean and from other inmates who had educated him, Joey was now waging a desperate battle to retract his confession, to distance himself from it. He *had* to deny the robbery; there was simply nothing else he could do.

The slopes at Hunter Mountain were all but empty and the early runs fast. The warming effect of the sun hadn't yet begun to melt the loosely packed powder, and Dean knew that conditions would deteriorate by midday, as the combination of more skiers and rising temperatures took its toll. He decided to try to ski hard, without a break, for as long as his out-of-shape legs could take it.

By his third run, Dean was at his peak, having worked the tentativeness out of his turns but not yet feeling the fatigue that he knew would come. A good athlete who hadn't taken up skiing until his twenties and had never taken a formal lesson (he abhorred lessons of any sort, taking absurd macho pride in mastering skills on his own), Dean knew he would never be a great skier. He liked to say that he skied intermediate slopes like an expert, and expert slopes like an intermediate, but the truth was that skiing for Dean was an exercise in trying to look like he knew what he was doing, while never being quite in control. Nonetheless, he fought this morning to keep his skis tightly together as he carved respectably parallel turns around slower, if steadier, skiers.

By the fifth run Dean's legs had begun to ache, and he found himself seeking out the gentler terrain of intermediate and even beginner trails, rationalizing to himself that they were prettier and longer than the steeper and shorter expert runs. The truth was he welcomed the respite of the long ride up the chairlift, acquainting himself each time with some new skier, gloating together over their good fortune to be able to take a day off during the week while the rest of the world worked.

On his sixth and seventh runs Dean was aware that his form had dropped off considerably. He began to substitute an occasional stem-christie for a parallel turn, went out of his way several times to navigate around a mogul instead of challenging it, and widened his stance on the steeper inclines. But each time he reached the bottom, the empty chairlift lured him back for one last run.

He didn't fall until midway down his eighth and *definitely* final run. Coming out of a turn on a slope humiliatingly named Belt Parkway, Dean happened to glance down at his skis, only to notice that they were slightly but decidedly crossed at the tips. Had his legs not been so tired, he mused to himself later, lying on his back in the first-aid station, he would have easily been able to lift the offending ski clear and replant it. Instead, he had been mesmerized into staring at the crossed tips, paralyzed in what seemed like eternal slow motion. He knew intellectually that he should be lifting his top ski, but the weight of it seemed absolutely awesome, as though the gravitational pull on it had increased twenty-fold. For a long moment nothing happened, and Dean actually had time to wonder if he might not be able to get away with it after all, to continue downhill in that fashion in defiance of the laws of nature.

He didn't have to wait too long for his answer. With alarming suddenness, Dean felt a tip catch and catapult him forward. Launched airborne, cartwheeling over his skis, he was able to tuck his left shoulder at the moment before impact. The move, an onlooker had told him later while helping to disinter him from the snow some twenty yards downhill, had probably saved him a broken collarbone or a dislocated shoulder at best. But it had done nothing for his right ankle, which the X rays disclosed was not broken but severely sprained.

"Of course," explained some ski patrol guy named Rolfe or Sven or Horst, "a schprain can actually be *verse* than a fracture, you know."

Dean knew. He knew then; he knew driving home, willing his left foot to simultaneously master brake, clutch, and accelerator, while his right leg stretched uselessly, immobilized by a cast, to the passenger side of the Jeep's floorboard. He knew because, determined to drive himself the three-hour trip home, he had been denied medication for the pain. And he knew that night when, having hobbled into his apartment on crutches generously loaned to him by the Hunter Mountain Volunteer Ambulance Corps, he made dinner of three frozen tacos, five aspirins, and a half bottle of red cooking wine. But at least, he realized as he finally succumbed to sleep sometime after midnight, not once had his thoughts wandered to the subject of Joey Spadafino.

EIGHT

If the pain from Dean's ankle was less noticeable by Monday, it was due only to the fact that his entire body ached. He felt as though he had spent an hour in a clothes dryer at high speed. On top of the pain, he had difficulty learning the rhythm of walking on his crutches, nearly falling twice on the way to court, once landing so painfully with his weight on his right foot that he saw stars and felt he might actually pass out.

And there was the humiliation of it all. Dean coped with that by upgrading the slope that he had wiped out on. Belt Parkway became Kamikaze, and the mishap had not been caused by crossed tips at all, but rather by an out-of-control madman who had sideswiped Dean but ironically emerged unscathed himself.

At the computer in his office, Dean prepared a set of motion papers on the case of the *People v. Joseph Spadafino*. In it he asked the court to inspect the transcript of the grand jury proceedings, which was still secret to the defense, to see if perhaps there had been insufficient evidence presented or some procedural irregularity committed that would require dismissal and representation, though he knew that Bingham would have been careful and the evidence supporting the charges plentiful. He moved for copies of lab reports, property vouchers, the 911 tape (the recording of any calls made to the Police Department on the emergency number, as well as the radio traffic among the units involved in the chase and arrest of the defendant), the sprint report (the computer log and printout of those same calls and radio traffic), the toxicology and serology reports that would be prepared by the Medical Examiner's Office, and the photographs of the crime scene (all of which the defense was entitled to for the asking at this stage), and for a long list of police reports (which it was not). He made a demand that the prosecution turn over any exculpatory material, information pointing toward the defendant's innocence, which it might have in its possession, formally referred to as Brady material after the case that first entitled the defense to it. He moved also for certain pre-trial suppression hearings, each deriving its name from a defendant whose case had established the right to challenge the constitutionality of how some item of evidence had been obtained: a Mapp hearing to test whether there had been sufficient probable cause for the police to stop Joey, search him, and seize the cash and knife found in his pockets; a Wade hearing to determine if any witnesses had been given an opportunity to view Joey after his apprehension under circumstances more suggestive than those at a properly conducted lineup; and a Huntley hearing to ensure that any statement made by Joey after he had been taken into custody had been preceded by a waiver of his right to remain silent and consult with a lawyer.

Then, because his ankle hurt too much for the prospect of negotiating the subway steps for the trip uptown, he thumbed through his Spadafino case file. It was already an inch thick. In addition to extra copies of the motion he had just prepared, it contained the original Criminal Court complaint, the computerized printout of Joey's criminal record, the indictment, the DA's Voluntary Disclosure Form, the autopsy report, the written statement given the detectives, Dean's notes of his interviews with Joey, pages with headings like "Things to Do" and "Thoughts," Joey's written account of the events leading up to his arrest, and finally, Joey's letter from jail. It was the letter that Dean ended up staring at absentmindedly, simply because it was the last item in the file, relegated to the back of the folder owing to its insignificance.

Dear Mr. Dean

Why are they sayin I robed the man I tole you I took his money but thats all I neuer robed him I neuer pult out my nife This is the Gods honist trueth Why wood they say those things And a nother thing I neuer tole the Dts that I rob the man They must of forgered page 2 of my statemint Please Please Please help me I haue no body but you

Dean leafed back through the file until he found the statement taken by the detectives. He looked at the signature at the bottom of the first page. He turned the page and studied the signature at the bottom of the second page. They certainly looked alike. He used his fingernail to straighten and remove the staple that joined the two pages. Separating them, he placed them so the signatures were side by side. The similarity left no doubt: whoever had signed the first had also signed the other. The detectives had not "forgered" the signature on page two.

But, knowing that his client would insist they had unless confronted with the proof himself, Dean took the two pages and limped up front to the copy machine. There he used the enlargement feature to blow up the signatures, one directly beneath the other, onto a single page.

Then he enlarged the enlargement, and finally the enlargement of the enlargement. When he had finished, he held in front of him a piece of paper containing virtually nothing but the two signatures, somewhat blurred but magnified to page-filling dimensions.

Dean stared at the paper in disbelief for a long time, but there was no getting around it.

They were identical.

Not just similar. Identical.

Identical in every stroke, every blur, every imperfection. Identical down to the dot over the I in *Spadafino*. Identical where the pen had skipped while forming the P in *Joseph*. Absolutely, perfectly identical. Copy machine identical.

They were the same signature, mechanically reproduced.

That evening, as he sat in front of his fireplace, his leg propped up on a pillow, Dean contemplated the significance of his discovery. There was no doubt in his mind that the detectives had somehow altered the confession they had written out for Joey Spadafino, making it look like he had signed both pages when in fact he had signed only one. A handwriting expert would be needed to prove the duplication, but for now Dean's own crude method would suffice.

Joey had admitted signing the first page and he freely acknowledged that everything it contained was true: he had been standing in the doorway on Bleecker Street; he had seen the man approach; he had thought about robbing him but had not hit him, cut him, or hurt him; he had taken the money and money clip while the man was lying on the sidewalk.

By contrast, Joey had denied signing the second page, insisting that he had never told the detectives the major admission it contained: that he had yelled, "Freeze, motherfucker!" to the man and demanded his money. Subsequently, Joey had consistently denied doing either of those things—to Bingham in the Q&A, videotaped barely a half hour later; and to Dean in both the narrative he had written out and the interviews since. So adamant had Joey been that he had finally accused the detectives of "forgering" his signature on the disputed second page, an accusation that had initially struck Dean as too absurd to take seriously, but one that now seemed supported by the evidence.

Buy *why* had the detectives doctored the statement to include the demand for money on Joey's part? Particularly when they had an ironclad case, complete with eyewitnesses, without that admission. It didn't make sense.

Or did it?

This was a big case, Dean reminded himself. The death of the Police Commissioner had been an extraordinary event, receiving headline coverage not only in New York, but across the nation. Within police circles, it was even bigger. No crime of this magnitude had ever touched the Department so directly; at One Police Plaza, it was nothing short of the Crime of the Century. The pressure to "solve" it was enormous. And with the suspect already in custody and admitting that the money in his pocket had come from the fallen victim, all that was left in terms of "solving" the crime was getting the prisoner to confess. When he had balked at the point of admitting having demanded money from the Commissioner, the detectives had simply gone ahead and put on paper the magic words they couldn't quite pry from his mouth. Then they had somehow reproduced Spadafino's signature from the first page onto the second.

Before he had been a lawyer, Dean had been a cop. For two and a half years he had worked the streets as an agent for the Drug Enforcement Administration of the U.S. Justice Department. As a gangly kid fresh out of college, his youthful appearance had enabled him to make undercover buys from mid-level heroin and cocaine suppliers who sized him up as too young to be a cop. Ironically, he had been slower to win the confidence of his fellow agents, who suspected him—with his law-school aspirations and ability to read serious books and write grammatical sentences—of being a "plant" placed among their ranks to investigate their own wrongdoings and report on them. For as Dean slowly gained their grudging respect, he learned that there was plenty of wrongdoings to report, had he been inclined to do so. Short of stealing money and reselling the very drugs they were sworn to seize (acts which were by no means confined to only a few of his peers) was the more common offense of tampering with the truth in order to make a search become legal or an arrest stand up in court (behavior which was virtually universal, and departure from which could actually cause an agent to be ostracized).

It was the latter course of conduct, and the fact that almost all in law enforcement whom he had encountered then or since embraced it, that intrigued Dean. The rationale was clear enough: police officers, almost to a man, believe that the laws were written and are invariably interpreted to favor the criminal; in order to balance the scales of justice, they have to do what they can to make sure that those few who do get caught aren't thereafter permitted to slip through the net on some absurd legal technicality. It's merely a classic application of the end justifying the means, and the fact that in many cases the means include false sworn reports and perjured testimony seldom bothers the officer involved, who invariably feels that he's the good guy, doing what he must in an us-against-them world.

And that same rationale, Dean recognized, was undoubtedly what confronted him here. A pair of detectives, who surely saw themselves as good and honorable men, had a two-bit, ex-con mugger who had caused the death of the Police Commissioner while robbing him. They knew he was guilty: he had all but confessed, though he'd cunningly shied away from admitting the magic words at the last moment. But they weren't fooled, and they weren't going to take any chances; they'd do it for him. Justice would be done after all. And if, in the process, the detectives themselves were to receive a bit of special recognition for extracting the perpetrator's signed confession, so much the better; the truth was they were overworked, underpaid, and they put their lives on the line for the rest of the people of this rotten city every day of the week. . . .

Dean awoke with a start, his ankle throbbing. Momentarily disoriented, he needed a moment to realize that he'd fallen asleep on the couch in his living room. He struggled to reposition his leg, then looked at the clock: 3:46.

Something was wrong with the way he had figured things out last night. He struggled to regain his train of thought, much the way he sometimes struggled, usually in vain, to recapture the thread of some erotic dream that had slipped away upon his awakening.

The detectives had altered the statement, rationalizing that the end justified the means. There was nothing startling about that. So what was Dean missing?

Nothing, as long as Joey Spadafino had in fact demanded money from Commissioner Wilson and afterward was simply too smart to admit it to anyone. But suppose that *wasn't* the case. Suppose just for a moment that the reason Joey kept denying the demand was because it had truly never happened. Joey's version was that he had thought about robbing the man but decided against it, that the man had suddenly grabbed his chest and collapsed. What if all that was true?

Bullshit.

Stop getting soft in the head, Dean told himself. Just because cops lie, it doesn't mean that criminals tell the truth. He struggled to raise himself on his elbows, rolled over into a new position, and closed his eyes.

Joey Spadafino senses that his lawyer isn't buying his story of deciding at the last moment not to rob the guy. He knows it's a bad thing to have a Legal Aid or an 18-B who thinks you're guilty, but he's got no money to hire a street lawyer. It's not that he doesn't like his lawyer; he does. It's just that if a guy thinks you did the crime, he's simply not going to fight for you the same as if he thinks you're innocent. Anybody knows that. So he decides to write a letter to the judge asking for a new 18-B.

But Joey knows he's not good at writing. So he pays two days' worth of desserts to an inmate they call Sleepy, who has hooded eyelids that make him look like he's always falling asleep, to help him write a letter to the judge. Joey tells Sleepy what he wants to say, and Sleepy puts it into long words and legal language. There are a lot of "most respectfullys," "wherefores," and "aforementioneds." It's going to be a very impressive letter. When Joey gets to the part complaining about how his lawyer has been out to Rikers Island only once to visit him, Sleepy stops him.

"He ackshully came out here?"

"Yeah," says Joey. "One fuckin' time is all."

"When?"

"Coupla Satadays ago."

"On a Sataday? You telling me your lawyer came out here on a Sataday?" Sleepy is incredulous.

In the end, they tear up the letter.

NINE

Walter Bingham's written response to Dean's motion on the Spadafino case arrived in the morning's mail. Bingham was getting prompt, apparently. It was pretty standard stuff. In the computer age, the New York County District Attorney's Office had developed a standard form to deal with defense motions. If a standard form could have a personality, this one was guarded and uninformative. It conceded that the judge could inspect the grand jury minutes, but promised that the inspection would reveal no insufficiency of evidence or procedural irregularity. It refused to provide names, addresses, and dates of birth of prosecution witnesses, none of which Dean had requested. It declined to provide police reports to which the defense was not entitled until the trial began. It conceded that pre-trial hearings might have to be conducted, but insisted that at no time had the defendant's rights been violated so as to warrant the suppression of any evidence.

Enclosed with the response was a copy of the autopsy report, which Dean already had. Stapled to this one, however, was the serology report, which Dean hadn't seen before. It contained the results of laboratory tests done on a sample of blood taken from Commissioner Wilson at the autopsy. According to the lab, every test they had run on the sample had proved negative—there was no trace of opiates, barbiturates, amphetamines—except for the presence of alcohol, which was calculated at .04 percent, or four parts per ten thousand parts of body weight. Well less than legally intoxicated, which New York State law presumed at .10 percent, and even under the level for impaired, which began at .05 percent. But not altogether insignificant: Wilson had had a couple of drinks that evening. Not that that fact had any legal significance.

Also enclosed were copies of the property vouchers filled out by the police. There were no surprises here: the Voluntary Disclosure Form, which Dean had received several weeks ago along with the indictment, had summarized them. The police had vouchered the money seized from Spadafino, which came to $288.15, broken down into various denominations; the Kool cigarette pack with nine remaining cigarettes; the knife; a jacket and cap Joey had been wearing, no doubt seized because witnesses had described them and would be asked to identify them at trial; and two books of matches. From the crime scene, they had vouchered eleven Kool cigarette butts, which, added to the nine remaining, completed a pack; they had also retrieved thirteen used matches. And finally, in a trash container on Seventh Avenue that the defendant had directed them to, the police had succeeded in finding the gold money clip with a miniature New York Police Department shield. The tiny number one on the shield identified it as belonging to none other than the Police Commissioner himself.

Dean flipped back to the list of items seized from Joey Spadafino. He focused his attention on the description of the knife.

1   Folding pocketknife with dark blue handle and stainless steel blade, overall length 6".

Dean recalled Walter Bingham's assertion at the bail application that one of the eyewitnesses to the robbery had been able to describe the knife. A six-inch folding knife had a blade of three inches at most. Joey's hand presumably would have been closed around the handle, which was dark in color at any rate. That would have left nothing exposed but a three-inch blade, in a snowstorm at two-thirty in the morning. Where could this eyewitness have been, Dean wondered, to be in a position not only to see the blade, but to be able to actually *describe* it later on?

Dean got out his Spadafino case file and found a copy of his written motion. He compared the list of documents he had asked for with what Bingham had supplied him. The property vouchers were all accounted for. He had the autopsy report and now the serology report. That meant he still needed the toxicology report, which generally took longer. Bingham had indicated that there were indeed photos of the crime scene, and copies would be forthcoming. Dean had the defendant's written statement to the detectives, complete with the altered signature on the second page, about which he had decided not to say anything yet. He also had his own copy of the videotaped Q&A.

That left the 911 tape and the sprint report printout of the emergency calls and police radio traffic relating to the case. Dean's interest in those items had been kindled by his skepticism over whether an eyewitness had truly been able to describe the knife in Spadafino's hand. If any witnesses had called 911, the calls would have been automatically tape-recorded, and the defense was entitled to hear them.

Dean picked up the phone and dialed Walter Bingham's number. Already he knew it by heart.

"Bingham," came the answer.

"Hello, Walter. Dean Abernathy."

"Hey, Dean. Howsitgoing?"

They exchanged small talk, male bonding stuff. Dean was actually fond of Bingham, in a way. He was real, he shared Dean's impatience with bullshit, and he was a Knicks fan.

"Got your response, Walter."

"Yeah? Pretty well written, wouldn't you say?"

"Spelling's okay, grammar could use some help. I'm afraid you lost a lot for lack of originality, though. Overall, I give it a C minus."

"Shit," said Bingham. "I thought I was doing better."

"Keep taking those review courses."

"You mean you think there's hope?"

"No, but keep taking them anyway. They're deductible."

"You're a hard man, Dean."

"Me? You send me nothing but a pile of property vouchers. How about the nine-one-one tape, the sprint report? How about the Fives?" said Dean, referring to the stack of DD-5's, the follow-up reports prepared by the detectives investigating the crime, which would include summaries of interviews with witnesses.

"You know you're not entitled to the Fives until trial, Dean."

"What's the big deal here?" Dean asked. "You let me have them on *Peralta*." Hector Peralta was a minor hit man whom Dean had represented; it had been Bingham's case.

"Peralta was different."

"How was Peralta different?" Dean wanted to know.

"Peralta didn't kill the Police Commissioner, last I checked."

"I actually suspected that," said Dean. "Why does that make a difference?"

"Get real, willya, Dean? It makes a difference because I've got every cop in the city with a rank of captain or higher calling me on this case every fucking hour of the day. I've got my bureau chief reviewing every piece of paper that crosses my desk. I've got the Old Man demanding weekly progress reports, for chrissakes. I've got three thousand reporters wanting exclusive stories. Yesterday I had a guy follow me to the fucking *toilet* for an interview. That's why it makes a difference."

"How did the interview in the toilet go?" Dean asked. "Good acoustics, I bet."

"It went about the same as all the others. I'm not giving anybody anything."

"Including me."

"Look, Dean. I'll get you the sprint report. I'm still waiting for the nine-one-one tape. As soon as I get it, you can have it. That's the best I can do right now."

Bingham was right about the DD-5s; the defense was not entitled to them until trial, so there wasn't much Dean could do about them. But the 911 tape and sprint report were another matter. Dean fished around in his file drawer until he found a blank subpoena and began filling it out. Those items he could obtain on his own.

The Spadafino case appeared for the first time in Part 56, where it would remain for all further proceedings, including trial.

Part 56 was the domain of Justice Harold J. Rothwax, who was universally admired for his ability and disliked for his temperament. He knew the law as well as any trial judge, and his rulings were invariably correct and generally fair, except when it came to matters of credibility; like the great majority of judges, Rothwax deferred to police witnesses and chose to accept their version of events when it conflicted with that of defendants, even when the officer's testimony seemed conveniently tailored to secure a conviction. It was, Dean knew, the judicial extension of the end-justifying-the-means doctrine: when you had a bad crime or a bad defendant, or both, you could expect most judges to do what they could to side with the prosecution. And the main thing they could do, without fear of criticism or reversal by an appellate court, was to say they believed the police. Rothwax tended to do just that.

He was a judge who worked hard and expected the lawyers who appeared before him to do the same. He was often disappointed on that score, and he displayed his disappointment in the form of a caustic, sarcastic humor that operated at the expense of defense attorneys, prosecutors, and defendants alike. His repertoire of one-liners included "You certainly have avoided the dangers of overpreparation," "You may go in now," and "If God were on your side, you'd be before another judge."

He was renowned for raising the bail of defendants whom other judges had released, and an absent or late defendant could expect to be remanded without any bail at all. He was coercive in plea negotiations: if a defendant refused an offer of a given amount of time in exchange for pleading guilty, the offer was promptly withdrawn and the time increased at the next court appearance. His demeanor had earned Harold Rothwax the imperious nickname of "Prince Hal," which some members of the defense bar expanded to the more ominous "Prince of Darkness."

Harold Rothwax and Dean Abernathy did have one thing in common. Rothwax, like Dean, preferred the bicycle as his method of transportation to and from the courthouse. Once, while presiding over the trial of Joel Steinberg, a lawyer accused of murdering his illegally adopted daughter, the judge had been sideswiped and knocked off his bike on the way to work. Breaking his fall with his hands, he had suffered two fractures to both wrists. But by early afternoon he was on the bench, sporting twin casts and telling the jury, "There are good days and bad days. So far this has been a bad day." Then, turning to the prosecutor, "Call your next witness." When the jury went on to convict Steinberg of manslaughter, Rothwax sentenced him to the maximum term the law permitted.

Dean Abernathy and Harold Rothwax got along. Dean's penchant for preparation earned him the judge's respect. As for Dean, when he had a complicated legal question or a difficult ethics problem, it was Rothwax he would go to for advice.

Once, on a plane to Colorado, Dean had struck up a conversation with the passenger he found himself seated next to. Upon learning that Dean was a criminal defense lawyer, the woman had asked him if he happened to know her friend Hal Rothwax. When Dean allowed that he did, she asked him for his opinion of the judge. Knowing that his remarks might find their way back to Rothwax, Dean had nevertheless been candid in his review. After describing some of Rothwax's strengths and weaknesses, he'd added the observation that the judge's sarcasm seemed to reveal a basically angry person, and Dean had been forced to conclude that his workday was, as a rule, unhappy.

Sure enough, not a month later, Dean was sitting in Part 56 when he heard himself summoned to the bench. "Abernathy!" the judge called out. "Step up, please."

After approaching, Dean listened as Rothwax brought the incident full circle. "It seems you were on a plane recently with a very close friend of my wife and mine," began the judge gravely. "And while she reported to my wife that you had some very complimentary things to say about me, she also related your impression that I appear to be unhappy in my work. Well, I just want you to know that, as a result, before I leave the house every day now, my wife shakes her finger at me and lectures me, 'Now, Harold, you make sure you smile a lot and have a happy day today.' So I must thank you for that wonderful addition to my life."

But if his wife's lectures had worked, their impact was not readily apparent. Harold Rothwax continued to be a tough judge with no sympathy for habitual offenders and little tolerance for relaxation in his courtroom. It had by no means been by accident that he had been selected by the administrative judge to preside at the trial in the case of the *People v. Joseph Spadafino*.

Once again the media had assembled, although there was no television camera in sight this time. Apparently the press had accepted the notion that there would be no further significant court appearances until the beginning of the trial itself, or at least the pre-trial hearings. Nonetheless, a good dozen or so reporters had come to get another glimpse of Commissioner Wilson's killer, and to try to pry a quotable comment or two out of the principals. Also present were two sketch artists, who had arrived early, taken seats in the front row, and were already busy re-creating the court-room in colored chalk.

On several occasions in the past, Dean had been involved in other "high profile" cases worthy of the sketch artists. Each time, the artists had called him afterward to ask if he might be interested in buying one or more of the sketches that included him. Once, his curiosity had prompted him to ask the price. The response, several hundred dollars, had astonished him. His lack of interest had led to a series of follow-up calls over the next week or two, each offering a further reduced price, culminating in an "absolutely final offer" of twenty-five dollars. Dean, who never even hung his diplomas on his wall, preferring nautical charts and drawings of sailboats, persisted in his refusal, but was amused to learn how nonexistent the market was for such stuff.

Justice Rothwax took the bench unceremoniously, as was his habit. Seeing both Dean and Walter Bingham in the front row, he inquired of his court clerk whether Joseph Spadafino had been produced yet by the Department of Corrections. Court language tended to dehumanize defendants, and they were "produced" rather than brought in. And to inform the clerk how many prisoners had been "produced," a corrections officer would supply the clerk with a "body count," a phrase that never failed to transport Dean back to the evening newscasts of the Vietnam War era.

Joseph Spadafino's body had indeed been produced, and the case was called. The defendant was ushered out of a door that led to the holding pens. Dean was struck again by how small and insignificant Joey looked. Justice Rothwax asked the lawyers to approach, and they walked up to the bench. Dean had mastered the crutches well enough to negotiate around the court reporter's table without incident.

"Is there an offer in this case?" Rothwax wanted to know, turning to Bingham.

"Yeah," replied Bingham. "Murder."

"I'll supply the sarcasm in this courtroom, Mr. Bingham," said the judge. Murder was the top count in the indictment; to "offer" it meant to make no offer at all.

Rothwax turned to Dean, fixing his eyes on him over his frameless half-glasses. Dean was ready for the drill. "If your client is interested, he can have the minimum today, fifteen to life. Next time it will be twenty to life. After trial he gets the maximum, twenty-five to life. Do you want a second call to talk with him?"

"No," said Dean, "he's not interested."

"Fine with me," Rothwax said, making some notations on a file card. "Okay," he said, looking up again. "Let's talk about scheduling." He was pleased to learn that defense motions had already been served, filed, and responded to. There was a brief conversation about pre-trial discovery. Bingham assured him in his sincerest voice that he was proceeding as quickly as he could but was still awaiting certain documents. "Okay," said Rothwax. "Why don't you gentlemen step back so we can give the press something to cover, before they file a complaint against me."

Dean resumed his place next to the defendant. He leaned over and whispered in Joey Spadafino's ear, "I can get you fifteen to life right now. You'd do twelve or thirteen."

"Fuck, no!" Joey answered, loud enough so that reporters and lawyers in the front rows laughed. Rothwax hit the top of his desk once with a gavel, and the courtroom quieted.

"I take it," the judge said, "that after careful consideration, your client has just voiced his opinion of the offer made to him, Mr. Abernathy."

Dean smiled. "It would seem so, Your Honor."

"Well, at least it has the virtue of clarity." That, too, was a standard Rothwax one-liner. "Very well," said the judge. "The record should reflect that defense motions have been made and responded to. The People will submit the grand jury minutes to me for inspection. There will be a Mapp/Wade/Huntley hearing prior to trial. The matter is adjourned until the twenty-third for a ruling on the grand jury minutes, and for the parties to continue the pre-trial discovery process. You may go in, sir. Next case."

It was vintage Rothwax.

The cast came off that Friday, and Dean traded in his crutches for a cane. An elastic support still covered his ankle and required him to wear a loosely laced sneaker on his right foot, but at least he could walk and tolerate the pain of putting some weight on the foot.

The same day, he received a letter from the Police Department's Legal Affairs Division. Dean's subpoena seeking the 911 tape and the sprint report had been rejected. Across the face of it, someone had written in red ink, "SUPPLIED TO DISTRICT ATTORNEY." It was the first time Dean had ever seen such a notation. He called Walter Bingham.

"No, I still didn't get the tape," Bingham assured him.

"How about the sprint report?"

"I think I've got that," said Bingham. "Let me see." There was a long pause, during which Dean could hear papers being shuffled. At one point he thought he could hear the muffled sound of voices, as though Bingham had placed the receiver, mouthpiece facing down, on an upholstered couch or chair. Or intentionally covered it with his hand.

After several minutes, Bingham came back on. "Yeah, I've got the sprint," he said. "How about I drop a copy in the mail?"

"No, I've got to come over to the building anyway," Dean lied. "I'll see you in fifteen minutes." He hung up without giving Bingham a chance to argue.

The usual seven-minute walk took Dean twelve minutes. He winced in pain each time he had to step off a curb and land on the street surface below. He had thought all sidewalks had sloped portions at intersections for wheelchair access; he was surprised to discover how many did not.

Dean knew the receptionist at the seventh-floor entrance to the District Attorney's Office, and she waved him through without asking his destination. He negotiated the one flight down and found Bingham's room. The door was open, but he knocked anyway as he entered.

"Hey, Dean. How's the cripple?"

"Getting along." It might have been Dean's imagination, but he thought Bingham covered some papers on his desk with a file before extending his hand to shake Dean's.

"This is the sprint report," Bingham said, handing Dean several pages containing small computer type.

Looking down at it, Dean could see that certain portions had been blacked out. "What's with the Magic Marker attack?" he asked.

"Oh, that. I've redacted it. All that's covered up is the names, addresses, and phone numbers of civilian witnesses. S.O.P."

"C'mon, Walter. That's standard when your witnesses need protection from an organized crime defendant or a drug dealer with nasty friends. My client's a fucking homeless guy, sitting in jail without bail, with no friends or family in the whole world."

"Sorry, Dean," said Bingham, and he looked to Dean as though he might actually be. "You know I'm not exactly calling all the shots on this one."

"Who is?"

"People who get paid a lot more than I do. Don't ask me questions I can't answer, Dean."

"What are they afraid of? This case is a goddamn grounder for you guys."

"If it's such a grounder, why doesn't your guy take the fifteen to life?" Bingham asked. "You know Rothwax will whack him out after trial. And I know you're not one to force it to trial for the publicity."

"What can I tell you, Walter? My guy says he didn't rob anyone."

"Right," said Bingham. They both smiled.

Hobbling back to his office, Dean wondered if his failure to encourage Joey Spadafino to plead guilty and take the fifteen to life might in fact have been motivated in part by his own desire for the publicity the trial would be certain to bring him. Lawyers did it all the time. Jean Harris might have plea-bargained and been out in three years for killing the doctor who was her former lover. Dean liked to think he was a cut above that, but who knew, really?

It was not until he reached his office and tossed his cane on his couch that it struck Dean that, in Walter Bingham's office, there was neither a couch nor an upholstered chair to muffle a telephone mouthpiece.

Dean spread the sprint report sheets out on his desk. Each page was subdivided into twelve boxes, two across by six down. The boxes in turn contained computer-printed lines made up of coded numbers and abbreviations arcane enough to stump an experienced cryptologist, but easily decipherable to someone with a working knowledge of police jargon.

Since each box referred to a single "job," or investigation, Dean's first task was to skim through them to determine which boxes related to the Bleecker Street incident and which related to other jobs altogether. The latter he drew a line through to eliminate. When he had completed the four pages, he was left with a total of thirteen boxes pertaining to the Bleecker Street job. Using scissors, tape, and the copy machine, Dean cut and pasted, copied, and enlarged until he had three pages containing all thirteen relevant boxes in sequential order and legible type size. Then he began the more arduous task of deciphering the coded lines of print.

The first entry began:

```
0228    911 Op 23 10-20 vicinty 76
        Bleekr x sts 6th & 7th
```

To Dean this meant that the job had begun with a call to the 911 operator at 2:28 A.M., reporting a robbery in progress in the vicinity of 76 Bleecker Street, between Sixth and Seventh Avenues.

```
0229    Any 13 Pct unit: 10-20 76 Bleekr
        6th 7th Ave
0229    Adam resp. Any further?
0230    No furth, Adam. Civ hung up. Any
        other units in area?
0230    Charlie on 7th Av hding S, ETA 2
        mins
```

The remainder of the first box told Dean that the operator, within a minute of receiving the 911 call, had put out a request for any radio car in the Thirteenth Precinct to report to the scene. Car A had been the first to respond, asking if the operator had any further information. No, the operator had responded; the civilian caller had hung up the phone. Answering a request for further cars in the area, Car C had radioed in to say they were on their way, heading south on Seventh Avenue, about two minutes away.

Dean continued through the boxes. The next several dealt

with radio traffic among the responding units and the central operator. Then the original civilian had called back.

```
0232      911 Op 06 Dupl Job: Fem clld
          earlier rpts perp took money fled
          rt on Bleekr towrd 7th Av. Perp
          is MW or Hisp 5-4 to 5-7 dark
          jak blue wool cap ID's self as
          ███████████████ tel ██████████
```

The operator had transmitted the description of the perpetrator to the responding units, together with the fact that he had headed right to Seventh Avenue. This time the caller, a woman, had left her name and phone number, though both items had been blacked out on Dean's copy.

Dean continued to read. In spite of the fact that he had been told that there were two eyewitnesses to the crime, he noted that no other civilian had called the 911 operator. All of the remaining entries chronicled the chase and arrest of the perpetrator. It had ended six minutes after it had begun.

```
0234      Adam to Central One under at 7th
          and Spring 4 units on scene No
          further, repeat no furth
```

Dean went back to the boxes containing the two calls from the female civilian. He did not know her name, address, or telephone. What he did know was that, somehow, he had to find her. Accentuate the positive, he told himself. What *did* he know? Unless she was calling from a phone booth on the street in a snowstorm at two-thirty in the morning, it meant she was in one of the buildings near 76 Bleecker Street, where the crime had occurred. Moreover, in order to be able to see that the perpetrator had actually taken money, Dean figured she had to be either in 76 Bleecker Street itself or directly opposite, more or less. Since 76 was an even number, it would be on the downtown, or south, side of Bleecker Street. If the caller was in that building, her window would face north, putting Seventh Avenue to her left. But she had told the 911 operator that the perpetrator had fled to the right—

no doubt meaning her right—toward Seventh Avenue. That placed her across the street from 76.

The District Attorney's Office might not want to give the defense the name of its eyewitnesses, Dean decided, but that didn't mean that the defense had to sit on its butt.

He got his address book out and looked under "I" for Investigators. He had used a number of private investigators over the years. They tended to be retired detectives who would work hard on the first case you brought them in on. But the rates they were paid to work on assigned cases such as this one were pitifully low, and they soon tired of putting in the creative energy and time-consuming canvassing that criminal investigations demanded.

Dean made two calls. The first was to Jimmy McDermott, a former federal agent who was pretty good when he was sober. If he was in, he was not answering his phone. The second was to Charlie Hayes, who had a cheerful message on his answering machine that promised he'd get back to the caller as soon as possible.

Patience was not Dean Abernathy's strong suit. He tossed the Spadatino file into a briefcase, along with an extra writing pad and pen. He decided to keep his suit and tie on instead of changing back into his more comfortable jeans-and-sneakers outfit. He figured he might appear a little less threatening in his lawyer costume. Then he headed for the subway to Greenwich Village, to find a female who lived across from 76 Bleecker Street. More or less.

It's not with the two Dominicans that Joey finally gets into his first fight. Instead it is with a black kid who can't be any taller than five-four, but who's built like a fire hydrant. It's on a Monday night, and they're in the TV room, watching a rerun of M*A*S*H. Something that Hawkeye says strikes Joey as funny, and he laughs. This black kid sitting in front of him turns around and says, "Why don't you shut your mouth, motherfucker."

Joey knows it's not a question that calls for an answer, but before giving it too much thought, he says, "Because it was funny. Lighten up a little, man."

The black kid says, "I ain't your man," and then, in one movement, he is up and on Joey, knocking him backward off his chair. Joey, falling, grabs the black kid by the front of his shirt and pulls him down with him. They roll on the floor together, too close to hit each other with any force. A CO shouts something that Joey can't understand, and he and other inmates grab at Joey and the black kid, trying to pry their arms loose. Just when Joey lets go of the black kid, the black kid butts him, forehead against forehead. Joey sees a flash of light, then feels the pain. His forehead is opened so bad it'll take seventeen stitches at the infirmary to close it. Meanwhile, the black kid doesn't even seem to be hurt.

Late that night, back in his cell and nursing a headache that'll last two days, Joey wonders if the black kid avoided injury because he was ready for the collision, or because black heads are somehow harder than white ones.

Lying on the two-inch-thick mattress of his bunk, he's aware that in some peculiar way, he's glad to have been in his first fight on the Block, relieved that it happened, that he didn't back down, and that he's survived it. It makes him feel like he can survive anything. He also kind of likes the idea that he'll have a mean scar across his forehead. He knows it's something that'll warn others not to mess with him: here's a guy who'll fight back, who doesn't give a fuck.

What's more, he's glad he's told his lawyer what they can do with that fifteen-to-life shit. Joey Spadafino didn't murder nobody, no matter what they say, and he ain't copping out this time around. They can bring on the whole fucking twenty-five to life; he's taking this one to trial.

TEN

Dean found 76 Bleecker Street without difficulty. He could readily see why Joey Spadafino had selected that particular doorway to stand in. It was deeply recessed and would have afforded its occupant a fair amount of protection from either the reach of swirling snow or the visibility of an approaching victim.

There was only one building directly across the street, 77 Bleecker, but instead of being a small brownstone like most of the buildings on the block, it was a larger apartment house. Good news and bad, thought Dean. Good because it increased the likelihood that his witness had to have been in it to see as clearly as she apparently had; bad because it was large enough to contain many apartments, instead of the four or five likely in a brownstone.

Dean noticed also that there was no pay phone in sight, in either direction.

Crossing the street to 77 Bleecker, he counted six stories including the one at street level. Except for the first, which was broken by the entrance, each story contained seven windows, though he could not determine where one apartment ended and another began.

An outside door, closed but not locked, let him into a vestibule that contained a panel of names arranged by apartment number and letter, each accompanied by a buzzer. There was also a telephone intercom. Dean counted twenty-three names in all, beginning with 1A and ending with 6D.

He tried the handle to the inner door but found it locked. He was about to reach for his wallet and try either a credit card or a small piece of venetian blind slat he had kept from his DEA days, when he heard a noise from within the inner door. Seeing someone approaching, Dean pulled out his keys instead, put them up to his mouth and held them between his teeth. Then he tucked his briefcase under one arm and leaned his weight in an exaggerated fashion on his cane, which he grasped with the opposite hand. When the inner door swung open, revealing a gray-haired woman led by a tugging dachshund, Dean released his bite on the keys, letting them land noisily on the floor. As he struggled to pick them up, the woman held the inner door wide for him, all the while bestowing a sympathetic smile upon him. The dachshund, not fooled for a moment, growled impatiently and strained at its leash toward the outer door.

Dean found the elevator and pushed the top button, being careful to keep his orientation with regard to the front of the building. Getting off on the sixth floor, he was able to determine that only 6A and 6B fronted on Bleecker Street, while the windows to 6C and 6D had to face the sides or rear of the building. Using the stairs on the way down, he saw that the pattern repeated itself on each floor except the first, where a storage room of some sort replaced the B-line apartment, leaving only 1A in the front.

Back in the vestibule, Dean removed a pad and pen from his briefcase and copied the information he needed from the panel. When he was finished, he had a list of eleven names.

1A NOVACEK (Super)
2A CIPPOLINO
2B H. DILLARD
3A KLEIN/RINER
3B J. KILLIAN
4A DEL VALLE
4B CHANG
5A DRABINOWITZ, S.
5B JACOBANIS-BREWSTER

6A A & M MANGIARACINO
6B ALTSHULER

Dean's first reaction was that he had stumbled upon a miniature United Nations in the heart of Greenwich Village. But he was pleased: all of the apartments had names to go with them, and that at least gave him a starting place.

Dean knew that he couldn't rush this, that he dared not charge in and go from door to door expecting that the lawyer for the murderer of the Police Commissioner would be given the time of day, much less the answer to who had witnessed and reported the crime. He had to be more patient than that. And more creative.

Back at his apartment, Dean decided to make himself a real meal for a change. Though he stubbornly refused to follow recipes (they reminded him of lessons), he considered himself an innovative cook and was not above using his talent to impress a female friend now and then. His philosophy was simple: if you used ingredients you liked individually, and didn't do anything to hurt them in the cooking process, you were bound to end up with something good. Another cardinal rule was to avoid garlic at all costs. He hated it in any way, shape, or form with a passion, and had come to believe that he could detect the most minute quantity in any food that contained it, the way a shark is said to be able to pick up one part of blood in a million parts of seawater.

On the way home, he had bought fresh pasta, bread, a red pepper (they were on sale), asparagus (the thin ones), and scallions. No garlic. Dicing the vegetables, a task most would consider tedious, gave Dean the same kind of mindless pleasure he got from mowing a lawn in perfect lines. He didn't own a food processor, preferring to use a knife and wooden cutting board, making little piles of red, green, and white, the essential food-color groups. Then, using chicken broth in place of oil, he sautéed the mixture while the pasta boiled, making certain not to overcook either. He tasted the vegetables as he stirred them, adding salt, red pepper, and pinches of various dried green leaves that filled a dozen or so tiny jars on his kitchen shelf. He drained the pasta but did not rinse it, then added the vegetables. The result, along with a half a loaf of sourdough bread and a tall glass of iced tea sweetened with sugar and soured with lime, was dinner.

If the meal was good, the ambience was decidedly second-rate. Dean had no dining room table or, for that matter, dining room. He ate sitting on his all-purpose couch, plate balanced on his knees, breadcrumbs accumulating on his lap. Every month or so, he vacuumed his apartment, and the things he discovered underneath the cushions were wondrous to behold. Forks, spoons, loose change that had escaped from his pockets, all sorts of dessicated reminders of long-ago meals. Once he had found what he was certain was a tiny fetus, carefully planted there by some militant right-to-life group, only to realize upon closer scrutiny that it was a cooked shrimp that had somehow slipped away from its companions.

Sitting with his second glass of iced tea, Dean toyed with the idea of lighting a fire. He needed a break from work. But his thoughts drifted back to the Spadafino case. A lawyer by profession, Dean was still an investigator at heart, a carryover from his DEA days that would forever shape his approach to his craft. And the Bleecker Street puzzle beckoned him.

In the end, he opted for both a fire and work. Leaving the dishes unwashed, he set about laying a fire. He rolled pieces of newspaper into tubes tight enough to burn slowly, but not too tight to prevent some air from circulating within the sheets. He ripped the ends of each roll to allow the flame a starting place. On top of the paper he placed a kindling of twigs, small branches, and splinters from logs. Those he topped with three split logs, recognizing each from having cut and split them: one piece of ash, easily identifiable from its thick, deeply furrowed bark; a red oak, which would last into the night; and a small cedar log, which he selected for the scent it would produce. He placed a single sheet of newspaper on top of the logs, and lit it first. It burst into flame, creating an immediate draft up the narrow chimney. With the same match, Dean quickly lit the lower rolls of newspaper, then sat back and watched with a child's pleasure as the fuel ignited in stages, bottom to top.

On the floor in front of the fire, Dean spread out his copies of the sprint reports and the list of tenants living in the front apartments at 77 Bleecker Street, one of whom had to be the 911 caller. First he studied the sprint entry that contained the blacked-out name of the caller.

```
0232      911 Op 06 Dupl Job: Fem clld
          earlier rpts perp took money fled
          rt on Bleekr towrd 7th Av. Perp
          is MW or Hisp 5-4 to 5-7 dark
          jak blue wool cap ID's self as
          ███████████████ tel ████████
```

Dean held the page up to the light, but the blackout totally obscured the name. He tried a magnifying glass, but that didn't help, either. Next he marked off the characters on the portion of the line immediately above the blacked-out name.

```
jak blue wool
█████████████
```

Including the blank space over the last part of the blacked-out portion, Dean counted thirteen characters. He turned to the 77 Bleecker Street list.

1A NOVACEK (Super)
2A CIPPOLINO
2B H. DILLARD
3A KLEIN/RINER
3B J. KILLIAN
4A DEL VALLE
4B CHANG
5A DRABINOWITZ, S.
5B JACOBANIS-BREWSTER
6A A & M MANGIARACINO
6B ALTSHULER

Although the list included no first names, and the thirteen characters blacked out on the sprint report undoubtedly contained both a first and last name, or at least a name preceded by a Miss, Mrs., or Ms., it was a start. Since there had to be a space between the first and last name, or the title and the last name, at least three characters could be accounted for before even getting to the last name. So the last name could be ten characters at most. That immediately eliminated Drabinowitz and Mangiaracino, and narrowed the field to nine apartments and eleven last names.

Dean rummaged through his hall closet until he found a Manhattan phone directory. Starting at the top of his list, he was able to find numbers listed for seven of the nine remaining names. He entered each number alongside the name it went with, together with the first name or initial listed in the directory. Looking at his watch, Dean saw it was 9:35. Too late to start making calls. He didn't want the added alarm of a nighttime call, and he also figured his chances of the woman caller's answering the phone herself—in case she lived with a man—would be better during the day. He wondered if that was sexist thinking, then said, "Fuck it," and reached for another log to put on the fire. From its weight he could tell it was another piece of oak even before looking at the split side. He placed it carefully on the already burning logs, leaving a narrow space in front of it for a draft. Within seconds, a blue flame appeared in the space, filling it from left to right in much the same way as the broiler flame of a gas oven ignites.

Sitting there on the floor in front of the newly invigorated fire, Dean settled back against the couch and began composing phone introductions to the good people of 77 Bleecker Street.

Janet Killian answered the phone on the first ring. She had just put Nicole down for her afternoon nap, and didn't want her waking up.

"Hello," she said quietly.

"Hello," said a man's voice. "Is this Janet Killian?"

"Yes."

"Miss Killian, this is Investigator Frye. I'm calling you about the reward in connection with the killing of Commissioner Wilson."

"Yes?" said Janet.

"Well, it seems you're entitled to a major portion of it. It *was* you who made the first phone call to nine-one-one, after all, wasn't it?"

For a moment, Janet said nothing. Then she said, "I'm afraid I don't know what you're talking about," and hung up the phone.

* * *

A mile and a half away, sitting at his desk, Dean Abernathy crossed another name off his list and said, "Shit," to no one in particular.

Janet Killian found the business card in the wallet in her blue handbag. As instructed, she dialed the number printed on the lower left-hand corner.

A man's voice answered. "Midtown South."

"May I speak with Detective Richard Rasmussen, please?" Janet said.

ELEVEN

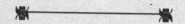

Dean felt as though he had reached a dead end. For one thing, he had whittled the 77 Bleecker Street list down to two names, Chang and Altshuler, neither of whom had a listed phone number. All of the others he had reached by phone, and none of them would acknowledge having been the 911 caller.

The most recent time he had been to the building, Dean had had to use his piece of venetian blind slat to slip the lock of the inner door. He was careful to look around before doing it, and made sure he could not be seen. When he came out some twenty minutes later, he noticed a dark blue Plymouth with two men sitting in it, three cars behind where he had parked his own Jeep. The men were white, fiftyish, and both wore sunglasses on what seemed, to Dean at least, a pretty overcast day.

As Dean pulled away from the curb, he watched the Plymouth in his rearview mirror, but it did not follow. Dean made a left on Sixth Avenue, then circled around to Seventh. Back at Bleecker, he pulled into a bus stop before turning into the block, where the Plymouth would now be in front of him. Walking to the corner, he saw that it had moved so that it was double-parked directly in front of 77 Bleecker Street. From the corner, it looked to Dean as though there was now only one man in the Plymouth, the driver. His impression was confirmed moments later, when the other man, still wearing his sunglasses, emerged from 77 Bleecker. He was a large man, broad-shouldered and beer-bellied. In the few seconds Dean had to observe him walking around the Plymouth and getting into it, Dean was certain he had seen the man before, but he could not quite place him. The two men sat in the Plymouth for a moment longer, then pulled away and drove off slowly.

Dean had walked back to his Jeep just in time to see a traffic department officer placing a fifty-five-dollar parking ticket on the windshield.

The building had not been the only disappointment, however. Despite repeated calls to Walter Bingham, Dean still didn't have the 911 tape. To be sure, Bingham had provided him with a steady trickle of other items. He had received, for example, a set of photographs of the crime scene, showing Commissioner Wilson lying dead in the wet snow, his open eyes eerily reflecting the flash of the camera lights. There had even been a shot of the trash basket on Seventh Avenue, its contents strewn on the sidewalk, and a closeup of the money clip recovered from exactly where Joey Spadafino had told the detectives he had thrown it.

Dean had also received a report from the Latent Print Unit of the Police Department. They had compared a partial fingerprint found on the knife recovered from Joseph Spadafino with those taken after his arrest, and found that the partial print was identical to that of the index finger of Spadafino's left hand, to the exclusion of all other persons. The report had hardly shocked Dean. After all, it was Spadafino's knife; Joey had told Dean that. What he continued to deny was that he had pulled it out before, during, or after the encounter with Commissioner Wilson. In fact, Dean had to admit that his client had been pretty persuasive on the point. "Hey," Joey had said in one of his recent meetings with Dean, "I'd forgot I *had* the fuckin' thing. Don't you think I woulda throwed it away before I got caught if I'd a used it to *rob* the fuckin' guy?" If it was not beautiful prose, it did seem to make a certain amount of sense.

Bingham had sent Dean some other worthless stuff as well. The Emergency Medical Service records contained the notes of the personnel who had responded by ambulance to where the lifeless body of Commissioner Wilson lay. The notes in turn depicted their efforts to resuscitate him until a Police Department surgeon had arrived and pronounced the Commissioner dead.

Then there were the usual two identification-of-body forms, one by a police officer, the other by a civilian who had known the deceased personally. In this case, it had been the Commissioner's nephew, Garth Wilson, who had responded to the morgue to verify that the body was indeed that of his uncle.

The death certificate, signed by Dr. Hans Van den Berg, the Deputy Medical Examiner who had performed the autopsy, certified that the Commissioner had died of a "massive coronary occlusion" at two-thirty in the morning. It listed the deceased's next of kin as his wife, Marie Crawford Wilson, of 76 Bleecker Street.

Finally, Bingham had sent Dean copies of the memo book entries of the various police officers who had responded to the robbery-in-progress radio run, participated in the chase and arrest of the defendant, or returned later to sift through the contents of the trash can on Seventh Avenue.

There were also copies of the memo book entries of a police officer named Jorge Santana, but instead of containing entries of times relating to the radio run or the events following it, almost all of its entries preceded the time of the crime. It was these entries that Dean turned to now, wondering what he was looking at.

1115	To garage to p.u. Dep. MV 226
1125	To res. of PC
1135	With PC to Chand S.H. W. 45th
1205	To 10th & 47th re refuel: 12.5 gals $17.50
1215	Ret to W. 45th
0215	With PC to res
0230	D.O. PC Bleecker & 7th
0300	D.O. Dep. MV 226 @ garage
0330	Off Duty

It didn't take Dean long to realize that Officer Santana's assignment that night had been as chauffeur to the Police Commissioner. He had dropped Wilson off a half block from his townhouse, five minutes before the Commissioner met Joey Spadafino and his death.

Working backward, Dean was able to reconstruct the events that led up to that moment. The drive to the townhouse had taken fifteen minutes, originating at West Forty-fifth Street. Except for a trip to Eleventh Avenue, Santana had waited for the Commissioner on Forty-fifth Street from around twelve until quarter after two in the morning. Although the exact location of where he had waited wasn't shown, it appeared that he had dropped Wilson off to visit with someone he referred to only as "Chand S.H." on West Forty-fifth Street. Dean smiled. To his cynical eye, the midnight rendezvous had all the earmarks of a lovers' tryst, and he noted that Officer Santana had discreetly omitted the full name and complete address. It made him wonder who the mysterious Miss Chand might be.

The single practitioner is denied the luxury of putting all other business aside to concentrate his efforts on the one case in front of him. To a certain extent, judges will permit him to do this when he is "actually engaged" in the trial of a case. At such times, he is allowed to submit an affirmation—a signed document that is the equivalent of an affidavit but requires no notarization—to other judges before whom he has court appearances, stating the case and court where he is on trial and requesting an adjournment to some date after his trial concludes.

But Dean was not on trial now, and even if he had been, the realities of earning a living and paying rent in New York City compelled him to seek, welcome, and attend to other cases. As much as he might have liked to turn down new matters and ignore old ones in favor of working on the Spadafino case, he had to remind himself that he would not get paid on it until after it was over, and that even then, in a day when a backhoe or crane operator might earn upward of $150 an hour, Dean's voucher would be based on a rate of $40 for in-court time and $25 for out-of-court.

So Dean took care of other business.

The other business he took care of was an attempted rape case in Queens. Dean's client, a Pakistani national named Kermani, had had a rent dispute with his landlady that had escalated into a shoving match. He had stormed out; she had called the police. When they arrived, she told them that Kermani had also "tried to have sex" with her. By the time the Sex Crimes Unit had finished interviewing her, the case had become an attempted forcible rape. What would have been a laughable example of overreaching ten years ago, the charge had to be taken very seriously in the heightened awareness climate of the nineties, and Dean set about reinterviewing witnesses, studying police reports he had read a dozen times already, and plotting his trial strategy.

Frank Ippolito, a former bank manager who had embezzled several hundred thousand dollars from his employers over a three-year period, came in, and Dean scheduled meetings with the bank's attorney and the assistant United States Attorney who was prosecuting the case. The defendant had never been in trouble before, had a military background, was a devoted husband and loving father, and was active in fund-raising for his church. In another time, a sympathetic judge might have largely looked the other way and imposed a stiff fine and some community service. But under the new federal sentencing guidelines, all that had changed, and Ippolito was looking at a three-year prison sentence.

Bobby McGrane, a tough kid from Hell's Kitchen who had traded a promising boxing career for a heroin habit, came in, referred by a former client whose name Dean could not place. It seemed that Bobby, already on parole from a manslaughter conviction, had been picked up by federal authorities investigating the role of organized crime in the Garment District. Knowing that even an arrest could jeopardize his parole status and lead to a violation and a return to prison, Bobby had cut a deal on the spot. Now he needed a lawyer to meet with the FBI agent he was working with, to ensure that his own involvement would go unprosecuted. Dean told him to set up the meeting.

Nathan Ramsey had an attempted murder case in the Bronx. A black man in his forties who had no prior record and held two jobs, Ramsey had been jumped by a group of Hispanics in Harris Park. He had run home to the safety of his apartment, where his family swore he had remained for two days, afraid to venture out but unable to call the police for lack of a phone. Sometime during the period, one of the Hispanics had been stabbed in the midsection, deeply enough to lacerate his spleen and almost cause death.

Ramsey had been identified as the stabber by two witnesses. Dean needed to talk to them.

And there were routine court appearances on two dozen other cases that were slowly working their way through the system: the drug sales, robberies, assaults, larcenies, and drunk drivings that filled Dean's calendar and more or less paid his bills.

Life goes on, as they say.

Life goes on for Joey Spadafino, too. The bandage is off his forehead, and the scar will be every bit as mean-looking as he figured. Not an ugly scar, like black people get, with the skin all puffed up around it. Just a long, thin line that gets attention, forces anyone to move their eyes up to stare at it, even when they try not to. It's almost like a tattoo on his forehead, he thinks, but better. A tattoo you would of had to put there. This got put there in a fight.

But aside from the gash on his forehead, it's not a good time for Joey. The days and weeks and months have begun to weigh on him. The novelty of being back on the Rock is over. The rapid-fire developments in his case are over—the arraignment, his One Eighty Eighty Day, his first appearance in Supreme Court, his offer from Judge Rothwax. By now his case had bogged down. The court dates are further apart, and when he does go to court nothing seems to happen. His lawyer has told him to expect this for a while and has explained some of the things that have to be done before the case can be ready for trial, but it doesn't help much.

Not being able to work doesn't help, either. Except for his lawyer, Joey has had no visitors. He's spoken to his mother twice and his sister once, but they sounded afraid to make the trip out, and Joey told them not to bother, that he was fine, if they could just send him some money for commissary so he can get cigarettes. With nothing to fill his days but meals and TV, he loses track of time, forgets what day of the week it is. He finds himself nodding off during the day, then has trouble sleeping at night. By the next day he's tired from not sleeping good, and he starts nodding off all over again. He wonders if they put stuff in the food, decides the coffee may be laced with some kind of drug. He cuts out drinking coffee, but that lasts only half a day. When there is nothing else to do, sitting five minutes with a cup of coffee is something he finds himself unwilling to give up, even if it means they're drugging him.

*   *   *

The Manhattan phone directory showed no listing for a Chand, S.H., on West Forty-fifth Street, or anywhere else, for that matter. Dean was not exactly surprised, though. Someone having a midnight rendezvous with the Police Commissioner would probably be the type to also have an unlisted number. Dean longed for the power and convenience of his DEA days, when such things as unlisted phones, names that went with license plates, and Con Edison subscriber information were all at his fingertips, a phone call or a computer search away.

He decided the walk would do him some good. He had been managing without his cane for a week now, and although he continued to limp slightly, he felt that was more from the habit of favoring his good ankle than from any pain or weakness in the bad one.

He began at Fifth Avenue, the dividing line between Manhattan's east and west sides. Determined to cover the whole stretch in a single afternoon, he proceeded to head west, zigzagging back and forth Forty-fifth Street, checking the directory boards in every apartment house on both sides of the street.

The first few blocks went fairly quickly. The buildings were large and commercial around Times Square, and many could be ignored altogether. Once he was past Eighth Avenue, there was a scattering of residential buildings to slow him down, and he had to check each one, often climbing a staircase to a second level before finding the directory. He noted two Chans and a Chang, but no Chand, S.H. By the time he reached Ninth Avenue, Dean had spent nearly two hours, and was still a few blocks from the Hudson River.

He crossed the avenue, feeling his ankle beginning to ache. He needed a phone to check his office for messages. In an era when his colleagues were beginning to carry beepers and pagers and cellular phones, Dean clung to his old habit of calling in periodically to his answering machine. He could not afford his own secretary, and found that answering services managed to lose more messages than they took in the first place.

He also needed a men's room. Badly.

He looked around. There was a McDonald's on the corner, but a sign on the door announced NO RESTROOMS. There ought to be a law, thought Dean, taking a deep breath and willing his knees to stop shaking. To the west was a parking garage, but the long ramp down looked uninviting to his ankle and unpromising to his bladder. Farther west and across the street was what looked like a restaurant. He squinted to make out the name.

CHANDLER'S STEAK HOUSE

It might have hit him right away had he not been so preoccupied with his urinary distress. Nonetheless, looking at the name, Dean sensed that it was significant, though he could not quite grasp how or why. Then it dawned on him, and his squint smoothed into a grin, which broadened into a smile before giving way to an outright laugh. One or two passersby craned their necks to stare at him, but the rest went about their business, taking no apparent note of one more New Yorker with his oars not quite in the water. To all of that, of course, Dean Abernathy was quite oblivious; indeed, the revelation made him momentarily forget the urgency of his need for a rest room, the body being the slave of the mind that it is. He had found Chand, S.H.

Checking his answering machine for messages that evening, Dean listened to the voice of Walter Bingham: The 911 tape had finally come in. There was also a call from a new client with a drunk driving case. And Bobby McGrane had set up a Friday night meeting with the FBI agent with whom he was working and he hoped that was okay with Dean.

Sure, Dean said to himself, why should I have a life?

On Friday morning Dean picked up his copy of the 911 tape at Walter Bingham's office. Holding it in his hand, he had an almost overpowering feeling of excitement. He wanted immediately to be back in his office listening to it, so certain he was that it contained some important clue—no, some *revelation*—that would begin to unlock the mystery of this case. For weeks now Dean had been experiencing a growing sense that there was something going on here, some other level of events beneath the surface of things that he could not quite see but could nevertheless *feel*. So the sensation of the tape in his hand was nothing less than electric, and the anticipation of playing it, hearing it, listening to the actual voice of the 911 caller, made his heart pound in his chest.

And yet it would have to wait. Three cases on the court calendar dragged out all morning. A seventeen-year-old was placed on probation for throwing rocks off a twenty-story rooftop, lucky that the only damage he had caused was to the roof of a car. A homeless woman accused of loitering and resisting arrest turned down a plea offer and got a trial date set. And finally, just minutes before the one o'clock recess, a bench warrant was issued for a minor drug seller who had failed to show up for sentencing.

Skipping lunch, Dean all but ran back to his office, forgetting about his ankle and jaywalking dangerously across Broadway. He postponed his habitual change back to jeans and sneakers in favor of hooking up a portable cassette player and inserting the tape. He closed the door to his room, took out a pen and notepad, and pressed the play button.

There was the usual introduction of date and time, as well as the date of the rerecording of the tape, followed by code numbers and technical data. Then Dean was listening to the 911 caller herself, to her own words, in her own voice, exactly as she had spoken to the emergency operator early that January morning, as she looked out from her window through the swirling snow and across Bleecker Street.

"Emergency Operator Twenty-three. May I help you?"

"Yes, I'm watching a crime."

"What sort of crime, ma'am?"

"A robbery, I guess, a mugging."

"Where is this occurring, ma'am?"

"Right across the street. Across from Seventy-seven Bleecker Street."

"What are the cross streets, ma'am?"

"What?"

"Seventy-seven Bleecker Street, ma'am. What streets is that between?"

"Oh. Sixth and Seventh."

"Sixth and Seventh. Ma'am, I'm going to ask you to hold on a moment. What's your phone number in case we get disconnected? Ma'am? Ma'am? Ma'am? Ma'am? Ma'am?"

Then there was a dial tone. A voice came on announcing that that concluded the first call, which had begun at 2:28 A.M. and ended at 2:29. The second and final call began at 2:32. This time the operator was a male; the caller was the same woman.

"Emergency Operator Six. May I help you?"

"Yes, I called a few minutes ago, about a robbery on Bleecker Street."

"Just a minute please." There was a pause, then, "Yes, Bleecker Street, between Sixth and Seventh Avenues?"

"Yes, that's right."

"Do you have anything else you can tell us?"

"He's gone. He took money from the guy and he left."

"Which way did he go?"

"To the right."

"Which way is right, Sixth or Seventh?"

"Seventh, he went toward Seventh Avenue."

"Can you describe him?"

"I don't know."

"How tall did he look?"

"He looked short, maybe five four, five five."

"Black, white, Hispanic?"

"White. Or Hispanic. I couldn't tell. Not black."

"Could you see what he was wearing?"

"He has a dark jacket and a dark wool cap, black or navy, I'm not sure."

"Okay. Could you give me your name, please?" (There was a break in the recording where the name had been erased.) "And your phone number?" (Another break.)

Again a voice came on announcing the end of the call. It was 2:33 A.M. Dean pressed the stop button. The rest of the tape, containing the radio transmissions to and from the responding police units, could wait. It was the voice of the 911 caller that interested Dean, and he knew it was a voice he had heard before.

He pulled out his Spadafino case file, which by now had

grown to two inches in thickness, and thumbed through the contents until he found the pages of notes he had made during his futile attempts to locate the apartment in 77 Bleecker Street from which the calls had been made. He found the list of the eleven tenants whose windows fronted on Bleecker Street, nine of whose names were followed by phone numbers. He counted the number of characters in the name Janet Killian. Including the space between the first and last name, there were thirteen, precisely the number of characters that had been blacked out in the copy of the sprint report Dean had been given. He dialed the number next to her name.

The 911 caller answered on the second ring.

TWELVE

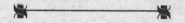

True to the promise he had made to Bobby McGrane, Dean had set aside that night to meet with Bobby and the FBI agent with whom he was cooperating. Dean had expected the meeting to take place at the FBI office at Federal Plaza, but Bobby had called to say that Leo—that was the agent's name—was working undercover infiltrating the Garment District mafia and couldn't risk being followed to or from a government building. Leo had suggested they meet a little bar and restaurant on the West Side called the Allstate Café. When he added that the FBI would spring for dinner, Dean readily agreed.

Dean found the Allstate, a long, smoke-filled room three steps below street level on Seventy-second Street. He saw Bobby at a back table, sitting with a good-looking man wearing a sweat-shirt and jeans. Bobby spotted Dean looking and waved him over. Sweatshirt stood up as Dean neared the table and extended his hand.

"Leo Silvestri," he said.

"Dean Abernathy." The handshake was firm.

"Hiya, Dean," said Bobby.

"Hello, Bobby."

"Well," said Dean, turning to Leo, "you sure don't *look* like a Febe. No raincoat, no suit—"

Leo laughed warmly. "That's the idea. Those days are over," he said. "We actually get our hands dirty from time to time."

Dean was surprised to find that the beer was cold and the food excellent. He ordered something called Southwestern-Style Paella, and the taste more than made up for the inauspicious name. Bobby tried to order lamb shark, and was disappointed to learn he had misread the menu and would have to settle for lamb shank. Leo had steak.

Leo explained that Bobby was providing important cooperation in the Garment District investigation. He had already succeeded in introducing Leo to some guys who were involved in trucking on Seventh Avenue. Trucking was the key in the business, Leo said: if you couldn't move your goods, you couldn't fill orders. And the wise guys had a stranglehold on the trucking routes. You did business with them, which meant on their terms and at their prices, or you didn't do business. It was that simple. Independent truckers who tried to break into the system found their trucks hijacked or sabotaged and their goods stolen, misdelivered, or mysteriously damaged.

Bobby and Leo had arranged a cover story that they had met in prison and done some burglaries together. It seemed to be working so far.

"How about his parole?" Dean wanted to know. "Do they know about this?"

"Yeah, I spoke with his PO myself. He's okay," said Leo. "As long as Bobby's straight with us, he's willing to ignore the little problem that brought him to our attention in the first place."

"And when does all this end?"

"Hard to say, Counselor. We figure Bobby owes us another month or two of solid work. After that, it's his choice. He wants to walk away, everything's squared up. He doesn't owe us, we don't owe him, and his PO doesn't violate him. On the other hand, if he wants to keep working, he'll get paid. Won't get rich, but it'll be enough to keep him out of trouble. Sound fair?"

Dean turned to Bobby. "Sound fair to you?"

"Yup."

"Sounds fair to me," said Dean. He asked Leo for a phone number.

"Well, the central switchboard number is 335-2700," said Leo, "but don't try to reach me there. When I'm deep undercover like now, I can't go near the office. Let me give you my beeper number and a special code so I'll know it's one of the good guys calling." He pulled out his wallet and extracted a business card. He wrote something on the back and handed it to Dean, who read it.

LEO N. SILVESTRI
Investor

LICENSED & BONDED   (212) 483-1927

On the reverse side Leo had written

#

"Punch that in after you enter your own phone number, okay?"

"Okay," said Dean, putting the card in his own wallet, which was already crammed with a dozen assorted others.

It was Saturday night before Dean got up the courage to go into Chandler's Steak House. He had resisted the temptation to walk right in and start asking questions. He had known he first needed a game plan, a strategy. Which meant he had to figure out what was to be learned by going in. So he had hailed a cab—an unusual step for Dean—and headed home, his knees jiggling tightly together the entire ride, in the manner of a small boy too shy to ask to use the bathroom.

In the end, he couldn't quite put his finger on what he hoped to learn at Chandler's. Commissioner Wilson had spent more than two hours there. Then he had been driven to within a block of his home. He had stepped out of the car, said good night to his chauffeur, Officer Santana, and continued on foot through the falling snow toward his door on Bleecker Street. He had never made it.

Dean wanted to talk to someone who had seen the Commissioner during the hours preceding his death. Had he looked all right? Had he complained of fatigue, of difficulty breathing? Had there been chest pain? Had he had too much to eat or drink? Departmental loyalty would prevent Officer Santana from answering these questions, but perhaps a waiter or bartender might be coaxed into providing some information.

He had waited all evening Saturday, the same night of the week that had been Wilson's last, and had walked into Chandler's just after midnight, hoping to maximize the chances that some of the same people who had seen the Commissioner that night would be there now. He was not to be disappointed.

Although dinner was no longer being served, the long bar was crowded and the place was noisy with the competition of voices and jukebox music. Roy Orbison promised that "anything you want, you got it, baby," and smoke hung thickly in the air. Dean stood by the end of the bar, ordered a beer, and bided his time. When a stool opened up some twenty minutes later, he took it and ordered another beer. Determined to nurse this one along, he swung around slowly and surveyed the crowd. This was a man's place; of the thirty or so patrons clustered in groups of three and fours, Dean counted only a half-dozen women. And the men had "cop" written all over them. Not beat cops, though; these were the brass, and this was their officers' club. Edward Wilson had spent his last evening drinking with the elite of the New York Police Department.

Dean's opening finally came when a barmaid—he had already decided it was no accident that two of the three bartenders were women—asked him what he did during the daylight.

"I'm a writer," said Dean.

"Oh? What kind of writer?"

"Freelance. Just now I'm working on a piece for *New York* magazine about Police Commissioner Wilson. Sort of a human-interest thing. You know, heartwarming and all that stuff."

"He was a nice man," she said.

"You knew him?" asked Dean. "I mean, I know he used to come in here. But you really knew him?"

"Sure," she smiled. "Ray knew him best though. Served him that night. You know, the last night he was in here." And with that, she called out, "Ray," and the lone male bartender came over obediently, drying a glass with a towel.

"Guy's writing a story about Commissioner Wilson," she said, introducing Dean to Ray with her eyes. "Needs some mushy stuff."

"Nice man," said Ray, shaking his head sadly.

"I understand you served him that last night," said Dean.

"Yeah, I'm afraid I did."

"Afraid?"

"Well, not *afraid* afraid," said Ray.

"Then?"

"Well," said Ray, "it's just that knowing what happened later, it's easy to say he might've had too much to drink that night. But, you know, how do you tell the Police Commissioner that?"

"I guess not." Dean smiled. He ordered another beer. "Really too much, or just . . ." He let the question complete itself.

"Oh, really too much," Ray said, then quickly added, "not that he was *driving*, you know. The Commissioner gets a chauffeur. But he was feeling no pain, if you know what I mean. Right, Sam?"

The barmaid, who evidently answered to the unlikely name of Sam, nodded in agreement. "That's for sure," she said.

"What did he drink?" Dean asked.

Sam's "Beer or wine" collided with Ray's "Jack Daniel's." Ray explained: "Usually he stuck to beer or wine, Sam's right. But that night they must've been celebrating. Putting away the good stuff. He was doing his share, and then some."

"They?"

"A bunch of the Big Brass."

Let it go, thought Dean. It didn't matter who was with him. "Did he seem sick or anything?"

Ray and Sam exchanged glances this time. It was Ray that answered. "He looked tired, is how I remember it. Like he'd been working too hard. He usually looked so energetic, you know. That night he did look sick, if you want to know the truth."

Thinking about it later, Dean had the uneasy feeling that it had all been just a bit too easy. For one thing, he had actually been more than ready to pay for information. After all, in the movies didn't the bartender always want a twenty before answering the reporter's question? But beyond that, this was a place where the brass came and spent their money. In return, they would expect the kind of loyalty an establishment bestows upon its regulars. The last thing they would want was for the help to share confidences with an outsider, particularly a reporter. Yet not one, but two bartenders, in the presence of each other, had done just that, readily admitting that their most valued customer had been drinking to excess the night of his death. And while Joey Spadafino corroborated their account by confirming that Wilson had been staggering drunk the morning of his death, there was the little thing of the serology report: at the time of his death, the Commissioner had had a blood alcohol level of only .04 percent. Hardly the reading one would expect of someone who had been knocking back Jack Daniel's for two and a half hours.

Unless, of course, the .04 percent figure was wrong.

Dean spent all of Sunday morning trying to come up with the best approach to get Janet Killian to talk with him. The first time he had reached her, going down his list of 77 Bleecker Street tenants and posing as a police inspector offering her a reward for having called the 911 operator, she had said she didn't know what he was talking about and had hung up on him. The second time had been Friday afternoon, when, having just listened to the tape, Dean had called her again to compare her voice with that of the 911 caller. When she had answered, Dean had asked for Miss Killington. He made the name close enough so that Janet would have to say something before realizing that it was a different name from hers and a wrong number. But the truth was that she hadn't had to say much; Dean knew immediately that the voices were one and the same.

Now Dean needed more. He needed to get her to talk about what she had witnessed that night, needed to know if she had really seen a knife in Joey Spadafino's hand, needed to find out if it had really been a robbery or if Joey's story about Wilson collapsing all on his own was true.

But Janet Killian seemed to have a compelling reason *not* to talk about the incident. She had hung up on a caller who wanted to give her *money* for having dialed 911. What would it take to persuade her to talk?

Dean concocted elaborate hoax after elaborate hoax. He was a reporter for *The New York Times* writing a retrospective piece about Commissioner Wilson. A professor at Columbia doing research on how New York citizens *do* get involved, Kitty Genovese notwithstanding. A filmmaker needing a shot of Bleecker Street from the exact angle of her window. But each time he played a scenario back in his mind, he had to admit that it was no better— and often far worse—than the reward hoax that had already failed.

In the end, he decided to settle for the truth. He would appeal to Janet Killian with his own heartfelt sincerity, the same sincerity he had mustered time and again in addressing juries at summation time. Of course there were some differences. For one thing, with a jury, Dean had his sincere good looks there to help him. He could stand in front of the jury box, making eye contact with each juror willing to meet his steady gaze. Over the years he had on occasion heard his voice crack with emotion and felt his eyes come close to spilling over with tears. But a jury was a captive audience. They could look away, they could yawn, they could even doze off (and Dean had seen just that happen more than once). But for better or worse they were stuck there sitting in front of him for as long as he chose to talk to them. *They couldn't hang up the phone.* This was different. What Dean needed was a grabber, a way to keep Janet Killian listening for a minute so that he could somehow get through to her, get her to trust him and talk with him.

Over and over again he practiced his introduction. He paced the floor, he spoke to his bathroom mirror, he cleared his throat. By the time he finally picked up the phone on Sunday afternoon, his shirt was wet with perspiration at the back and under the arms. He was reminded of phone calls made long ago, of calling to invite the class beauty to the junior prom, of phoning to find out whether he had been accepted or rejected by the college of his choice, of inquiring from a pay phone to hear whether that desperately needed job was his, of calling to learn whether he had passed or flunked the bar exam. He cleared his throat one final time and dialed. The phone rang once, twice, three times.

"Hello?" It was her.

"Miss Killian?"

"Yes?"

"Miss Killian, my name is Dean Abernathy and I'm a lawyer and I *beg* you to listen to me for a minute. You don't have to say a word, just please listen to what I have to say."

There was no response, but there was no click, either. Dean pushed on.

"I'm the lawyer they've appointed to defend the guy who's charged in the death of the Police Commissioner. I called you once before and lied to you about there being a reward. I apologize, I shouldn't have done that. I'm also the one who called on Friday and asked for Miss Killington. I apologize for that, too. I shouldn't have done that, either, but I had to hear your voice. Miss Killian, I need to speak with you. I give you my word I'm not going to harm you, I'm not going to endanger you in any way. I just need to ask you a few questions, and then I'll leave you alone, I promise." Dean took a breath. He had gotten through his preamble without getting hung up on. On the other end there was still silence.

Then, finally, she spoke. "Would you spell your name for me, please?"

"Sure," said Dean. "A-B-E-R-N-A-T-H-Y. The first name is Dean, D-E-A-N."

"And your phone number?"

Dean gave her both his home and office numbers.

"I'll get back to you," said Janet Killian.

Around the corner from Dean's building was a homeless man who begged for change. Dean sometimes gave him a quarter. On the occasions he did not, he would say "Sorry" to the man, who would then respond with "Thank you for at least listening to me."

"Thank you for at least listening to me," Dean now said to Janet Killian.

* * *

It was almost eleven when his phone rang. Dean was working on the Sunday *Times* crossword puzzle. The theme was opera, which had put him at a great disadvantage, but, working at it on and off all day, he had filled in all the long answers, and was missing only about four or five small words. He was trying to come up with a seven-letter word for a Muslim ascetic for 86 across, and had _E_VIS_, when the sudden ring made him jump.

"Hello," he said.

"Dean Abernathy?" said a male voice.

"Yes."

"Mr. Abernathy, this is Det. Richard Rasmussen. Forgive me for calling you at home, and so late in the evening."

"That's okay," said Dean, trying to place the name.

"I understand you'd like to speak with a Miss Janet Killian with regard to the Wilson homicide." If the ringing of the phone had caused Dean to jump, this brought him to his feet.

"That's right, I really would."

"The woman's been through a lot," said the detective. "She really doesn't want to talk to anyone else."

"I can appreciate that," Dean said, trying to imagine what she had been through that was so difficult, but not wanting to be confrontational. "All I want is about ten minutes of her time. I just want her to tell me what she saw."

"And then what?"

"What do you mean?"

"She tells you what she saw. She tells you she saw your client pull a knife on the victim, saw the victim grab his chest and go down, saw your client go through his pockets and take his money. Then what?"

"Then," said Dean, struggling for the right answer, "then I can tell my client once and for all that he's full of shit and it's time to cop out. That's what."

"It's very irregular, you know, Counselor?"

"What's that?"

"Me trying to work it out so you can talk to a witness who don't wanna talk to you in the first place."

"Look," said Dean, lowering his tone to sound like the Voice of Reason, "I don't want to try this case. It's going to be a fucking bloodbath, I know that. Get me ten minutes with the witness. You pick the spot. You sit in. She answers my questions. I talk to my client. He cops out. She never has to come to court and testify. Why don't you tell her that?" And then, pulling out all the stops, he added, "C'mon, I'm not going to bite her. I'm not such a bad guy, I used to be On the Job." Police speak for: I used to be a cop.

"I know," said the detective to Dean's surprise. Then, "I'll get back to you in a day or two, Counselor."

For the first time in nearly three months, Dean fell asleep feeling hopeful. He was acutely aware that he had been expending an enormous amount of energy on a case that was probably completely hopeless to begin with. Was he on to something with these tiny clues he was picking up, or was he just grasping at straws? If you looked hard enough at something, you could always find some irregularity, some infinitesimal incongruity from which you could begin to see the seeds of doubt germinate and begin to sprout. Hadn't half a nation come to believe that Oswald hadn't killed Kennedy? Weren't there those who insisted, against overwhelming evidence, that the Holocaust had never happened, that HIV didn't cause AIDS, and that man had not evolved from the apes?

But even in his awareness that he might be denying the obvious to the point of being a sore loser, Dean couldn't help feeling hopeful. Hopeful because now he was on the verge of finding out one way or another what had really happened that night. He was about to gain access to the star of the prosecution's case, the very eyewitness who placed the knife in Joey Spadafino's hand and, in doing so, put the lie to his story that he had been but an innocent bystander to the Commissioner's death. As soon as Dean heard the truth in her own words, he could put an end to this absurd charade of innocence being played out between insistent client and skeptical lawyer. "Okay, Joey," he heard himself saying, "it's over," and Joey, nodding in agreement, pleading for Dean to get back the fifteen-to-life offer he had earlier so foolishly turned down.

Joey Spadafino is anything but hopeful. As Dean falls asleep on a ...uch in front of his fireplace on the West Side of Manhattan ...lies sleepless on his bunk in C-93's B Block on Rikers ...Dean, Joey doesn't live alone on his island. He shares his nine-by-twelve-foot cubicle with two cellmates, who at this moment snore and fart and toss in their sleep. Joey doesn't sleep. He's been on the Rock nearly three months, and he sees no end in sight. Other inmates come and go, get bailed out, take pleas, hit the street, or move on upstate. Joey stays. In three months he's gone from being New Kid on the Block (an expression that takes on a very literal meaning in prison) to Longtimer. It's a change in status that brings with it some measure of physical security, since the newcomers tend to defer to those inmates who've been here long enough to have made friends and forged alliances with others. But Joey can't shake the feeling that he's going to be here forever and that time—which is something that exists only on the outside—is passing him by.

His court appearances are now three weeks apart. The routine is the same. They wake him up at four in the morning by clanging a metal pipe against the bars of his cell. He isn't permitted a shower, and because he's got only two changes of clothes, he turns out in whatever he's slept in, tucking in his shirt and slipping into his sneakers. When he walks he's got to curl his toes to keep his sneakers from falling off, because either they've stretched or Joey's feet have gotten thinner as he's steadily lost weight. He can't lace up his sneakers, because inmates are not allowed laces for fear they might use them to hang themselves or strangle one another.

Joey's losing weight because he can't eat the food. It's all milk and potatoes and bread, everything white. He'd been living on the street, and he longs for a hot dog with onions, a slice of pizza, even a piece of fruit scavenged from a Dumpster outside a supermarket. His stomach aches and rumbles all day because he can't go to the bathroom. In the cell there's a bare commode for pissing and shitting, but Joey finds it impossible to take a shit in front of other people. He waits until night when his cellmates are asleep, but even then he imagines they're awake and listening to his noises.

On court days he gets led out of his cell at four-fifteen and locked into the day room with twenty other inmates. There are seats for eight. Joey, who's white and therefore in the minority, finds a spot on the floor to sit, a corner if he's lucky, a wall if he isn't. He can sit like that for as much as four hours until his name is called out and he's led, in the early-morning darkness, along with five or six others, to a bus with torn seat cushions and grates on the windows. He rides for an hour or more, breathing the stink of forty other inmates, none of whom has showered or brushed their teeth or taken a shit since the night before. He rides in a din of snoring, belching, farting, grumbling men. There's no joking, no small talk. Each man on the bus is apprehensive about going to court, wondering if his lawyer will show up this time, knowing he may sit all day and never even be brought into the courtroom, but also knowing that this may turn out to be the day he fears, the day they try to railroad him, to fuck with him.

By the time they arrive at Centre Street it's light out. The bus can wait in line for another hour before pulling into the unloading bay. There the inmates are handcuffed in pairs and led off into a freight elevator. Joey, headed for Supreme Court, rides up to the twelfth floor, where he's booked in at the Bridge, still handcuffed to another inmate who he may or may not know, may or may not like, who may be black, white, Hispanic, or other, may or may not speak a word of English. From there they're led to a holding pen in the middle of the floor, where they're uncuffed and locked in with anywhere from ten to thirty others who have court appearances in any one of the four courtrooms that are on the middle of the eleventh floor below or the thirteenth floor above.

Because his lawyer always shows up early, Joey's generally called out by ten or ten-thirty. With two or three others, he's led down a back flight of stairs to a smaller feeder pen just off Part 56. There Dean comes in, talks to Joey through the bars, and tells him what's going to happen in the courtroom, which these days is usually nothing.

Next he's led into court by a court officer, placed in front of the defense table, told to sit in a wooden chair with arms and pull the chair all the way up to the table so he can't get up. One court officer takes a position directly behind him, while others stand at either end of the table. Joey sits there while his lawyer and the DA go up and talk to the judge. Joey can't hear most of what they say, and understands little of it even when he can. Then they step back, the judge announces the adjourned date three weeks away, and Joey's led back to the feeder pen. His court appearance has lasted less than three minutes. Dean usually comes back to the feeder pen and talks to him for a couple of minutes more, and—if he isn't too busy with other cases—may come upstairs and spend a half hour with Joey in the counsel room, where they sit and talk through the steel mesh that separates them. Then Joey's returned to the twelfth-floor holding pen, where he rejoins the other inmates. Joey spends the rest of the morning with them while they wait for their lawyers, who'll show up later in the day or not at all.

The routine is broken only by lunch. Bologna sandwiches and cheese sandwiches, made with white bread and wrapped in wax paper. Sometimes there are packages of mustard. There are containers of black coffee, half full and lukewarm.

At one o'clock, those inmates who are finished in court are led out for the early bus back. Joey's lucky to be one of them, because those that are left behind don't get onto a bus until somewhere between seven and nine o'clock, which means they can get back to Rikers after midnight, back to their cells at one in the morning. For the ones who are to be "turned around"—due back in court the next day—they'll do well to catch two hours of sleep before the routine begins all over again at four.

THIRTEEN

Dean did not hear from Detective Rasmussen the following day. And, with the exception of reading the toxicology report, which arrived in the mail, he did nothing on the Spadafino case, turning his attention instead to other cases that needed catching up.

The toxicology report was essentially negative. It described the findings of the postmortem examination conducted on samples of brain, liver, and bile taken from the body of Edward Wilson at the time the autopsy was conducted. As had the blood sample reported in the serology report, all of the tissue samples tested negative for the presence of opiates, amphetamines, and barbiturates. There was .01 percent of alcohol in both the liver and bile. Dean knew from previous cases that the figure, lower than the .04 percent found in Wilson's blood, did not necessarily represent an inconsistency: alcohol simply took longer to show up in the liver and bile than it did in the bloodstream.

The report revealed virtually no other positive findings. Traces of aspirin and something called dibenzepene were present in the liver sample, and there were also traces of aspirin in the brain tissue.

*　　*　　*

Rasmussen did not call the day after, either, and Dean wrestled with the idea of calling the detective himself, but resisted. He would give him one more day.

On Wednesday afternoon, Dean got stuck in court until four-thirty. A woman charged with passing more than two hundred bad checks finally pleaded guilty in exchange for a promise of a one-year jail sentence, after much coaxing from Dean and the judge.

By the time he got back to his office, there were six messages on Dean's answering machine. He rewound the tape before even taking off his coat. The first was from a new client, worried he was about to be arrested for making payoffs to a taxi emissions inspector. The second was his mother, inviting Dean to a Passover seder. The third was a hangup. The fourth sounded like an insurance salesman or a stockbroker looking for customers. The fifth was his father, inviting him to Easter Sunday dinner. The sixth was Detective Rasmussen.

"Mr. Abernathy, this is Detective Rasmussen. Sorry it took me so long to get back to you. I've been working nights. I spoke to the Killian woman, and I've convinced her to talk to you. I gotta say, she's very nervous and very reluctant to do so. But she says if I can be present and it's not at her place, she's willing to do it." The message ended with a phone number for Dean to call back.

The meeting took place at the edge of the Hudson River, at the end of Christopher Street. Rasmussen was very specific in his directions. Dean was to meet him three o'clock sharp Friday afternoon. Rasmussen would have "the Killian woman" with him; they would be in his car, which was blue. Dean should come alone. No tape recorder, no camera, no signed statement, no notes of the meeting. Take it or leave it.

As soon as he arrived, Dean spotted the blue car. It was the same blue Plymouth he had seen on Bleecker Street the afternoon he had left the building and circled back in his Jeep. As he approached the driver's side now, Dean recognized the man behind the wheel as the big guy who had come out of 77 Bleecker Street that day. Instead of getting out, the man reached back and pulled up the button on the back door. Dean got in and closed the door behind him. In the front passenger seat sat a woman with curly blond hair. She wore sunglasses and stared straight ahead. She blew a stream of cigarette smoke out her half-opened window, then stubbed the cigarette out in the ashtray. She looked very nervous.

"Mr. Abernathy," said the man, "I'm Detective Rasmussen. This is Janet Killian."

"Hello," said Dean. "I appreciate your doing this, both of you." Janet Killian nodded but did not speak.

"Janet's agreed to answer your questions, Counselor. No personal stuff, no cross-examination. Short and sweet. Fair enough?"

"Fair enough," said Dean.

"Janet?"

"Okay," said Janet to the detective.

"Miss Killian," Dean began, "rather than fire a bunch of questions at you, I'd really just like you tell me what you saw that night, in your own words."

Janet Killian turned slightly but not enough to face Dean. She cleared her throat. "I was having trouble sleeping, so I was looking out the window, watching the snow. I saw a man walking along. All of a sudden I saw another man, a smaller man who I hadn't noticed until then, jump out of a doorway and hold a knife to the first man's throat. I know he said something, the one with the knife, but I couldn't hear what it was. Then I saw the other one grab his chest and collapse on the sidewalk. He moved a little at first, like he was in pain, then he stopped. As I watched, the one with the knife bent down and went through the pockets of the man on the sidewalk. I saw him take a wad of money from him. I could see it was money, 'cause he held it up to the light to look at it.

"I got my phone and called the police. I told them what I'd seen. They asked me where it was, what were the cross streets, stuff like that. Then we got disconnected. Then the man who had taken the money left. I called the police again. It was a different operator this time. They wanted to know which way the man went. I told them he went to the right, toward Seventh Avenue. They asked me what he looked like. I described him as best as I could, like how tall he was and what he was wearing. I remember he was short and had a dark jacket and cap."

"Anything else?" Dean asked.

"They asked me for my name and phone number, and I told them. That's all I can remember."

"What did the knife look like?" Dean asked.

"It had a silver blade and a dark handle," she said. "Maybe dark blue."

"What did he do with it?"

"He held it at the man's throat."

"No," said Dean, "afterward. What did he do with it afterward?"

"I don't remember."

Rasmussen coughed loudly. "Anything else, Counselor?" he said pointedly.

But Dean was a defense lawyer, and "Anything else, Counselor?" was a question he heard from judges all the time and had come to ignore almost automatically.

"Did the guy walk away or run away after it was over?"

"I'm not sure," said Janet. "I don't remember. I was very frightened, and it was several months ago."

"Remember what we said about no cross-examination, Counselor?" said Rasmussen. "Remember we're doing you a favor here, and I think the favor is about over."

"One more thing," said Dean. "Then I'll get outa here."

"One means one," said Rasmussen. He would've made a pretty good judge, thought Dean.

"Are those prescription glasses you're wearing?" Dean asked. "I mean, do you wear prescription glasses and did you have them on that night?" If he was down to one question he was going to make it count.

"These are just sunglasses," Janet said. "I have twenty-twenty vision." And she lowered her head, took off her sunglasses, and handed them over the backseat to Dean. As she did so, she turned to face him more fully and smiled. Dean held the glasses up and looked through them. They were plain sunglasses. Looking just above them, he could see that Janet Killian was pretty, though there was a certain hardness to her looks. He handed her the sunglasses and she put them back on.

Walking away, Dean felt as if he had just struck out with the bases loaded and two out in the ninth. Janet Killian was a devastating witness. She completely put the lie to everything Joey Spadafino had told Dean about not pulling out his knife and not saying anything to the man. She was pretty, she was intelligent, she was articulate, and—unlike Joey Spadafino—she had absolutely no reason to lie about what had happened that night. This case was over.

In the second week of April, Dean went to trial on a minor drug case. The defendant, a Rastafarian named Dexter Churchwell, had a pleasant smile and a singsong voice that made him easy to like. He had been accused of selling two vials of crack cocaine to an undercover police officer. When the backup team had arrested Churchwell they had found four more vials in his right rear pocket. Churchwell readily admitted that the four vials were his. He said he had bought them ten minutes earlier to share with his woman, a three-hundred-pounder named Tanya. But he vehemently denied selling the two vials, or anything else, to anyone, and Dean was inclined to believe him.

Luckily enough, upon close inspection it turned out that while the four vials in Churchwell's pocket were "redcaps," so called because the tops were made of red plastic, the two vials bought by the undercover cop were not only "bluecaps," they were also "jumbos," larger vials that contained more crack and went for more money. Dean put Churchwell on the stand, and the jury seemed to like him as much as Dean did. In summation, Dean argued long and hard that the discrepancy cast tremendous doubt on Churchwell's being the seller. When it was her turn, the prosecutor suggested that Churchwell had simply sold his last two bluecaps to the officer, and had nothing but redcaps left when arrested fifteen minutes later. But the jury was not buying it. They found the defendant guilty of possession, but not guilty of sale. Which was fine with Dean, since the possession was a misdemeanor and carried a maximum sentence of a year. The sale, a felony, could have cost Dexter Churchwell eight-and-one-third to twenty-five years.

The Spadafino case came on once again in Part 56 just after Dean had finished trying Dexter Churchwell's case. But Judge Rothwax was busy trying a rape case and adjourned all other trials to May.

Upstairs on the twelfth floor, Dean faced Joey through the familiar mesh of the counsel room. He confronted Joey with Janet Killian's version of the incident.

"She's lying, Dean," Joey said. "On my mother's honor, she's lying." Dean wondered if this was the same mother who hadn't been out to visit Joey in the three months he had been locked up. He didn't say anything, though. You had to be careful when it came to people's mothers. A defendant who would sit passively while you called him a liar to his face could suddenly lash out at the first suggestion that you were putting down his mother. And many a prison stabbing was attributed to the careless use of the epithet "motherfucker," where some other equally profane term might not have drawn a glance.

Dean turned instead to the subject of alcohol. How drunk had the guy really seemed to be, he asked Joey, remembering the .04 percent reading from the serology report and how it contrasted with the account of the bartenders at Chandler's.

"Man, he was *smashed*," said Joey.

"What makes you say that?"

"What makes me say that is that's why I thought about takin' him off in the first place, that's why. He was so drunk he was *beggin' to be a vic*."

Interesting, thought Dean. But then again, it was Joey Spadafino talking.

The brisket at his mother's seder was overcooked and falling apart, the way Dean liked it, and the reading of the Passover Hagadah was abridged enough to be tolerable. The Four Questions were answered by Dean's nine-year-old nephew, who did well enough but had a bit of trouble explaining why on this night it was necessary to eat reclimbing.

Then, four days later, Dean's father, not to have his god upstaged, cooked both a turkey and a ham for Easter. The holidays were a rather schizophrenic time for the half-Jewish, half-Catholic Abernathy family, but they got through them in good enough humor. And they provided a good break for Dean, who had come to realize that he had spent far too much time and effort on Joey Spadafino, who, it turned out, deserved neither. "He shouldn't've been robbing the *schvartze* in the first place," scolded Mrs. Abernathy, and Dean had to admit she had a point there, after all. By Sunday night, Dean was back at his apartment, five pounds heavier, his refrigerator uncharacteristically full of little plastic containers and foil packages of brisket, matzoh brei, turkey, and ham.

* * *

Easter Sunday is observed at Rikers Island, too. In place of the usual menu, the inmates are served ham, mashed sweet potatoes, and green beans, in addition to the ever-present white bread and containers of milk.

Joey Spadafino has never liked meat or potatoes that taste sweet. He tries to eat a piece of ham, but it is covered with sticky raisin sauce. He has to chew it a long time before he is able to swallow it. He ends up trading the rest of it, along with his sweet potatoes, for an extra portion of green beans. The beans are over-cooked and gray, and water comes out of them when you stick a fork into one or bite into it, but they taste okay.

Easter Sunday is also a big visiting day, but, as always, Joey has no visitors. He tells himself that's the way he prefers to do his time, alone. He's made no friends to speak of on B Block. He keeps to himself as much as possible. His lawyer has told him he may not under any circumstances discuss his case with anybody, explaining that there are many inmates who would gladly say he admitted his crime to them and testify against him in exchange for a reduced sentence on their own cases. But it's not just that. C-93 is a detention facility, which means that everybody here is waiting to go to trial or cop out. The average stay is nine weeks. So as soon as you get to know somebody, they're outa here.

Of course Joey himself has been here for about three months already. But some of the older inmates tell him that's not unusual. In the old days you used to have to lay up a year before getting a trial on a murder case.

It isn't the waiting that gets to Joey, however. It's that his lawyer doesn't believe him. With no visitors, no friends in Popula-tion, and a lawyer who doesn't believe him, Joey feels completely cut off from the rest of the world. He now knows he's going to blow trial. His lawyer has explained that the DA's got a witness who's going to testify she saw him pull his knife and hold it at the guy's throat. Joey isn't stupid, after all. He knows that the jury will believe her, knows they'll convict him. But he also knows he didn't kill the guy, and there's no way he's going to cop out and say he did.

So Joey Spadafino spends Easter Sunday waiting, as he spends every other day waiting, for the trial he knows he will lose, and the life sentence he knows it will bring him.

FOURTEEN

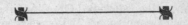

Dean had a habit of downplaying his chances as a trial approached. To colleagues and friends and family, he had been quick to say that the case against Joey Spadafino was overwhelming, that he didn't have a prayer, that he didn't even have a *theory* of a defense to work with. And in most respects, he believed all this to be true. But in quieter moments, he knew he was deliberately painting a picture somewhat more hopeless than the facts themselves warranted, if indeed that was possible to do in this case.

He recalled his days as a student, walking out of a classroom where he had just taken a written exam. Dean had not been one of the theatrical moaners and groaners who consistently insisted that they had failed, but if anyone had asked him how he thought he had done, he would have bent over backward to avoid any appearance of confidence. "Terribly" would have translated into a C, "not very well" suggested a B, and "not too bad, I hope" meant he had absolutely aced it, though he never dared say so.

Old habits died hard. Now years later, Dean the lawyer continued to paint bleak pictures to the rest of the world, and in doing so, avoided the sin of hubris and protected his ego at the same time. If the case he was trying was impossible, losing it would be no disgrace. Winning it, on the other hand, would be nothing short of miraculous.

The weekend over, Dean sat at his desk now, wondering just how much ego protecting he was doing with respect to the Spadafino case. To be sure, he knew that the prosecution had a devastating witness in Janet Killian. They also had the physical evidence: the money, the money clip, the knife, the clothing. They had the statements. And Dean had a defendant who was homeless, not too smart, and had a criminal record.

On the other hand, there was the little matter of the duplicated signature of Joey Spadafino on the written statement to the detectives, which strengthened Joey's denial of the robbery to Walter Bingham on the videotaped Q&A. And there was the discrepancy between Commissioner Wilson's apparent intoxication and the low blood alcohol reading on the serology and toxicology reports. It wasn't much, but it was something.

So Dean forced himself to get out the file again. He began going through it, document by document, page by page, paragraph by paragraph, line by line. Every time he came across something even slightly helpful, or something that he thought merited further investigation, he made a note of it on a yellow pad. It was tedious work, and he had to will himself to concentrate. More than once he was tempted to put a marker in the file and put it away, but he stayed with it to the final page. It took him an hour and a half.

He looked at the yellow pad. He hadn't even had to tear the front sheet off, so little did he have to work with. One page had been more than enough to list every positive lead he had developed in more than three months of work on the case.

Good Stuff

1. Forged signatures on written statement
2. Denial of robbery during Q&A
3. Alcohol: Bartenders/Joey (drunk) v. Serology (.04%)
4. Toxicology: (a) aspirin
            (b) dibenzepene
5. Knife: difficult to see dark handle @ night

And that was it. One end-justifies-the-means instance of cheating by overzealous detectives, one self-serving denial of guilt by the defendant, one discrepancy in how drunk the Commissioner had been that night, two drugs to check out, and an otherwise credible witness who exaggerated what she had been able to see on one minor point.

Dean closed the file, tossed the yellow pad onto a cabinet in the corner, and called it a day.

Most of that week was spent on Nathan Ramscy's stabbing case in Harris Park in the Bronx. With Ramsey's help, Dean located two witnesses who corroborated Ramsey's version that the Hispanics had chased him home and beaten him at his doorway, and that that had occurred at two o'clock in the afternoon, not seven o'clock in the evening, when the victim claimed Ramsey had stabbed him. It didn't make sense; *somebody* had stabbed the guy. Finally, Dean confronted Ramsey and asked him point-blank if he had in fact stabbed the victim at the doorway in self-defense earlier that afternoon. Ramsey put his head in his hands and started crying softly. It was true, he said. But his first lawyer had told him to deny it, since he had an alibi for seven o'clock, the time when the victim insisted he had been stabbed.

It was suddenly all too clear to Dean. The victim, stabbed once in the belly, had walked away from the scene and gone about his business, not reporting the incident because he himself had been one of the aggressors. But as the afternoon wore one, he began to feel weak, and around seven o'clock, in some distress, he had walked into the hospital, insisting the stabbing had taken place only minutes earlier, in the park.

So Dean went to the assistant district attorney handling the case and suggested to him that both the complainant and the defendant had been lying. He agreed to look into it further.

It was Thursday by the time Dean came across the yellow pad on the corner filing cabinet in his office. He looked again at the list of leads he had made. Of the five items listed, he had done about all he could on four of them. The only one he had not checked out was the fourth, the traces of aspirin and dibenzepene noted in the toxicology report.

The aspirin was easy. Everybody took aspirin, whether for a headache, a toothache, a sore back, or arthritis. Besides, Edward Wilson was known to have had a heart condition, and Dean knew that an aspirin a day was often routinely prescribed as an antico-agulant for people with heart problems. It was the dibenzepene, whatever that was, that he needed to check out.

Larry Jacobs, one of the laywers in the suite, specialized in personal injury law, and the shelves in his office held as many medical treatises as they did law books. It was to him that Dean went now. Dibenzepene turned out to be something Jacobs had never heard of, but he handed Dean his *Physician's Desk Reference* and *Merck Manual* and said, "If it's not in these, it doesn't exist."

Back in his own room, Dean thumbed through the books. Each one ran nearly three thousand pages, including life-size, full-color photographs of virtually every prescription and over-the-counter medicine available in the country, under brand names and generic listings.

But no dibenzepene.

Dean dialed the number he had for the New York County Medical Examiner's Office, and asked to speak to Dr. Mustafa, the pathologist whose signature appeared at the bottom of the toxi-cology report.

"I'm sorry," the secretary said. "Dr. Mustafa has taken a leave of absence and cannot be reached."

Great, thought Dean. Next he tried his own doctor, Larry Davidson. He was a family practitioner in his late sixties who was as much Dean's friend as his physician. His office was in Hacken-sack, New Jersey, but when Dean needed to see a doctor he would make the drive. He liked Davidson because he was low-key and not overly impressed with himself. Even now, during office hours, he took time to talk to Dean.

"So, what can I do for you?"

"You can tell me what dibenzepene is."

"That's what you think." Davidson laughed. "Dibenzepene? Never heard of it."

"Neither has the *PDR* or the *Merck Manual*," said Dean. At Davidson's request, he spelled out the name of the drug to make sure Davidson had it right. Then he explained that it had shown up in toxicology samples in a murder case he was working on.

Davidson knew the case, even knew that Dean was representing the defendant. Unlike some physicians, he read the newspaper.

"Can you give me a day or two?" Davidson asked.

"You can have a week," said Dean. "My client's not going anywhere in a hurry, I'm afraid."

That night Mark Wexler called to report to Dean that a mutual friend, Angelo Petrocelli, was getting married upstate in a couple of weeks. Mark was trying to organize a bachelor party and wanted Dean to help out.

"What do you have in mind?"

"The usual," Mark said. "Sex, drugs, rock 'n' roll."

"Good luck with the sex and drugs," said Dean. It was widely believed that Angelo, who at twenty-eight still lived with his parents in Rhinebeck, New York, was a virgin who was "saving himself" for marriage. As for drugs, he would not take an aspirin for a headache, insisting that proper diet, meditation, and pure thoughts were all the medicines the body required.

"I'm working on getting a couple of hookers," said Mark.

"Forget about it. He'll never come."

"Very funny."

"I meant he'll never show up."

Larry Davidson called back on Wednesday, which was unusual in itself. Doctors in New Jersey recognize Wednesdays much the same as Christians recognize Sundays. The few that see patients work at most a half day, and it is a foolish person indeed who has the misfortune to pick a Wednesday to fall ill. Precisely what the medical establishment does while the rest of the world toils remains a mystery to many. But it is no secret, and probably no coincidence, that the parking lots of golf courses and motels experience no dearth of M.D. plates on these midweek holidays.

Larry Davidson was not a golfer, however, and apparently not a regular frequenter of motels, either.

"Well, I found your dibenzepene," he said. "Apparently no one sells it in the U.S. But it's been in clinical use in Europe since 1966. They market it there under the brand name Noveril. It's a fairly strong antidepressant, prescribed in tablet form. Was your Police Commissioner known to be depressed?"

"I don't know," said Dean.

"Well, I've ordered a reprint of a technical paper on it. Should have some information as to dosage, contradictions, toxicity, that kind of stuff. As soon as I get it, I'll send it to you."

"Terrific, Doc. What do I owe you?"

"Your life, your firstborn, your estate. That'll do for now."

"You got it. And thanks."

Dean hung up the phone. He wondered what Commissioner Wilson had been depressed about. And why he had been taking a drug available only in Europe? That seemed to make no sense at all.

Then again, did any of this make any difference? Felony murder was felony murder, Dean reminded himself, and it made no difference if the victim had a heart condition, was depressed, or was taking medication from Mars, for that matter. So who was Dean kidding?

The Assistant District Attorney in the Bronx called to say he wanted to meet with Dean's witnesses in the Nathan Ramsey stabbing. Dean's landlord called to say that the May rent was due, and Dean still hadn't paid for April. Mark Wexler reported that he couldn't get any hookers for the bachelor party, so they'd have to settle for stag films instead.

There are no stag films on B Block in C-93. Nor are there any bachelor parties. Sex is just one more thing that Joey Spadafino is deprived of on Rikers Island, along with privacy, food he can eat, and the right to come and go as he pleases. Even during the six weeks he had spent on the street after losing his room, Joey felt like he was part of the world. Here he feels cut off, alone.

Here there are no pleasures. On the street he could beg, hustle, steal if necessary. There were no big scores, but there was always money if you were enterprising enough. And money meant you could get high whenever you wanted, could eat when you were hungry, drink when you were thirsty. Could even get laid now and then.

Not that there are no drugs here. There's plenty. Some come in on family visits, smuggled inside balloons or condoms concealed in visitors' mouths and given to inmates in kisses right under the noses of the COs. But most are brought in by the COs themselves, to be distributed by a trusted inmate or two. After a while, the roles reverse, and it becomes the inmate who owns the officer. If the officer stops bringing stuff in, the inmate snitches on him. So the flow continues. Coke, crack, speed, heroin, uppers, downers. You name it. Marijuana can be a problem 'cause of its telltale odor when being smoked, but you can get that, too. All it takes is money. Something Joey has none of.

There's booze, too. It's called pruno, though Joey can't say why. The kitchen crew brews it in a makeshift still that looks like it's part of the refrigeration unit. Joey's seen it and even tasted it. There are two varieties, white and killer. White is clear like gin or vodka. It tastes like pure alcohol but burns your throat as it goes down. Killer is a dark brownish purple color, thick and syrupy. It's said to be a 150 proof, and lives up to its name.

As for sex, for the first two months he was here, Joey had no sex drive at all. Then, gradually, he began to remember sex, began to actually get horny. Lately, he spends a lot of his time replaying his sexual experiences in his mind, starting with the most recent and working back as far as he can recall. Lying awake this night, he tries to relive every sexual experience he's ever had, all the way back to the time he was fourteen and his cousin Emilia—who was only fifteen herself, but was a head taller than Joey and already in high school—had unzipped Joey's pants, reached into his undershorts, and began stroking his cock. Joey's whole body had gone rigid right along with his cock, and his mouth had opened like he had lockjaw, making Emilia laugh as she watched him. But she hadn't stopped, she'd kept stroking him until he thought his head would explode, kept stroking him until he came in agonizing, excruciating spurts that he thought would last forever. Then she had dried him off, stuffed him back in his shorts, zipped up his pants, and kissed him on the cheek, smiling sweetly. The whole time, Joey couldn't say a word. Afterward, he'd wanted to say, "I love you," or "Thank you," or something, but he'd been totally unable to speak, and neither of them has ever talked about it since that day.

Although he hasn't seen her in ten years, it is his cousin Emilia that Joey makes love to tonight, rubbing himself under his blanket, softly at first, then harder, harder, until at last he cries out in ecstasy and pain and loneliness and despair.

"Will you shut the fuck up before I come over and cut that thing off for you!" comes an angry voice from the bunk across from his.

Just as he had been unable to say anything fourteen years ago, half his lifetime away, Joey can say nothing now. He lies motionless in the semi-darkness, afraid to make a sound, feeling the warm stickiness spread slowly between his legs, and cries silently in the night.

FIFTEEN

"Dean, have you got a fax machine?"

It was Thursday afternoon, and Larry Davidson was on the phone.

"Yeah, why?"

"I just got the reprint of the dibenzepene article. I think you're going to like it."

"What does it say?"

"Well, for one thing, it says there've been a number of deaths reported from overdoses. That may be why they don't market it here. For another, an overdose—let me read this to you. 'Overdosage with dibenzepene results in severe circulatory collapse and cardiac arrest. Postmortem presentation will mimic nonspecific heart failure, with microscopic studies of the circulatory system required for differentiation.' "

"What the hell does that mean?" Dean asked.

"It means that if there was enough dibenzepene in his system, your Commissioner may just possibly have died from taking too much. But you're going to have to disinter the body and get another autopsy to find out."

"Wow," Dean said softly.

"But that's not the best part." Davidson was on a roll. "Didn't the papers say whatshisname had a heart condition?"

"Yeah," said Dean, wondering where this was going.

"Well, listen to this. 'Contraindications: obesity, coronary disease, respiratory disease, alcohol consumption.' "

Dean didn't need any of that explained to him. It meant that Wilson, having suffered a heart attack a year earlier, probably should never have been taking the drug in the first place. And that he *certainly* shouldn't have been drinking while he was on it. It meant that, for the first time, there was the possibility, ever so slight, that he had died not from a second heart attack, but from the combination of a drug he shouldn't have been taking and alcohol he shouldn't have been drinking.

"Fax that stuff to me, Dr. Einstein," Dean said, knowing that there was enough there to take to Walter Bingham and enlist his help in getting a court order to dig up the body of Edward Wilson. And probably enough to get Justice Rothwax to sign an order if Bingham opposed it.

The fax arrived within minutes. Dean would never understand how such things happened. He could not program a phone with a memory, hook up an answering machine, or reset a digital watch, let alone record on a VCR. But he had no time now for marveling. He glanced at the pages as he walked back to his room. There were a lot of technical data he didn't understand, drawings resembling benzene rings he remembered from college chemistry days, and tables of levels of concentrations of various demethylated metabolites found in tissues of overdose victims. There were the contraindications Larry Davidson had read to him over the phone. And there was a list of references, mostly from European forensic toxicology publications, many of them in German.

He dialed Walter Bingham's number. Walter picked up on the first ring.

"Walter, Dean Abernathy."

"Hey, Dean. What's up?"

"I need to see you right away. Can I come over?"

"Now?"

"Yes, now. As in immediately."

"Bad time, Dean. I've gotta see the Old Man in fifteen minutes."

"This is more important," said Dean.

"Right," Bingham laughed. "I can always find another job. What's going on? Did Lee Harvey Oswald confess to killing Wilson?"

"What's going on is you and I are going to get an order exhuming the body so we can do another autopsy."

"Not a chance."

"Wait'll you see what I've got, Walter."

"I don't care what you've got. Edward Wilson was cremated three months ago."

Dean sat stunned. Once, some years back, he had come home to what was then his apartment. As soon as he had put his key in the lock, he had known something was wrong. Dean was no more neurotic than the average New Yorker, but he always double-locked his door, even if he was going no farther than the laundry room downstairs. This time he had found the door completely unlocked. He had been living alone at the time, and no one else had a key.

He had pushed the door open slowly, ready for combat. But, probably luckily, he was too late. Whoever had ransacked the apartment had apparently been unwilling to believe that the occupant had *nothing* of value, and he—or they—had torn it apart, whether in frustration or retaliation. But to Dean, who placed enormous value in his thrift-shop surroundings, in his collections of seashells, driftwood, and old bottles, the violation had been deep and personal.

He sat now, crushed as he had been then, feeling as he had then that the world had collapsed around him.

Was this some sort of roller-coaster ride he was on? Every time he developed a lead and found some small cause for hope, things would dramatically nosedive. The signatures duplicated by the detectives had turned out to be, in all likelihood, nothing more than typical police overreaching. The painstaking search for the 911 caller and tracking down Janet Killian had succeeded only in the discovery of a witness who would completely demolish the defense at trial. And now the possibility that Wilson's death might actually have been caused by an accidental overdose of a drug he shouldn't have been taking and alcohol he shouldn't have been drinking, was suddenly rendered unprovable because his body had been cremated following the autopsy.

It was almost enough to make a guy feel paranoid, thought Dean.

With no cases scheduled for the following day, Dean turned on the radio that evening to hear the weather forecast. While listening to the business news, the traffic-and-transit report, and the late-breaking headlines, he decided he would place his fate in the Gods at AccuWeather. If the Oracle of WINS 1010 said tomorrow was going to be rainy, Dean would take that as an omen that he should go to the office and catch up on paperwork and filing and that sort of stuff. If, on the other hand, sunny skies were promised, that would be a definite sign that he should go climbing.

He walked to his window and craned his neck to peer upward in an attempt to spot the tiny portion of sky visible from his apartment, but the gray patch told him little and almost caused him to miss the weather report, which his ear picked up just in time to hear "mostly sunny, with highs in the low eighties. Tomorrow night, becoming cloudy, with a chance of showers." As omens went, that was a definite A+.

Dean called his regular climbing partner, Mark Wexler, but Mark had to be in court the following day. Next he tried Jordan Miller, a much better climber than Dean himself, but got no answer. Finally he called Gary Ranier, who was less experienced than Dean—a fact that meant Dean would have to act as lead climber rather than follower, an arrangement that raised Dean's level of anxiety considerably, and one he accordingly tried to avoid whenever possible.

"Yello," came Gary's trademark greeting.

"Gary. Dean. Howyadoin'?"

"Nothin' much. Whatchupto?"

"Sameold sameold."

"Me too."

Not quite as articulate as the way a couple of women friends might bring each other up to date on the course of their lives over the past five weeks, but it would do.

"What are you doing tomorrow?" Dean asked.

"Going to the doctor, my favorite thing." Gary had AIDS. He had survived a tumor in his neck and two bouts of pneumonia.

He was between crises now, and he went to the office where he worked as an accountant as often as his health permitted him to. "Why, got something in mind?"

"You up for a trip to the Gunks?"

"Dynamite!" Gary shouted.

"Pick you up?"

"You bet. What time?"

"How does seven sound?"

"Sounds horrible," said Gary, "but I'll deal."

Dean busied himself checking his climbing gear and laying out his clothes to save time in the morning. He picked out a rope of brightly woven orange and black nylon laid over a solid core, the combination of which was capable of withstanding an impact of several thousand pounds, a very relevant requirement when one considered the momentum generated by a free-falling human body and the need to stop that body in midair in a fraction of a second. He packed a harness, a sling, various lengths of nylon webbing, several dozen carabiners, or snap-rings, an assortment of nuts and chocks to wedge into the cracks of the cliff face, a chalk bag, and a second bag containing emergency equipment: knife, whistle, flashlight, lighter, water bottle, and first-aid kit. He checked his climbing shoes and backpack and selected several layers of clothing that would enable him to keep warm in the early-morning shade and gradually peel down for the strenuous business of climbing in the heat of the afternoon sun.

The morning found Dean and Gary headed north on the New York State Thruway, approaching the New Paltz exit. There, far off to the west, the first section of cliff came into view, marked by the Mohonk Tower.

Located fifteen minutes out of New Paltz, the Shawangunk Mountains are a conglomerate of granite-like sedimentary rock roughly 400 million years old. They are a portion of the Appalachian chain that rises slightly to the north and extends as far south as Alabama. But only in its northernmost reaches do the cliffs soar dramatically to their full height and is the rock hard enough to form the premier technical climbing site in the eastern United States, drawing climbers from all over to a mile or so of vertical wall known affectionately, as well as pronounceably, as the "Gunks."

Dean aimed the Jeep west on Route 299, then north on Routes 44 and 55. Immediately the road began to climb, and after a hairpin turn and a short uphill stretch, the cliffs rose sharply on the right. Dean continued up until he found a spot between two trees, into which he was able to maneuver the Jeep. They got out, packed up their gear, and began a short hike to the base of the cliff.

The very first route they came to was a favorite of Dean's, a short, single-pitch 5.7 climb. Under a universal rating system that graded climbs by degree of difficulty, Dean considered anything from a 5.0 to 5.3 something he could safely free climb. A 5.4 to 5.6 route was still within his comfort range, though he would not attempt one without a rope. The 5.7 to 5.9 range provided him with all the challenge he needed, and though he'd managed one or two 5.10's, he didn't consider himself a 5.10 climber, certainly not when he was in the lead. There were climbs in the Gunks rated as high as 5.13, and even a 5.14 or two, but Dean resigned himself to the role of admiring spectator at that level of the sport.

They set up at the bottom, Gary tying onto a tree with a length of webbing and wrapping the rope around his body in a belaying stance. Dean stepped in a harness and slipped a sling containing carabiners, webbing, hardware, and chalk bag over one shoulder and across his body bandolier-style. He tied one end of the rope to a carabiner connected to the harness at his waist and stepped to the base of the cliff.

In a stylized manner used by virtually every English-speaking rock climber and duplicated in a hundred languages around the world, Dean checked to see if Gary was ready to catch him should the need arise.

"Belay on?" he called.

"On belay," came Gary's response.

"Climbing," Dean announced.

"Climb."

The climb began with a four-inch-wide vertical crack, into which Dean wedged the toe of one climbing shoe. Then, placing a hand on either side of the crack, fingertips pointed together as though he intended to rip the crack apart, he pulled himself up from the ground and began his ascent. On this route, the crux—or most difficult—move came very quickly, and he wasted no time placing protection in case of a fall. At fifteen feet he wedged a hex nut into a V-shaped groove so that a downward force would serve only to tighten it. The nut was pretied to a short piece of webbing that held a carabiner at the other end. This carabiner Dean now snapped onto the climbing rope. The result was that were he to fall at this point, Gary could catch him right where he was, saving him a fifteen-foot drop to the ground below.

Dean continued upward to the crux move. There he placed his left fist thumb up into the crack and then turned it ninety degrees, wedging it into the opening as a jamb. Working quickly to avoid the fatigue of hanging on to the cliff, he leaned back to test his hold. The crack hugged his wrist snugly while refusing to let his wider fist come free. Satisfied, he shifted all of his weight to his fist, simultaneously reaching high above him with his right hand and walking up the vertical surface of the rock with both feet. As his right hand found an outcropping of rock above him, he turned his left fist and released it from the crack, transferring his weight to his right hand. As his feet kept contact below him, he was able to reach up with his left hand to a good handhold. He placed both feet in the crack beneath him, one atop the other, and thus secured, he paused to place another piece of protection. That done, he was able to climb easily to an alcove, where he rested for a moment before making a simple traverse to the right, from where he continued on up to the top. He had completed the forty-foot ascent in fifteen minutes, the only price having been a set of raw knuckles on his left hand.

Once on the top, Dean unclipped the rope from the carabiner on his harness and shouted, "Off belay!" to Gary. He heard an answering "Belay off!" which told him that Gary would be unhooking from the tree and tying his end of the rope onto his own harness in preparation to climb. Dean found a tree to tie himself to, took a sitting position, wrapped the rope around his body and pulled up the slack in the rope. When he felt tension he called, "On belay!" Moments later he heard Gary's "Climbing!" and answered, "Climb away!"

Within twenty minutes from his start, Gary's face came into view and he pulled himself up to Dean's level. Even within sight and reach of each other, they completed the ritual of "Off belay" and "Belay off" before permitting themselves to sit back and enjoy the view they had earned. Then, while Gary rested a bit longer, Dean set up a rappel for their descent. He had learned long ago that climbing down could be much harder than climbing up. Unlike the upper portion of the body, the lower portion had no eyes, and climbing down a difficult route entailed placing the feet blindly each step of the way. It also meant leaving behind protection needed for the final climber's descent, or a bottom belay running up and around a tree at the top, then down to the descending climber, an arrangement that sometimes jammed and was never good for the rope. So, like most climbers, Dean preferred to rappel.

He located the midpoint of the rope, where the color pattern changed to identify it. He found a solid tree near the edge of the top and dropped first one and then the other end of the rope to the ground, leaving a single strand around the back of the tree while creating a double strand on the downhill side for the rappel.

Gary had caught his breath and was ready to hook up. Dean helped him tie onto the doubled rope with a figure-eight to add friction to the system. Unlike Marine Corps commercials featuring sudden drops and dramatic kicks against the cliff, rock climbers' rappels were tightly controlled maneuvers, meant to minimize the wear on the equipment, which tended to heat up considerably during a rapid descent, and Gary backed over the cliff carefully and disappeared from view.

Gary's "Off rappel!" several minutes later signaled that he was down and Dean was free to hook up. He used a brake-bar, a straight piece that fitted across a carabiner for added friction. By threading the doubled rope over the brake-bar within the carabiner, attaching the carabiner to the one at his waist and running the rope around his back as though he were in a belay stance, Dean was able to move himself to the edge of the cliff and lean backward out over it, feet planted so that he faced the tree uphill that secured the rope. As he increased his lean, his body became almost horizontal and his view changed from the tree to the sky above him. Then, overcoming a moment of fear—and for Dean there was always that moment of fear—he gradually opened his arms to reduce the amount of rope touching his back. The resulting decrease in friction freed him to begin walking down the cliff in a nearly horizontal position while supported by the rappel rope. If he needed more tension he simply brought his arms forward and together; for less he opened them and held them behind him. Once underway, Dean's momentary fear vanished, replaced by a sense of exhilaration in his ability to defy gravity, and he walked his way down the cliff as deftly as any spider might have.

They tackled two other climbs, an easier but longer 5.5, and a 5.6. Gary opted out of the final climb, so Dean rappelled down after completing the first of its two pitches. They found a large flat rock to stretch out on. The sun was hot, and they were exhausted, thirsty, and hungry. They broke open their food and spread it out.

"Sure beats working for a living," Gary observed. It was a hard statement with which to disagree.

On Monday Dean met with the Bronx Assistant DA, who was "interested" in Dean's "theory" that Nathan Ramsay had stabbed his victim in self-defense. He agreed to look into it. Dean sensed that this case was going to be an uphill battle. But at least he'd managed to buy some time.

Three Mexican law students, part of a group visiting New York, got into a fight outside the Sheraton. Something in Midtown, and Dean promised the Mexican vice-consulate that he'd represent one of them.

Mark Wexler called to ask if Dean would buy the beer for the bachelor party next weekend. Dean said he guessed he could do that.

It rained for four straight days, flooding streets and shortening tempers.

And Dean went back to the drawing board.

He got out his file again and began to leaf through it for the umpteenth time. He stared at the list of "Good Stuff" he had made two weeks ago, the same list that had prompted him to call Larry Davidson about the dibenzepene.

Good Stuff

1. Forged signatures on written statement
2. Denial of robbery during Q&A
3. Alcohol: Bartenders/Joey (drunk) v. Serology (.04%)
4. Toxicology (a) aspirin
              (b) dibenzepene
5. Knife: difficult to see dark handle @ night.

He focused on items 3 and 4. He knew now he would never be able to prove that the drug had caused Commissioner Wilson's death. But that didn't stop him from *suspecting* that it had. And right above that item on the list was the alcohol controversy. Dean still didn't know whether to believe Joey and the bartenders at Chandler's, who said Wilson had been intoxicated, or the serology report, which indicated that he hadn't been. He put the list to one side and continued through the file.

The document that stopped him was the death certificate. Not that he hadn't seen it before; he had read it at least a dozen times, noting the cause of death listed as "massive coronary occlusion," and the time of death as "2:30 A.M." What stopped him now was the next of kin.

Marie Crawford Wilson
76 Bleecker Street
New York, N.Y.

Who was in a better position than the Commissioner's widow to know what medication her husband had been taking just prior to his death and what his drinking habits had been? Then again, Dean realized just as quickly, who would be less likely to talk to the lawyer who spoke for the man accused of murdering her husband? No matter; he knew he had to give it a shot.

Dean received a phone call from the managing editor of Courtroom Television, a cable-network program that covered trials of interest to the public. Would Dean agree to an in-depth, on-camera interview regarding various aspects of the Wilson case? Dean said he'd think about it and asked that they get back to him in a day or two.

He straightened out his desk, caught up on paperwork, paid some overdue bills, and filed some others that he didn't have the money to cover. He ordered a half keg of beer for Angelo Pertrocelli's bachelor party, using a credit card that would give him a month to find some way to pay for it.

Then he turned his attention to Marie Crawford Wilson.

He went to the library and spent three hours in the microfilm section, going over old *New York Times* articles about the Commissioner. Finally he found what he was looking for: a cover story in a Sunday magazine section profiling Wilson. Toward the very end of the article he came upon a paragraph devoted to Mrs. Wilson. It described her as an articulate, energetic woman, whose interests included theater, opera, and charity work. She served on the board of directors of the American Cancer Society, the American Foundation for AIDS Research, and the Pegasus Society.

Bingo.

The Pegasus Society was a foundation devoted to drug treatment. Somewhat smaller than Daytop, Odyssey House, Phoenix House, and several other better-known organizations, Pegasus enjoyed a good reputation for working with black and Hispanic inner-city heroin and crack addicts who were generally considered tougher cases than their white, suburban, marijuana-abusing counterparts. Pegasus offered a variety of services but was known best for its tough two-year residential program. Many entered, few stuck it out. But of those who did, the five-year recidivist rate was said to be less than fifteen percent, an astounding figure in a landscape of statistical disaster.

Bingo, not just because Dean had had clients in Pegasus programs, and as a result knew a handful of counselors and at least one assistant director. Bingo, because Dean knew Judge Patricia Washington.

Patricia Washington was a Criminal Court judge, now presiding over felony trials as an acting Supreme Court justice. Dean had met her when she had been assistant United States attorney in the Southern District of New York, the federal counterpart of an Assistant District Attorney. As adversaries, they had tried several cases against each other, including a lengthy drug trial that had twice ended in hung juries. When Patricia Washington had been approached regarding an offer of a Criminal Court judgeship, her lack of familiarity with the New York State court system had left her uncertain as to whether or not she wanted the appointment. One of the people she had called for advice was Dean Abernathy.

In spite of Dean's advice, Patricia had responded with interest, and had been appointed by the Mayor six months later. She had risen to acting Supreme Court justice after three years, earning a reputation as a demanding judge who was tough on prosecutors and defense attorneys alike. Her high standards and low tolerance for sloppiness earned her more admirers than friends. Recently her name had surfaced as a candidate for a federal judgeship, but her Harlem roots and liberal politics had combined to disqualify her in the mind of the junior senator of New York, whose turn it was to pass on the nomination to the White House.

Through it all, Patricia Washington remained tough on the bench, cheerful off it, and good friends with Dean. He knew from conversations with her that she played tennis, rode horses, took fencing lessons, and sat on the board of directors of the Pegasus Society.

On Wednesday, Mark Wexler called to report that he had rented four porno movies for Angelo Petrocelli's bachelor party.

"Four?" exclaimed Dean. "No sane person can sit through more than two of those things. There are only a certain number of orifices in the human body, you know."

"Yeah, yeah," said Mark. "But this way we got choices."

"Choices?"

"Yeah. We got *Naughty Nipples*, we got *When Carry Met Sally*, we got *Sweet Cheeks*, and—my favorite of all—*Inside Teenage Vixens, Part Two.* How'd I do?"

"You missed your calling, Mark."

Later that day, Dean dropped into Part 43, the courtroom of Patricia Washington. He sat in the front row, where she would be sure to see him, and waited while she completed several matters on her calendar. Then she called him up to the bench with an official-sounding, "Step up, please, Mr. Abernathy."

At the bench she dropped the formality.

"How are you?" she asked, her face breaking into a warm smile.

"I'm good," said Dean. "But I have to warn you: I'm here to ask a favor."

"Not because you love me?"

"Of course I love you. But honesty compels me to be straight with you."

"Bullshit. Tactics compel you." Her smile was infectious, and they both laughed. Then, to the courtroom, Judge Washington announced a ten-minute recess. She got up, and Dean followed her into the jury room just outside the court. It served as her robing room.

"So," she said, taking one of the twelve chairs arranged around the long table, lighting a cigarette, and motioning Dean to sit, "what's this favor?"

"I want to talk with Marie Wilson."

"Mary Wilson, as in Mrs. Edward Wilson?"

"Yup."

"Marie Wilson, as in the widow of your celebrated client's victim?"

"Yup again."

"Marie Wilson, who no doubt would like to rip out your heart?"

"Three for three."

Patricia Washington pursed her lips, raised her eyebrows, and exhaled loudly. Finally she said, "You're going to owe me *big time* for this, Abernathy."

The meeting took place Thursday evening at the Wilson townhouse on Bleecker Street. Patricia Washington had called Dean that morning to tell him that the Commissioner's widow would talk with him, and had supplied him with her phone number. If it had taken a lot of doing, Patricia had not made a point of telling Dean. She had simply repeated, "Big time." They had both laughed.

Dean had dialed the number. Marie Wilson had answered, had recognized his name, and had suggested he stop over at the end of the day. Dean had said he could be there at seven.

A tall, attractive black woman with graying hair answered the door. Dean introduced himself to her.

"I'm Dean Abernathy."

"Yes, come in, Mr. Abernathy. I'm Marie Wilson."

He followed her into a living room with thick carpeting on the floor and books on every wall. He sat when she motioned to a sofa.

"I'm just making some tea. Do you take milk or lemon?" Refusal was not offered as an option.

"Lemon would be fine," said Dean.

Marie Wilson disappeared into an adjoining room. Dean was struck by the absurd civility of the scene. Here he was, the defender of the man accused of murdering this woman's husband, and she was serving him tea in her living room. He felt as though he were acting in a movie. He crossed his legs, straightened his tie, and tried to look good for the camera he knew was not there.

Marie Wilson returned carrying a tray. She served tea not in delicate china cups, but in large mugs with comfortable handles.

"So," she said. "Patricia twisted my arm pretty good. She thinks a great deal of you."

"Patricia is one of my favorite people in the world," said Dean.

"We have something in common, then. What can I, of all people, do for you?"

"Well," Dean began, putting his mug down on the coffee table in front of him, "I feel very awkward about this, but certain things have come up in this case that strike me as contradictory."

"Isn't that usually the way?"

"Yes and no," said Dean, trying to buy time while he composed an answer. "I'm not talking about normal variations, such as where one witness remembers the perpetrator as five-six, and another says he was five-nine. I'm talking about things that I can't reconcile in my own mind as simply perceptual differences."

"For example?"

"For example," said Dean, "there's a major conflict in the evidence on the matter of what your husband had had to drink that night. On the one hand, I've got a toxicology report showing he had had maybe two drinks at the most. On the other hand, I've spoken with several people who served him that night. They describe him as intoxicated. Uncharacteristically intoxicated." Dean purposefully omitted Joey Spadafino's account of the Commissioner's staggering down the block. He looked at Mrs. Wilson. She said nothing.

"For another thing," Dean continued, "I'm surprised that your husband had been drinking at all, given the fact that he was taking an antidepressant that you're not supposed to mix with alcohol."

One of Marie Wilson's eyebrows arched ever so slightly. Still she said nothing.

"Furthermore, your husband had a history of heart disease, and the antidepressant he was on is contraindicated in such cases.

And it's not even sold in this country. So I guess I don't understand why he was taking it in the first place."

"Is that all?" Mrs. Wilson asked. Dean, painfully aware that it wasn't much, braced himself. He considered it likely that she was about to abandon her politeness and throw him bodily out of her apartment.

"I'm afraid so," he admitted.

"Where does this lead to?" Mrs. Wilson asked. She gave no sign of throwing anyone or anything.

"I don't know," Dean confessed. "It's led me to you. I'm hoping you can clear it up for me."

Marie Wilson stood and walked to a window that was framed on all sides by bookcases. Dean had the feeling he was about to be dismissed. When she spoke, she looked not at Dean but out the window.

"I'm not aware of any antidepressant medication my husband was on. His doctor had him on an aspirin a day. He sometimes took something for indigestion."

"Was he depressed?" Dean asked gently.

"Not to my knowledge. He was an active man. He had a stressful job, and he got frustrated and upset from time to time. But I wouldn't have called him depressed."

"And the drinking?"

"My husband drank very little. Beer at a ball game. A glass of wine at dinner. I've been married to him for twenty-seven years, and I've never seen him drunk." Dean wondered if she realized that she'd shifted to the present tense.

"Jack Daniel's?"

"Never," she said, turning to look at him.

"Not even celebrating some occasion?"

"No way. He'd sooner have drunk motor oil."

"The medication, Mrs. Wilson. It's called dibenzepene. It's sold under the brand name Noveril. Strike a bell?"

"Absolutely not. How much was in his system?"

"That's the tricky part," said Dean. "The toxicology report doesn't say. And apparently the only way to know if it was a significant amount would be to do a thorough examination of his circulatory system. And the cremation makes that impossible, of course."

"Yes, that was very upsetting."

"I'm sorry," said Dean, realizing he had offended her with the implication of a second autopsy.

"No, I mean the cremation was upsetting."

"I don't understand," said Dean.

"I never requested it. In fact our church is opposed to cremation. But apparently there was a mixup of some sort. Someone in the department thought I wanted my husband's body cremated, and it was done right after the autopsy. I was very upset at the time. But I find I've been getting upset at all sorts of foolish things lately. I'm told it's part of the healing process, working through the anger."

"I'm sorry," Dean said, feeling stupid.

"So what does all this mean, Mr. Abernathy?"

"I wish I knew," said Dean.

For Joey Spadafino, no tea is served on B Block in C-93 on Rikers Island, either in china cups or mugs. But on this Thursday, as Dean Abernathy meets with Marie Wilson in her Bleecker Street townhouse, Joey's notified that he has a visitor, his first in four months. He's summoned not to the general visiting area, where inmates receive visits from family members and friends whose names they have listed on their visit permission sheets. Instead he's brought to the counsel room. His visitor is an attorney.

"Hello, Mr. Spadafino," says a tall, tanned man with silver hair and a matching, carefully trimmed beard.

"Hello," Joey says, not knowing what to make of this stranger. He had expected Dean.

"My name is Leonard Winston. I've been asked by a mutual friend to speak with you. I'd like a half hour of your time. Don't worry, I'm not going to ask you any questions about the case. I simply want to introduce myself and let you know why I'm interested in your situation. Okay?"

"Who's the mutual friend?" Joey asks, looking into Leonard Winston's eyes. They are a brilliant blue.

"I'm afraid I'm not at liberty to divulge that," says Leonard Winston. "Let's just say he's someone who thinks you're being railroaded, someone who cares about you. Willing to listen to me for a few minutes?"

"I'm listening," says Joey.

"Wonderful. Mr. Spadafino, I know you didn't murder any-one. I know you're not guilty. I know you have a lawyer right now who's, well, let's just say he's in over his head. He's someone they assigned to you. He gets paid by the court. In other words, he's part of the system that's out to get you. Understand?"

"I'm listening," Joey repeats. But the truth is that what he's hearing makes a lot of sense. It's all occurred to him before, of course, but he's never been able to put it into words as neatly as Leonard Winston.

"I'm not part of the system," says the man. "I fight the sys-tem every day. I take cases like yours. Little people with no one to fight for them. I take cases like yours, and I win them."

"Why? What do you want from me?" Joey asks. "I got no money."

The man laughs. "I don't want any money," he says. "I've got all the money I need. I want to defend you against unfair charges. I want to win your case. And I'll be honest, I want the publicity that comes with getting an innocent man off. After I do that, who knows, maybe we'll write a book together, you and me, and you'll end up a rich man, too."

"And if you fail?" Joey asks.

"I won't fail." The man smiles confidently. He is very good-looking. "I've picked your case because I know I can win it."

"What do I have to do?"

"Nothing but sign on the dotted line," says Leonard Win-ston, reaching into his inside jacket pocket and producing a wad of papers stapled together. From the other inside pocket he pulls out a pen. He unscrews the cap and places it on top of the writing part of the pen. It's a fountain pen. Joey hasn't seen one like it since grade school penmanship classes. It's dark green, with wavy lines through it. It looks like it's made out of marble. Leonard Winston slides the pen and the wad of papers in front of Joey. Joey looks down at them. The papers are folded in such a way that the page for his signature is on top. He begins to shuffle through the other pages. They're printed like the pages in a book, only the let-ters are much smaller and closer together. There are almost a dozen pages.

"Don't worry about the fine print," Leonard Winston says with a smile. "That's just legal language."

Joey suddenly has a headache. The things this man is saying sound good, but he seems a little too smooth, too slick. Joey feels confused and stupid.

"Can I keep the papers?" he asks the man. "Read them over and let you know?"

"I'm afraid I have only one set," explains Leonard Winston. "Tell you what. Sign this set. As soon as I get back to my office I'll have one of my secretaries make a copy for you and send it right out to you, Express Mail. You'll have it this time tomorrow. Can't beat that, can you?"

It sounds good, but again Joey feels somehow that he's being conned. He remembers one time a black kid from Fourteenth Street wanted to sell him a twenty-five-inch RCA color TV for fifty bucks. It all sounded so good until the kid asked him for half the money up front and said Joey would have to wait while the kid went to get the set. He knew then that he was about to be taken, and knew enough to not part with his twenty-five dollars. He has the same feeling now, even though this man is a lawyer and not some black kid from Fourteenth Street.

"What do you say, Mr. Spadafino? Do we have a deal? Do I beat this case for you or not?" The smile is still there.

Joey speaks slowly. He says, "The deal is, you leave the papers here with me to read. If that's no good, you can go shit in your hat."

Joey watches the smile disappear. "You're an asshole," says Leonard Winston. "A stupid, ignorant asshole. I hope you get twenty-five to life. I hope you die in jail. I hope—"

But Joey Spadafino has already stood up and begun to walk away, and he doesn't hear the rest of what the man has to say. He feels angry at the man. But at the same time he feels good, like he's just saved himself twenty-five dollars all over again.

The half keg had already been tapped by the time Dean arrived at Mark Wexler's on Friday night, and the odor of beer and marijuana smoke filled the apartment. Dean was late because at the last moment he had remembered he was supposed to bring a gift. Worse yet, the gift was supposed to be something silly, twenty dollars or under, and accompanied by a poem written by the giver.

In a panic, Dean had decided to approach the task backward. He had quickly given up trying to think of words that rhymed with Angelo or Ange, and settled on something he pretentiously entitled, "To Angelo, on the Eve of the Big Plunge."

> *Behold the great Ange Petrocelli!*
> *His pits may be damp and smelly,*
> *And his knees shake just like jelly.*
> *But he never eats meat*
> *And refuses to cheat,*
> *So there's nothing wrong with his belly!*

It wasn't much, but it was a poem. Then Dean had rushed to a health-food store on Broadway, where he had spent $19.38 on the most absurd products he could find. He bought concentrated carrot juice, garlic mints, fortified millet, unsulfured organic sun-dried raisins, and blue sesame seaweed candy. The yogurt-covered dried carob clusters would have put him over the twenty-dollar limit. Then he violated his rule against cabs and was still an hour late getting to the party.

Dean, it turned out, knew few of Angelo's friends besides Mark Wexler. So he spent the first hour or so pretty much in the background, an observer to the beer-guzzling, marijuana-smoking, joke-telling rituals of male bonding that were the order of the evening. A six-foot hero sandwich arrived, and an impressive amount of it disappeared. Poems were read, gifts were presented to cheers and laughter. A cake created and decorated at a place called the Erotic Baker was brought out. It was made to resemble a naked woman lying seductively on her belly, rear end on display. All who knew Angelo's fiancée Stephanie agreed it was a remarkable likeness of her, though Angelo insisted Stephanie's buns were cuter. Someone disagreed, and good-natured ribbing followed. Photos of the cake were taken from all angles, body parts were served and eaten, and crude jokes abounded. In spite of himself, Dean found himself mellowing and joining the fun, not without the help of several mugs of beer and even a hit or two of premium Wexler weed.

Then the movies came out, with more laughter and a heated argument over selection. *Naughty Nipples* and *Sweet Cheeks* had few supporters, it turned out. It came down to a runoff between *When Carry Met Sally* and *Inside Teenage Vixens, Part Two*. Dean cast his vote for the Vixens, based purely on the improbable campiness of the title. But the Vixenistas were narrowly outvoted by the Carryites. In the days that followed, Dean would wonder about fate, destiny, and the long arm of coincidence. At the moment it happened, he simply accepted the election returns good-naturedly and settled back on the sofa, feeling no pain from the pleasant buzz of cold beer, fattening food, and top-grade marijuana. He watched Mark Wexler work the VCR controls, and waited for his first glimpse of Carry and Sally.

The truth was, Dean secretly liked pornography. Not the graphic closeups of sweaty body parts endlessly slapping together and merging, but the foreplay: the seduction, the teasing, the undressing. Unfortunately, there was precious little of that in what he had been exposed to. He concluded that his tastes must be strange, or at least in the minority, and that the average porno viewer (whoever that might turn out to be) was eager to zoom in with the camera and focus on organs, orifices, and orgasms.

Even before Carry could meet Sally, there were previews of coming attractions, with the inevitable comments on the use of the word *coming*. Promising scenes from *Heather in Leather* and *Rear View Mirror* raised complaints that Mark should have included them in his selections. Then, finally, the feature attraction.

In a heavy-handed parody of *When Harry Met Sally*, the movie began with the two principals being introduced and setting out on a cross-country drive. Only Carry and Sally were both young women. Gorgeous young women. Pornography had come a long way, Dean thought to himself, not only in the quality of the production, but in the selection of the performers as well. Gone for the most part were the pale, overweight actors and actresses with bad teeth and sagging breasts, replaced by young California types with Nautilus bodies and toothpaste smiles. One of the women, a curly-haired blonde—Sally, he thought, though he had not paid close attention to the dialogue and might be mistaken— Dean knew he had seen before, right down to the sunglasses she wore, a fact that surprised Dean. He wondered if he had been watching too much pornography, might be in danger of becoming addicted. Was there a program he could join, a Voyeurs Anonymous? Should he contact Clarence Thomas?

On the screen, the car's air conditioner gave out in the middle of the desert. To combat the heat, the women were forced to shed various items of clothing. In time, the engine overheated, and an emergency stop had to be made. Off came the rest of the clothing, and Carry and Sally got down to meeting for real.

It was not the slow unbuttoning of Sally's blouse that did it for Dean, or the discarding of her bra, though the effect of the latter act was spectacular enough in its own way. Nor was it the wriggling free of her jeans, or even the lowering of an absurdly tiny pair of black panties. It was instead the removal of her sunglasses that did it. Dean reacted in stages. First he experienced a vague but undeniable sense of déjà vu, an awareness that things had somehow shifted to slow motion, that all this had happened to him before. But his mind seemed to be working at half speed, as though he were underwater, trying to reach the surface and break through.

Sally smiled (at Carry? at *him*?), then lowered her head between Carry's breasts. The camera shifted to Carry's face, thrown back in exaggerated, eye-closed ecstasy. Still Dean felt submerged, separated from the real world or recognition. He watched hypnotically as Sally kissed each of Carry's breasts in turn before lifting her head. The camera caught her smile.

"That's her!"

The shout brought Dean up and out of his reverie with a jolt. It took him a second to recognize the voice of the shouter as his own.

"That's her," he repeated inanely.

"Who?" someone was asking.

"Stephanie?"

"Hillary Clinton?"

"Your mother?"

"That's her," Dean said a third time. "That's Janet Killian."

SIXTEEN

It had certainly turned out to be a strange way to end a bachelor party. There had been a loud chorus of "Who-the-fuck-is-Janet-Killian?" followed by complaints that Dean's epiphany had sure managed to destroy everyone else's mood. The tape was rewound and begun twice, then finally permitted to run its course. Carry met Sally again and again, and by the end of the movie the two seemed best of friends. Dean was forced to explain just who Janet Killian, better known to those present as Sally, was, and how she had witnessed the murder of Commissioner Wilson. He succeeded in commandeering the tape from Mark Wexler in exchange for a solemn promise to reimburse Mark out of the check he would receive after the case was over. Even then, Mark looked dubious.

Despite the beer and marijuana, despite the fact that it was after two in the morning by the time he got home, Dean could not fall asleep. He lay on his back in the darkness, hands folded behind his head, eyes wide open. He watched the occasional lights of a passing car reflect across his bedroom ceiling, and he thought about Janet Killian and the tape.

He forced himself to believe that the tape was important, though he was unable to figure out just why. But by *assuming* that it could significantly help his client, Dean was compelled to turn his attention to the question of just *how* it could best be used.

The first thing that came to him, he had to admit, was blackmail. He could get word to Janet Killian that if she testified against Joey Spadafino, the whole world would be watching *When Carry Met Sally* on the six o'clock news. Of course, he could also get arrested for that, lose his license to practice law, and end up in prison. Not to mention that it was a sleazy thing to do in the first place. Other than that, a fine idea.

Or he could sit tight and use it at trial. Chances are Janet Killian was not going to take the witness stand and volunteer that she was a porno star. She would be much more likely to say she did something else altogether, whether waiting tables, tending bar, or working as an office temporary. If she had no such other job to cite, she would still be inclined to describe herself as an actress doing bit parts, studying filmmaking, or in between roles. Then, on cross-examination, Dean would ask her if she had appeared in pornographic films. If she said yes, she would drop a notch in the eyes of the jury, and Dean would get credit for his perceptiveness. If she said no, he would raise an eyebrow in surprise and ask her if she was certain. Hearing her yes, he would walk over to the defense table, fumble around looking for something, find a manila envelope, withdraw a videocassette, and study its title.

"Miss Killian," he would ask, almost matter-of-factly, "have you ever heard of a film called *When Carry Met Sally*?" There would be a dramatic silence in the courtroom as the jury stared at her, waiting for her answer. And the beauty of it was that whichever way she went at that point, he would have caught her in a lie.

But not a big lie.

Showing the jury that the prosecution's star witness had appeared in pornographic films, even coupled with the fact that she had lied under oath to conceal the fact, was hardly the stuff to produce an acquittal in an otherwise overwhelming case. The jury might well disapprove of Janet Killian, but they were hardly likely to disbelieve her testimony because of their disapproval. And if Dean played the card too heavily and tried to make a major issue of it, the tactic could even backfire and cause the jurors to feel sympathy for a beautiful young woman who had been compelled to do compromising things in front of a camera in order to support herself.

So using the film to embarrass Janet Killian wouldn't pay big dividends for Joey Spadafino. There had to be some other use of it, some other significance it held for the defense. But try as he might, Dean couldn't figure out the answer to the riddle he had created. Yet he continued to force himself to remain convinced that an answer did exist. . . .

Monday morning Dean called Dr. Larry Davidson to tell him that the body of Edward Wilson had been cremated and that therefore no second autopsy would be possible.

"What did they save from the one they did?" he wanted to know.

"What?" Dean was confused.

"What samples did they take from the body for toxicology? Liver, brain, stomach contents?"

Dean thumbed through his file, which was getting thick and needed to be subdivided under headings. He found the autopsy and the toxicology reports. "Brain, liver, and bile," he read to Larry Davidson.

"And where did our friend dibenzepene show up?"

"In the liver sample," said Dean, looking at the toxicology report.

"Okay, you're going to need a toxicologist. He'll have to examine the sample, and do dilutions to see if he can calculate the level of metabolites. From there he may be able to work backward and estimate the amount of dibenzepene. It's not precise, but it might be able to give you an idea. Like, was it just traces, or was it enough to suggest an overdose?"

"Know any toxicologists?" Dean asked.

"Not on a first-name basis. They tend to wear thick glasses and live under rocks," Davidson explained. "But I'll ask around."

"Thanks, Doc."

Dean dialed Walter Bingham's number. Bingham was on another line but promised to get right back to Dean.

Dean called him back twenty minutes later.

"Sorry," said Bingham. "What can I do for you, Dean?"

"I've come for your liver."

"Excuse me?"

"I've got a toxicologist," Dean stretched the truth a bit. "I'd like to get him access to the liver sample that was saved from the autopsy."

"No can do," said Bingham.

"How's that?"

"They tell me the sample was used up in the analysis. There's nothing left of it."

The line that separates being appropriately suspicious and being downright paranoid can sometimes be a thin one, and Dean Abernathy sat at his desk, wondering just which side of that line he was on at that moment. Walter Bingham, who had tried a lot more homicide cases than Dean had, had gone on to assure Dean that it happened all the time, that tissue samples removed from a body by the pathologist at the time of the autopsy were routinely used up by the toxicologist. After all, there were a lot of tests and only a small sample of tissue. They look for alcohol, all sorts of dangerous drugs, and a whole list of prescription drugs. By the time they're finished, there's little or nothing left. That was often the case, Bingham explained, particularly in a situation such as this, where at the time of death there had been no basis to believe that there had been an "exotic" cause of death. Not that there was any basis to believe so now, either, Bingham reminded Dean.

Maybe Bingham was right. But was it coincidence that the body could no longer be examined, having been cremated on orders from someone other than the Commissioner's widow, and that now the tissue samples had been destroyed as well? Being paranoid was disabling for the average person, but for the criminal defense attorney a little paranoia was a healthy thing.

The phone rang.

"Hello," said Dean.

"Dean, Walter Bingham again."

"Yeah."

"Dean, I've been thinking. What do you figure the chance is that your guy might be interested in a plea?"

"He already turned down the minimum, fifteen to life."

"No," said Bingham. "I mean a *real* plea."

"What do you have in mind?" In fact, Dean wasn't sure what Bingham was driving at, but it sounded as though he was about to make a real offer in the case, something he hadn't done until now. Something he certainly hadn't done on any of the occasions the case had been in court, in front of Judge Rothwax. Was he embarrassed about the destruction of the body and the liver sample and afraid that Judge Rothwax might get on his case about it or, worse yet, that a jury might make something of it?

"Well, I can't offer him manslaughter, because the only murder here is felony murder, and I know he probably didn't intend to hurt Wilson. So there's really no lesser plea possible to the murder count. But I might be able to give him the Rob One. It's a B, the same as Man One, so as a practical matter there's no difference. But the label's a lot better."

"I doubt my guy's into labels too much," said Dean. Jail had a way of creating pragmatists, and a defendant generally cares far less about what he's pleading guilty to than what his sentence will be. "What kind of time are we talking about?"

"C'mon, Dean. I'm offering you a Rob One on a murder case I can't lose. He'd have to take the max."

The "max" on first-degree robbery was, for someone with a prior felony conviction like Joey Spadafino, twelve-and-a-half to twenty-five years. Better than fifteen to life, the minimum on murder, but not exactly time served.

"Why the sudden change of heart, Walter. Do I detect a touch of human kindness?" The truth was, he wanted to know what this development was all about.

"Don't bust my chops, Dean. Why don't you run it by your guy?"

"I will," said Dean.

So Dean devoted another Saturday to visiting Joey Spadafino at Rikers Island and conveying to him Walter Bingham's offer.

Not that there was much point to it. Having rejected in the strongest possible terms a plea that would have given him fifteen years to life, Joey was not likely to jump at this new offer of twelve-and-a-half to twenty-five years. And even though Dean continued to see the case as a loser at trial, something in him wasn't entirely unhappy at the prospect that Joey was certain to reject this new offer in favor of holding out for something better, or to reject *any* offer for that matter, however reasonable, and to insist instead upon going to trial despite the odds against him. Nonetheless, he recognized his obligation to inform Joey of the development.

Dean believed that too many lawyers took over the decision-making process for their clients. In doing so they often failed to recognize that what was the right choice for the lawyer was not necessarily the right choice for the client. Under the mistaken impression (because often the thought process was subtle and unconscious) that they were acting in the best interest of their clients, lawyers went to trial in high-profile cases for the publicity, while talking other clients into pleading guilty when a trial would be too time-consuming, expensive, or inconvenient. Dean tried his hardest to divorce himself from such considerations, but he knew that sometimes he succumbed to the pressures of the real world. He made a conscious effort to avoid being overly paternalistic when it came to decisions that rightfully belonged to the defendant. Even when a client faced with a difficult decision turned to Dean and asked him whether he should take a plea or go to trial, Dean liked to say, "Hey, it's your case, it's not mine. You've got to decide."

So Dean drove out to Rikers Island to present Joey Spadafino with a choice. And basically because he had nothing better to do.

His investigation was at a standstill. He had nobody to look for, no witness to interview, no body to exhume, no liver sample to reanalyze, no theory to pursue. He was caught up on his other cases. The top of his desk was visible to the naked eye for a change. At home, he had washed the pile of dishes in his sink, made his weekly pilgrimage to the laundry room, and performed the monthly vacuuming of his apartment.

His social life had reached ground zero. He had had one date in the past month. A nice enough person with the unlikely name of Iphegenia Houdranian, she was a teaching fellow in the classics at Columbia University whom Dean had met over the cantaloupe section at Fairway. She had caught Dean pressing the melons, testing them for ripeness.

"Smell it," she had said.

"Excuse me?"

"Smell it," she had repeated. "It's not enough to feel it. Smell the end where the stem was. If it smells good, it'll be ripe."

Together they had smelled cantaloupes, laughed, and introduced themselves. Dean had ended up with her phone number and something approximating her name. A real New York Story. A respectable week later he had called her, and they went out for dinner, a Greek Syrian and an Irish Jew at a Japanese restaurant.

Only it turned out they had little to talk about. Joey was ignorant when it came to the classics, and try as she might, Iphegenia Houdranian could not approach or even appreciate Dean's intensity as he described to her the various twists and turns in Joey Spadafino's case. She ended up appearing somewhat bored and more than slightly bewildered at Dean's concern for this worthless ex-convict who had brought about the death of another man.

He drove her back to her Morningside Heights apartment and walked her to the door, where they shook hands. The dinner had been pleasant enough, and the fact that Iphegenia Houdranian had insisted on splitting the check had helped ease Dean's latest fiscal crisis. Not to mention that for the rest of his days he would be an expert when it came to selecting ripe cantaloupes.

So he drove his Jeep out to Rikers Island to tell Joey Spadafino that he could have twelve-and-a-half to twenty-five years on a robbery plea.

"Fuck that shit, man."

No need for paternalism after all. It appeared that Joey was going to be able to make this decision on his own, without too much difficulty.

"So what's goin' on?" Joey wanted to know. "What's new with the case?"

Dean had already told Joey about the cremation of the body. He now explained to him that the liver sample had been destroyed as well, making it impossible to determine if Commissioner Wilson's death had been in any way related to medication he had been taking.

"Great," said Joey. "It's just one thing after another. I can't buy a fuckin' break, can I?"

"Well," said Dean, "there is one thing."

"Whatsat?" asked Joey without looking up.

"The woman, the eyewitness—the one who saw you pull the knife on the guy—"

"I didn't pull the knife."

"You're right. I'm sorry." Dean corrected himself. "The one who *says* she saw you pull the knife. It turns out she makes skin flicks. Porno movies."

"Makes 'em, or is *in* 'em?"

"Is in them."

"Howdya know?"

"It's my job to find these things out," Dean explained with a smile. "I investigated. I've even got one of her movies."

"So whatasat mean?"

"I'm not sure it means much of anything," Dean admitted. "We can embarrass her with it."

"That ain't right," said Joey.

"Since when are you Mr. Morality?"

"Whaddayou mean?"

"Nothing," said Dean. He realized that Joey operated on a very literal level, that he never seemed to know whether Dean was speaking seriously or ironically. He wondered if it sometimes seemed to Joey that Dean was making fun of him. At the thought, Dean's Jewish half delivered him a pang of guilt.

"Whyn't you bring it to her?" Joey's voice brought Dean back to the interview. "You know, like a peace offerin'. Tell her you won't use it if she'll tell the truth."

"Suppose she's already telling the truth?" Dean asked.

"Fuck you, Dean. You wasn't there. I was there. She says I pult the knife, she's lyin'. You tell her I said that. If you're my goddamn lawyer, you tell her that to her face. Else I'll hire that other guy."

"What other guy?"

"Nobody," Joey mumbled.

"What other guy?" Dean repeated.

"Some lawyer came to see me," Joey explained.

"Who?"

"Some sleazebag. Winton? Winters?" Joey groped for the name.

"Leonard Winston?"

"Yeah."

Dean knew of Leonard Winston, and sleazebag was not too far off the mark. Sometimes referred to as the Silver Fox, Winston was generally regarded as short on legal skills but good at theatrics and playing to the media. He had first gained publicity as a lawyer with the Patrolmen's Benevolent Association, where he had successfully represented police officers accused of committing crimes. More recently he had landed several high-profile clients. The vanity plate on his Rolls-Royce read WINS TONS.

"Who sent him to see you?" Dean asked.

"I dunno," said Joey. "He wouldn' say."

"That's Leonard Winston, all right."

"So you gonna do it?"

"Do what?" Dean was still trying to figure out Leonard Winston's interest in Joey Spadafino.

"Go see her. Tell her you'll forget the nasty movies if she'll tell the truth?"

"I'll think about it," said Dean. "You want to think about the twelve-and-a-half to twenty-five?"

"No way, man. He can stick that up the Hershey Highway."

Joey thinks about all of it that night. He lies on his bunk in the dark, feeling encouraged. He now knows he was right to refuse to plead guilty to murder, just as he's right to refuse to plead guilty to robbery. Other inmates have told him this: no matter what lawyers and judges say, if you can hang tough they'll offer you less and less time as it gets closer to trial. And he now sees they're right. First they offered him fifteen to life. He turned it down. So next they offered him twelve-and-a-half to twenty-five. He figures next they'll offer him ten to twenty. He'll hang tough all right. When it gets down to something he can deal with, then he'll think about it. Maybe two to four. He could do that.

Also, he's kind of glad he told Dean about the other lawyer. He could see Dean was a little upset about that. Meaning Dean is afraid Joey might fire him and get a street lawyer. That's good, Joey knows, because it'll make Dean try harder. Maybe get him to take the movie to the woman and get her to say he didn't pull the knife.

Being a lawyer can't be so hard, Joey decides. He wonders if maybe he should think about acting as his own lawyer on this case. He's heard about a guy in C Block who represented himself on a burglary case and beat it, got found not guilty on the whole thing.

For one thing, if he was the lawyer he'd know what to do about this woman. You go to her and you get her to say she didn't see him pull the knife, that's all. What's the big deal about that? How hard can that be?

SEVENTEEN

Dean went to trial on a stolen-car case. The defendant, a twenty-year-old Korean named Bong Kao, had been stopped driving a car that turned out to have been stolen a month before. Bong claimed that a girlfriend had loaned him the car an hour earlier. He testified that he had seen her driving the car off and on for about a week, and assumed it was hers. She had given him the ignition key, but no door or trunk key, explaining that she had lost those. Dean argued in summation that the jury could convict Bong only if they were convinced beyond a reasonable doubt that he knew the car was stolen. Apparently they were. It took them the better part of two days of deliberations, but in the end they found Bong guilty.

The day after the verdict, Dean stayed home. Facing his colleagues at the office or the courthouse after winning a case was glorious; facing them after a client had been convicted was unbearable. In fact, Dean realized that over the years he had even adopted an entirely different language to describe the two results: when the jury returned a not-guilty verdict, Dean would answer inquiries about the result with a proud "I won"; when the jury's verdict was a guilty one, Dean would explain that "they convicted him," immediately distancing himself from the outcome.

But while staying home protected Dean's bruised ego from the queries of his colleagues, it failed to distract him from thinking about work. And thinking about work meant thinking about Joey Spadafino's case.

For one thing, Dean found the business about Leonard Winston upsetting. Although all lawyers had clients who drove them crazy and cases they wished would somehow disappear, no lawyer liked being knocked out of a case, even when it was a court-appointed case and the client or his family found the money to retain a private attorney. So the notion that another lawyer had tried to hustle his biggest case away from him angered Dean. His dislike for Leonard Winston—whom he had seen but never met—further fueled that anger. What puzzled him was Winston's interest in the case. Surely it wasn't money; neither Joey Spadafino nor his family had any. Nor did Joey's case strike Dean as a particularly attractive case from a publicity standpoint. Certainly there would be media attention during the trial, but media attention was something to which Leonard Winston had easy access without the Spadafino case. Joey Spadafino himself was hardly the type of client with whom a publicity seeker would want to identify. And because the trial seemed inevitably headed for a conviction, the long-range effect of any publicity was bound to be negative.

Finally, it struck Dean as curious that Winston, with his old ties to the PBA and the Police Department, should be interested in representing the man accused of murdering the Police Commissioner. But then again, Dean knew that trial lawyers were basically mercenaries, gunslingers who were able to switch sides at the drop of a hat, without losing any of the fervor it took to represent either party to a lawsuit with total dedication. The toughest assistant district attorney would leave his job and would suddenly be representing accused criminals with the same vigor with which he had been prosecuting them a month earlier. The only common denominator seemed to be an intense desire to win. To those who cited this chameleon quality of the litigator as proof of the moral bankruptcy of the legal profession, Dean agreed up to a point, but he also insisted that it was that same intense desire to win that produced the best trial lawyers. A lawyer, after all, was an advocate. If he stopped to ponder the moral strength of his client's position, and allowed his estimate of it to dictate how hard he fought in court, he was worthless to all but those few whom he was convinced were totally innocent of any wrongdoing. Dean believed mightily in the system. He believed that even society's lowest member, accused of its very worst crime, was entitled to one advocate in his corner. It was the job of that advocate, short of cheating, to give his client one hundred percent of his effort. The rest of the world could—and no doubt would—be affected by its loathing for who the defendant was and what he had done. The only person who could not be affected, who could not pull his punches and try less hard to win, was the defense attorney.

For better or worse, Joey Spadafino was such a defendant, a lowly ex-con accused of murder, and Dean Abernathy was his lawyer. He found it hard to believe that Leonard Winston wanted the case because his desire to win it was greater than Dean's. And it pissed him off that some slick hustler with ulterior motives was trying to steal it from him.

To distract himself from his growing anger over Leonard Winston, Dean forced himself to think about other aspects of the case. But with his investigation at a virtual dead end, he kept coming back to Janet Killian and *When Carry Met Sally.*

Try as he might, Dean couldn't think of a constructive use for the movie. His mind game of assuming there *was* such a use, and then trying to discover it, had failed him. Joey had suggested he go back to Janet Killian and present her with his copy of the movie, as some sort of peace offering, a barter in exchange for her telling the truth. The problem was that Dean was firmly convinced that she *was* telling the truth, that she'd actually seen what she described to Dean that afternoon in Detective Rasmussen's car. Joey, of course, did not like that particular truth.

So what Joey was really suggesting amounted to extortion. Dean's bringing the movie to Janet Killian would be nothing more than a way of letting her know that he had it. Even as he presented it to her, she'd know that he was aware of her pornography career and could easily locate another copy of the movie—or other movies in which she might have appeared—to expose her on the witness stand. The message would be clear enough: if she'd back off from the truth in her testimony, Dean would keep quiet about her secret. That's all there was to it.

Unless.

Unless the premise behind all that thinking was wrong.

Unless Joey Spadafino was the one who was telling the truth and Janet Killian was lying.

And slowly it came over Dean that he wasn't giving that scenario a chance, much as he hadn't believed Joey's claim that the detectives had forged his signature on the second page of his written statement—the page that had Joey demanding money from Wilson—until the copy-machine enlargements proved that Joey was right after all.

And in that moment, Dean knew that he was wrong to preclude the possibility, however unlikely it seemed to him, that Janet Killian was lying. Dean owed it to Joey to go back to her. Notwithstanding her reluctance to talk to him and his own understanding with Detective Rasmussen to leave her alone, Dean had an obligation to his client to confront her point-blank about whether she had really seen Joey pull out his knife and threaten the man with it, or whether she was adding that crucial detail to the things she had actually seen because the police had convinced her to do so. If Joey was wrong about everything else, he was right about one thing: Dean had to go back to her and ask her.

The problem, once again, was one of strategy.

Dean rejected the idea of bringing her the videotape. Even presented as an unconditional peace offering, it implied a threat. At the very least it would put Janet Killian on the defensive at a moment when Dean would be asking for her cooperation.

He rejected also the notion of calling her ahead of time as he had before. He knew what would happen if he did. She would hang up the phone and call Detective Rasmussen, and shortly Dean would get a call. "Counselor," he could hear Rasmussen scolding him, "we had a deal. A deal's a deal. The lady doesn't want to talk to you. Stop harassing her." And that would be that.

In the end he settled on a harmless enough ploy. He needed to get access to Janet Killian's apartment in order to take photographs from the vantage point she had had as she observed the crime that night. If she would simply give him five minutes at her window, he could shoot looking down across the street to the spot where Joey Spadafino and Edward Wilson had confronted each other five months ago. She'd see the camera in his hand, the tripod under his arm, and know his intentions were legitimate. If necessary to persuade her to let him in, he'd promise to refrain from asking her any questions.

Then, while setting up the tripod (he'd bring it along precisely because the business of setting it up and adjusting it would buy him extra time) and peering down to the street below, Dean would muse aloud at how surprising it was that she could have seen the knife at that distance so as to be able to describe the color of its handle in the man's hand, in the dark, with the snow falling. He'd snap a few pictures, change lenses, make further adjustments. Finally he'd turn to her and look her straight in the eye. "Miss Killian," he would say as softly as he could, "you never saw a knife that night, did you?"

And whatever her answer, at least he would have taken his best shot.

The following day Dean received two unexpected phone calls. The first was from Marie Wilson.

"I wanted you to know, Mr. Abernathy. I called my husband's physician. He never prescribed any antidepressants for Edward. And I checked our medicine cabinet and Edward's dresser. There were no pills that I can't account for. So if he was taking diben—"

"Dibenzepene."

"Dibenzepene. If he was taking dibenzepene I have no idea where he was getting it or where he was keeping it."

The second call was from Walter Bingham.

"So, did you ask your guy about the robbery offer?"

"Yeah, Walter, I did."

"And?"

"And he says you can take your twelve-and-a-half to twenty-five and stick it in your ear." Dean was being charitable; if he remembered correctly, Joey had been a little more graphic in his phraseology.

"Doesn't he know I've got him cold on felony murder?"

"He's not exactly a rocket scientist, you know."

"I know, but let's be reasonable about this," said Bingham. "What's he looking for?"

"Oh, we'd settle for a twenty-five-dollar fine, two days' community service, and a strong reprimand from the judge."

"I'm serious, Dean. What would it take to get rid of this case?"

"Seriously?" said Dean. "At four to eight I'd break his arm."

*　　*　　*

As Dean thought about the conversation afterward, he was baffled. A general rule of thumb in negotiations involving criminal cases—or negotiation of *any* sort, Dean assumed— was that the party with the weaker hand bore the burden of initiating the negotiations. Prosecutors with strong cases didn't have to make offers; they enjoyed the luxury of being able to wait for defense lawyers to come begging to *them* on behalf of clients who would have no chance at trial and whose only hope, therefore, lay in getting a plea to a lesser charge and the reduced sentence that came with it.

But Bingham had now come to Dean, not once but *twice*. Twice he'd called Dean with the express purpose of making plea offers. Furthermore, rebuffed the first time, he'd now called back to find out *what the defendant would take*. "What would it take to get rid of this case?" he had asked. A question that interested Dean not so much in terms of what Joey's answer might be, but in terms of why the question was being asked at all. A prosecutor wanted to "get rid of" cases that were nuisances, those too old, too trivial, too complex, or too boring to try. This case was none of those. That left only one explanation, as far as Dean was concerned: that to Walter Bingham, despite his air of supreme confidence about the strength of his evidence, for some reason this case was too *risky* to try.

Or to someone calling the shots for Walter Bingham.

For hadn't Bingham remarked about the close interest his supervisors and the police brass had taken in the case, that he had even heard from the *Mayor*? Bingham wouldn't have the authority to make offers on his own in this case. Which meant that someone up the ladder had to be telling him to "get rid of this case." And for some reason that Dean could not begin to comprehend.

That evening Dean returned his copy of *When Carry Met Sally* to Mark Wexler, symbolically removing any temptation he might otherwise have had to use the videotape as a trump card.

The following day he gathered his camera and tripod, an extra lens, a couple of filters, and three rolls of 35 millimeter film, and headed to 77 Bleecker Street. He found a parking place up the block, a legal one this time. He looked at his watch. It was ten-fifteen, late enough in the morning so that he would not be waking anyone, even a sometimes movie actress.

Resisting the impulse to sit in his Jeep and hope that Janet

Killian would fortuitously stroll out the front door, and leaving his strip of venetian blind behind, Dean walked directly to the front of the building and opened the outer of the two doors. He didn't try the inner door. Instead, he pressed the button alongside the listing on the board that read 1A NOVACEK (SUPER). Nothing happened. He pressed it again. Still nothing. He reached for the button again and was about to press it a third time, when he saw a door open onto the lobby beyond the inner door. A large man dressed in dark work clothes moved toward the door and cracked it open. Standing in the doorway, he looked Dean up and down. Apparently satisfied that Dean did not present an immediate menace to him, he pushed the door open and stepped into the vestibule area, joining Dean but continuing to hold the door open behind him.

"Vut can I do for you?" he asked in what Dean took to be an Eastern European accent.

"Are you Mr. Novacek?" Dean was careful to pronounce the third syllable "check." He knew of both a professional tennis player and a tight end for the Dallas Cowboys whose names were spelled the same and pronounced that way.

"That's me."

"I need to see Miss Killian, Janet Killian," Dean explained. "I need to take some photographs from her apartment."

"She expects you?"

"Sort of," Dean said. "I've spoken with her several times, and we've met."

"So?" said Mr. Novacek, holding the inner door open and allowing Dean to enter the lobby. "Ask her."

"Thank you," Dean said, and began walking toward the elevator.

"Ask her," Mr. Novacek repeated, and when Dean stopped in midstride to look at him, he saw that the man was pointing across the lobby in the direction of what appeared to be a mailroom. The only person in sight was propped up in a baby stroller and looked to be about six months old. Dean looked back at the super and thought he saw the man roll his eyes upward slightly.

"Janet," he called, making it sound like "Zhanet."

"Yes?" came a voice from within the mailroom.

"Young man to see you," called Mr. Novacek.

Dean braced himself for the appearance of Janet Killian. At their first meeting he had appraised her California blond good looks only in the context of how she would strike the jury as a witness. Now he felt his heart beat in anticipation and what he recognized instantly as pure lust for her other persona, the uninhibited, unclad co-star of *When Carry Met Sally.*

So he was totally unprepared for the appearance of the dark-haired, fine-featured young woman who emerged from the mailroom and fixed her gaze on him.

"Yes?" she said.

Dean returned her stare. "Ah—I'm looking for Janet Killian."

"I'm Janet Killian."

Dean stared at her. A lawyer, a college graduate, a person of at least average intelligence, Dean prided himself in the fact that he rarely if ever said things that could be classified as completely stupid. Nonetheless, he now distinctly heard himself say, "Are you sure?"

"Reasonably," replied the young woman. She moved to the baby stroller and focused her attention on its occupant. Then she turned back to Dean. "And who do you think you might be?"

"A moment ago I'd have sworn I was Dean Abernathy. Now I'm totally confused."

"Dean Abernathy," the woman repeated slowly. "The man's lawyer."

"Yes."

"And photographer."

Dean looked down at the equipment in his hands. "I can explain this," he said. And as if to demonstrate, he held out the camera. But in doing so, he managed to tangle the strap with one of the legs of the tripod, which had apparently not been completely closed. He shook the camera to free it, but the strap remained snagged. He shook it again, harder, and it broke free. Too late, Dean realized he had no grip on it. The camera, launched from his hand, rose a foot or two in the air and seemed to float there before finally succumbing to gravity and beginning its inevitable descent to the lobby floor. Instinctively, Dean lifted his right foot, the way a soccer player would use his foot to catch a ball that had bounced off his chest, to control it before letting it reach the ground. But Dean's soccer days were well behind him, and his timing was off. Instead of breaking the camera's fall with his foot, Dean succeeded in kicking it squarely and lofting it across the lobby. He watched it land hard and slide to a rest. He looked sheepishly at the woman, who was fighting to suppress a smile.

"I hope you're a better lawyer than you are a photographer," she said. The smile won.

"I meant to do that," Dean said, walking to the camera and retrieving it. "I never liked this camera." The woman's smile broadened, causing Dean to wonder if his clumsiness might prove worth the price of the 35 millimeter, which in truth was second-hand and somewhat temperamental at best.

"Do you do things like that often?" she asked.

"Only when I'm trying to make a total fool of myself. Not more than once or twice a day."

"We were supposed to meet with Detective Rasmussen," the woman said, her attention again turned to her baby. "Only you changed your mind."

"Who told you that?"

"Detective Rasmussen. He set it up, then he called me back to say you had changed your mind. You decided you didn't want to talk with me after all."

"He lied," Dean said.

She looked back at him. "Why would he do that?"

"I'm not sure. But he did more than that. He got somebody to play your part."

"Play my part?"

"Miss Killian—Mrs. Killian," he corrected himself, glancing at the baby in the stroller.

"Miss Killian," she corrected the correction.

"Miss Killian, I need to speak with you. What's more, I think you need to speak with me."

"Would you like to come upstairs?" she asked.

"I thought you'd never ask."

Upstairs was a comfortably furnished one-bedroom apartment that the real Janet Killian shared with her six-month-old daughter, Nicole. Dean sat on a sofa in the living room, which doubled as Janet's bedroom, while Janet did whatever one did with a six-month-old in the other room, which she described as a combination nursery and attic. "I've decorated it in pink clutter," she explained, but to Dean's eye it looked pretty orderly.

When she emerged, Janet held her index finger to her lips and whispered, "I *think* she's asleep." Before she would turn her attention to Dean, however, she insisted on making tea. "I can't help it." She shrugged. "It's the Irish in me, I guess." He found himself following her into the kitchen, where he looked on as she went through her ritual. She seemed to derive pleasure from it, and he enjoyed watching her.

She was maybe five-five or five-six, and slender to the point of being almost skinny. Her skin looked lightly and evenly tanned. Her hair was somewhere between dark brown and black, with a hint of auburn visible only when she passed in front of the window. It was straight, but looked soft to the touch. Her nose was a bit too sharp and her lips a trifle too full, but both of those flaws disappeared when she smiled, revealing small white teeth that looked like they belonged on a dental health magazine cover. But it was her eyes that captured Dean. They were disproportionately large, giving her, along with the fullness of her mouth, the hint of a street urchin capable of breaking into a pout at any moment. They were blue—but not the blue that eyes usually come in. They were a darker slate-blue color, more suitable perhaps for the exterior of an expensive car or the hull of a sleek sailboat. The combination of these unlikely components caused Dean to catch himself staring for long moments at this young woman he had just met, and who now brought them tea that smelled slightly of orange and cinnamon.

Dean was reminded of being served tea by Marie Wilson, and wondered if there was something about him that inspired mothering in women, triggering some primitive need to brew dry leaves in steaming water.

Back in the living room she sat on a chair opposite him and watched as he examined his camera.

"Is it going to live?" she asked.

"I don't know. It's not going to be taking pictures for a while, that's for sure."

"Sorry."

"That's okay. It's not really why I came here in the first place," he confessed.

"Oh?"

"It was a ploy."

"I see." She sipped her tea, her tongue testing its temperature. "And why did you need a ploy?"

"Because you didn't want to speak with me again—at least the person playing you didn't want to."

"I think I better explain why someone's been playing me," she said.

Dean did his best. He told her about the irregularities he had discovered in investigating the case, about the forged signature of Joey Spadafino, the presence of an exotic drug in the toxicology report, the conflicting reports regarding the drinking habits of Commissioner Wilson, the mysteriously ordered cremation. He described his meeting with Detective Rasmussen and the blond "Janet Killian."

"So who is she really?"

"An actress of some sort." Dean did not elaborate.

"Why would they do that? Why would they go to all that trouble?"

"I don't know yet," Dean confessed. "Except that they obviously felt it was very important to keep you away from me. If you're willing to tell me what you saw that night, maybe we can figure out what they don't want me to know."

Janet Killian sipped her tea again. Then she said, "The man you're representing is guilty." When Dean didn't say anything, she added, "I mean he did it." She looked at him almost apologetically.

Two Janet Killians, Dean thought, and they *both* have to blow my client away. But he shrugged and said, "That tends to happen a lot in my business. Why don't you tell me what you saw."

"I was nursing Nicole," she said. "I mean I still am, but I was nursing her that morning. It must have been about two-thirty. I had just put her down. I went to the window and looked out. I do that sometimes. It was snowing. I saw a man bending over something. I couldn't see what it was at first. After a moment my eyes got accustomed to the darkness, and I realized it was another man lying on his side. He wasn't moving. And I saw the first man— your client—going through his pockets.

"I dialed nine-one-one. I have one of those cordless phones, and I was able to keep watching at the window while I called. I told the operator what was happening. She asked for my phone number. I don't think I gave it to her.

"After a moment the man—the one going through the other one's pockets—he looked up, like he realized people were watching what was going on. I saw him put something in his pocket. I'm pretty sure it was money. Then he started walking away, toward Seventh Avenue. He walked quickly, then he sort of broke into a run.

"I had got disconnected from the operator, so I called back. A different operator answered, a man. He asked me for a description of the man who took the money. I described him as best as I could. I don't remember exactly what I said, except that he was short and had a dark jacket. Oh, yes—he had a cap on, a dark cap. I think I said that, too."

"Anything else?" Dean asked.

"Well, I'm sure he had pants on—"

"No, I mean, do you remember anything else that happened between the two men?"

"Like what?" Janet asked.

Dean hesitated, then reminded himself that this wasn't a trial; there was no need to refrain from asking the dangerous questions, the ones that might hurt his client. It was the truth he wanted. He needed to know.

"Like a knife?" he said, and held his breath in spite of himself.

And Janet Killian said, "Oh, no."

Research studies have shown that a type of mental paralysis, an actual inability to cognate, can result from the simultaneous bombardment of the brain with two equally powerful but competing reactions to a single stimulus. Thus we sometimes find ourselves figuratively "frozen in our tracks" when confronted by some emergency we want to at once both rush to confront and flee to avoid.

So Dean now sat dumbly on the sofa for what seemed like minutes, unable to fully absorb either of the two messages that tried to penetrate his thought process.

He could win this case.

And, *What was going on here?*

Years of being a trial lawyer—of battling to win, of fighting desperately to avoid losing, of being an adversary, a competitor, a *gunslinger*—made the first reaction almost instinctive and inevitable, but he struggled to get past it, to get to the second one. And realized even in the process that he was afraid to ask the question. So he stalled.

"You never saw a knife in my client's hand?"

"No," Janet said firmly. "I never saw a knife at all. Why?"

"Because they had your stand-in say you did."

"Why would they do that?" Janet asked.

There it was again, stated in slightly different terms. The Question. Why was it so important that they put a knife in Joey Spadafino's hand? Dean knew now that Joey had been telling the truth all along, that the knife had been in his pocket the whole time. Having a folding knife in your pocket wasn't illegal; it became a crime only when you did something with it that demonstrated an intent to use it unlawfully against someone else. But it meant more, it meant that Joey was to be believed about *everything*. He had taken the money from the fallen body of Edward Wilson, taken the money clip. He had run when he realized he had been seen. He had gotten rid of the money clip and been caught with the money. He was guilty of larceny, grand larceny if he had taken the money while Wilson was alive, because then it had been "from a person." If Wilson was already dead, he was no longer "a person" in the eyes of the law, and it was only petit larceny, a misdemeanor that carried a maximum of a year in jail. But whichever it was, without the knife, without the threatening words that Joey had always denied saying—a denial that Dean finally knew was honest—there was no robbery in a legal sense. And without a robbery there was no felony murder. *Joey Spadafino was absolutely innocent of every charge in the indictment.* But that still didn't explain why someone was willing to go to great lengths to make it look like Joey was guilty. Who, after all, was Joey Spadafino, and why should anyone want to frame him for something he hadn't done?

"Mr. Chang didn't see a knife, either."

"What?" said Dean, snapped suddenly out of his mental wanderings.

"Mr. Chang, from Four-B." Janet pointed toward her ceiling. "He didn't see a knife, either."

The other witness, thought Dean. He moved to the edge of the sofa. "How do you know he didn't?" he asked.

"I talked to him the next day. He saw the whole thing, even more than I did. From when the Commissioner was first coming up the block."

"Are you serious?"

"Of course I'm serious. And the detectives were much more interested in him than they were in me."

"What makes you say that?"

"Because they were," Janet said. "Mr. Chang told me they had him downtown three separate days, for hours at a time. They said they knew he had seen more than he was telling them. They kept insisting that he must be too frightened to tell them everything. But he swore to me he told them everything he had seen."

"Where is he now?" Dean asked. "Is he home?"

"Nobody seems to know. He disappeared about three weeks ago. He doesn't have any family here, as far as anyone can tell. Mr. Novacek said he thinks he's in the hospital, but nobody seems to know for sure."

"We've got to find him," said Dean.

"What you mean, *we*, Paleface?"

"I mean we," said Dean, "because you're involved in this whether you like it or not. Janet, someone went to a lot of trouble to make sure I would never meet you, would never speak with you, that I would never find out that you could clear my client. People have lied under oath, falsified reports, and forged signatures. *They've even hired an actress to play your part.* Mr. Chang probably told them the same things that you did. They tried to get him to change his story, but he wouldn't. Now he's disappeared."

"You're frightening me," said Janet.

"I'm sorry," said Dean. "But until we figure out what's going on here, you've got good reason to be frightened. And you better watch yourself."

Joey Spadafino, also with good reason to be frightened, has been watching himself, too. But Joey's precautions prove to be his undoing. Somebody—Joey doesn't know who, but he's got a pretty good idea it's the two Dominicans that continue to menace him—drops a dime on him, snitches on him, and on the way to break-

*fast he's stopped by two COs and searched. From the thorough-
ness of the search Joey knows right away it's not routine. Which
means they'll find his shiv.*

*They pull him out of the mess line and into a small office
that contains a desk, a chair, a computer, and a telephone. They
have him extend his arms and spread his feet. One of the officers
pats him down while the other sits on the desktop and smiles.
When the one patting him down finishes, he tells Joey to drop his
trousers. Joey does so.*

"Your undershorts."

*Joey lowers his undershorts, trying as he does so to keep the
upper parts of his legs together. But with his feet spread it's impossible, and the sharpened piece of coat hanger falls from his crotch
and lands incriminatingly between his sneakers.*

*"Whatdowegot here?" says the CO, seeming to enjoy every
minute.*

*Whatever he could say would only get him into more trou-
ble. So he says nothing.*

*The two officers walk Joey back to his cell. He knows he'll
get written up for this, but he can deal with that. He long ago decided it was better to take a chance getting caught by the COs
with a weapon, than it was getting caught by the Dominicans
without one. At the moment he's annoyed with the fact that he'll
miss breakfast, which is the only meal where he can ever find
anything to eat. It means he'll go nearly two days without food,
instead of one.*

*Back at his cell, Joey's made to stand outside the bars with
the same CO who sat on the desk earlier, while the other CO
tosses the cell. This is because there's a rule that gives an inmate the right to be present when his cell is searched. Before there
was such a rule, inmates were all the time getting told that contraband was found in their cells, and they had no way of arguing
that it was found under another inmate's bunk or in another
inmate's stuff.*

*Joey feels pretty secure about the search. The only thing he
has is some oatmeal cookies he palmed from the mess hall at last
night's dinner and a couple of photographs of some inmate's girlfriend putting a bottle up her twat. The inmate had broken up
with his girlfriend and didn't want the photos anymore, and was
about to throw them out, so Joey took them. Both food and*

pornography are contraband, but neither is a big deal. Joey has heard inmates say it's a good thing to have some sort of minor contraband for the COs to find, so they don't get too pissed off when they can't find anything, and trash your belongings. In this case, Joey figures they'll just eat the cookies and take the photos, anyway. He even knows an inmate who keeps Ex-Lax in a Hershey wrapper, so if anyone swipes it and eats it they'll get a good case of the runs.

So Joey's surprised when the officer tossing the cell ignores Joey's bunk and personal items, and instead goes straight to the commode. He reaches around behind it and comes up with something that looks like an envelope with tape on it. Joey's never seen it before.

"Lookie, lookie," he says as he walks over to Joey and the other officer. Standing in front of them for both to see, he pulls out several small glassine bags containing a white powdery substance.

This time Joey, who knows he's been flaked, says something.
"Fuck."

EIGHTEEN

Thursday came, and with it another call from Walter Bingham.

"I'm going to make you my final offer," he said to Dean. "Five to ten. As the beer commercial goes, it just doesn't get any better than that."

"What's going on here, Walter? Why all this sudden compassion for my client?"

"Two reasons," said Bingham. "For one thing, I realize Spadafino never intended to kill Wilson. Or even harm him, for that matter. It was just his dumb luck to pick a victim who goes and has a heart attack on him and drops dead, and who happens to be the Police Commissioner. But I have no reason to believe he knew who his victim was, either, so how much more can I penalize him for that? But that's only part of it, Dean. I might as well level with you."

Dean found himself counting his fingers. He had long ago learned that when an adversary said, "I might as well level with you," it was time to get ready for the Big Lie.

So he braced himself and said, "By all means, Walter. Level with me."

"My people want to wrap this thing up," said Bingham in his most confidential tone. "Between you and me, rumor has it the Mayor wants to name a new Police Commissioner. He'd rather the

Spadafino case be out of the way before he does it. So they're telling me to give away the store if necessary. What they really wanted me to do was to offer you ten to twenty, see if you'd take it. Then seven-and-a-half to fifteen if you wouldn't. Finally five to ten, take it or leave it. But I told them I've got too much respect for you, that I didn't want to play games."

"And if I leave it?"

"You won't," said Bingham. "You can't."

"My client might."

"Then I'll convict his stupid ass and Rothwax'll give him twenty-five to life."

Thinking about the conversation later, Dean had the peculiar sensation that Bingham had had other people in the room with him on his end of the phone. Maybe that's who he had been referring to when he had said "my people." Then again, maybe Dean was imagining the whole thing.

Dean had asked Janet Killian to call him that afternoon. She had agreed to ask Mr. Novacek, the superintendant, what hospital Mr. Chang was in. When Dean had asked her the second part of the question—if she would go with him to talk to Mr. Chang—Janet had hesitated. He had found it hard to blame her.

But she did call, promptly at one.

"They took him to St. Vincent's," she said, and Dean thought he detected a note of pride in her having completed her assignment: "At least that's what Mr. Novacek says, and he's into everyone's business around here. We call him 'Nosey Novacek.' "

"Good work."

"Only he's not there anymore. I called."

"Where is he?"

"They'll only tell me he was transferred," she said. "They say they're not allowed to tell me where unless I'm immediate family."

It had been raining that morning, and Dean had left his bike home and driven to work. But by late afternoon the sun was out and the temperature reaching toward ninety. Knowing he would get stuck in traffic on the way uptown, Dean decided he might as well enjoy it, and he put the top down on the Jeep. He liked the fresh air, fresh being a relative term in the city. He also liked the increased visibility it gave him. His convertible top was six years old, and the plastic windows were so scratched that he could barely see out of them. With the top down he rediscovered his rearview mirror, which actually allowed him to see the traffic behind him for a change.

He first became aware that he was being followed around Fortieth Street. He was heading north on what would eventually become the West Side Highway, and had just changed lanes to make a light before it turned from yellow to red, when he noticed that a dark red sedan behind him, with two men in it, also went through the intersection. Dean watched in his mirror as the sedan pulled over to the curb and stopped. He would have given it no more thought, but several blocks later he looked in the mirror, and there it was again. It was one of those generic American cars, a Chevy or a Ford or a Plymouth or a Pontiac—he could not make out which. And to Dean, the two occupants had "cop" written all over them.

At Fifty-seventh, instead of getting onto the elevated highway or turning right toward Eleventh Avenue, Dean threaded his way through traffic another two blocks. His right turn took him up a little-used street. He was halfway up the block when he saw the red sedan turn into it behind him. He toyed with the idea of pulling over to force the sedan to drive right by him, but decided against it. He had made the tail; there was no reason to let them know he had done so.

At West End Avenue he made a left and continued uptown. The red sedan kept going straight, its occupants apparently not wishing to "burn" or reveal themselves, or perhaps simply content to assume that Dean was headed home.

That evening Dean phoned a college classmate, David Leung. It was a somewhat uncomfortable call to make, because Dean had not spoken to David in several months, and now he was calling to ask a favor.

"I need you to call St. Vincent's Hospital," Dean explained after they had caught up on news. "Your brother Po Wen Chang was admitted there about three weeks ago. He's been transferred to another hospital, and you need to know where."

David was an eager accomplice. He made his living as an accountant and envied the excitement that seemed so present in Dean's work and so totally lacking in his own. When Dean had worked as a DEA agent after college it had been almost too much for David to bear, and he would routinely corner Dean and make him tell stories of undercover buys and Midtown stakeouts.

David phoned back twenty minutes later. He had had no luck. "They say they can't give out any information over the phone," he reported. "I've got to go down there and bring proof that I'm Chang's brother. What is this guy, an international terrorist or something?"

"You'd think so," said Dean. "But he's really just a guy who happened to be looking out his window one night."

"I guess I'll stick to watching TV."

"Good idea," said Dean.

David promised to go St. Vincent's in person after work Friday, even though Dean told him to forget it, he'd try to locate Mr. Chang some other way.

Some other way turned out to be a burglary.

Dean called Janet Killian on Friday morning. He told her he needed to talk to her again, and asked if he could stop by on his way uptown after work. She agreed. She didn't question him as to why he couldn't ask her whatever he needed to know on the phone, which was fine with Dean. The truth was he was beginning to feel very paranoid. If someone was following him, they could also be listening in on his telephone. He preferred not having to share such thoughts with Janet, however, since if they were listening in on his phone they were probably doing the same with hers. Whoever *they* were.

He took the bike this time. And he made sure no one was following him. He watched carefully in his mirror, so carefully that at one point he almost rode into a cab stopped in front of him. Rather than taking Broadway uptown, he zigzagged through the maze of downtown streets. He deliberately went the wrong way on several one-way streets, and at one point even walked his bike into the lobby of a large office building and out the side door. No one seemed to be following him.

Janet buzzed him in, and Dean took the elevator to her third-floor apartment, bike and all.

She was bathing her daughter, and he watched while she finished. When she had dried and powdered and diapered Nicole with cloth diapers ("They're cheaper than Pampers," she explained, "and not as bad for the environment"), she handed her to Dean while she did things with baby food in the kitchen. Dean managed not to drop the child, despite the fact that she squirmed and seemed intent on pulling his nose off. She had apparently never been around someone with a full-sized nose and was not about to miss her chance.

Over mashed banana and applesauce, Dean explained that his Chinese connection was having difficulty locating Mr. Chang. It was Janet who suggested breaking and entering.

"I bet Novacek will give us the key," she said. "He'll do anything for money."

"How much money?" Dean asked. "They tend to frown on reimbursing lawyers for expenses incurred in committing major felonies."

"Twenty bucks might do it," Janet said, her blue eyes shining with the excitement of a life in crime. "I'll chip in half."

"You sure you're up for this?"

"Absolutely," she said, smiling. "How much time could they give us, anyway?"

"For a first-degree burglary? Not more than eight-and-a-third to twenty-five."

"Piece a cake," said Janet.

So when Nicole had been fed and nursed and put to bed, Dean played baby-sitter while Janet, armed with two crisp ten dollar bills, went downstairs to find Mr. Novacek. Dean paced the living room while he waited for her, trying to digest the idea of suddenly having a partner in his investigation. He was so used to working alone, so accustomed to calling the shots without having to consult anyone else, that his first reaction over this new development was mixed with uncertainty. For example, in addition to his strip of venetian blind, Dean had a full set of lock picks, and at one time in his DEA career he had been pretty good with them. His preference would have been to leave Mr. Novacek out of things, to try to get into Mr. Chang's apartment on his own. If in fact he had decided he wanted to get in there at all.

But here he was, waiting in a strange apartment with a six-month-old child for a woman he barely knew, who had not only decided that they needed to get into Mr. Chang's apartment, but was at this very moment out in pursuit of the burglar tool of *her* choice, while in the process alerting the general public to their criminal enterprise in what he was reasonably certain would prove to be a futile attempt to get the key, anyway. He would set her straight as soon as she returned.

It took her about fifteen minutes. When he let her back in and saw that she was empty-handed, he tried to hide any trace of smugness from his voice. "No luck, huh?"

Janet said nothing. She closed the door behind her, kicked off her shoes, and looked straight at Dean. Then she reached down the front of her blouse and, to a triumphant "Ta-dahhh!," extracted a set of keys. "And," she said, opening her fist and revealing a neatly folded ten dollar bill, "I saved half our bribe money. I figured we might need it for bail."

"You're unbelievable," Dean said, in spite of himself.

Janet got Mrs. Del Valle from Apartment 4A to baby-sit Nicole. Janet insisted in dressing in all black—black jeans, black turtleneck top, and black sneakers—saying she wanted to feel like a cat burglar. Dean managed to talk her out of blackening her face with mascara. "It'll make trying to explain this as a spur-of-the-moment thing a little difficult if we get caught," he said.

"We're not going to get caught," Janet assured him. But she relented on the mascara.

They had to take the elevator down because Mrs. Del Valle insisted on seeing them off, bestowing motherly smiles on them. Dean guessed her weight at upward of three hundred pounds and didn't want to do anything that might upset her.

"She's so happy for me," Janet explained. "She thinks I'm going out on a date."

"Yeah," said Dean. "My mother would be thrilled." But the truth was, it was Dean that was having a hard time hiding his excitement at being with this young woman he didn't quite know how to deal with.

They got off the elevator at the second floor and took the steps back up to the fourth. As Dean followed Janet up the stairs, taking them quietly, two at a time, he felt like he was back in high school, prowling the building at night in search of the answer sheet to the next day's math test. He had an almost uncontrollable urge to reach up and grab her rear end as she took the stairs in front of him. He fought the impulse by picturing himself the subject of a

Congressional inquiry on sexual harassment, trying to explain to Orrin Hatch and Arlen Spector that he had meant no harm.

Janet cracked open the door to the fourth floor, peered out, and motioned Dean to follow. They paused at the door to Apartment 4B and listened. There was no sound from within. Janet unlocked the two locks, and they stepped inside, closing the door behind them.

The interior reminded Dean a little of his own apartment. It had an informal, lived-in quality, and Dean took an immediate liking to this Mr. Chang, who was obviously comfortable enough with himself to leave his things around in a casual way.

"Oh, my God," Janet whispered. "Someone's torn the place apart!"

"Are you sure?"

"Yes, I'm sure. Mr. Chang is compulsively neat. He'd never leave his things like this."

So much for the informal, lived-in quality. Dean walked into the bedroom and had to agree with Janet's version. The mattress had been pulled halfway off the bed, and the linens tossed to the floor. All the drawers of a dresser had been pulled open, and one was removed altogether and left on the seat of a wooden chair. Articles of clothing were scattered about, personal items dumped in piles on the bare floor.

"Someone's been looking for his money," said Janet. "He told me he didn't trust banks. In China the government can decide to take your money out of your account any time they want, and that's it."

Dean kneeled down and began sifting through the piles of Mr. Chang's belongings. "I don't think it was his money they were looking for," he said, showing Janet a billfold with several fives and tens in it. There was also a gold pocket watch that was heavy enough to be worth something.

"What *were* they looking for, then?"

"I'm not sure," said Dean.

"What are *we* looking for?"

"I'm not sure about that, either. Wasn't this your idea?"

"Oh, sure," laughed Janet. "Blame me."

"Shut up and search, you. We're looking for something that'll give us a clue where the inscrutable Chang is at the moment. There's got to be something here."

And there was. It took them close to a half hour, but Janet finally came up with a packet of letters neatly tied together and stored atop a bookcase in the living room. The letters themselves were written in Chinese, but the envelopes were addressed in English. On the back of each one was a neatly printed return address:

Edna Chang
133 Hillcrest Road
Brimfield, Mass. 01010

Dean copied the information onto a separate piece of paper and returned the packet to its hiding place.

Another twenty minutes of searching turned up nothing further, and Dean announced that it was getaway time. Janet was going through kitchen containers, insisting she was looking for opium of microfilm, and pleaded for another ten minutes. Dean told her she had five, and wandered over to the window.

It had turned dark outside, and streetlamps lit up Bleecker Street below. Dean looked across to where Joey Spadafino had encountered Edward Wilson nearly six months ago. From Mr. Chang's apartment on the fourth floor, the doorway where Joey had been huddling from the storm was even easier to make out than it was from Janet's window one floor below; the added height actually improved the perspective, much the way you could sometimes see the playing field of a ballpark better if you sat up higher in the grandstand.

Pedestrians were visible in the lights as they made their way along the narrow sidewalks on either side of the street. An Italian restaurant featured specials on a blackboard propped up out front. Taxis cruised by. A dark blue car sat at a hydrant across the street, about five parking spaces to Dean's right. And even though he could not distinguish its make or model from the distance, Dean knew immediately that it would be a Plymouth. Squinting into the glare of the lights, he could see that there were two people in the front seat. And though it was impossible to tell if they were male or female, black or white, young or old, he knew that they would be Detective Rasmussen and his partner, Detective Mogavero. As his eyes adjusted further, Dean thought he could make out eyeglasses on the occupant of the passenger seat. As he strained to see better, he saw the passenger lower them to his lap, and Dean realized they were not eyeglasses at all. They were binoculars.

Dean pulled back from the window, knowing he'd been seen. When he was thirteen or fourteen he had been spying on Mrs. Felcher undressing in her bedroom across the way one night, when she had suddenly and unexpectedly looked straight at him from her own window. He pulled back now as he had then—too late—feeling caught, discovered, and very much in trouble. For days he had lived in dread anticipation of a midnight knock on the door, followed by his parents' summoning him to face the inquiries of the police. He prayed for deliverance, swore off his Peeping Tom ways, and made a secret pact with whatever powers might control things that, if only he could be spared this one time, he would never again lust after Mrs. Felcher or any other woman as long as he lived.

"Turn off the lights," he said to Janet, and the urgency in his tone brought an almost immediate response. In the darkness, Dean stood at the side of the window but back a step, in shadow, as he studied the blue car on the street below. A fragrance of what seemed like peach, or perhaps apricot, reached him, and though she said nothing, he felt the presence of Janet Killian standing close behind him.

"See the blue car?" he said.

"Yes." She was so close to him he could feel her nod.

"That's your friend Rasmussen."

Now he felt a shiver go through her body, and he reached back with his hand. She took it in her own, which felt small and cool to the touch. She closed the distance between them even more, and they continued to stand like that in the shadow by the window, the front of her body lightly touching the back of his.

"What are they doing here?" she whispered, though they were well out of earshot.

"Watching us."

"Why?"

"Because they're afraid of us."

"For a minute there," Janet said, "I thought you said *they're* afraid of *us.*"

"I did," said Dean.

"Why?"

There it was again: the Question, reduced this time to a single word. Dean tried his best. "Because they've done something," he said, "and they think we're on to it."

"Something," Janet echoed. "Like what?"

"I don't know," Dean admitted. "Something to do with Joey Spadafino and Commissioner Wilson and you and Mr. Chang. But I don't know quite what yet."

"They're moving," Janet said. And she was right; the blue car pulled away from the curb and into traffic. It slowed down as it came abreast of the building entrance, then accelerated and continued up the block and away from them.

Dean looked at his watch. It was nine-thirty. "What time do you have to be back?" he asked Janet.

She laughed. "Mrs. Del Valle told me I should stay out all night. She expects me to be at least engaged by the time I return. But if I don't get back to Nicole by two, my breasts explode."

Dean suppressed his interest and let her comment pass. "I'm starved," he said. "Let's spend our ten bucks' bail money on dinner somewhere."

They found a Mexican restaurant on Bank Street. Janet would not drink while she was nursing Nicole, so Dean was forced to down a margarita for each of them. They wolfed down chips and salsa and shared an order of vegetarian fajitas. And they talked. Janet, it turned out, had been orphaned at nine when her father, an alcoholic, had raced a locomotive to a crossing in the family car, killing himself, Janet's mother, and two of her four brothers. She had looked after her two younger brothers since she had been fourteen. One was in college in Boston, the other writing poetry in Ireland. She herself had worked as a waitress, barmaid, lifeguard, aerobics instructor, and housepainter, earning enough money to put herself through nursing school at night. It had taken her five years. She had lived with one man for two years and spent two more waiting in vain for another one to leave his wife. Three days after that ended, she had gone to the Museum of Natural History and picked up the best-looking man who ventured into the Hall of Fishes that afternoon, taken him home, and gone to bed with him. She had never asked or learned his name. When Nicole was born and Janet had been asked the father's name for the birth certificate, she had replied with a straight face, "Ralph Barracuda." She was presently working in the post-operative recovery room at Mount Sinai Hospital, because they had a good day-care facility, where she could leave Nicole and even nurse her on her lunch break.

Dean insisted on paying the check, even though it came to somewhat more than ten dollars. "Mrs. Del Valle's liable to ask you if I treated," he explained, "and I don't want her getting angry and sitting on me or anything."

They walked back to her building hand in hand, Dean and this woman he had already fallen in love with.

For Joey Spadafino, there's nobody to hold hands with. Joey sits in the darkness in a six-by-nine-foot cell in what is officially designated by Rikers Island management as the Administrative Segregation Unit. Among the inmates it's known simply as the Hole.

Joey's in the Hole for fifteen days, the punishment for possession of a dangerous instrument, and a Schedule One Controlled Substance. The decision to treat the incidents administratively, rather than refer them to the Bronx County District Attorney for prosecution in court, is supposed to be appreciated by Joey as a break, but he regards it as an admission of sorts by the corrections authorities that he has been "flaked"—the cocaine put on him by the CO's.

In the Hole, Joey's in lockdown for all but one hour a day, which means he spends the remaining twenty-three hours sitting in his cell. There's no bed; he's provided a mattress and a blanket. He sleeps on the mattress at night; during the day he folds it against the wall and uses it as a chair. There's no other furniture in the cell. There's a hole in one corner of the concrete floor, to be used as a toilet. There's a discolored sink with a single faucet that drips lukewarm water. A twenty-five-watt bulb lights the interior of the cell from within a protective cage attached to the ceiling. There's no window. The metal door has a six-inch-square opening in it for the duty officer to look in on him. A vent in the opposite wall lets a blast of hot air in during the day, a trickle of cooler air at night.

For one hour a day, Joey's led out into a small yard and permitted to exercise, along with half a dozen other inmates he assumes are also in the Hole. He's permitted to walk with them, to run laps with them, even to lift weights that are provided. He's forbidden to talk to them. One word of conversation results in all of the inmates being immediately returned to their cells, as has happened once, even though the rule was not explained to Joey in advance. But it was another inmate who spoke, not Joey. Joey has no way of knowing whether the rule had been explained to the other inmate, and dares not ask.

On rainy days there are no yard privileges.

Twice a week Joey's led out and escorted to the shower area, where he's allotted five minutes of water, the same lukewarm water that drips from the faucet of his sink.

Three times a day, meals are passed to Joey on a plastic tray slid through the small square opening in the door of his cell. Everything on the tray is room temperature—meat, potatoes, vegetables, coffee, milk—as though it's been sitting somewhere for an hour before being brought to him.

Joey tries hard to finish his food because the tray from one meal isn't collected until the next one's delivered at the following meal. The leftover food draws roaches and reminds Joey of a science experiment in sixth grade, where a magnet attracted iron filings in pretty patterns. At first Joey squashes the bigger roaches with the soles of his sneakers, but the dead ones only manage to attract more live ones. So he ends up leaving them alone, lets them come and go as they please. He's begun thinking of them as his cellmates. Once he even catches himself talking to one of them, asking it if it wants some of his leftover cooked peas.

He worries that he's beginning to crack up. He thinks it's even possible that he talks to the roaches a lot, only he's not aware of it, except for the one time he caught himself.

To pass the time, Joey dreams. Not just when he is asleep, but when he's awake, too. If he wakes up from a dream, he tries to continue it while he's awake. He finds he can do this if he concentrates real hard when he first wakes up, while the dream is still fresh in his mind. If he waits even a few seconds, it's too late, and the dream gets away from him.

He dreams now he's at an amusement park, though he's not sure which one, or even if it's any one in particular that he's ever been to. He's on the Ferris wheel, sitting next to a pretty girl. Each time they get to the top he has the feeling the car they're in is going to come unbolted and sail forward, out over the park below. But each time they stay attached and begin to drop, slowly at first, and then faster and faster, as though in free fall, and as they drop Joey feels like his insides have been left at the top, and the feeling is so intense, so excruciating, that it's all he can do to keep from crying out.

NINETEEN

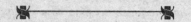

Dean slept until after ten Saturday morning. He had walked Janet home, said good night to her and a beaming Mrs. Del Valle at the door, and headed carefully home, the two margaritas being one more than his customary self-imposed limit when he was biking. It had been after two when he climbed into bed, but still he had lain awake for at least an hour. The intrigue of searching Mr. Chang's apartment, the panic at almost certainly having been spotted by the detectives, and the general excitement over spending the evening with Janet Killian had combined to produce an adrenaline level in Dean that was totally incompatible with sleep. The last time he had looked at his clock it read 3:11.

He took three aspirins for his morning headache, reminded of his father's kidding him that when it came to alcohol, Dean took after his mother and drank "like a Jew," meaning he was better suited to eating. He showered, shaved, made a pot of espresso. He had just sat down on the couch with a cup of it when the phone rang.

"Hello," he said.

"Hello, Dean." Dean recognized David Leung's voice.

"How'd it go?"

"Are you sure you want to know?" David asked.

"That good, huh?"

David explained that he had gone to St. Vincent's Hospital Friday afternoon, as he had said he would. He had identified himself as the brother of Mr. Chang, and had even been able to produce some phony identification he had made up in case he was asked to show some. When he had asked about the whereabouts of his brother, he had been ushered into an office and asked to wait while the files were checked.

"After about fifteen minutes, some guy in a suit from Administration comes in and starts asking me a bunch of questions. I had the impression he was stalling for time, and it turns out I was right. About ten minutes later, two detectives arrive, along with two uniformed security guards. They want to see my identification. I'm worried now, so I act all indignant and refuse to show it to them. I keep saying, 'This is America,' and start threatening to call my lawyer. They want to know who my lawyer is. I make up a name for them."

"Good thinking," said Dean.

"They want to know who I'm working for. I keep saying I don't understand, I'm not working for anyone, I just want to find out where they've sent my brother. Then they ask me if I'm the only family he has. You can call me crazy, Dean, but I had the feeling that if I'd said yes they would've killed me on the spot. 'Big, big family,' I said. 'Mother, father, brothers, sisters, cousins, aunts, uncles, all the works.' Finally they ask me for my phone number and tell me they'll call me with the information. But I'm too scared by this time, so I gave them a wrong number. After an hour or so they let me go."

"Jesus, David, I'm sorry."

"Well, I'm sorry I failed in my assignment. What the hell is this all about? Nuclear secrets? Alien invaders?"

"Over dinner some night," Dean said, aware that they had already said too much on the phone. "I owe you one."

After hanging up, Dean called Information for Brimfield, Massachusetts. He was pleasantly surprised when they were able to supply him with a number for an E. Chang at 133 Hillcrest Road.

A woman answered on the second ring.

"Hello," said Dean, in his most official voice. "I'm Mr.

Frasier in the records department at St. Vincent's Hospital in New York. I'm trying to reach Edna Chang."

"This is Edna Chang."

"Oh, good. Miss Chang, we've located some additional portions of Mr. Chang's chart, and we'd like to forward them to the hospital he was transferred to, but I'm afraid nobody entered the name and address of that hospital in our computer. I wonder if you could assist us."

"Yes," said the woman. "He's at the Tall Oaks Recuperative Center. If you hold on a minute, I'll get you the address."

"Please."

After a moment the woman came back on with the address. Tall Oaks was on Route 303 in Congers, New York. "That's in Rockland County," said the woman.

"Yes, I know," said Dean. "May I ask how Mr. Chang is doing?"

"About the same," said the woman.

"Well," said Dean, "let's hope for the best. In the meantime, I'll see that these records get sent right out."

"Yes, thank you."

Dean hung up and dialed Janet's number. Already he knew it by heart.

"Hello," she said.

"So did Mrs. Del Valle approve of me?"

"She's giving you one more date to buy me a ring."

"That's what I like," said Dean. "A nice, relaxed timetable." Then, "What are you doing today?"

"I don't know," she said. "I thought maybe we'd break into the White House, kidnap the President."

"You up for a ride?"

"Where to?"

"Secret."

"How's a girl to know what to wear?"

"Don't ask so many questions," said Dean. The truth was, he figured the chances were pretty good that one or both of their phones were tapped. "I'll be over in an hour, if that's okay."

"Should I get a sitter?"

"I think so," said Dean, adding, "I'll pay this time."

"No need. Mrs. Del Valle wouldn't take any money last night. Said I should think of it as going toward my dowry."

* * *

Janet was wearing shorts and a T-shirt when Dean arrived in a gray suit. "I see I guessed wrong," she said. "What'll it be, bullet-proof vest? Bathing suit? Ballroom gown?"

"Work clothes."

"My work clothes are all white," Janet said.

"Work clothes," said Dean.

She disappeared into the bedroom while Dean went to the window and checked the street below. There had been no sign of anyone following him over, and he saw no suspicious cars now.

A few minutes went by before Nurse Killian emerged from the bedroom. Dean looked her up and down. He wanted to tell her she looked gorgeous, stunning, sexy, irresistible. He contained himself and said, "Excellent," as professionally as he could.

Mrs. Del Valle arrived and smiled approvingly at Dean. Janet gave her instructions and said she wouldn't be late since she had to work that night.

They put the top down on the Jeep and headed uptown. Dean drove without talking for the first ten minutes, watching his rearview mirror for a tail. He saw nothing obvious. He got onto the West Side Highway at Fifty-seventh Street. He exited at Seventy-ninth Street, took the circular ramp down into the Boat Basin, and as soon as he was out of sight from the traffic behind him, pulled over to the curb. No one followed. Satisfied, he pulled away and back onto the highway and headed to the George Washington Bridge.

"Hi, Janet," he finally said.

"Gee, I thought you'd become autistic."

"Just paranoid," he assured her.

"So what's the mission of the day?"

"Ever hear of a place called Tall Oaks?"

"Nope."

"Me, neither," said Dean. "But that's where we're going."

"You've found Mr. Chang?"

"I think so," said Dean.

The air felt ten degrees cooler on the New Jersey side of the bridge, and the trees that lined the Palisades Parkway offered a welcome contrast to the concrete corridors of the city. Dean reached for one of Janet's hands that rested on her lap. She took his hand and squeezed it slightly; he returned the squeeze.

At Exit 5, Dean took Route 303 north. They were in New York State again, passing through towns like Orangeburg and Valley Cottage. Congers, Dean remembered from long-ago visits to a favorite fruit-and-vegetable stand mysteriously called Dr. Davies, was only a few miles up the road, and he lightened the pressure of his foot on the accelerator to make the drive last a little longer.

The Tall Oaks Recuperative Center was a cluster of stone buildings set back from the road and hidden by not only oak trees but maples, ash, birch, tulip, and cedar. A gravel driveway opened into a circular parking area that contained a half-dozen cars and an antiquated Cadillac ambulance.

A small sign in front of the centrally situated building said RECEPTION, and Dean and Janet entered. A gray-haired woman sat behind a counter and reminded Dean of his grade school librarian. There was no one else in sight.

"Hello," said Dean. "I'm Dr. Braithwaite and this is Nurse McCarren. We've driven up from St. Vincent's in New York. We had promised to look in on Mr. Chang."

"Do you have an appointment?" said the woman.

"We were told there wouldn't be a problem," said Dean. "At the time of the transfer we said we'd be making a follow-up visit. We were told to come on a Saturday morning, when things wouldn't be too busy."

"Well, let me see if I can reach Dr. Warshaw."

"Thank you," said Dean.

Within minutes, a short, nervous man arrived. He was wearing a white lab coat and dark slacks and carried a clipboard. He walked over to Dean and Janet. "I'm Dr. Warshaw," he said. "May I be of assistance?"

"Yes," Dean said. "I'm Dr. Braithwaite." He took the man's hand and shook it unnecessarily hard. "This is Virginia McCarren. We're from St. Vincent's in New York. We transferred a Mr. Chang to you awhile ago, and at the time we said we'd have a look in on him after he was settled in here. Our guidelines auditors require it, as I'm sure you know. So we're here to do our duty."

"I'm afraid this isn't a very good time," said Dr. Warshaw.

"That's why we'll just take a minute and be on our way," said Dean, and he turned and moved toward the door. Janet took her cue and fell in behind him. With nothing else to do but be left standing there, Dr. Warshaw followed. Dean opened the door and held it for the others.

In spite of what seemed like great reluctance, Dr. Warshaw led them to one of the buildings that flanked the first one. A sign atop the entrance read simply WEST BUILDING. As they entered, Dr. Warshaw cleared his throat and appeared to be about to say something, but Janet beat him to the punch.

"How's he doing?" she asked.

Dr. Warshaw stopped inside and looked at them in turn. Again he seemed on the verge of challenging them. Dean looked at his watch in an exaggerated display of annoyance.

"Mr. Chang," Janet said. "How's he doing?"

"About the same," said Dr. Warshaw finally, and led them into a large room. The interior was dimly lit, with the overhead fluorescent fixtures casting a violet hue. There was a hum from the air-conditioning, punctuated periodically by electronic beeps and hissing noises from around the room. Two rows of eight beds each filled the room, sixteen in all. Each bed was occupied by a patient, or more precisely a body, which was in turn connected by a series of plastic tubes and colored wires to various monitoring, feeding, and collecting devices. Although a few of the bodies were elevated slightly on their mattresses, none of them showed the slightest sign of movement or, for that matter, life.

Janet and Dean followed Dr. Warshaw to a bed in the second row, where a gaunt Chinese man lay on his back with his eyes open. Thick plastic tubes ran from his nostrils to a machine that alternately compressed and expanded like an accordion, but instead of music it emitted a rhythmic hissing sound. An intravenous hookup dripped a clear liquid from a plastic bag suspended above the bed into a thinner plastic tube that ended under a patch of tape on the back of one hand. A stenciled card attached to a chart holder at the foot of the bed informed them what they already knew: the body was that of P. W. Chang. Dean heard Janet catch her breath and watched her momentarily grasp the siderail of the bed before her training took over and she regained her composure.

"About the same" turned out to be a polite euphemism for comatose. As Dean and Dr. Warshaw stood by the bedside, Janet made her way to the foot of the bed. With his size advantage, Dean was able to position himself between the two of them in such a way as to block her from Dr. Warshaw's view. Janet picked up the chart, as Dean tried to ask doctorlike questions to distract Dr. Warshaw.

"Any change in his vital signs?" he asked.

"No."

"What do the EEG's show?"

"Virtually flat."

"Any idea what brought this on?"

"Can't say." Dr. Warshaw was not exactly a wealth of information. "And I'm afraid I have my rounds to complete now," he added.

"By all means," said Dean.

Dr. Warshaw stepped away from the bed, where Mr. Chang continued to lie, motionless and unseeing. Dean moved too late to block his view of Janet leafing through the chart. Dr. Warshaw extended his open hand toward her like a teacher who had just caught a schoolchild in the act of passing a note. "I'm afraid that unless you're on staff here, Miss—"

"McCarren," said Janet, to Dean's relief, since he himself had forgotten the name he'd assigned to her. She finished reading the page she was on before handing over the chart.

"I'm sorry about your neighbor," Dean said to Janet as soon as they pulled out of the driveway. "But while it's fresh in your mind, I need you to tell me what you found out from the chart."

"What I found out was that most of it's missing. But he's brain-dead, that much I saw. Been like that since before they admitted him. Massive circulatory collapse resulting in anoxia. That's a fancy word for when your organs are deprived of oxygen. One of those organs happening to be the brain. By the time they got him to St. Vincent's and coded him, there had already been massive, irreversible brain damage. He's been on a ventilator ever since."

"Prognosis?"

"He lives like this, or he dies," said Janet. "They usually pull the plug when the insurance runs out. In this case it doesn't make much difference; he's got about as much brain activity as a cucumber.

"Any clue as to the cause?"

"The chart says 'Suspected overdose of unspecified antidepressant medication,'" said Janet. "But Mr. Chang never seemed depressed to me. And it doesn't make any sense, because he never would have taken medication even if he was. He believed in ginseng and garlic and herbal teas. I've never known him to take an aspirin for a headache. I can't for the life of me believe he took an overdose of anything."

"He didn't," said Dean.

"What do you mean?"

"I mean he was poisoned."

They rode in silence while they each absorbed what was now painfully but unmistakably true, at least to Dean. For all intents and purposes, Mr. Chang had been murdered for what he saw the night of Edward Wilson's death, or for what he *didn't* see and wouldn't say he did. How safe could the young woman sitting next to Dean now be, given that she had seen almost as much as Mr. Chang and was now almost certainly known to be cooperating with Dean in an effort to unravel the entire business? The thought sent a shudder through his body.

It was Janet who finally spoke. "We have to go to somebody."

"Like who?"

"The police?"

Dean laughed. "They *are* the police."

"The District Attorney?" she said. "That Mr. Brigham, he seemed honest."

"Bingham," said Dean. "And I can't be sure he's not part of this. He's acted very strange lately. He's been trying to get my client to take a plea on this case in the worst way. Like he's petrified at the thought of going to trial, when he should be looking forward to it as his moment in the limelight. I end up not being able to trust him."

"How about the FBI?"

The thought hadn't occurred to Dean. He wasn't a big fan of the FBI, and he traced his wariness of them to his DEA days, when the two agencies had been rivals with overlapping jurisdiction in drug cases. He tended to think of the Febes as guys who wore suits and carried attaché cases, and were afraid to get their hands dirty. He remembered saying as much not too long ago to one of them.

"Leo Silvestri," he said.

"Excuse me?"

"Leo Silvestri," Dean repeated. "I've got a client, Bobby McGrane, who's cooperating with the FBI. I met the agent he's working for, Leo Silvestri. He seemed like an okay guy. I guess I could call him."

Dean dropped Janet off a block from her building. He had noticed no one following them at any point during the day, but in case they were watching her building he didn't want them seeing her with him. He figured he had put her in enough danger already.

Back home, he spent an hour searching for Leo Silvestri's phone number. After looking through stacks of notes and scraps of paper, he emptied out his wallet. There, among a dozen or so business cards, was the one he was looking for.

LEO N. SILVESTRI
Investor

LICENSED & BONDED   (212) 483-1927

He turned the card over. On the reverse side Leo had written the code Dean was to use when calling him:

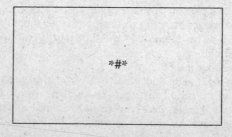

#

Dean dialed the number. When he heard a long beep, he entered his own phone number, followed by *#*, and hung up.

It took only three minutes for the phone to ring.

"This is Leo. You beeped me?"

"Yes. Thanks for calling back, Leo. My name is Dean Abernathy. I'm Bobby McGrane's lawyer."

"Yeah, sure, we had dinner with Bobby," said Leo. "Smart boy. How you been, Dean?"

"I'm okay, thanks."

"Bobby's doing real good for us. Good kid."

"Good."

"What can I do for you, Dean?"

"You can let me buy you dinner this time. I've got something I want to talk to you about."

"You got it, except the buying part," said Leo. "The Bureau's too rich for that. Tonight soon enough?"

"Sounds good," said Dean.

"You name the place."

"Same as last time?" Dean didn't want to name a place, in case someone was listening in.

"Eight o'clock?"

"Eight o'clock."

The Allstate Café was crowded when Dean arrived, and he didn't spot Leo Silvestri. He worked his way to the bar and asked what kind of beer they had on tap.

"Try the Newcastle Brown Ale," said a man's voice behind him. Dean turned to see Leo Silvestri.

"I'll try the Newcastle Brown Ale," Dean said to the bartender. To Leo he said, "Hello, Leo. Thanks for meeting me."

"My pleasure," Leo said, smiling. He held what looked to be a club soda with lime. Catching Dean eyeing it, he lifted the glass slightly and said, "On duty."

The Newcastle Brown Ale was good. They stayed at the bar until a table opened up in the corner, where they could talk without being overheard. Leo had arranged it.

"Try the roast chicken," said Leo. "They make it nice and moist." Dean ordered the swordfish, no garlic.

"So what's on your mind, Dean? You sounded serious on the phone."

"You got an hour or so?"

"I got all night."

Dean began at the beginning, how he had been assigned to represent the man accused of the felony murder of Police Commissioner Wilson. How it had seemed at first to be an open-and-shut case. How inconsistencies began popping up. The signatures forged by the detectives, the dibenzepene in the toxicology report, the mysterious cremation, the used-up liver sample. He took Leo through the meeting with Detective Rasmussen and the first Janet Killian, Dean's accidental discovery that she was an actress, and his success in contacting the real Janet. He described being followed and even expressed his concern that both his and Janet's phones might be tapped. He talked about the increasingly attractive plea offers made by the District Attorney's Office. By the time Dean concluded his story with the locating of the comatose Mr. Chang, Leo Silvestri could barely contain himself.

"Jesus Christ, Dean. This is *big*. This is *awesome*. Who else have you told this to?"

"Nobody, really, besides Janet and now you."

"Well," said Leo, "I'd like your go-ahead to talk to the New York field director about this. I can tell you this much: he's going to want to meet with you, and probably Janet, too. This thing is dynamite."

"What do you make of it?"

"Me?" said Leo. "I'm a stupid field agent, what do I know? But it sure sounds to me like the NYPD is up to no good here."

"You and me both," Dean said, nodding.

"So what do you say?"

"About what?"

"Can I go to the Director?"

Dean thought for a minute, but the truth was he could think of nothing else to do. Besides, that was the whole idea, wasn't it? "I suppose so," he said. "But be careful."

"Me?" Leo laughed. "You're the one who better be careful, you and this Janet woman. These guys, whoever they are, seem to be playing for high stakes. Take my advice and back off a step or two for the time being. You don't want to end up like Charlie Chan."

"Chang."

"Chang," echoed Leo. "I'll talk with the Director first thing Monday morning. Meantime, anything happens, you know how to reach me, right?"

"Right," said Dean. He picked at the remains of his swordfish, which had proved to be a bit on the dry side. Leo Silvestri's roast chicken looked moist and tender.

For Joey Spadafino, there's no swordfish and no roast chicken. Joey picks over his food slowly, trying to drag out each meal as long as he can, since meals have become just about his only activities.

He figures he's down below 120 pounds, but he doesn't worry about it too much. He knows he doesn't need much strength or energy to sit in a cell twenty-three hours a day.

So, sometime during his second week in the Hole—he's not certain exactly when, because he loses track of the days frequently now—Joey Spadafino reaches and passes the six-month mark of his confinement on Rikers Island.

TWENTY

Dean's phone was ringing as he arrived at his office Monday morning. He balanced his bike against a file cabinet and picked up the phone just as his answering machine clicked on.

"Hello," he said, switching off the machine.

"Dean?"

"Yes."

"Hey, Dean, Leo Silvestri. Surprised to catch you there this early. Figured I'd leave you a message."

"I'm an early bird. Listen, Leo, I just walked in. Give me a number, I'll call you back in three minutes."

"No need," said Leo. "I'll hang on. Take your time."

Dean removed his backpack, tossed his helmet onto the sofa, circled around his desk, and lowered himself into the chair.

"Thanks," he said into the phone. "What's up?"

"Well, I got to thinking yesterday," said Leo. "And I decided this thing we talked about Saturday night was too big to wait on. So I called the New York Director and ran it by him. He's *very* interested. So interested that he got on the phone to Washington last night. They think you're really on to something here. And they also think you, and the Killian woman, for that matter, may be in real danger. So get this. The Deputy Director for Investigations is coming up on the shuttle this afternoon. He wants me to set up a meet with you, Killian, himself and me. Nobody else, top secret, away from the office."

"When?"

"ASAP," said Leo. "As in tonight, if you can."

"Give me a time and place," said Dean. "I'll call Miss Killian and see if it's good with her."

"How about eight o'clock? We'll have a car, and we'll pick you up any place you say. Then, so we can talk in absolute privacy, we'll go to a safe house." He put the accent on the word *safe*.

"You at a phone where I can get back to you?"

"Just beep me," said Leo. "You've got the number?"

"I've got the number," said Dean.

Dean waited until eight-thirty to call Janet. She had worked a four-to-midnight shift Sunday night, and he didn't want to wake her. He needn't have worried.

"Been up since six," she said. "Nicole doesn't seem to understand about rotating shifts."

"Will she understand if I take you away from her again this evening?"

"Is this a proposition?"

"Not a very romantic one, I'm afraid. I got a call from Agent Silvestri," said Dean, who had already filled Janet in on his Saturday-night meeting with Leo. "Some bigshot Deputy Director is flying up. Wants to meet with both of us this evening at eight."

"Where?"

"A safe house," said Dean, accenting the word *safe* as Leo had. "They'll pick us up, probably in an armored personnel carrier or something."

"Sure," Janet said. "Why not?"

"How about I come to your place about seven?"

"Deal," she said.

Several minutes before noon on the fifteenth day of his confinement, Joey Spadafino is released from the Administrative Segregation Unit of C-93, the Hole. He's led out of his twenty-five-watt cell into a small yard, where the dazzling sunshine forces him to squint. He's unable to shield his eyes with his hands, which are handcuffed behind his back. He remembers a scene from a movie he saw long ago, in which an army colonel POW was kept locked up in a tiny cell out in the fierce tropical sun. When his captors finally released him, the colonel was almost unable to walk, but he managed to stagger back toward his fellow prisoners, having survived the worst the enemy could throw at him. So Joey Spadafino feels now, emerging from the Hole into the blinding sunlight. He holds his head high, he wears his handcuffs proudly. He's been set up and framed but has refused to complain or whimper. He's done his bit in the Hole. He's taken his captor's best shot, and he's still on his feet. He wishes he could remember the music they played in the movie when the colonel staggered back toward his men so he could play it in his head now as he's led back to B Block and his old cell.

The day seemed to drag on forever. Dean had two cases in court, and he was at the building before nine-thirty. One client, Pedro Quinones, had made bail; the other, Darnell Smith, was in jail. Pedro didn't show up until after eleven, explaining that the trains were broken. By the time he got there, the sign-in sheet was two pages long, and it was twelve-thirty before the case was called and adjourned. Darnell Smith wasn't produced by Corrections until quarter of one; by that time it was too late to get his case called until after the lunch break. Dean went back to his office, where he opened mail, returned phone messages, and took two aspirins for a headache that the morning's frustration had cost him. One of the calls he made was to Leo Silvestri's beeper number. When Leo called back three minutes later, Dean told him they were on for tonight. Leo said to be at Famous Original Ray's Pizza on Sixth Avenue and Eleventh Street at eight o'clock, and to make sure no one followed them there.

He walked back to court at two. It was twenty to three by the time the courtroom reopened. Darnell Smith's case was called at three-fifteen and adjourned. Dean finally got back to his office at quarter of four. Both cases had been adjourned; Dean had accomplished absolutely nothing.

For his four and a half hours sitting in court, Dean would ultimately be reimbursed 180 dollars before taxes. There were a lot of people who did worse, he told himself, as he downed two more aspirins.

*   *   *

By six o'clock Dean gave up the notion that he was going to get any work done at the office that day. He also was anxious to see Janet. It had been more than forty-eight hours since he had dropped her off Saturday afternoon, and he missed her. He changed into jeans and sneakers, and walked his bike out to the service elevator.

Janet greeted him at her door, Nicole on one hip. "You're early," she said.

"I missed you."

"Well, you're just in time for bath time."

"You're going to seduce me with a scented bubble bath and exotic oils from the East?" Dean said wishfully.

"Not me," Janet laughed. "It's Nicole's bath time. It's the high point of her day."

Dean watched as Janet partially filled a plastic tub and placed a naked, squealing Nicole into the water. Although he stood behind Janet during most of the process, he was almost as wet as the two of them by the time it was over. All three were laughing as Janet wrapped her daughter in an oversized white towel and said to Dean, "Take your shirt off."

"I'll never fit in that tub," he protested.

"You're probably right," she agreed. "But imagine the pain if I iron your shirt dry while you're still inside it."

He complied and took off his half-soaked work shirt. As she reached for it, she ran her index finger down his chest, causing him to shiver involuntarily.

"Easy, big fellow," she laughed.

"Was it good for you, too?"

"Best ever."

Dean occupied Nicole while Janet ironed his shirt. When she handed it back to him it was warm, dry, and fresh. "Wow," he said, buttoning it up. "I've got this apartment you might want to tackle next—"

"Thanks very much, but I got a mental image of your apartment the moment you announced that you thought Mr. Chang's place looked normal. I think I'll pass."

Janet used the bathroom to change into fresh jeans and a ribbed top. "Do we tell these FBI guys everything?" she wanted to know.

"I think so," said Dean. "They seem to be taking it very seriously."

The doorbell rang. "Get that, would you?" Janet said. "It'll be Mrs. Del Valle."

Dean opened the door, and Mrs. Del Valle presented him with her warmest smile yet. As she walked by him, she reached up and pinched his cheek, affectionately yet painfully, causing Dean to pull back and say, "You're not Jewish by any chance, are you?"

Dean explained the plan to Janet. He would leave first while she watched from her window to see if anyone followed him. He would make a stop somewhere along the route to Sixth Avenue and Eighth Street, then fall in behind her to see if she was being tailed.

"Check," she said, in her most melodramatic fashion.

When they met up at Famous Original Ray's fifteen minutes later and compared notes, neither had anything suspicious to report. Dean looked around. There was no sign of Leo Silvestri. "How about a slice?" he said.

"Sure. Mushrooms."

Dean jostled for a position at the counter and managed to come away with two slices in under five minutes. "I read an article once that said there are over fifty Ray's Pizza places in the city," he said. "And forty-eight of them claim to be the original Famous Original Ray's."

"Yes," said Janet, burning the roof of her mouth on melted mozzarella cheese, "but this is the best. Everyone knows that."

It was hard for Dean to argue, especially with his mouth full.

"We could have got you some real food, you know," said a familiar voice behind Dean.

Before he turned, he knew it was Leo Silvestri.

After introductions, Leo ushered them outside to a black Lincoln Town Car with tinted side and back windows that made it impossible to see inside. He held the back door open for them to climb in. A distinguished-looking man in a gray suit sat in the front passenger seat; Leo got behind the wheel and pulled away from the curb.

"Hello," said the man, in a voice that sounded like that of a network anchorman. "I'm Bennett Childs. I appreciate your meeting with us."

They drove downtown and entered the Holland Tunnel. Once in Jersey, Leo took side streets to an area Dean was unfamiliar with. The neighborhood gradually changed from factories to brownstones to row houses to private homes with small lawns and attached garages. They turned into a driveway and Leo pushed the button on a transmitter clipped to the sun visor above his head. The garage door opened, and he pulled the car in, stopping alongside a maroon Chevrolet. Leo cut the engine and pushed the button on the transmitter again. They waited in the car until the garage door closed.

A door led from the garage into the house, and Leo knocked on it three times. Almost immediately it swung open. A thirtyish-looking clean-cut black man wearing a shoulder-holstered revolver over his white shirt and tie held the door open while the others entered. Inside was the comfortably furnished ground floor of a suburban home. It looked like the occupants might be due back any moment except for the fact that all of the windows were completely covered with drapes.

"Mr. Abernathy and Miss Killian," said Bennett Childs, "this is Agent Jeffries. Please make yourselves comfortable," he added, gesturing to a sofa.

Dean and Janet seated themselves. Childs took a chair, as did Leo Silvestri. Jeffries excused himself and disappeared.

"So," said Childs, "Agent Silvestri tells me you're on to something, Mr. Abernathy. He also says, I might add, that he's concerned for the safety of both you and Miss Killian."

Neither Dean nor Janet said anything.

"I'm here from Washington, representing the Director. I want you both to know that anything you tell me will be kept in strictest confidence. That means I report only to the Director, nobody else. I also want you to know that we're prepared to offer you round-the-clock protection if you cooperate with us."

"What does that mean?" Dean asked.

"Teams of agents assigned full-time to—"

"No," Dean interrupted. "What do you mean by 'cooperate'?"

"Ah," said Childs. "Initially, tell us everything you know. Let us evaluate it, set up a discreet investigation. We'll need your help in that, whether on an active or passive level. It may require some fairly dangerous undercover work on your parts. On the other hand, it may come down to doing nothing more than staying out of our way. Whatever it is, you give us that help." He smiled at Dean and said, "That's what I mean by cooperating."

Janet and Dean exchanged approving glances. "Sounds okay," Dean said.

"Why don't you begin at the beginning?" said Bennett Childs, pulling a pipe and tobacco out of his side jacket pocket.

Dean began at the beginning. As he had with Leo, he told the whole story of his involvement in the case, from his initial contact with Joey Spadafino and his early assumption that Joey was guilty as charged. As Childs puffed thoughtfully on his pipe, filling the room with the sweet aroma of what Dean thought he recognized as Captain Black, Dean recounted his awareness of the first inconsistencies, his mounting suspicions, leading to the discovery of the two Janet Killians, and culminating in the trip to Tall Oaks to find the comatose body of Mr. Chang.

When he was finished, Dean sat back. Bennett Childs tapped his pipe to empty its bowl into an oversized glass ashtray. Then he said, slowly and quietly, "Wow."

"I told you this was hot stuff," said Leo.

"You may be guilty of gross understatement," Childs told him. He looked very serious. Then he turned to Dean and Janet. "It is essential, absolutely *essential*, that you both carry on as though you have not met with us. For the present time, no heroics. Let's just sit back for a few days and see what they do next. If there are any developments whatsoever, you should report them immediately to Agent Silvestri. That should be your exclusive method of contact with the Bureau."

"Who are 'they'?" Janet asked.

Childs took a moment to answer. "I hesitate to say this," he said presently, "but 'they' seem to be a bunch of detectives in the New York Police Department who have developed their own agenda. I think you can imagine how volatile a situation that presents us with." To Leo he said, "As of this moment, you're temporarily relieved of all other duties. You're to coordinate this investigation full-time. I'll see you get everything you need.

"Miss Killian, Mr. Abernathy, I'd like your permission to put a detail of men on you." When they hesitated, Childs added, "Believe me, you'll barely know they exist."

"Is it really necessary?" Janet asked.

"I'm afraid it is. If Mr. Abernathy's story is true—and I have every reason to believe it is—they've already silenced another witness, Mr. Chang. You could be their next target. Or you, Mr. Abernathy, if they realize you're on to them."

"Okay," said Janet in a small voice.

Childs looked at Dean, who said, "I guess we have no choice."

"Good," Childs said, standing up. "Agent Jeffries!" he called, and Jeffries reappeared on cue. "Jeffries, I want you to drive Miss Killian and Mr. Abernathy back to Manhattan. Take them wherever they want to go. Make sure you're not followed, and make sure *they're* not followed after you drop them off. We'll have other teams on them by midnight. Agent Silvestri, you'll take me to the airport. I'll be meeting with the Director tonight."

Childs walked over to Dean and Janet, who stood as he approached. He extended his hand. "I'm very grateful to both of you," he said, shaking their hands firmly in turn. "You've done a very heroic thing in coming forward with this information. I promise you won't be sorry."

Jeffries began to lead Dean and Janet to the door that connected with the garage, when Leo held out a set of car keys. "Take the Lincoln," he said to Jeffries. "We'll use your car."

"Okay," said Jeffries, taking the keys and handing Leo the other set. Dean and Janet followed him into the garage, took their seats in the back of the Lincoln, and were soon on their way back toward the lights of the city.

Back in his cell on B Block, Joey Spadafino recuperates. His fifteen days in the Hole behind him, he finds himself regaining his old strength. He's able to sleep at night for the first time in months. His appetite comes back with a vengeance, and where he once gave much of his food away to other inmates, he now looks around for portions that go uneaten. He begins to put some of the weight he's lost back on, so he starts working out. In the weight room one day he gets another inmate, an Irish kid named Eddie Clancy, to show him how to do curls and presses with weights, something Joey never learned in his boxing days. He does pushups on the floor of his cell first thing in the morning and last thing at night, and works himself up to where he can do seventy-five in a set. One afternoon when his cellmates are both signed out to court, Joey jerks off in the corner of his cell, not out of depression but out of actual horniness, and he comes with a force that makes him laugh. He begins to shave every morning, and brushes his teeth more regularly. One day, he phones his mother in Jersey and asks her to come visit him. She promises to try, if she can get his uncle to drive her. He hums the theme song from Rocky *as he jogs and shadowboxes with new energy each day in the yard. Getting strong now . . .*

On Wednesday the Spadafino case appeared in Part 56, and Dean stood in court with Joey beside him for perhaps the twelfth time in the past six months. The press had long since lost interest in these routine calendar calls. They would presumably reconvene when there was a promise of something newsworthy. By now all of the pre-trial discovery had been completed, leaving as the next order of business the setting of a date for the hearings that would immediately precede the trial, and the trial itself. Dean's guess was that, in view of vacation schedules and the difficulty in getting jurors to sit on all but the shortest of cases during July and August, the court would probably suggest a September date. He was wrong.

"Any reason we can't start this case next week?" Judge Rothwax asked the lawyers at a bench conference.

It was Walter Bingham who protested. "Judge," he said, "I've got about a dozen cops and five or six detectives I've got to call, not to mention ballistics people, an ME, and some civilians. There's a new departmental regulation that requires them to use their vacation time by the end of the year or lose it. There's no way I can coordinate their schedules on such short notice."

" 'Short notice,' says Mr. Bingham," Rothwax mimicked. "I was led to believe that the arrest in this case occurred over six months ago. But of course I may be mistaken."

"You're not mistaken," said Bingham.

"So I take it that you're caught by surprise that at some point we would proceed to trial?"

"Well," said Bingham, "to a certain extent, I am, now that you mention it. I had made a pretty generous offer to Mr. Abernathy, and I'm frankly quite surprised at his client's stubbornness in turning it down."

"And what was this generous offer, if I may be so bold?" Rothwax asked.

"Rob One," said Bingham. "Five to ten. I'd even go along with the minimum, four-and-a-half to nine, if he wants to take it today."

Rothwax turned to Dean. "And your client has displayed the good judgment to reject that offer, Mr. Abernathy?"

"I'm afraid so, Judge," said Dean.

"Do you understand the felony murder rule?" asked Rothwax, his voice rising in anger.

"Of cour—" Dean began.

"This isn't for you," Rothwax whispered. "I'm doing this for your client's benefit. Believe me, I know *you* understand." Then, raising his voice again, "I appreciate the fact that there is no evidence that your client ever intended to kill Mr. Wilson. If it were up to me, I might decide that this shouldn't be a murder case at all. The law, however, is much smarter than I am. It recognizes that robbery is one of those felonies that are considered so dangerous that victims sometimes die even when their deaths are unintended by the perpetrator. In Mr. Spadafino's case, it takes his intent to *rob* his victim, and it says, 'That's enough.' If your victim happens to die while you're robbing him—or fleeing from having robbed him—that intent to rob him will be sufficient to convict you of murder. So all Mr. Bingham here has to prove is a simple robbery. Then he brings in someone from the Medical Examiner's Office, who, with the aid of a Russian or Indian interpreter, testifies that Mr. Wilson is dead. That seems to be something that even Mr. Bingham should be able to manage."

"Thanks," Bingham mumbled.

"And once that's done," continued Rothwax, without missing a beat, "Mr. Spadafino will have the next twenty-five years to life to figure out what went wrong with the jailhouse advice he's been listening to. This case is adjourned one week, for the defendant to reconsider the offer that's been made to him, and to pick a date for hearings and trial. The offer will stay open until next Wednesday. After that it will be withdrawn and there will be no further offers made in this case. Is that understood?"

"Yes, sir," said Bingham.

"Yes," said Dean.

Rothwax looked at the defendant and said, "You may go in now, Mr. Spadafino."

* * *

The first letter arrived the following day.

Dean had returned to his office from court and found the day's mail on his desk. There was a bank statement, which he tossed unopened into a drawer. Every six months or so he would open all his statements, spend a half hour trying unsuccessfully to balance his account, and give up, shoving the statements into the back of a desk drawer. There was a phone bill that could wait. A fingerprint card of a client whose case Dean had got dismissed. A college alumni bulletin, an Eddie Bauer catalog, and a solicitation from a life insurance company. And an envelope looking like it had been addressed by a child. In place of a typed or handwritten address, the information had been spelled out, letter by letter, number by number, using characters clipped from newspapers and magazines and then pasted carefully onto the envelope.

His first thought was that it must be the work of his niece or nephew. But Dean's birthday was several months past, and no holiday or special occasion came to mind. He tore open the envelope. Inside was a single sheet of white paper, adorned with a message created in identical fashion to the address on the envelope.

you are in Big danger
watch out

Dean looked at the envelope again. There was no return address. The postmark indicated that the letter had been mailed the day before, from New York, NY 10028.

By the time it occurred to him that his new FBI friends might have been able to have lifted fingerprints from the letter, Dean had been handling it for ten minutes. He photocopied it, along with the envelope. The originals he put in a file that he marked simply LETTER and placed in a file drawer. The copies he folded and put in his shirt pocket. Then he dialed Janet Killian's number. When her answering machine picked up, he left a message asking her to phone him. He toyed with the idea of calling Leo Silvestri and at one point actually dialed his beeper number, but when he heard the tone, he hung up without entering his own number. He would show Janet the letter before he did anything else. They were in this thing together; if he was in danger, so was she. That meant she had the right to help decide their next move. Besides which, he readily admitted to himself, it gave him a wonderful excuse to see her again.

It was almost five when Janet phoned him back. "What's up?" she asked.

"What's up is that I want to see you. What can I bring you for dinner?"

"And here I was all set to unleash my considerable culinary skills on a Lasagna Primavera Lean Cuisine."

"You can still eat that if you want," said Dean. "I was thinking of food, myself."

"Like what?"

"Like takeout from Hunan Empire Mandarin Szechuan Garden Balcony Emporium East."

"Ooh," said Janet. "Scallops with black bean sauce? Brown rice?"

"Might be able to manage that," said Dean.

He also managed moo shu vegetables, green onion pancakes, and an order of lichees, all of which he held out to Janet in a slightly leaking paper bag when she opened the door of her apartment. They ate out of the cartons spread out on the floor of Janet's living room while the food was still hot. Nicole did an admirable imitation of adults' eating, taking particular delight in flinging rice in all directions and squeezing lichees in her tiny fists. By the time Janet picked her up for bath time, it looked like a wedding had taken place.

It was only after Janet came back into the living room from nursing her daughter and putting her to bed that Dean showed her the copy of the letter that had arrived in the morning's mail.

"Is this some kind of a joke?" she asked.

"I don't think so," said Dean. "Someone spent a considerable amount of time doing this. Whoever it was wanted us to get the message without the risk of being identified. None of my friends has a sense of humor that strange."

"What do we do?"

"I don't know," Dean confessed. "One obvious option is to turn it over to Leo Silvestri."

"I suppose we could do that." Janet nodded somewhat tentatively, Dean thought.

"You don't seem convinced, either." Without being able to put his finger on it, Dean—and now Janet, it appeared—had some vague misgiving about running to the FBI with the letter. It wasn't that they didn't trust the agents; they did. It was rather, they finally agreed, their fear that the FBI people might overreact and want to begin monitoring their mail, listening in on their phone calls, and following them more closely rather than at the present comfortable distance. Those were things neither Dean nor Janet wanted to put up with. And after all, wasn't the writer simply warning Dean that he was in danger, something both he and the FBI already recognized? In the end they agreed that they could risk holding off calling Silvestri, at least for the time being.

Though they tried their best to spend the remainder of the evening together like two normal people, the letter and the warning it contained hung over their heads like a cloud that would not disappear. They turned on the TV and tried watching a Chevy Chase–Goldie Hawn movie, *Foul Play*, but the story kept reminding them of their own plight, and the funny parts didn't seem funny. They switched to a *Cheers* rerun, but the episode centered around Cliff Clavin's social life and proved no more diverting. When Nicole woke for what would be her eleven-thirty feeding, they decided to call it an evening. They held hands at the door, then kissed good night. It was an almost brotherly-sisterly kiss, lips coming together, barely touching, then withdrawing, but it was more than enough to pump testosterone through Dean's body the entire drive home.

The second letter arrived four days later.

The envelope was addressed in the same newspaper and magazine print collage. As before, there was no return address. Again there was a New York City postmark; the zip code this time was 10003.

Dean remembered to handle the letter inside with care, removing it from the envelope with a pair of tweezers he borrowed from one of the secretaries in the office. He managed to unfold the single page and flatten it out on his desk without touching it with his own fingers. The lettering was virtually unchanged from that on the envelope or in the earlier letter, but the message was somewhat more elaborate.

they are planning an accident for you or her they mean business be very careful

The upsetting ingredient was the addition of "her," an unmistakable reference to Janet. It meant that the writer was not just a good Samaritan concerned with Dean's welfare while he was handling a high-profile case, or even an irate member of the public uttering a harmless threat. It meant instead that whoever was cutting and pasting these letters knew what Dean was up to, and also who—and therefore what—he had found. And while the "you" of the first letter could be read as either singular or plural, depending on whether one wanted to come to terms with the fact that Janet might be in danger as well as Dean himself, the second letter left no room for doubt.

Again he called Janet to tell her he wanted to stop by.

"Something's the matter," she said as soon as she heard his voice, "isn't it?"

"No," Dean lied. He had become more suspicious than ever that their phones might be tapped, and he didn't want to say anything about the letter.

"Are you sure?" Either she was very perceptive, or Dean sounded as concerned as he felt.

"Absolutely," he said. It certainly sounded upbeat enough to convince him.

But apparently not her.

"So what's the matter?" Janet asked him when she let him in. "And don't ever play poker."

Dean handed her a photocopy of the second letter. "Welcome to the Two-Most-Wanted List," he said as she studied it. "I think we've got to turn these over to the FBI," he said. Her reply was limited to a nod. It was the first time Dean had seen her at a loss for a lighthearted comment.

Dean used Janet's phone to call Leo Silvestri's beeper. When Leo called back four minutes later, Dean told him he had received a couple of letters he thought Leo might be interested in.

"Threats?"

"More like warnings," said Dean.

"Have you handled them?"

"Not the second one. I didn't know what the first one was until I had opened it and got my prints all over it."

"Okay," said Leo. "When can I get them from you?"

"First thing in the morning," Dean said. "I'm in my office by seven."

"No chance tonight?"

"No, I left the originals downtown. I didn't want to be carrying them around."

"All right," said Leo. "Your office at seven-thirty. See you then."

"See you."

Dean hung up and glanced at Janet. She stood in the kitchen doorway, staring off into space. She looked small and vulnerable. He walked to her and said softly, "Are you okay?"

"I'm okay," she answered. "But I'm all Nicole has."

"I know," said Dean.

"So I can't afford to pretend I'm brave. If something happens to me, she's all alone."

Joey Spadafino is thinking he's all alone when he walks into the weight room of C-93 at Rikers Island. It turns out he's wrong. And the man who's there somehow seems to have been waiting for Joey, seems to have arranged the meeting. He's a large black man they call Big Brother, with almost black skin, in his late twenties or early thirties. He's lying on his back on a padded bench, lifting a weighted barbell over his head over and over again. He wears a pair of shorts and is bare-chested. His upper body glistens with sweat over muscles so sharply defined as to remind Joey of pictures he's seen in bodybuilding magazines.

The man finishes his set and walks over to where Joey's toweling off after doing curls with hand weights. "You Spadafino?" he asks.

"Yeah," Joey answers, tensing and trying to sound tough, though he knows he's going to take a beating if that's Big Brother's pleasure.

"Well you better be watchin' that little white butt of yours, you know what be good for you."

"Yeah?" is all Joey can think of to say.

"Yeah. You the one's got the Po-leece Commissioner's body, right?"

"That's what they say," Joey says.

"Well, they also say there be a pretty good price on your ass. Seems some folks don't want you to have no trial. Seems it's worth five figures to them to see you don't get one." And then he walks off. Joey doesn't thank him or call after him or ask for more details. He knows he's been told everything he was meant to hear. You don't say thank you in jail, or ask stupid questions when somebody risks his own life to go out of his way to warn you about yours.

Five figures means that there's a ten-thousand-dollar contract on Joey. Not that a contract like that is ever paid off in jail; whichever inmate was to step forward and kill Joey for the money would surely be the next victim, both to avoid the need to pay him off and to silence the link back to the requesting party. But there are a lot of inmates who don't know that part of the deal, or don't believe it could happen to them, and Joey has to worry about that, too.

Faced with no other choice, Joey demands to see a captain that evening and fills out a written request to be placed back in administrative segregation. Even though it'll keep him in contact with the COs, he'll be isolated from other inmates, which means that the COs will be unlikely to harm him with nobody but them to be held accountable. Joey's forced to lie on the form, first so he doesn't have to identify Big Brother as the source of his concern, then to put down enough to constitute "actual injury and/or threats of actual injury." In the blank where he's required to name the inmates who injured or threatened him, he inserts nicknames and descriptions of guys he used to know out on the street and adds, "Ackshual names un-none."

Joey's request to call his lawyer from the captain's office is granted, but it's late and Dean isn't there. Joey hangs up without leaving a message on the tape.

Around midnight, Joey's awakened and told to gather his belongings, taken out of his cell, and led back into the Hole.

TWENTY-ONE

True to his word, Leo Silvestri was at Dean's office by seven-thirty the following morning. He had with him four clear plastic evidence envelopes, complete with locks and FBI labels, and his own set of tweezers. He carefully placed each of the letters and each of the envelopes in its own evidence envelope. Only then did he read the pasted-on messages, shaking his head from side to side as he did so.

"This worries me a lot, Dean," he said.

"You and me both, Leo."

"I want you to give us permission to screen your mail."

"What does that mean?"

"It's no big deal," Leo explained. "You authorize the Postal Service to deliver your mail to us for the time being. We examine it, pull out anything that looks suspicious, and forward everything else to you."

"What do you do with the suspicious stuff?"

"We dust it for prints, X-ray any packages, bring in the K-nine unit for anything that could be a bomb—"

"Open and read any suspicious letters?"

"Certainly anything that bears the same characteristics as these two," Leo said.

"And how long before I get the rest of my mail?"

"A day, two at the most."

"I need to think about it," Dean said. He wanted to be helpful, and certainly didn't want to seem ungrateful for the Bureau's concern. But the truth was, Dean was having a hard time seeing things the way that Leo was: that the letter writer was likely to progress from warning Dean that he and Janet were in danger to sending a bomb through the mail. And perceiving no such threat, Dean was reluctant to surrender his privacy, expose his other clients to having their mail opened and read, and accept an additional day of delay in the arrival of his mail.

"Please do," said Leo. "This guy sounds like he plays for keeps." He promised to inform Dean whether or not the lab succeeded in lifting any prints from the letters, and left.

Judge Rothwax had adjourned the case in order to give the defendant one final opportunity to accept Walter Bingham's plea bargain offer. Now it was Wednesday, the point of no return in the case of the *People v. Joseph Spadafino*. If there was ever going to be a plea, it had to be now. Today it was robbery, four-and-a-half to nine years. After today, it was murder, twenty-five years to life.

The media showed up, perhaps alerted by some reporter who had been phoned by a court officer in exchange for a twenty dollar bill, perhaps responding to a sixth sense that told them something newsworthy might be brewing in Part 56. A half dozen of them were waiting on the eleventh floor when Dean stepped off the elevator. There was a television crew and a sketch artist, as well. It was Mike Pearl of the *Post* who approached Dean.

"Is he going to take a plea?" Mike asked.

"I don't know" was Dean's truthful answer. "Let me talk to him. I'll let you know."

Inside the courtroom Dean checked with court officers and learned that Joey had been produced. Rather than waiting for him to be brought down to the feeder pen alongside the courtroom, Dean went through the pen area and took the stairs to the twelfth floor so that he could talk with his client in the counsel visit room. He took a seat on one side of the mesh window and waited for Joey to be admitted to the other side.

He was startled by what he saw when Joey arrived. The prisoner had dark semicircles under his eyes, and the pupils looked dull. His face was drawn and thin, and his clothes seemed to hang on his body, suggesting that he had lost a lot of weight. His hair was messy and looked unwashed. He clearly hadn't shaved in several days.

"Jesus, Joey, you look like hell. Are you all right?"

"Yeah. No." Back to the multiple-choice answers of their early interviews. "I been in the Hole. Twice now."

"What happened?"

"First time they flaked me," said Joey. "Put a package in my cell. Gave me fifteen days."

"Why didn't you call me?"

"With what, my toothbrush?"

"They won't let you make a phone call to your lawyer?" Dean was incredulous. "You're entitled to a hearing."

"I'm lucky they let me take a piss."

"And this time?"

"I just decided it'd be easier."

"How many days you got left?"

"I don't know." Then, with a crooked smile, he added, "Fuck 'em, I can do it. I done worse than this."

"You sure?"

"Yeah."

"What about the case, Joey? Today's D-Day."

"Yeah, I know."

"What do you want to do?"

"I want outa here," said Joey, and the simplicity of his answer caught Dean off guard, and for a second he thought he might cry. For once he was grateful for the obscuring presence of the mesh that separated them.

"I know," said Dean.

"Can we beat this thing, Dean?"

Dean hesitated. Ask me anything but that, he thought. Don't ask me to decide for you. Sure they could beat this thing. Dean knew enough now to turn the case upside down. He had detectives forging his client's signature on a confession, substituting a porno actress for one witness, and rendering another one braindead. He could have a field day with this case. He could drive a truck through it. But he also knew they could just as easily lose it. A jury could ascribe Mr. Chang's condition to coincidence and attribute all of the other irregularities to the understandable zeal on the part of the police to nail down the conviction of their commissioner's murderer. In spite of everything Dean had to work with, he had no way of saying that a jury might not believe that Joey Spadafino was robbing·Commissioner Wilson when Wilson suffered a fatal heart attack.

"Maybe," he said weakly.

"Maybe?" said Joey. "Seven months you been workin' on my case and all you can say is 'Maybe'?"

Joey was right. He was entitled to more. "Yes, we can beat it," Dean said in a firm voice. "We can kick the shit out of them. And I want nothing more than a chance to do it. But a trial is always a roll of the dice, and the only thing I know for certain is that when it's over they'll let me go home. They're offering you four-and-a-half to nine on a murder case."

"If we blow trial, will he really give me the max?" Joey asked. "Twenty-five to life?"

"He might."

"I'd be fifty-three," said Joey in a small voice. "I figgered it out."

"Yup."

"What would you do if you was me, Dean?"

Dean thought for a moment. "I don't know," he said.

"Would you be angry at me if I took the cop-out?"

"No, Joey." Dean smiled. "I wouldn't be angry at you at all. Whatever you decide to do, I won't be angry at you."

Joey said nothing for what seemed a long time. When he finally broke the silence, it was to ask Dean a question.

"Didja know I was in the Golden Gloves once?"

"No."

"Seventeen years old. Hundred-and-nineteen-pound class. Novice. I had six fights," said Joey, sitting back and smiling as he relived that time of his life. "Won the first five. Three by knockouts. Sixth fight, regional semifinals, Madison Square Garden. They bring in this black kid, six-foot-one. So skinny I figure I could blow him over. Trouble was I couldn't get·near him. He had these arms that were about a hundred feet long. Two and a half rounds he held me off with his jab. Wasn't really a jab, more like a push. People booin', everything. Finally I say, 'Fuck this shit, I'm goin' to go down fightin' if it kills me.' So I lower my head and charge the motherfucker. I figure we'll mix it up for a half a round, see what happens. Only Stretch, he spreads his arms wide and I go crashin' into his gut, head first."

"What happened?" Dean felt like he was playing straight man.

"What happened is Stretch, he goes flyin' through the ropes ass first into the front row of the audience. Me, I get disqualified and banned for life from the Gloves. 'Conduct unbecoming a sportsman,' or some such shit. But you know what?"

"What?"

"I went down fightin'."

"I have a feeling there's a message in that story," Dean said with a smile.

"Yeah." Joey returned the smile. He looked more like himself. "And the message is: Tell those cocksuckers we're comin' in head down and full speed ahead. If we're goin' to go down, we're goin' to go down fightin'."

"Calendar Number Fourteen, Joseph Spadafino," called the clerk. Dean stepped forward into the well area as Joey was led into the courtroom from the side door that led to the feeder pen.

"This case is on," announced Judge Rothwax, "for the defendant to accept or reject an offer that has been held open until today, and which will be withdrawn if the defendant declines it. What is your pleasure, Mr. Abernathy?"

"We'd like a trial date, Your Honor."

"And you shall have one. There will be no further offers in this case. Hearings and trial, September seventh."

Outside the courtroom Mike Pearl stopped Dean again. "Anything you can tell me?" he asked.

"Yes, as a matter of fact, I can give you a direct quote." As Mike reached for his notebook, Dean whispered in his ear, "'Tell those cocksuckers we're comin' in head down and full speed ahead.'"

The third letter arrived on Friday.

Contained in the same type of envelope as the first two and created out of the same type of characters, cut from newspapers and magazines and pasted into words, it was crafted less neatly than the first two, suggesting to Dean that its author was either in something of a hurry or had simply grown less preoccupied with the artistic aspect of his—or her—creation.

they killed wilson they
tried to kill
the Chinaman you 2 are
next
we need to meet

S.

Dean sat at his desk, stunned. There, fully contained in the first three words of the message, was the inescapable conclusion to which he had known for months his investigation was leading him. But until he saw the words spelled out before him, childlike, in the bizarre magazine and newsprint collage that had by now become familiar to him, Dean had utterly refused to accept it. Yet forced to confront it now, he knew immediately that it had to be true. There had been no heart attack; the dibenzepene in Commissioner Wilson's body had come from no accidental overdose; the mysteriously ordered cremation and the destruction of the tissue samples had been no mystery after all. They had been the intentional acts of a cover-up. And the cover-up had sought to shield an event so staggering that Dean could not even begin to comprehend it. But one thing he knew, finally, absolutely: the police had killed their own.

Dean forced his eyes to the remainder of the letter: the confirmation that they had tried to murder Mr. Chang as well, the warning that Dean and Janet were next, the suggestion of a meeting, and—for the first time—a sign-off: the letter S.

He picked up the phone and dialed Leo Silvestri's beeper number. When his phone rang two minutes later and he heard Leo's voice on the other end, Dean said simply, "Come on over. I've got another letter."

Leo examined the letter gravely. "It's time to stop fooling around," he said to Dean. "We're prepared to move the two of you to a safe house immediately. We need to start screening your mail and put a tracing device on your phone. We just can't wait any longer."

"Let me meet with him."

"What?"

"Let me meet with S.," Dean repeated. "See what he wants to tell me."

"No way," said Leo. "It's a setup if ever I saw one. You meet him, they run you over on the way home. No dice."

"I'm willing to take the risk," Dean said.

"I'm not," said Leo. "I'm going to run this stuff over to the lab. When I come back, it'll be with permission forms for the mail and phone. Do you want me to tell Miss Killian, or do you want to?"

"I'll tell her," Dean said.

Driving his Jeep up to Janet's building late that afternoon, Dean was acutely aware of the FBI agents who were following him, something he had not sensed in the week or two since the meeting with Bennett Childs at the safe house in New Jersey. Obviously their concern was mounting with the receipt of each letter, just as Leo Silvestri had been telling Dean, and they were stepping up their efforts to protect Dean and, presumably, Janet.

He made no attempt to evade the surveillance, realizing it was there for his own good, but his awareness of the agents shadowing him made him feel foolish. He remembered a time back in grade school, the first day his parents had finally given him permission to bike to school instead of taking the bus like the little kids. He had pulled out of the driveway feeling brave and independent, backpack strapped on securely, a ten-year-old adult imagining himself on a crucial mission behind enemy lines. He had threaded his way along familiar streets with a sense of importance and purposefulness never before imagined. He was about to pull onto Grove Street—he remembered it to this day—a maneuver that required him to look back to his left for oncoming cars. Looking over his shoulder, he spotted the familiar form of his father's blue Oldsmobile creeping along well behind him. Then, as now, he had done nothing but continue on, but in that instant he had been reduced to a boy again.

Janet greeted him with a hug and handed him a giggling Nicole. "Entertain her a minute," she said. "I'm trying to get her dinner ready and she only wants to nurse. Poor kid, can't decide whether she wants to grow up or not."

"I know the feeling," said Dean.

Nicole's ambivalence continued, and her dinner consisted of alternating spoonfuls of orange and green mushy stuff, which she would seem to swallow, only to spit back out what seemed like minutes later. Dean marveled at her ability to store the food for such lengths in her tiny mouth, and was convinced that, during the process, it somehow increased in volume.

"I swear that for every spoonful that goes in, at least three come out," he observed.

"Yes," Janet agreed. "But somehow she manages to swallow some of that. I can show you dirty diapers to prove my point."

"That won't be necessary."

After about five minutes of spoon-feeding, Nicole would pull her head back, shake it from side to side to avoid the spoon, arch her back, and fidget until Janet would pick her up and nurse her. This Janet did in front of Dean, without the least sign of embarrassment. Nicole would immediately settle down, sucking quietly while looking all around with deep blue eyes that missed nothing. For his part, Dean felt as awkward looking away as he did watching. He wanted to see Janet's breast, experienced a sudden surge of excitement at the glimpse of her brown nipple, and caught himself feeling lecherous and almost un-American in his lust.

After twenty minutes or so of the pattern, Nicole's dinner was declared over. "I have this image of breast-feeding her until she's thirty," Janet said. "Like taking a time-out during her wedding ceremony?"

Bath time was next, and Dean again found himself in the role of designated drier, wrapping a squealing, slippery Nicole in an oversize towel and more or less letting her squirm herself dry inside it.

It was getting dark by the time Nicole was placed down in her crib, and Dean, thoroughly exhausted by his minimal participation in the evening's ritual, marveled at Janet's stamina and unflagging good humor.

"Don't you ever get wiped out?" he asked.

"Only twenty times a day or so," she answered, smiling.

"You're terrific with her."

"Thank you," she said simply, displaying yet another talent for Dean to wonder at and envy—the ability to accept a compliment. He let it go; enough was enough. Besides which, they had things to talk about. He reached into his shirt pocket, unfolded a copy of the third letter, and handed it to her.

"Today?" she asked as she studied it.

"Yup."

"My God," she said softly. "This means the police murdered the Commissioner."

Dean nodded silently.

"And your client? What does it mean for him?"

"It means all he's guilty of is larceny. He took some money from a guy lying on the sidewalk. The guy might have been alive, he might have already been dead. But he didn't rob him. And if there was no robbery, there's no felony murder."

"Have you told Leo?"

"He's got the original. He's very concerned for us. Wants to put us in a safe house, intercept our mail, trace incoming calls. His men were on me like glue on the way up here."

"And you?"

"I don't know," said Dean. "I feel like I should be frightened, but I really don't think I am."

"Who is this S.?"

"Beats me," said Dean. "I only know he wants to meet with me."

"What does Leo say about that?"

"He's sure it's a setup, a trap. I don't see that. But what's the difference? I don't have any way to contact the guy."

"He'll contact you again." Janet sounded certain.

"I guess so," Dean said. "Though Leo wants to screen my mail. If I give him permission, he may not let any more letters get through to me."

"Since when do they need your permission to do stuff to your mail? They're the FBI."

"I'm a lawyer," Dean said. "That puts them on their best behavior."

"You may be a lawyer," Janet said, "but they're the law. They're going to do whatever they want to do, whether you give them permission or not."

She was probably right, Dean realized, but he didn't acknowledge it.

Janet made them bacon and eggs for dinner. "I know it's evil to eat stuff like this," she said. "But I've got to be at work at midnight, so it's breakfast for me. And my arteries are feeling a little soft, anyway."

Mrs. Del Valle arrived at eleven-thirty, and Dean drove Janet uptown to Mount Sinai. Before she got out of the Jeep, she looked at him seriously and said, "Please be careful, Dean." Then she leaned over and kissed him gently on the mouth. He forgot to look for his FBI friends the entire way home.

The days pass slowly for Joey Spadafino back in the Hole. With only a few weeks left before his trial is to begin, he figured doing his time there would be a piece of cake. He figured wrong.

Afraid because of the contract on him, Joey gives up his daily yard privileges, meaning he's in lockup twenty-four hours a day. The only time he comes out is to shower, and he's even reduced that to once or twice a week. He's aware that his body has begun to smell like the boys' locker room in high school, but like most smells, he finds it bad and good at the same time. He catches himself smelling his armpits now and then and wonders if he's going crazy, like some of the weirdos he used to see when he was living on the street. Doesn't matter, he decides. Better to smell bad and talk to himself than to be cut up in the weight room.

It's not so much that he's afraid of dying, Joey decides. What he's afraid of is being cut, the pain of a knife or a razor slicing through his skin, ripping his flesh, hacking him down to the bone like a piece of meat, making blood pour out of him.

He counts the days until his trial starts. With the trial so near, Joey expects Dean to come see him, or at least have him brought over to the courthouse for a counsel visit. He needs to tell Dean that he wants to take the stand at his trial, tell what really happened. He has a little dream-fantasy that he plays over and over in his mind. He's on the stand, testifying in front of the jury, telling his story. The DA is cross-examining him, the big guy, Mr. Bingham. Every time the DA asks a question, Joey kills him with his answer. The jury understands perfectly. They nod in agreement at every point he makes, smile at his honest explanations, cheer when he finishes. The judge orders all of the charges thrown out, then rises from his seat to shake Joey's hand as he steps down from the witness box. Flashbulbs go off, and the TV people surround Joey for interviews and autographs. The only thing he can't explain is that Dean is nowhere in the dream. . . .

TWENTY·TWO

For a while nothing happened. No more letters arrived. No more requests were made that Dean permit his mail to be screened and his incoming calls to be traced. The teams of agents assigned to follow him receded into the background, and he was seldom aware of their presence. Walter Bingham didn't call with any new plea offers. Mike Pearl didn't stop him in the hallway and ask him for a quote.

His calendar lightened, a reflection of the usual August slow-down at the Criminal Court Building. There were days when he had a single case in court, and days when he had none at all. Only one of his trials, the Bronx attempted murder stabbing, was scheduled to begin before September, and the chances that it would actually go were slim. He caught up on his paperwork, organized and reorganized his files, rearranged his office furniture, and straightened the pictures on his walls, until there was nothing left to do but get down to the business of preparing for trial in the case of the *People of the State of New York v. Joseph Spadafino.*

He broke his file down into subfiles, and inked titles on them: JURY SELECTION, OPENING, LEGAL PAPERS, PROSECUTION WITNESSES, DEFENSE WITNESSES, PROPERTY VOUCHERS, 911 CALLS, MEDICAL EVIDENCE, and SUMMATION. He grouped police reports according to whichever officer or detective he would need to question regarding them. He actually took photographs of the doorway of 77 Bleecker Street, both from street level and from Janet's third-floor bedroom window. He had the photos developed and had enlargements made of the ones he intended to use, which he then arranged and cataloged. He brought an order before Judge Rothwax, *ex parte* so he wouldn't have to alert Walter Bingham, to authorize the appointment of a handwriting expert for the defense, and he phoned and met with Herman Lopat, a former Secret Service agent, who agreed to analyze the two signatures on Joey's statement to the detectives. He called Larry Davidson, the doctor who had educated Dean about dibenzepene, and asked him if he would testify as an expert on the basis of his readings about the drug and its toxicity in overdose, particularly when combined with alcohol or administered to a heart patient. He reviewed reports, made notes from them and then reviewed the notes. At night, lying in bed, he thought about his summation, sometimes working himself into an emotional pitch that made sleep impossible. He found himself watching the late movie for distraction, and eventually the late late movie. All part of the process, long a ritual with Dean, of getting ready.

TWENTY-THREE

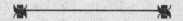

Dean hadn't seen Janet for nearly a week. It was the Friday before the trial was scheduled to begin. He called her from his office and invited her to come over to his place for dinner. She could not, she said, she was working the midnight shift again. But she did have Saturday off and accepted his second offer. Which was better anyway, Dean decided, because it would give him time to clean up his apartment, which had pretty much reached the critical stage. But that was something he could put off until Saturday. His immediate attention he directed to what he would make for dinner.

He very much wanted to please Janet, wanted to impress her with his cooking. Which meant making something creative but failproof. He knew that, despite her bacon-and-eggs relapse, Janet was not much of a meat eater. He rejected chicken, considered vegetarian, and settled on seafood. He would make a fish stew or casserole of some sort, combining shrimp, mussels, clams, scallops—whatever looked best at the market without doing serious violence to his budget. In fact, he decided, he could even save money by shopping in nearby Chinatown, where the curbside selections were so fresh that the fish could sometimes be seen flipping about on the crushed ice beneath them, and the prices were usually a dollar or two less than uptown.

He walked up to Canal Street and was immediately enveloped by the short-sleeved afternoon crowd of tourists, merchants, peddlers, hawkers, and hustlers. He headed east, past stalls of five dollar watches, baseball caps, batteries, T-shirts, jewelry, videotapes, and perfumes. Crossing Lafayette, he encountered the first of the Chinese grocers, displaying strange-looking cabbage, ginger, and bok choy. Past Centre, the lettering on storefronts changed from English to Chinese, and the pushcarts featured mysterious meat offerings in place of pretzels and ices. At Mulberry Street he paused at one fish market, but the dull eyes of the red snapper warned him that they weren't all that fresh. At the second market things looked better. Though they had no scallops, there were lively blue crabs, small mussels, and, according to a hand-lettered cardboard sign, JUMBOE SHRIMPS $7.95 POUND." He wondered briefly if Dan Quayle worked there, but managed to keep his joke private, deciding it would be lost on the two clerks, whose eagerness to please far outstripped their command of English.

"Try the squid," said a voice behind him. "They're small and very sweet."

Dean turned to see a thirtyish Hispanic man, slightly shorter than he, looking clean-cut in a sport jacket and open-collared shirt, and wearing aviator-style sunglasses. "Thanks," Dean said, "but I don't do squid. The legs are all right, but the rest of it makes me think I'm eating rubber bands."

"That's a shame," the man said. "You don't know what you're missing."

"I'm sure you're right, but I'm going to pass. But thanks anyway."

"No problem," said the man. "Perhaps I could be of help in some other way." And he reached into his inside jacket pocket and withdrew a business card, which he extended to Dean.

Feeling a bit put upon, but not wishing to insult the man, Dean took the card in his own hand. He looked down at it and saw that it was completely blank, except where the letter S—cut out from a newspaper or magazine—had been pasted squarely in the center.

Dean looked up at the man, but there was no making eye contact; the man's attention was fixed somewhere over Dean's shoulder.

"Who are you?" Dean asked.

"I can't tell you that." The man's eyes, visible even behind his sunglasses, swept the crowd around them. "Walk with me a minute," he said, and when Dean hesitated, he added, "You can trust me," in a way that caused Dean to fall into step with him.

"What's going on?" Dean tried a different tack as they threaded their way farther east on Canal Street.

"Just like I told you," the man said. "They killed Wilson. They killed the Chinaman. They'll kill you and the woman if you get in their way."

"Why? What's this all about?"

"The file," the man said, suddenly reversing his direction and heading west, causing Dean to pivot into a tiny Chinese woman bearhugging a sack of rice half her size. He struggled to catch up to the man, who was cutting through openings in the crowd as soon as they appeared.

"What file?" Dean almost called out from behind him.

"The Brandy File," the man answered over his shoulder. Then he stopped, put a hand on Dean's upper arm, and said, "Stay on this side," and before Dean could ask what the sides were and which one he was on, a black man was suddenly in front of them, closing in on the run. Dean recognized him as Jeffries, the FBI agent who had driven Janet and him back from New Jersey. The Hispanic man wheeled around, and Dean saw a revolver in his hand. Dean watched him dart from the sidewalk out into Canal Street, jumping acrobatically between speeding cabs and swerving trucks in a dash across five lanes of traffic toward the uptown side. Two men appeared out of the crowd and gave chase, and Dean heard a screech of brakes and the loud thump of an impact just as he took the force of Jeffries's charge and fell backward into a sidewalk fish display, causing hundreds of pounds of fish, ice, water, crabs, and seaweed to explode in every direction. He ended up on his back on the pavement, unhurt but dazed, and covered with what seemed like half of the north Atlantic. A good-sized carp did flips on the pavement next to him, looking only slightly more out of his element than Dean felt.

Agent Jeffries, who had managed to remain on his feet despite the collision, bent down next to Dean and said, "Sorry, are you all right?"

"I'm great," Dean managed, allowing himself to be helped to his feet. He smelled like low tide. "Somebody help him," he added, pointing in the direction of the carp, who had thus far eluded his pursuers.

"He'll be all right," Jeffries assured him, causing Dean to wonder momentarily if the carp might not be one of them. "Let's get you some clean clothes before you start attracting cats." And Jeffries steered him around the corner and into the backseat of a white car. The sudden chill inside against his wet clothing made him shiver, and even as Jeffries walked around to the front passenger side, Dean begged the man seated behind the wheel to turn off the air conditioner.

"Sure thing, Dean," said the familiar voice of Leo Silvestri as Jeffries joined them. "Sorry about the takedown back there."

"What was it for?" Dean asked. "That was 'S.' He was starting to tell me what this thing is all about. Why did you guys have to break it up?"

"We saw him pull a gun," Leo said, pulling away from the curb. "I thought you were about to buy the farm, and I couldn't take a chance. I gave the order. Agent Jeffries here wanted to make sure you weren't in the line of fire if there were shots."

"You saw his gun," Jeffries added, "didn't you?"

"Yes," Dean acknowledged weakly. He had seen the man's gun.

"What did he tell you?" Leo asked, taking side streets and heading in a southwest direction.

"Something about a file," Dean said. "I think he called it the Brandy File. Mean anything to you?"

"No," said Leo. "What else?"

"Just what was in the letters, that the police had killed Wilson and the Chinaman. And that Janet and I will be next. Who is he? Or was he?"

"I don't know yet." Silvestri had picked up Lafayette Street from Worth, and now he pulled over to the right in front of FBI headquarters at 26 Federal Plaza." I've got to report to the Director," he said, "and run this Brandy File thing through our computers, see if we've got anything on it. Agent Jeffries, take Mr. Abernathy home, or back to his office, or whatever he wants."

"Right, Lou," said Jeffries.

"And Dean?"

"Yes?"

"Be careful," Silvestri said. "That was a real gun that guy had. Chances are it had real bullets in it." He got out of the car and walked toward the entrance to 26 Federal Plaza.

Jeffries slid over behind the wheel and adjusted the rearview mirror. "Where to?" he asked.

"Home, I guess." There was a good fish market on Seventy-fifth and Broadway. And, anyway, at the moment, chicken was sounding pretty good.

Back at his apartment, Dean peeled off his wet clothes and climbed into the shower, where he scrubbed his body for a good twenty minutes. When he got out he was still convinced that he smelled of fish. He headed for the laundry room in the basement and threw his clothes into a washing machine, using extra detergent and even some Clorox. He didn't care if his things got bleached out; anything would be better than smelling like a flounder.

Dean inspected his refrigerator and could locate nothing that even remotely resembled food. He found a jar of peanut butter in the cabinet, and some pita bread in his freezer. He made two sandwiches, which he ate standing in the kitchen and followed with three handfuls of Grape Nuts. Maybe it was his imagination, but everything seemed to taste vaguely of sushi. He made some iced tea, extra strong so he could chill it with ice without its becoming too diluted. That way he didn't have to wait for it to cool. He rubbed his fingers with the piece of lime he added to the tea, but the fishy smell stubbornly refused to disappear. He drank one glassful of iced tea still standing in the kitchen, then poured himself another one, which he took with him when he finally walked into the living room and collapsed on the sofa. The tea felt cold inside his chest, no doubt where it had run into an impenetrable mass of peanut butter, dough, and Grape Nuts. His brother had probably been right when he'd warned him he'd be dead of terminal indigestion before his fortieth birthday.

Propping his feet on the cross section of a log that served as his coffee table and resting his head on the back of the sofa, Dean replayed the afternoon's events. He couldn't remember being aware that he was being followed as he left his office and walked east along Canal Street. But then again, he paid little attention to such things lately; he knew the agents were there, but regarded their presence as something benign and even protective, rather than threatening. He had been unaware of the stranger at the fish market until he had heard a voice behind him suggesting that he try the squid. He had politely rejected the idea, and the stranger had then produced the business card with the letter S. Dean didn't even know if he still had the card or if he had lost it in the events that followed.

He recalled S. repeating the warnings contained in his letters. In response to Dean's questions about what was behind all of this, S. had mentioned a file, and had specifically referred to it by name. It had been the Brandy File, or something like that, Dean could no longer be sure. He remembered S. nervously scanning the Chinatown crowd and starting to move through it, telling Dean to follow him. Had he already spotted the agents in the crowd? Then his abrupt about-face, and finally his command to Dean to stay on that side of Canal Street, while he bolted into traffic, revolver in hand, pursued by what must have been FBI agents. The screech of brakes and the sickening thud. Finally, the image of Agent Jeffries bearing down on Dean, crashing into him, producing his own dramatic backflip into the fish stand.

Dean drained his second glass of iced tea. He supposed he should be grateful for Jeffries and Leo Silvestri and the rest of the agents. S. had pulled a gun, after all, though Dean had trouble recalling when in the course of events he first became aware of it. But afterward, in the car, Leo had explained that it was the sight of the gun that had prompted him to give his men the order to move in, and that Jeffries had responded by tackling Dean to get him down and out of the line of fire in case shooting started.

In any event, they had learned something. They had a clue now as to what this whole business was all about—this Brandy File, or whatever. Leo had seemed very interested in that, interested enough to drive himself directly to his office so he could report to the Director and begin a computer search. And he had been decent enough in telling Jeffries to drive Dean wherever he wanted to go, sparing him the humiliation of wandering about in his soaking, smelly clothes.

Was there something else? Had Dean missed some detail? he wondered. He had the uneasy feeling that something else had happened that was important, and he closed his eyes tightly in an attempt to blot out the distraction of his living room and picture the scene once again, trying at the same time to ward off the first deep blue wave of fatigue that came rolling in. . . .

In his dream, he was falling backward underwater, slowly, interminably. Sea creatures swam by him and floated around him on all sides. Red snapper, bluefish, mullet, fish he couldn't identify. Eels wriggled by close enough to reach out and touch. The ominous shapes of sharks and manta rays loomed overhead near the more brightly lit surface. Beside him, a carp did strange flips in the water. . . .

He awoke in darkness, without any idea what time it was or how long he had been asleep. He lifted himself painfully from the sofa. His neck felt like it had been permanently bent to the contour of the sofa back. One foot was asleep where it had rested atop the other one, and he favored it as he half hopped across the living room, afraid to put weight on it, remembering reading years ago that you could get a stress fracture by doing so.

He turned on the TV set, more to find out what time it was than to locate any particular program. One of the channels—the Weather Channel, he thought—always displayed a digital clock as part of its format, but he couldn't recall what channel number it was. He rejected, in turn, a *Star Trek* episode, an old black-and-white Fred Astaire movie, an MTV offering of Bon Jovi singing while repeatedly pointing at a screaming crowd of teenagers, and a commercial for something called the Touch-of-the-Orient Escort Service. He paused at a stand-up comedian in front of a brick-wall backdrop, allowing him two jokes before moving on. A Mary Tyler Moore rerun featured Mary in conversation with Ed Asner, giving in on an argument and saying, "Right, Lou."

And he froze right there.

The fishy smell was back in his nostrils, the cold wet clothes clinging to his body all over again, as he sat shivering in the backseat of the air-conditioned car. "Right, Lou," Agent Jeffries had said in response to the instruction that he drop Dean off wherever he wanted to go.

Only he had said it to a man whose name happened to be Leo.

Dean's grogginess disappeared, replaced in an instant by a jolt of pure adrenaline. Jeffries, the field agent, had addressed Silvestri, his supervisor, as Lou. Had he called him Tom, Dick, or Harry, Dean might have dismissed it as a harmless slip of the tongue. Or Moishe or Leroy or José or almost any other name in the world. But not Lou. For in the stylized, quasi-military world of law enforcement, the nickname Lou wasn't up for grabs; it was the exclusive province of one group, and there were no exceptions to the rule. Lou was what every officer in the New York Police Department used when addressing his lieutenant.

These guys weren't FBI agents.

They were cops.

New York Police Department cops.

Dean struggled to grasp the full significance of what he now was sure of. There were many things going on that he didn't fully understand, but he realized one thing only too well: if the police had indeed killed Commissioner Wilson and Mr. Chang, and had reason to kill Janet and Dean, they were his enemy in all of this, and he had played right into their hands. He had told them everything he had found out during his investigation of the Spadafino case. He had reported every subsequent development to them over the past two weeks. He had turned over the letters from S. to them, when it now appeared that S. was trying his best—even risking his own life—to warn Dean about them. He had all but invited them to follow him, probably intercept his mail, maybe even listen in on his phone conversations. He had confided in them that he knew it was the police who had killed Wilson and Chang and might kill Janet and himself, and he had even told them that he had learned from his aborted conversation with S. that the killings were related to something called the Brandy File. In other words, Dean realized, he had made it clear that while he still lacked the details to bring down whatever cops were involved, he already had the knowledge—and a certain amount of proof to go along with it—to go public and make life very difficult for at least one ranking lieutenant, several detectives, and maybe a bunch of other cops as well. Which meant that Dean was, in their eyes at least, nothing short of a walking, ticking time bomb, waiting to explode at any moment.

He sat down, trying to calm himself and collect his thoughts at the same time. The one thing he still had going for him was that the police couldn't yet know that Dean had seen through their FBI cover. That tiny edge might be all that was keeping Janet and him alive at this moment, and he couldn't afford to jeopardize it. But he also realized that he had to alert Janet. He looked at his phone. She would be at Mount Sinai now, working the midnight-to-eight shift. He could call her, arrange to pick her up when she got off, and tell her then. Together they could go directly to the real FBI.

But even such a call might alert the police if they were listening in, particularly if they were waiting for some sign that the afternoon's events had awakened Dean to the fact that the FBI agents who were protecting him were in reality the very police who were so threatened by what he knew. No, he needed to avoid making waves for the moment, to stay within his routine as much as possible so as to let the police think that nothing had changed. In the morning, he would even call Janet and say things into the phone calculated to reassure them that they had nothing new to fear from him.

At the same time, however, he remembered Janet's words, how she was all Nicole had, and he knew he somehow had to get to her, whatever it took.

Dean awoke a little after seven. He made coffee and drank it black and sweet. He knew Janet would be getting home around eight-thirty, and he wanted to call her then with his everything's-fine message. But he knew he had to sound convincing, much more convincing than the last time, when her first words had been "Something's the matter, isn't it?" So he composed a speech, even jotting down notes on a yellow pad. He felt a bit silly doing it, but he reminded himself that their very lives might depend on how convincing they sounded to whoever might be listening in.

By the time eight-thirty came, Dean figured it was as good as it was going to be. He dialed Janet's number, notes in front of him. She picked up on the second ring.

"Hello," she said.

"Hi, it's Dean."

"Hi," she said, sounding genuinely glad to hear from him. "What's up?"

"Nothing much, I'm doing laundry. It seems I went swimming on Canal Street yesterday."

"Excuse me?"

Dean told her the story. When he got to the part about Jeffries's flying tackle, he engaged in a touch of revisionism. "One of the agents—you remember Jeffries, the one who drove us back from Jersey that night?—grabbed me to make sure I didn't get shot, and I landed in a fish display. It was pretty embarrassing. But I've got to hand it to those guys, they were really on the ball. As soon as they saw a gun, they were there to protect me. From now on, I tell you. I let them do the detective work. This is all too scary for me."

"Good," said Janet.

"And Leo was there, too. I told him about the file the guy mentioned, and he went straight to headquarters to bring the Director up to date and run it through their computer system."

"Good," Janet said again. "So what do you think?"

"I'm finished thinking," Dean said, trying to sound convincing. "I'm going back to being a lawyer. When the trial comes up, I'll try it. Until then, my investigator days are over."

"Well, I'm glad you're okay."

"How about you?" Dean asked. "How was work?"

"Okay," said Janet. "The usual craziness."

"What are you up to this morning?"

"I've got some errands. We'll go out for a while, before it rains. Nothing too exciting. Then I've got a dinner date at some guy's place tonight."

Jesus, thought Dean, he had completely forgotten she was coming over later. If the police were listening in, could he afford to let them know they had plans to be together later in the day? Might that not send the police into a panic, that Dean and Janet were scheming to go public with what they knew?

"Oh, yeah," Dean said, changing the intensity of his voice slightly and hoping that Janet would pick up on it. "That guy you met at the museum, right? What's his name, Ralph Barracuda or something?"

There was the tiniest of pauses, and then Janet said softly, "Right. You've got a good memory."

"Yeah," said Dean, now wanting to end the conversation before she asked him what was going on. "Well," he said, "have a good time. I'll talk with you sometime, okay?"

"Okay," said Janet, and Dean hung up. If she was mystified, she gave no sign of it on the phone.

Dean showered and put on old jeans, sneakers, and a sweatshirt. He found his venetian blind slat and his lockpick set and tossed them into a small backpack. He added a pair of sunglasses and an old full-brimmed fishing hat. He slung the backpack over one shoulder, stepped out of his apartment, double-locked the door behind him and took the fire stairs to the roof.

Like the roofs of many small buildings in Manhattan, the one atop Dean's apartment house provided a breath of fresh air and enough room to spread out a few lounge chairs and soak up some harmful ultraviolet rays in summer. If you craned your neck you could even see a bit of the Hudson River to the west. When the tall ships had sailed up toward the George Washington Bridge one recent Fourth of July, Dean had climbed halfway up the water tower to a perch from where he could watch with an old pair of binoculars he used for sailing. From there he had seen clipper ships and schooners and barks, and even a full-rigged brigantine. He had watched the spectator fleet and the police boats and the harbor patrol and a Coast Guard cutter and even a fireboat spraying great arcs of water in the air. And, when his attention had wandered, he had watched the traffic on the side streets below, and finally the other watchers on other rooftops. In doing so he had noticed how his own roof was one of a series of eight or nine of identical height, separated by gaps of a few feet at most. It had reminded him of his DEA days, when an adjoining roof often provided the least noticeable entry to a building where an arrest had to be made or a search warrant executed.

Today it would provide him with the least noticeable exit from his own apartment house.

The first three gaps were easy enough, and he took them from a standing position. The height didn't bother Dean: he was a rock climber, accustomed to working a ledge several hundred feet up a vertical wall. The six-floor drop to street level represented maybe eighty feet at most, roughly half the length of a fifty-meter rope, a height well within his comfort level.

The next gap was no wider than the others, but the building Dean had to jump to was several feet lower than the one he stood on. No problem. He stepped back, and his three-step approach allowed him to easily reach the lower rooftop. But a quick visual inspection confirmed his fear: the next jump had to be *up* as well as across. He gauged the distance as about three feet across, but two feet up. He looked around for a board or a ladder that he might use as a gangplank, but there was nothing in sight. He removed his backpack and tossed it across. He paced off eight steps back from the edge, the way he had seen high jumpers do it at track meets. He imagined the next morning's *Daily News* headline,

LAWYER DIES IN FALL
(See Pics in Centerfold)

before going for it. To his surprise, he not only lived, but managed to clear it with room to spare.

The last three roofs were a piece of cake. He now stood atop the westernmost building on the block, nearly a full avenue from his own apartment house. He walked to the front edge and, showing as little of himself as possible, looked down over the edge. None of the cars beneath him was occupied; no one was sitting on a stoop or hanging out on the corner. Back up the block, a man wearing a sport jacket and sunglasses held what looked like a container of coffee as he stood by the driver's side of a black Ford, in conversation with the driver. They might as well have been in uniform, Dean thought.

He tried the door that led from the roof to the stairway and found it locked. But it was a simple latch bolt, the kind with a beveled tongue, and his venetian blind strip slipped in easily and tripped it open on the first pass. He closed the door carefully behind him and descended the stairs silently on his sneakers. At ground level he put on his hat and sunglasses, stepped out onto the sidewalk, and turned the corner in the direction opposite the surveillance team up the block.

Which was the easy part, of course; the hard part would be getting into Janet's building unnoticed.

He hailed a cab and directed the driver to head downtown to Broadway and Twenty-second Street. When they got there, Dean paid the fare, got out, and proceeded to circle the block on foot to check for a tail. Twice he stopped abruptly and reversed his direction. Satisfied finally that there was nobody following him, he completed his circle and slipped into a store called the Gordon Novelty Company. He had been in it once several years ago, when a last-minute need for a costume had forced him to do a Yellow Pages search, which in turn had led him to Gordon's.

It hadn't changed much. Masks of every sort lined the walls, famous people, monsters, ghouls. Costumes that could instantly transform one into anything from a ballerina to a gorilla. Grass skirts, flowing capes, magic wands, halos, devils' pitchforks—it was all there, jammed together onto three walls of floor-to-ceiling display.

The line Dean had waited on just before Halloween had been twenty deep; Saturday morning in late summer was a different story altogether.

"May I help you?" asked a fiftyish man with sixties sideburns turned gray.

"I hope so," Dean said. "I'm looking for a disguise. I've got to go to a party and look like a regular person—you know, not like a clown or anything—but not be recognized. Any suggestions?"

"Do you want a mask?" Sideburns asked. "Some of our full rubber masks are very lifelike."

"Maybe," Dean said. "But I don't want a Ronald Reagan or anything identifiable like that."

"Aaaah," the man agreed theatrically. "Something in the obscure for the gentleman! Do you have a few minutes?" When Dean said that he did, the man called for a clerk to replace him on the floor. "I need to go into our *archives*," he whispered to Dean conspiratorily.

Dean spent the time studying the masks on the walls and identifying to himself as many of the likenesses as he could. There were JFK and LBJ, a beaming Ike and a scowling Nixon. Bogart winked and Brando pouted. Even George Bush did the smile thing. There were Marilyn Monroe, Dr. Ruth, Sigmund Freud, and Albert Einstein. There was Ross Perot, interestingly juxtaposed with Alfred E. Newman of *Mad* magazine fame. And Freddy of *A Nightmare on Elm Street*, several Frankenstein monsters, and an assortment of Count Draculas.

After about fifteen minutes, he felt a tap on his shoulder. He turned to see a sixtyish man, quite bald on top, but with black hair. "Adlai Stevenson," Dean said.

Adlai pulled his mask off and revealed Sideburns underneath. "Not bad for a youngster," he said. "But how about these?" With a flourish, he spread out several others on the counter. Of those, Dean quickly identified Dan Quayle and Lee Harvey Oswald; he was less certain with Walter Mondale, Nelson Rockefeller, and a rather poor likeness of Warren Beatty. But the one that stumped him completely was Spiro Agnew.

"How much for old Spiro?" he asked.

"Well, let's see. We don't get many calls for him. How does fifteen dollars sound?"

"Ten sounds better," Dean said.

"Twelve and it's a deal."

"Done," said Dean, wondering where on his voucher he was going to list a twelve-dollar expense for a Spiro Agnew disguise. "Investigation" was always worth a shot.

It was a curious-looking man who got out of a cab and entered 81 Bleecker Street. The brim of his hat was turned down all around, and sunglasses shaded his eyes. What was visible of his face suggested a rather rubbery texture to his skin, and his expression seemed frozen between a smile and a sneer. But it being New York City, and indeed Greenwich Village, no one seemed to pay him any mind, certainly not the two men eating jelly doughnuts in a maroon Chevrolet across the street and four doors down.

Once in the vestibule, the man used something in his hand to slip the inner door. He walked to the elevator and rode it to the sixth floor. From there he found the stairway, which he took one flight farther, stepping out onto the roof. Earlier, he had asked the cab driver to make one pass through the block before dropping him off, and had selected the building as the farthest one of similar height that connected to 77 Bleecker Street. His visual inspection now confirmed his street-level reconnaissance.

He took off his sunglasses, hat, and mask before jumping first to 79 Bleecker, and then to 77. Then he put them back on. He appeared to have difficulty with the lock on the door to the stairs and soon rejected whatever implement he had used previously. In its place he withdrew two flattened, slender metal tools from his pocket. One he slid directly into the keyhole of the lock; the other, which had a ninety-degree bend in it, he inserted up to the bend, then worked the protruding portion back and forth with his free hand. Within fifteen seconds there was an audible click. A turn of the knob pulled the door open and the man was inside.

Dean removed his sunglasses and took the stairs down to the third floor, where he rang Janet's bell. He waited, then rang it again. He could hear the chime tone it made inside the apartment, and when there was again no response he retreated to the stairwell to consider his options.

The roof lock had been child's play. Dean seriously doubted that his skill was sufficient to pick the more difficult locks on Janet's door, one of which was a Medeco deadbolt. Even if he succeeded, the process would take time, during which he would be vulnerable to being spotted by someone suddenly getting off the elevator or coming out of an apartment. In addition, the doors had peepholes, and any noise he made might attract attention. The risk of someone calling the police, however slight, was a risk Dean judged he could not afford.

He thought about ringing Mrs. Del Valle's door, which he knew was 4A. She might have a key to Janet's apartment, and he could probably coax her into letting him in. If not, she might at least let him into her own apartment, where he would be safe, and from where he could phone Janet until she picked up. But he was reluctant to involve Mrs. Del Valle, and involving her might also mean involving anyone else who happened to be with her at the moment.

Still, he felt very exposed in the stairway. The third-floor landing, from which he could keep an eye on Janet's door if he held the stairway door open a crack, placed him in the way of anyone who might decide to take the stairs for a couple of flights rather than wait for the elevator. So he decided to sacrifice the convenient view of Janet's door for the greater safety of the highest—and therefore least traveled—portion of the stairway, that connecting the sixth floor to the roof level.

His choice required periodic trips back down to the third floor and left him vulnerable each time he stood at Janet's door hoping she would answer his rings. But it turned out he needed only three such trips before her "Who is it?" rewarded his patience.

"Spiro Agnew," he answered.

He heard a slight noise within and saw a blue eye appear in the peephole. "Who?" he heard.

"Spiro Abernathy."

The door opened.

"I must've slept late and it's Halloween," Janet said after she had let Dean in and closed the door.

"Very funny," Dean said, as he struggled to pull the mask up and off his head.

"And you're about the last person in the world I expected to be ringing my bell. I thought you blew me off for dinner. And what was with the Ralph Barracuda business?"

"Sorry about that," said Dean, wiping off the sweat that the mask had left on his face and walking to the window, where he adjusted the blinds so the two of them couldn't be seen from the street below. "But I was afraid to let them know you were coming over tonight. This thing has gotten very complicated. I've got a lot to tell you."

They sat in Janet's living room, where Dean turned up the volume on the TV news, afraid the apartment might be bugged. He explained what S. had told him about there being something called the Brandy File at the heart of it. Then he told her about Jeffries's referring to Leo Silvestri as Lou and the significance of the slip, that their FBI agent-protectors were in reality the very police behind the murder of Wilson.

"Oh, my God," Janet said.

"And I've been so stupid," Dean added. "I've had us playing right into their hands this whole time. Telling them everything we know, letting them follow us, turning the letters over to them, even telling them what S. told me."

They sat in silence for a moment, the only sound being the muffled voice of the newscaster on the television.

"What do we do now?" Janet asked slowly. But Dean hardly heard her. His attention was focused over her shoulder, upon the TV screen. The smiling photograph of a young police officer, uniformed but hatless, filled the screen. His face looked familiar, and Dean's first thought was that he might have testified at one of

Dean's trials. He raised a hand to command Janet's silence. She turned, and together they listened to the newscaster.

". . . struck by a truck as he pursued a fugitive across Canal Street Friday afternoon. He was pronounced dead at Beekman Downtown Hospital. Officer Santana was twenty-seven. Among his recent assignments, he had served as the chauffeur for the late Police Commissioner Edward Wilson, and was the last officer to have seen Wilson before the Commissioner's untimely death at the hands of a mugger. Officer Santana is the fourth member of the force to be killed in the line of duty this year. He leaves behind a wife and two small children. The fugitive escaped. No charges have been brought against the truck driver. In other news , . ."

"That's him," Dean managed to say, numbly. "That's S."

"Was," Janet corrected.

"Was," Dean echoed. "He knew what had happened and was trying to tell me. Leo and his men saw that and ran him into the street. They killed him, too."

Janet was shivering. "What do we do, Dean?" she almost begged him to have a plan.

"We call in the *real* FBI," Dean answered, trying to speak with conviction. "But we can't do it from here. We've got to assume they've got both of our phones tapped."

"They'll kill us, too, won't they?" Janet's shivering grew worse, and Dean put an arm around her.

"Not as long as they think we're still buying their cover," he said, but he was aware that his voice carried a bit less conviction this time. "That's why I gave you all that I'm-letting-the-professionals-handle-this business when we were on the phone before. I want Leo and his people to feel secure that I'm not about to do anything rash."

"Like call the real FBI?"

"Like call the real FBI. Or even get together with you to try to figure things out."

"How do you know they didn't follow you over here?" Janet asked. "Do you really think that silly mask fooled them?"

"I'm not even sure they saw me. I've also been leaping tall buildings at a single bound."

"That sounds like fun."

"It was, actually."

"Do we call the real FBI now?" Janet asked.

"Yes. Let's ask Mrs. Del Valle if we can use her phone."

Janet reached for her own phone, but Dean stopped her. "Nothing on this one."

"I need to call my sister," Janet said. "I want her to take Nicole for a few days, until we know we're safe. Can't I at least do that?"

"Yes," Dean said. "It's a good idea. But not from here. You'll do that from Mrs. Del Valle's, too."

So Janet gathered up a sleeping Nicole, and the three of them climbed the stairs to the fourth floor. Janet rang the bell to 4A. A bald, heavyset man answered the door and invited them in. Somehow Dean had not counted on a Mr. Del Valle. He explained in broken English that his wife was out.

"Her at bodega."

"Can we use your telephone, please?" Janet asked him.

"Yes, but no," Mr. Del Valle replied. "Is broke." He made them follow him to the kitchen, where he took the receiver off a wall phone and handed it to Dean, who held it to his ear. Silence. It was indeed broke.

Janet asked Mr. Del Valle to send his wife to her apartment when she got back from the bodega. He seemed to understand. Nicole woke up and took in the surroundings somewhat apprehensively. They walked back downstairs. Once they were inside Janet's apartment, Dean triple-locked the door. Janet noticed, and a visible shiver ran through her body.

Dean walked to the phone and picked it up.

"I thought you said—"

"Shit," was what Dean said. Her phone was dead, too. "I guess they aren't taking any chances."

"Can they really do that?" Janet asked.

"They can probably knock the whole building out. Can you buzz the super on the intercom and see if his phone is out, too?"

Janet buzzed Mr. Novacek.

"I know, I know," came his voice over the intercom. "The phones are out. It's the whole building. The phone company knows. They're trying to locate the problem."

It was twenty minutes before the doorbell rang and Janet let Mrs. Del Valle in. She listened carefully to Janet's instructions on how to take Nicole to Janet's sister's on Long Island. She was to leave in an hour, when Nicole would be asleep, carrying the baby in a bag to hide her. She was to be absolutely certain that nobody followed her. She seemed to sense the seriousness of the situation and asked no unnecessary questions. She fussed over Nicole while Janet went inside to pack the things her daughter would need. When Janet came back out her eyes were dry but red, and her hands were trembling slightly.

"You don't have to to this, you know," Dean said. "I'll be okay. You can go with Nicole to your sister's until this blows over." God only knew when that might be, of course.

"And let you fall into a fish tank again?"

"It wasn't exactly a fish tank."

"Whatever," she said, drying her eyes and taking a deep breath. "As they say in the movies, we're in this mess together."

Dean didn't argue. He stood by helplessly as Janet hugged her daughter tightly, and then surrendered her to Mrs. Del Valle, who crossed herself quickly before stepping out into the hallway.

At the third-floor window, Dean parted the blinds just enough to watch the Del Valles emerge from the building. They appeared to be carrying several large bundles, which they placed carefully in the back of a rusted Toyota station wagon. When they pulled away from the curb, no one followed.

"She'll be okay," Dean told Janet with some measure of confidence.

The more difficult question was whether the two of them would be okay, and he was grateful to her for not asking it.

With no working phones in the building, they needed to slip out without being detected, get to a phone to call the FBI, and locate a place to hide while the FBI began the business of identifying and apprehending the various Police Department people involved in the killing of Commissioner Wilson, the poisoning of Mr. Chang, and the suspicious death of Officer Santana.

"Suppose they don't believe us?" Janet asked. "Suppose they think we're nuts?"

The thought had certainly occurred to Dean. After all, he was the lawyer for the very man charged with killing Wilson. It would be easy to dismiss as a total fantasy his claim of a police conspiracy to murder their own.

"You may be right, but we've got to do *something*. Can you think of a better plan?" he said.

"No."

"I've tried," he said, "and I can't either. But it's not going to take Silvestri and his friends forever to figure out I'm not in my apartment. If they know we're here together, they could panic, and we're sitting ducks."

The last thought seemed to get to Janet, and she offered no further resistance to his plan, or what there was of it. She changed into jeans, sneakers, and a sweatshirt. Dean had her find a pair of sunglasses and a scarf to cover her head. From her closet he selected a coat that was almost floor-length. These items, along with his own mask, hat, and sunglasses and some toiletries Janet had assembled, he placed in a canvas bag.

Dean checked the street below. The maroon Chevy was still there, two men still seated in it. Farther down the block was a Frozfruit vendor. Yuppie surveillance?

He left the window and went to the front door to check the peephole. No one was visible. He had Janet open the door and step out. She signaled to him that all was clear.

They retraced Dean's earlier route, taking the stairs to the roof. It turned out Janet was agile and sure-footed and able to leap tall buildings with the best of them. They crossed from 77 Bleecker to 79, and from there to 81. The next building, a double-wide one, was about five feet away and six feet lower, a combination that made the jump easy but the landing tricky. Dean asked Janet if she was game.

"Why not?" She shrugged nonchalantly.

Broken bones, head injuries, death, thought Dean. But he kept such thoughts to himself, knowing that they must have occurred to this brave young woman next to him as well.

"You first," said the brave young woman.

Dean laughed. "As long as you promise not to chicken out," he said. "I've got no way to get back to you once I'm down there."

"I promise," she said. "Unless you don't make it."

"Fair enough," said Dean.

He tossed the canvas bag to the lower roof, well to the side of what he had picked out as his landing area. He stepped to the very edge of the roof they were on. Then he rocked his weight forward and back several times by swinging his arms in exaggerated arcs, before pushing off with both feet. He cleared the distance easily and landed without incident.

"Piece of cake," he said to Janet, being careful not to raise his voice.

She stepped to the edge and looked across at the lower roof. As a climber Dean knew the visual problem that greeted her. A five-and-a-half-foot person looking at a drop of six feet actually confronts a distance of eleven feet, the six-foot drop plus the additional five feet from foot to eye level. Looking down eleven feet is suddenly serious business, because the eye refuses to make the intellectual adjustment that no part of the body—be it eyes or feet or whatever—will have to descend more than six feet during the jump.

But if the sight terrified Janet, she refused to allow it to paralyze her. She mimicked Dean's swinging motion, describing longer and longer arcs with her arms. Once, twice, three times. And on the fourth she pushed off deftly, clearing the air space with ease and landing lightly on the lower roof, where Dean grabbed her in a bear hug.

"Terrific!" he told her.

"No sweat," she said.

He could feel her entire body trembling in his grasp.

A look at the next building confirmed what Dean already knew. It posed the reverse problem: five feet across, but six feet *up* to the next rooftop. And out of the question. They had jumped their last roof.

Dean turned his attention to the door leading to the stairwell of the building they were on. Again he needed his lockpick set, but his touch had not deserted him, and he had the door open in less than a minute. They donned their disguises, Dean becoming Spiro Agnew again, while Janet added thirty years or so with a kerchief, dark glasses, the long coat, and the slouch of a crone.

They walked down the steps to the ground floor and out the front door. Arm in arm, they turned right, away from the maroon Chevy, away even from the Frozfruit vendor. As they rounded the corner, an empty cab sat by the curb, its driver resting against the hood.

"You working?" Dean asked the man.

"Depends." A Middle East accent of some sort. "Where do you want to go?"

"Anywhere but east," said Dean.

"Sure, get in."

At Dean's instruction, he took them down Seventh Avenue to the World Trade Center, where Dean paid him and they got out. They headed to a large bank of public phones outside the nearer of the Twin Towers. Dean stepped to an unused phone; Janet alongside him. He picked up the receiver and dialed Information. When an operator answered he asked her for the number of the FBI.

"I'm sorry, Mr. Abernathy," said a familiar voice behind Dean, "but I can't let you do that." He turned to see Leo Silvestri, flanked by Jeffries and another man whom he recognized as Detective Rasmussen. They looked like they meant business.

TWENTY-FOUR

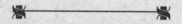

Dean and Janet were led to a gray van and directed to get in through the back doors. The inside consisted of two facing padded benches along either side. Jeffries motioned for them to sit, then closed the doors behind them, leaving them in sudden and total darkness. They heard the doors being locked from the outside and felt the van shift slightly as someone got behind the wheel. Front doors slammed shut, the engine started, and they were moving.

"Are they going to kill us?" Janet asked Dean softly in the dark.

"Of course not," he said, then added more loudly, "these guys are FBI agents." As he spoke, he groped for her in the dark, and when he located her face he placed his index finger against her lips to quiet her, against the possibility that there was a microphone somewhere in the back of the van. "They're on our side," he continued. "They must have felt we're in danger, that's all." He felt her lips kiss his finger softly.

For a while Dean tried to keep track of the turns the van made, but he soon found it impossible. At one point the traffic noise changed and seemed to echo, and Dean guessed that they were going through a tunnel. At another point the van bounced sharply, as though it had struck a pothole, causing Janet to slide into him on the bench. He put an arm around her to steady her and kept it there the rest of the way.

After about a half hour, they were aware of the van slowing, then descending a steep incline before leveling out and coming to a stop. The engine was cut off, and they heard the sound of the front doors of the van opening and closing. Noises at the rear of the van told them the doors were being unlocked. Fluorescent light suddenly streamed in, causing them both to squint, but Dean was able to see that they were in an underground parking garage.

Leo Silvestri led the way while Jeffries and Rasmussen ushered them through a door that connected the garage to the remainder of the building, and they were directed to a freight elevator. Leo pressed the top button, and they rode up in silence. When the elevator door opened, they were led down a long corridor containing doors to offices. Most of the doors were wooden, a few with opaque glass panels; all had numbers, running from 700 to 714. Only one had a name that Dean could make out: D. M. FERGUSON. The door at the end of the corridor was dark wood, broken only by a peephole and the brass numerals 714. It was there that Leo unlocked the door and held it open for the rest of them to enter.

Inside was a small hallway that opened onto a large conference room. The only furniture in the room was a long imitation mahogany table, surrounded by chairs of chrome and black leather. Leo motioned for Dean and Janet to sit; he, Jeffries, and Rasmussen found empty seats themselves. Of the dozen or so others present, Dean recognized Bennett Childs from the first meeting, as well as Rasmussen's partner, Detective Mogavero, and several others who, Dean was fairly certain, had been among those following Janet and him over the past weeks. To Dean's even greater surprise was the presence of Bobby McGrane, the client who had first introduced Dean to Leo Silvestri.

"*Bobby?*" Dean asked incredulously.

"*Detective* Bobby, to you."

"Yes," explained Leo. "When we found out you were starting to snoop around on the Spadafino thing, we thought you might get lucky and put two and two together. We figured at some point you'd feel the need to reach out to some other agency. We created

Bobby McGrane for the express purpose of giving you a friendly FBI agent you could turn to if that need occurred."

"And it did," said Dean.

"And it did," Leo agreed. "Unfortunately, we didn't figure on you're being quite as lucky as you were."

"Or as smart," interjected Bennett Childs.

"Sorry," said Dean.

"We are, too," agreed Childs. "Thereafter, we did everything we could to keep you out of the position you now find yourself in. We sent in another lawyer to try to hustle the case away from you—"

"Leonard Winston?"

"Yes. But Mr. Spadafino wanted no part of Mr. Winston, I'm afraid," said Childs. "Not that I can blame him. Winston is a rather sleazy creature."

"And not much of a lawyer," added Dean.

"That, too, I suppose. Then we arranged a series of incredible plea offers for your client that any reasonable man would have jumped at."

"Unless he happened to be innocent."

Childs ignored the remark. "And now we've come down to this," he said, gesturing to the roomful of men who surrounded Dean and Janet.

"This?"

Childs took out his pipe and tobacco, and there was silence as he went through the ritual of filling it, packing it down, lighting it, and beginning to puff on it. This was clearly his meeting, and he was going to make it his show, as well. "This," he said finally, "is where we tell you what you *don't* know and try our best to appeal to your sense of reason."

"I want you to know I'm feeling very reasonable," Dean said.

"For my part, Mr. Abernathy, I'm prepared to level with you. For your part, how about you sparing us the bad jokes?"

"Sorry."

The sweet aroma of Captain Black filled the room as Childs began his narrative. "Some years ago, back in the early eighties, actually, the Police Department hierarchy—meaning the then Commissioner and his top deputies—decided that the laws dealing with such things as search and seizure, admissibility of confessions, and the like were weighted far too heavily in favor of the criminal. It was a time when violent crime was on the increase, the crack epidemic was beginning, and handguns were everywhere. Parks were no longer safe places, people were afraid to go out after dark, whole neighborhoods were being taken over by drug pushers. Gunfire became a commonplace thing, with handguns falling into the hands of teens and even preteens. Saturday Night Specials were replaced by nine-millimeter Mac-tens and uzis. You couldn't pick up a newspaper without reading about an innocent woman or child getting killed in crossfire. And yet our courts continued to operate on laws drafted in the nineteenth century, hamstrung by rules that were hopelessly out of date and totally inadequate to deal with the crisis.

"As police officers—and we are all police officers, as you've probably figured out by now—we knew we couldn't sit idly by and watch criminals walk free because of technicalities while our city was destroyed in the process. So we did what we could. We lied a little here, we cheated a little there. When we made a good collar we'd do our best to make it stick. If we didn't have a search warrant, we'd say we found the drugs in open view. If we didn't give a suspect his rights, we'd later say we had. Nothing major. Certainly nothing that you and every other defense lawyer hasn't been aware of for years."

"And every DA and judge, too," said Dean.

"Exactly. But we were the ones who always had to do the dirty work," Childs continued. "We had to be the liars, the perjurers, the cheats. And when one of us would get caught at it, some politically ambitious prosecutor would go after him with a vengeance, some holier-than-thou judge would take away his shield and send him to prison, and the media would chime in with a chorus of righteous indignation about dishonest police. That was the height of hypocrisy, and that was what we set about to correct. If you want us to do our job in a particular way, make it legitimate: Change the laws so the men who enforce them don't have to be criminals.

"But how to do this?" Childs asked rhetorically. "That was the problem. We couldn't very well come out and tell the world that we'd been falsifying evidence and expect everyone to pat us on the back and say keep up the good work. So the suggestion was made that we begin the process of keeping track, at least in serious cases—those involving murder and other violence, or large amounts of hard drugs—of precisely what falsification we engaged in and how it was necessary in order to ensure a conviction. The ultimate goal was to assemble enough data to convince even the most extreme bleeding-heart liberals that under their rules almost all of those major felons would have gone free, and that the laws must be changed so that we can obey them and at the same time get convictions on guilty felons.

"After a great deal of discussion, the study was approved. In every major case that qualified under the guidelines, the arresting officer or detective was interviewed by an inspector, precinct commander, or captain, under an absolute guarantee of confidentiality. The interviewer than prepared a report, usually a single page or two, of what liberties had been taken in the case in order to obtain a conviction. That report was forwarded to the Commissioner's office, where it was analyzed and the data contained on it was entered into a computer program. The program was accessible to no one under the rank of inspector. The individual reports themselves were kept under lock and key in a secure vault in the Commissioner's office, under the heading of the Brady File."

"As in *Brady v. Maryland*, the case that requires exculpatory material to be turned over to the defense," said Dean.

"Precisely," Childs said, nodding. "Though it seems our Officer Santana somehow confused it with an after-dinner drink and called it the Brandy File instead. We figured it was only a matter of time until you realized his mistake."

"Right," agreed Dean, though of course it had not occurred to him.

"In any event," Childs resumed, "the data began coming in. And it was very impressive data. Drug kingpins, terrorists, serial murderers, Mafia hitmen, Central Park rapists—in virtually every case we learned that the officers or detectives involved had been forced to engage in at least some minor fabrication in order to ensure a conviction. The statistics run to about ninety-two percent. Know what that means? That means for every ten major criminals behind bars for the most violent crimes and biggest drug conspiracies committed in this city in the past dozen years, nine of them would have walked if our men hadn't been willing to bend things a bit."

Childs paused to relight his pipe. "The next problem was how to reveal the data to the politicians who write the laws without blowing the whistle on ourselves and jeopardizing the very convictions that had been obtained. Everybody agreed that this was the tricky part. But we had to do it. Our men deserved better than to be turned into criminals for doing what no one else was willing to do. No less than four Commissioners, beginning in the early nineteen eighties, supported the plan and worked to implement the next phase, the lobbying of the legislature."

"Until Wilson," Dean said.

"Precisely," said Childs. "As Chief of Patrol, the highest rank he held before that of Commissioner, Wilson had been out of the loop. He had never *heard* of the Brady File, much less been involved in its creation. As Commissioner, he had to be brought in on it sooner or later. Those of us who knew him best were afraid to trust him. He was so zealous in his anticorruption campaign that we were frankly afraid that he'd see this as a corruption issue, when in fact it has nothing to do with corruption and never has."

"What does it have to do with?" Dean asked.

"It has to do with good cops trying to do a job against a stacked deck, trying to keep this city out of the hands of the animals out there in the jungle."

"But Wilson didn't see it that way," Dean said.

"I'm afraid not," Childs agreed. "We kept him out of it for over two years, despite the fact that the file was sitting there in his office the whole time. When we finally needed to bring him in on it, we sat him down and explained the situation to him in as fair and honest a way as we could, hoping to persuade him to support the plan."

"But he wasn't buying."

"Not for a moment. Wilson was a good cop," Childs said, as though he meant it, "but he couldn't see the forest for the trees. All he kept saying was that cops had lied and that the department had withheld material that should have been turned over to the defense in hundreds of cases, thousands of cases."

"He had a point," said Dean.

"Perhaps," Childs agreed, "but it was a very technical point when compared to the damage that would have been done if we suddenly had to turn over the entire Brady File to the courts. Can you imagine the consequences?"

"A lot of bad guys walking out of prison?" was Dean's guess.

"And a lot of good cops walking in to take their places," added Childs. "Talk about an Alice-in-Wonderland situation."

"So . . ."

"So we couldn't let that happen," Childs said. "Our statisticians created a computer model from which we were able to estimate that, given the number of violent criminals whose cases would have to be reversed and who could no longer be tried, we'd have an additional four hundred and fifty murders over the next five years. *Four hundred and fifty murders!* Mostly of innocent victims. And that's a conservative estimate, without the assaults, the rapes, and the robberies, let alone the drug traffic.

"We did everything humanly possible to try to convince Wilson. He even agreed with our statistics, more or less. But all he would say was that he was sworn to uphold the law and let the chips fall where they might."

"Something to be said for that, I suppose," Dean said.

"Bullshit!" Childs roared. "These aren't chips, these are human lives!" He repacked the bowl of his pipe as though to regain his composure. "In the weeks before Wilson's death, we tried everything we knew to persuade him to at least hold off going public for a while. But he was adamant. The night of his death, he told us he'd be calling a press conference the following day. We had to make a judgment: hundreds of lives, or one."

"So you poisoned him."

Dean thought he noticed Childs nod ever so slightly, but certainly no explicit spoken confirmation was forthcoming. When Childs put down his pipe after a long moment, he said simply, "One life."

"Until Joey Spadafino decided to go through Wilson's pockets," Dean said.

"Yes," Childs said. "Your client certainly managed to be at the wrong place at the wrong time, as they say. But for him, everything would have gone down smoothly. Man with a heart condition exerts himself by partying too late, drinking too much, walking in the snow. Has a second heart attack, a fatal one. End of story. No criminal case, no snooping defense lawyer."

"And Mr. Chang?" Dean asked.

"Yes, poor Mr. Chang. Regrettable. But Mr. Chang was very stupid and kept insisting that your client never robbed the Commissioner, only picked his pocket as he lay dead on the ground."

"And why was that so terrible?"

"Ordinarily, it might not have been. But by the time we located Mr. Chang, our detectives had already committed themselves to saying that your client had confessed to robbing Wilson while he was alive and standing up. They couldn't very well all of a sudden retract their grand jury testimony, or make your client's written confession disappear, could they?"

"And Officer Santana?" Dean asked.

"That was truly an accident, the lieutenant here tells me," Childs said, pointing with his pipe to Leo Silvestri.

"We didn't know who was sending you the letters," Leo picked up the narrative. "We followed you along Canal Street at a distance. I recognized Officer Santana when I saw him strike up a conversation with you. All we were trying to do was keep him from telling you too much for your own good. In a way, you might say we were looking to protect you."

"Thanks," Dean muttered sarcastically.

"We had no intention of harming Officer Santana. We could have dealt with him, gotten him to see the big picture. How were we supposed to know he'd panic and go one-on-one with a dump truck?"

"Sounds like three down so far," said Dean, "If you count Mr. Chang."

"Yes," Childs agreed, "and I can tell you I speak for the entire department when I say how terribly sorry we are that innocent lives have been lost. If it helps any, you should know that Mrs. Wilson and her family will be generously taken care of. So, too, Officer Santana's widow and children. In due time, we'll even do the right thing for Mr. Chang's relatives, though any payment to them will be made anonymously.

"Mr. Abernathy, we very much want there to be no further casualties. Three is already too many. We are moral people, and we never intended a number like that, even if it is far less than four hundred and fifty. The point is, it's got to end."

"Meaning?"

"Meaning," said Childs, pausing again to relight his pipe, "we're prepared to do anything within reason to avoid further casualties."

Dean thought for a minute. He was suddenly aware that he was holding Janet's hand in his under the table between them. He had no idea how long he had been doing so. When he finally spoke, he said, "My job is pretty straightforward here. I represent a man who says he's innocent of all charges, except perhaps a simple petit larceny he's not even accused of. He wants a trial."

"He doesn't want a trial, Mr. Abernathy," said Childs with a smile. "He, like most defendants, wants to go home."

"He, unlike most defendants, has no home," corrected Dean.

"Then he wants to hit the street," Childs said. "Suppose we could arrange that?"

"How?"

"Several possibilities come to mind. If Mr. Spadafino is willing to forgo a trial, the department could release newly discovered tissue studies that suggest that Commissioner Wilson's death actually resulted from a condition unrelated to the robbery. Based on those studies, the DA will offer your client a plea to precisely the petit larceny you suggest. I believe," Childs added, "that could be done as what you lawyers would call a lesser included charge under the robbery count." Childs was right, Dean knew; he had done his homework. "Since petit larceny is only a misdemeanor, the maximum sentence is a year, on which you do eight months. By the time of sentencing, your client will have done it already. Time served, I believe they call it?"

"And if my client insists on a trial?" Dean asked.

"Well," said Childs, between puffs, "it seems to me that there are two very different trials that could take place here, under the circumstances. In the first, you behave yourself, and Miss Killian stays completely away. No talk of any Brady File, no accusations of any conspiracy or cover-up or any department involvement whatsoever. Toward the very end of the trial, that same tissue study surfaces. If you like, we'll supply it directly to you, let you pull the rabbit out of the hat, so to speak. The DA will be compelled to dismiss all charges but petit larceny. Maybe the jury convicts your guy, maybe they acquit him. Either way, he comes up a winner. Worst case scenario is the same as the other way: time served. And you're a hero. Every criminal in the city will be knocking down your door looking for you to represent him."

"And the other kind of trial?"

"The other kind of trial," said Childs softly, "is if you go for broke and try to prove what you know."

"What happens then?"

Childs thought a moment. "Let me emphasize once again, Mr. Abernathy," he said at length, "that we are good men. Not perfect, certainly, but good. We've done some things we're not particularly proud of. We're not anxious to continue doing those things. But I think you can imagine that if the situation demands, we'll do whatever we have to do to contain this business. We're simply not going to stand by while you turn the key that lets thousands of murderers, rapists, and drug dealers loose on the streets of our city to prey upon our weakest members. Understand, it's not the police who have the most to fear; we're armed and able-bodied, and most of us live on Staten Island or Long Island or in some other part of the suburbs. It's the people of this city who stand to lose. The very young, the very old, the frail, the unarmed. The usual victims, you might say. Four hundred and fifty of them. And that's only by the most conservative estimates—and only the deaths—in the first five years alone. That only scratches the surface."

"I'm going to need some time to think about this," Dean said.

"You'll get as much as you like," Childs replied.

"How does that work?" Dean knew they weren't simply going to let Janet and him go home to decide. He recognized that Childs and his people needed a way to keep them from contacting other law-enforcement agencies.

"Very simple," said Childs. "As soon as you're ready to leave, Mr. Abernathy, you'll be brought back to the city. Miss Killian will remain with us." Dean felt Janet squeeze his hand. He tried to give her a reassuring squeeze back, but he doubted that it served its purpose.

"I'm a hostage?" Janet spoke for the first time.

"I prefer to think of you as insurance," Childs said.

"You think of it however you like," Janet said, her voice breaking from the strain. "This is kidnapping!"

If Childs was flustered by the comment, he gave no sign of it. "I can assure you," he said, smiling, "that you'll be the most comfortable person who's ever been 'kidnapped,' as you insist on putting it." Then, turning to Detective Rasmussen, he said, "Richie, why don't you show Miss Kilian to her quarters? Mr. Abernathy, you may accompany them to assure yourself that Miss Killian will be comfortable. I don't want you to be under the im-

pression that we'll be keeping the lady locked up in a dungeon."
Childs picked up a set of keys from the table and handed them to
the detective.

Janet and Dean followed Rasmussen out of the meeting
room and back down the corridor, past the wooden doors with
only numbers on them, past D. M. Ferguson's door, until they
came to a door without a number. Unlike the others, it was metal.
There were no less than four locks on the door, including a massive slide bolt that worked from the outside. It took Rasmussen
several minutes to match the various locks with the proper keys.
It certainly seemed like a dungeon so far.

Inside, however, it was a totally different story. A flick of a
wall switch revealed a well-appointed, if somewhat Ramada
Inn-ish, suite, complete with living room, bedroom, kitchenette,
and bath. There was a large color TV and VCR, a coffeemaker,
and an AM/FM radio. Conspicuously absent was any sign of a
telephone. A bookcase was filled with titles running from *Moby-
Dick* to *Silent Spring*, and there were even attractive prints on the
walls. While Janet looked over what was meant to be her living
quarters, Dean turned his attention to possible escape routes. He
didn't like what he saw. The only door was the one through which
they had entered, and he knew already that its locks were well beyond his very amateur level of expertise. The windows in the living room and bedroom, which were covered by both venetian
blinds and heavy drapes, were of the nonopening variety; fresh air
was apparently supplied by a central ventilation system.

"Okay to use the bathroom?" Dean asked.

"Sure, Counselor, why not?"

Dean stepped into the bathroom and closed the door behind
him. He lifted the toilet seat noisily and turned on the faucet of
the sink while he checked the window. It was small, no more than
nine or ten inches wide, certainly too narrow for his body to fit
through. The glass was frosted, making seeing out impossible.
But, unlike the others, it was designed to open. He turned off the
faucet, flushed the toilet, and left the seat up. He figured Rasmussen could relate to that.

Back in the living room, Dean asked the detective if Janet
and he could spend a few moments together.

"Okay, Counselor, but make it quick. I'm supposed to bring

you back." And with that, Rasmussen walked to the door, where he stood with his arms crossed, well within earshot.

"What are we going to do?" Janet asked Dean.

"We have no choice," Dean answered. "I have to act in my client's best interest. Joey Spadafino's going to jump for joy at the idea of time served. I can't deprive him of that, even if I think these guys are dead wrong. And I'm not so sure I do." Then, despite the fact that Janet was dry-eyed, he added, "Now don't start crying."

She looked puzzled for only an instant, then broke into a breathless sobbing, which she punctuated with a running commentary on how much she missed her baby. Dean took her in his arms as though to comfort her, and as she nuzzled her head against his shoulder he lowered his mouth to her ear.

"I'll think of something" was all he could think to whisper to her.

To Rasmussen, it must have seemed nothing more than a weepy broad and a guy trying his best to score.

"Okay, lovebirds, break it up," called Rasmussen. "Miss Killian, a woman detective will be looking in on you later to see what you need. Counselor, you come with me."

Back in the meeting room, Bennett Childs laid out the ground rules to Dean. "You'll be driven home now," he explained. "You'll be free to go about your life, attend to your business. Wherever you go, we'll be there, close by. Whoever you call, we'll know instantly. As for Miss Killian, we shall retain custody of her until this thing is over. From this point on, however, in a very real sense we are no longer responsible for her life. You are. Do I make myself clear enough?"

"Yes," said Dean.

With nothing further said, Dean was blindfolded and led out of the room by Rasmussen and, he supposed, Detective Mogavero. They walked him to the elevator, which the three of them rode down to the basement-level parking garage. Dean was helped into the back of what he assumed was the same van that Janet and he had arrived in.

As soon as the doors closed, Dean pulled the blindfold off, but the interior of the van was as black as it had been earlier. When the engine started and they began moving, Dean groped around the floor, hoping to find paper and something to write with, so that he might record the turns they made and the approximate length of travel between each one, in order to get a crude idea of where he had been. But though he found a single square of thin paper under one of the benches, he was unable to locate a pen or a pencil. He tried to keep track nevertheless, but the disorientation produced by the darkness prevented him from being able to gauge the turns with any degree of certainty and he soon had to give up the attempt. He settled for trying to time the trip as best as he could and be alert for any clues along the way.

He noticed that, unlike the earlier trip, the return trip contained a toll booth, evident from the van's coming to a stop, then inching forward for the next several minutes before suddenly accelerating. Immediately thereafter, there was a downgrade, followed by the same echo sensation he had experienced on the way out. Then an incline, leaving Dean with the distinct impression that they had, as before, emerged from a tunnel.

Once again, the trip took roughly a half hour. As Rasmussen opened the back doors of the van, Dean shielded his eyes to protect them from the light he expected to stream in, but he was surprised to find that it was dark outside. He lowered his hands and recognized his own street, his own building.

Rasmussen left Dean with a warning. "Don't do anything dumb, Abernathy. There's a lotta people back in that room hoping you'll try."

"You tell them they're going to be disappointed, okay?"

"I'll tell 'em," Rasmussen said, "but they're not going to believe it. The betting is three-to-two you're going to get carried out before this thing's over."

Upstairs, Dean collapsed in exhaustion on his sofa and kicked off his sneakers. He emptied the contents of his pockets onto the floor next to him, slipped out of his jeans, and curled up on his side in a fetal position, hands between his knees. He had seen James Dean fall asleep that way in *Rebel Without a Cause*.

Had he been a counter of sheep, he might have reached three or four.

Sometime during the night, Joey Spadafino gets awakened from his sleep by the blinding beam of a flashlight. It takes him a few seconds to realize where he is. Then he recognizes the floor of his cell alongside his thin mattress and remembers he's in the Hole.

He shields his eyes with his hands to try to see who's holding the flashlight, but a sudden blow to his right side, just under his armpit, that he identifies as a kick, informs him that he's not supposed to see who his visitor is. He brings his knees up against his chest, readying himself for whatever kick or cut or blow's coming next. But instead of an attack, the second message is delivered in words.

"Spadafino," says a voice he doesn't recognize but which bears the unmistakable arrogance of a CO or someone else in power, "you betta not make waves, you hear? You take that time served and you keep your fuckin' mouth shut. Anything else, you're one dead Eye-talian. Got it?"

Joey's afraid to answer, so he doesn't. A second kick, to the same spot as before but even harder, causes him to cry out.

"Yessir," he manages to say to the flashlight, "I got it."

Only later, after the CO has left him alone with his broken ribs and is out of earshot, does Joey manage to mutter his answer. "Fuck you and all your asshole buddies" is what he says.

Dean half awoke during the night to the sound of rain. He was vaguely aware that he'd been dreaming of castles and dungeons, of knights on white horses and damsels in distress. He rolled over and kept his eyes tightly closed, fighting off the impulse to look at the clock, knowing that no matter what time it turned out to be, his awareness of the hour would then keep him awake. Instead he listened to the raindrops landing on top of his air conditioner until exhaustion settled over him again.

The same rain that falls on the west side of Manhattan also falls on Rikers Island. But Joey Spadafino, locked down in the Hole, is unaware of it. Joey's also unaware that in addition to the broken ribs he suffered when he was kicked in his side, he's sustained a partially punctured lung, the result of a tiny sliver of rib piercing the lower lobe of his right lung. He knows something is wrong, because along with the knifelike pain in his side that gets worse every time he moves, he's having trouble breathing. It isn't so much that he can't breathe—he can, though it hurts—as that his breaths somehow fail to supply him with enough air.

TWENTY-FIVE

Dean awoke to darkness. This time he allowed himself to look. The little dots blinked repeatedly at 4:45, and after a while he wondered if the clock might be broken. But at some point, though he missed the transition, he noticed it was finally blinking 4:46. He knew it was September and decided the darkness meant it had to be morning. The ache in his lower back told him he'd spent another night on his sofa.

Many years ago, as a college student, Dean had got very drunk one night, a rarity for him even then. At one point he'd sat down hard and heard a crunch from the vicinity of his back pants pocket. Upon inspection, he realized he'd sat on his reading glasses, smashing both lenses. The following morning, he'd awakened with a terrible hangover, but somehow remembered his glasses. He'd groped around for them, hoping they'd been broken only in some dream, and that now, in the morning, they'd be intact. The sight of shattered glass had assured him it had been no dream.

Now the memory of leaving Janet locked up in some strange building came back to him, and for a moment he lay in the dark, trying to transform the events of the previous evening into a dream. But it hadn't worked in college, and it didn't work now. He needed no broken glasses to tell him that it had all been real—Leo

Silvestri, Bennett Childs, the ride in the van with Janet, and the ride home without her.

He swung his feet to the floor, managed to get to a more or less standing position, and steered himself toward the shower.

The warm water felt good against his skin, and slowly his eyes began to focus and his mind to clear. But with the clearing came the full recollection of the previous day's events and the sobering realization that at this very moment Janet was being held hostage, and Dean didn't even have a clue where she was. All he knew was that it was time for him to make another trip to Rikers Island to talk some sense into Joey Spadafino.

He dried off, made a pot of strong coffee, and drank two cups of it, black and sweet. He got dressed, grabbed his wallet and the keys to his Jeep, and headed downstairs.

By Sunday morning the pain in Joey's side isn't quite as bad as it was the night before, but he feels like he's leaking air when he breathes. When his breakfast tray is delivered around seven o'clock, he asks the CO to put his name on the list to see the doctor. The CO grunts something Joey can't make out.

At the corner newsstand, Dean picked up a copy of the Sunday *Times* out of habit. He was a crossword enthusiast. He limited himself to one puzzle a week, but that was the one in the Sunday *Times* magazine section, and he cherished it. He did it clipped to a piece of masonite board. He did it in ink. Well, sort of: he did it with an erasable pen. And he did it, more often than not, to completion. He knew that a "Loan follower" was a "shark," that "Pay the pot" called for "ante," and that the "Heavenly hunter" was "Orion." He loved clever themes, hated stepquotes, and could usually intuitively tell from the clues whether the author was a man or a woman, before looking to see if he was right.

Tossing the paper onto the backseat of the Jeep, Dean doubted he'd get around to opening it before the day was over, much less doing the crossword puzzle. His thoughts returned to reality and to Janet. Her reward for being a responsible citizen had been to be locked up as a hostage, separated from her daughter and completely cut off from the rest of the world. How could he have involved her in all of this? How could he have let things reach a point where her very life was now in danger? They sure didn't teach you about stuff like this in law school.

He pulled away from the curb and headed uptown for the Triborough Bridge. A quick check of his rearview mirror assured him that he'd have company on the trip. He figured that would be pretty much the case from now on.

At the first red light, Dean got out of the Jeep and walked directly to the tan Pontiac that had pulled up behind him. The "client" Dean had thought was named Bobby McGrane was driving; Dean didn't recognize the man in the passenger seat, but knew he had to be one of them, too.

"In case we get separated," Dean said, "I'm going to Rikers Island."

"Thanks," Bobby said, shifting a toothpick he'd been chewing on from one side of his mouth to the other. "'Preciate it."

"You look lousy, Joey." It was something Dean hated to tell anyone in jail. Inmates had enough to deal with without having to worry that they might be sick, too, and Dean tended to go out of his way to tell them they looked good, even when they didn't. But the truth was, Joey looked worse than lousy.

"Yeah, I'm not doin' so good," Joey wheezed, shifting his position in his chair.

"Maybe you should see a doctor. Really."

"Yeah, later. What's new with the case?"

"Lots," Dean said. He'd spent the drive planning just how he'd tell Joey about the new development. Normally, when there was a new plea offer in a case, Dean would present it to his client as an option to going to trial, and he intended to do that with Joey. At the same time, he'd decided he had absolutely no intention of taking this case to trial if there was the slightest chance it could cost Janet her life. Furthermore, he'd decided that Joey had no need to know everything that went into Dean's reasoning: Joey's decision needn't be based on Janet's safety, or even Dean's; those considerations could only serve to complicate things for him and prevent him from doing what was in his own best interest. What Dean owed Joey was a simple, straightforward presentation of his choices, and that was what he'd give him. But he was also going to do it in a way that dictated the outcome.

In other words, he was going to make Joey an offer he couldn't refuse.

So when Joey asked, "So how do my chances look at trial?" Dean's answer was direct and to the point.

"There's not going to be a trial, Joey. I got you petit larceny and time served." Even as he said the words, Dean knew he should be presenting it as an alternative and not as a fait accompli. But he didn't care. It was over and Dean knew it. He told himself it wasn't a weakness to know when to fold, it was a strength.

"What's the catch?" Joey asked. Apparently he didn't share this particular strength of Dean's.

"There's no catch. It's a lesser included charge under the robbery count. And it's exactly what you did: You didn't rob anyone, but you did steal money. That's larceny."

"And if I still don't wanna cop out? If I refuse?"

"You're not hearing me, Joey. I'm walking you out of here tomorrow morning. No strings, no probation, no parole. Time served on a misdemeanor. It's over. We won."

"No trial?"

"No trial."

"How come?"

This one made Dean hesitate. But he decided he could make an end run around it and answer it without really answering it. After all, that was what lawyers did, wasn't it?

"Because if we were to have a trial it's what might very well happen anyway," Dean explained. "I think we'd be able to prove that Wilson was already dead when you took his money. The judge would have to dismiss all the other charges. The jury would end up finding you guilty of petit larceny. Same result. Only this way it's risk free."

Joey seemed lost in thought for a moment. Dean was frankly surprised he hadn't fallen all over himself jumping at the opportunity to walk out of jail. But he figured Joey'd been through a lot and wasn't exactly a rocket scientist to begin with. So there was no need to bully him. Let him think about it for a minute, let him feel like it was his own decision to take the plea, rather than Dean's forcing it on him.

But when at last Joey spoke, it was to ask another question, one Dean wasn't ready for. Joey, the street kid, the ex-con who'd never gone past ninth grade and hadn't even earned his high school equivalency diploma upstate, who could barely read and write, and who knew everything there was to know about prison sentences but nothing about grammatical ones, said, "What aren't you tellin' me here, Dean?" He closed his eyes as he said it, as though he were in pain.

It was the last question in the world Dean wanted to hear. Because this one couldn't be sidestepped; this one left no room for another narrow, evasive interpretation. So Dean tried the only thing left: He countered with a question of his own, pretending he hadn't heard what Joey had asked, hoping that if he ignored Joey's question it might simply go away.

"So what do you say, Joey?" he said.

"I say, what aren't you tellin' me?"

It hadn't gone away. Which meant, in the strange world of legal ethics that Dean took so seriously, that Joey, having asked, now clearly had the right to know. And that Dean had been trapped. He no longer enjoyed the luxury—or had the right, when it came down to it—to keep from his client what he himself knew. Ethics could get in the way like that sometimes.

He took a deep breath. "Joey," he said, "not only did the police forge your signature on the confession to make it look like Commissioner Wilson died of a heart attack while you were mugging him, they did more. They've gotten rid of one witness who saw you didn't mug him, and they're threatening to kill another one if we expose them."

"Who?"

"The woman."

"The one who lied first?" Joey asked.

Dean nodded absently.

"She's tellin' the truth now?" Again Joey seemed to wince.

"Yes," Dean said. He felt suddenly too tired to explain to Joey how there were two Janet Killians. It was all too complicated, too difficult.

"Can't she hide out?" Joey asked. For him, there were always answers.

"It's too late for that. They're holding her hostage somewhere. We expose them, they'll kill her."

"Where do they got her?"

"I don't know." Dean's voice cracked slightly as he said it.

"How come they're doin' all this?"

Here it comes, thought Dean, here it all comes. But there was no turning back now.

"Because they're the ones who killed Wilson," he said softly. "He wasn't drunk when you saw him coming up the block, he was dying. They'd already poisoned him."

Joey said nothing. Maybe he was too sick to be understanding this. Maybe it was all too much for him. They sat in silence for a while.

"What you're sayin'," Joey said finally, "is that they killed the guy themselves, an' now we're sposed to protect them."

Dean had to smile. "Something like that."

Again, Joey didn't speak right away. It was almost as though his brain worked in slow motion. It seemed to take extra time for Dean's words to sink in, for a response to then occur to Joey, and for the response to finally find its way back into spoken words. Dean found himself wondering if it was the years of drugs, or the alcohol, or the cold nights on the street that had taken their toll, or being sick or hurt or whatever Joey was now, or some combination of all of those things and much, much more.

"This woman," Joey said after a while. "She somethin' special to you?"

Slow maybe, but not stupid.

Dean didn't say anything. Joey seemed to take that for an answer. Maybe drugs and alcohol weren't so bad for you, after all.

"I guess there's nothin' I can do," Joey said. "Me bein' in here and all."

Dean thought he might have missed something. "What does your being in here have to do with anything?"

"I'm locked up. *You're* not." He winced again, shifting positions in his chair.

"So what's that supposed to mean?" Dean asked.

"It means if *I* was on the street, I'd fuckin'-A find her ass and spring her so's we could go to trial and nail those fuckin' cocksuckers. That's what that means."

"I told you, Joey. I don't even know where they've got her."

"Hey, you the one seen they copied my signature?"

"Yes." Dean nodded wearily.

"You the one figgered out it wasn't me who killed the guy?"

"Yes."

"You the one solved this whole thing, came up with the idea the cops killed the guy themselves, even know it was fuckin' *poison* they give him?"

Dean nodded again.

"An you mean to say after all that you can't find one lousy fuckin' broad?"

Dean said nothing. But Joey didn't seem to care; he was on a roll now.

"Me, *I'd* find her, Dean. That's what *I'd* fuckin' do."

"Easy for you to say" was all Dean could think to mutter.

"*Easy?*" said Joey. "*Easy? Nothin's easy* here, man. It ain't easy to fart in here, or take a shit, or close your fuckin' eyes without some dude maybe comin' up behind you an' stickin' a knife three feet up your ass. *Easy?* You wanna swap places with me for twenny-four hours? You come sit here in the fuckin' Hole, man. I'll go find the broad. How 'bout that? I'll show you *easy!*" When he stopped talking, it seemed more like he was out of air than out of anger.

Dean was too tired for the lecture.

"Joey," he said, "I give up. You tell me: Do you want the time served or not?"

"No, I don't want the time served! They can offer me the Congressional Fuckin' Medal of Honor, and I don't want it. I want a trial," Joey hissed. "I want a trial where we can stick it to those bastards just like they been stickin' it to me. Only diffrence is they're dirty. They got it comin' to them, an' I didn't."

Outside the interview room was a small waiting area, and since it was still pretty early on a Sunday morning, it was empty, except for a row of plastic chairs, a soda machine with a cardboard OUT OF ORDER sign, and a pay telephone on the wall. Bobby McGrane and his friend had apparently been satisfied to wait by Dean's Jeep in the parking lot, where they'd pulled in alongside him.

Dean collapsed onto one of the chairs, overcome by fatigue. He'd come out to Rikers Island to get Joey's decision, and he'd gotten it. Only it was the wrong decision, the exact opposite of what Dean had tried so hard to push Joey into doing. Dean had made Joey an offer he couldn't possibly refuse, but Joey had refused it. And what was worse, Dean knew that in some way Joey was right. Not for Dean, and certainly not for Janet, who stood to die because of it. But some small part of Dean knew that what Joey had said made perfect sense for Joey. The same cops who'd been ready to frame Joey and put him away for the rest of his life without a second thought were now asking him to come to their rescue and protect them from the deserved consequences of their own murderous acts. And Joey wanted no part of it. Who could really blame him when you looked at it that way?

But in the process, Joey was turning down an opportunity to walk out a free man, and making a choice that—for somebody charged with murder—was almost unheard of. Dean tried to put himself in Joey's position but found it all but impossible. Who knew? Maybe freedom wasn't all that it was cracked up to be when you were on the street, with summer over and nothing but cold weather ahead. Maybe it was having all of life's good stuff stripped away, until you were left like Joey Spadafino, without all that much to gain or lose one way or the other, truly free to figure out what was the right thing to do.

But where did that leave Janet?

Dean stood up and tried to fend off the panic that accompanied the thought. Ignoring the OUT OF ORDER sign on the soda machine, he inserted three quarters, stepped back, and gave it a solid kick with the bottom of his shoe. A can of Pepsi dropped into the opening with a pleasing *thud!* He opened it, drained half of it in a single swallow, and pinched the bridge of his nose to deal with the sudden pain from the cold. Then he walked to the pay phone and, using the rest of his change, dialed the number Janet had given him to phone her sister.

"Hello," answered a woman who could have been Janet herself.

"Hi," said Dean. "I've got a message from your sister."

"Yes?"

"That little package we had sent out to you yesterday?"

"Yes?"

"Did it arrive?"

"Yes, it did."

"How is it?"

"Just fine. A little damp at first, but just fine."

"Good," said Dean. "Please listen carefully. Your sister needs you to take care of it for a while. She can't call you, and it's important that you don't try to call her. In fact, it might be safest for you to move the package somewhere else altogether, where no-body'll know where it is. Understand?"

"I think so. Is she okay?"

"She's fine," he lied, trying to sound as reassuring as he could. "Can you do this for her?"

"Yes, I can," the woman said with an air of competence that told Dean there was more to the sisters' resemblance than a simi-lar voice.

In the parking lot, Dean stopped by the two cops sitting in the tan Pontiac. His "client" Bobby McGrane sat behind the wheel, sip-ping from a container of coffee. Bobby had gotten rid of the toothpick, but now he had powdered sugar and a drop of purple jelly on one side of his mouth.

"I'm going home, fellas," Dean said. "And you can tell your people that their dirty little secret is going to be safe. My client will take the time served. He was thrilled." He figured this bit of misdirection might take some heat off Janet for a while.

Bobby wiped his mouth with the back of his hand and smiled. "Smart boy," he said.

"Yeah, I guess he is," Dean agreed.

"Not him. You."

Back at his apartment, Dean went into his manic phase and began straightening up. He figured the activity might make him forget Janet and her predicament for an hour or so.

He gathered all the dishes and glasses that had somehow worked their way into the living room over the past week. He washed them, along with friends of theirs that were already in the kitchen sink. In the living room, he turned over the cushions on the sofa and fluffed them so they didn't look quite so slept on. He picked up the loose change, paper clips, and a scrap of paper he had left on the floor the night before. He looked at the scrap of paper, recognized it as a credit card slip for the purchase of gaso-line, but couldn't remember where it had come from. Certainly it wasn't his; he didn't own any gas credit cards. He read the writing on the slip,

KELLY'S FRIENDLY MOBIL STATION
1050 Pearson Blvd.
Jersey City, NJ

21.7 GALS $25.00

and wondered how it had ended up in his apartment. It was a lot of gas, he thought. His Jeep held only fifteen gallons, most cars no more than twenty. More likely a truck or a bus. And suddenly he remembered the van: it was the scrap of paper he'd found in his blind search of the back of the van. He looked at it again. Jersey City was just the other side of the Holland Tunnel. Dean remembered the tunnel he was certain they had gone through. They had paid a toll only on the return trip to Manhattan, a fact that eliminated the Brooklyn Battery Tunnel and the Midtown Tunnel to Queens, but was consistent with the Holland and Lincoln Tunnels, both of which had one-way tolls. The Lincoln Tunnel had a long, spiraling ramp on the Jersey side, and Dean had no recollection of being aware of such a feature on either trip. That, plus the Jersey City gas receipt, convinced him that it had to have been the Holland Tunnel they'd used.

Dean felt his heart pumping in his chest. God damn it, Joey had been right. Dean *was* going to find Janet! Already he had a start, and starting was always the hardest part, wasn't it? The rest would be easy.

But what else did he have? An office building of seven stories, not too far from the Jersey side of the Holland Tunnel. Not much to work with. But there was the name, Dean suddenly remembered, the name on the door of one of the offices off the seventh-floor corridor. Only thing was, he couldn't remember it.

He resorted to a time-tested method. He began working his way slowly through the alphabet, A, B, C, D, E, F— At F, he felt a definite tug. He continued through, experiencing a similar feeling at T. He repeated the process, again getting a strong positive response at F. He added vowels to create sounds, trying FA, FE— and immediately came up with Ferguson, and knew in an instant it was right. There'd been initials with it, and they came back to him quickly as D. M., which he had associated at the time he saw them on the door with the author D. M. Thomas, an association Dean now realized probably explained the positive reaction he'd felt at the letter T.

Having no desire to forget the name he'd retrieved, Dean wrote "D. M. Ferguson" on the back of the gasoline receipt and pocketed it. He knew it wasn't much, but, along with a general location, it was all he had. Then he went next door and rang the bell to the apartment of Everett and Val.

An affected "Who *is* it?" answered from within.

"Dean."

The door swung open and Everett greeted him with a "Dean, how *are* you?" and ushered him in with a theatrical sweep of his arm. Val was in the living room, talking on the phone, but took time to wave and blow Dean a kiss. Everett, a choreographer whose last name Dean didn't know, and Val, a best boy in the the film industry who used the last name Halla, were lovers, two gracefully aging hippies who'd been lucky enough, or careful enough—or perhaps both—to have escaped the decimation of the city's gay population, spared to live out their lives in a contented, if not legally recognized, monogamy. They were also good neighbors and animated conversationalists, and Dean had spent more than a few evening hours with them, trading stories from their very different worlds. They found his work as a defender of the downtrodden noble and exciting, and were thrilled to learn that he'd come to ask for their help.

"What sort of help?" Val asked, his phone call completed.

"Well, I'm being followed, for one thing. And I'm pretty sure my phone is tapped. So for starters, I'd like to use your phone to make some calls, or maybe even have you make them for me. Then, I may need your help getting out of the building without being spotted."

"Who's after you?" Everett asked. "The Mafia? Arab terrorists? Extraterrestrials?"

"The police, I'm afraid."

"Oh, wow!" Val exclaimed. "Of *course* we'll help you!"

They spent the next hour taking turns making phone calls. They started calling New Jersey Information to see if there was a Jersey City listing, either business or residential, for a D. M. Ferguson or a D. Ferguson; there wasn't. They got out a road map and expanded their search to Newark and Bayonne, but although there was a number of Fergusons, none of those listed had the first initial D. When they tried Hoboken, however, they struck it rich. There were several Fergusons, but one in particular interested them. The good news was that it was right on the money: a business listing for a D. M. Ferguson. The bad news was quick to follow.

"I'm sorry, that number is unlisted at the subscriber's request."

"How about the address?" Dean asked. "Can you at least give me that?"

"I'm afraid we can't give that out, either." The next thing Dean heard was a dial tone.

"Great," Dean muttered. "No number, no address."

"What kind of business has an unlisted number?" Everett asked.

"A police kind of business," Dean said.

Dean put in a call to Jimmy McDermott. Until recently, Mc-Dermott had been an agent with ATF, the federal agency that investigated violations of the alcohol/tobacco taxes and firearms laws. Too much drinking and too many women had led to an early retirement for McDermott, and now he did some private investigating between binges. Dean called him because Jimmy still had contacts in the government and with many of the agencies and utilities with which it dealt, and because when he was sober he was good.

The phone answered on the fifth ring.

"McDermott." It sounded like the one word was all he could manage.

"Are you awake?" Dean asked.

"Who wants to know?"

"Dean Abernathy. How you doing, Jimmy?"

"I was doing good till you woke me up. What time is it?"

"About one o'clock," Dean said.

"What day?"

"About Sunday."

"Wow." He sounded truly surprised.

"What were you hoping for?"

"No, no," said McDermott, "Sunday's okay. Sunday's good."

"You all right?"

"Yeah. Who is this?"

"Dean. Dean Abernathy." It was becoming apparent that this wasn't going to work.

"Hey, Dean! Whatsup?"

"I need you to check out something for me, Jimmy. But only if I can really count on you. What do you think?"

"Gimme fifteen, Dean? I'll call you back."

Dean gave him Val and Everett's number before hanging up. Dubiously, he looked at his watch. Then he opened his address book and began looking through it for other investigators. He'd give Jimmy twenty minutes, but no more.

The phone rang in less than ten. Val handed it to Dean.

"Hi, Dean. Jimmy McDermott here. What can I do for you?" Cold sober, wide-awake, all business. Amazing, thought Dean.

"Jimmy, I've got a name of a business—or at least the name of some guy with his name on the door of an office—in Hoboken. I need an address. In the worst way."

"Try the phone company?"

"Yeah," Dean said. "Unlisted number, unlisted address."

"Gimme what you got."

Dean gave him the name, D. M. Ferguson, and the city, Hoboken. Even as he did so, he was struck by how little he had to work with.

"That's it?"

"That's it. That and the fact that he's on the seventh floor."

"In Hoboken."

"In Hoboken."

"I always like a challenge," said McDermott. "I'll be back to you within the hour, okay?"

"Thanks, Jimmy."

"No problem."

"Problem."

It was Jimmy McDermott on the phone.

"I got a source that can always get me these things," he said, "and I mean always. Only not this one. It comes back no public record, refer all inquiries to 212–374–6710. So I call it. Turns to be a number at One Police Plaza, for the fuckin' chief of operations. I hang up, figured I better check with you first. You in some kinda trouble, Dean?"

"Not exactly."

"Okay, so then I try PSE&G. That's the utility company that serves Hoboken. No record. Dunn and Bradstreet, TRW: no record. Postal Service Inspector General's Office: no record. Department of Motor Vehicles: no record. Who is this guy, the Fuckin' Phantom of the Opera?"

"Worse: NYPD brass. The whole floor of the building, evidently. And all of them wrong."

"I'll check with the Department of State in Trenton first thing in the morning," McDermott said. "But we both know what they're going to tell me."

"No record."

"Ten-four," McDermott agreed. "You get me a phone number, Dean, even an unlisted one—I don't care—I'll get you an address. But until then, no can do. I'm at a dead end."

Which made two of them.

Joey Spadafino finally sees the doctor at eight-thirty Sunday night, twenty hours after being kicked in the ribs and thirteen and a half hours after he'd asked to be seen. A small dark man who wears a turban and speaks little English, the doctor places a stethoscope against Joey's back and listens for several minutes before writing "posibil pneumothorax" on a piece of paper in the blank that calls for diagnosis. In the space calling for treatment he writes "obsurve"; under cause he notes "fall"; and under Rx he prescribes "Tylenol t.i.d." Quite aside from his spelling, his handwriting is almost impossible to read, not only because he's a doctor and has been taught poor penmanship in medical school, but because throughout the examination he wears three pairs of latex gloves. As a result, no one will check the inmate thereafter for a pneumothorax, and no one will "obsurve" him. But he will get some Tylenol.

Back in his cell, Joey can do nothing more than avoid exerting himself, which is easy, and try to find a comfortable position, which he finds all but impossible. In spite of the fact that in the outside world his condition would be considered life-threatening and require emergency surgery to repair the lung puncture, and antibiotics and a drain to ward off infection, Joey's left to himself with nothing but a couple of pills for his pain. He lies down on his bunk, hugging his arms tightly around his sides for support, trying to find a position where he can breathe. He knows he's due in court in the morning, and he wants to get an hour or two of sleep before four-thirty, when they'll wake him up for the bus.

TWENTY-SIX

With his name on the court list and no notation on his card that he might be too sick to travel, Joey Spadafino's awakened for the bus to Manhattan Supreme Court at four thirty-five Monday morning. And it's okay with him. It's been seven months since the memory of his arrest on a snowy night in late January. Winter's ended, and so has Spring. Summer's come and gone, and though it's been weeks since he's seen the light of day, Joey figures it must be September, and that means his case is finally about to begin for real. So in spite of his fatigue, in spite of his weakness, in spite of the continuing aching in his ribs, in spite of the fact that he's facing a murder charge and the real possibility of a twenty-five-year-to-life prison sentence, he's ready.

The media was back in full force. Dean knew it even before he entered the courthouse. Two network vans with telescoping antennas, one from *Eyewitness News* and the other from *Live at Five*, were parked right on the sidewalk in front of the courthouse steps. Dean wondered cynically what would happen if he ever tried to park there. "Freedom of the press" had its own perks, he guessed.

Blue wooden barricades had been set up, extra police and court officers were everywhere, and long lines of the curious waited to pass through the metal detectors on their way into the building.

The eleventh floor was no better. Lights were turned on and cameras aimed at Dean as soon as he got off the elevator. Microphones were thrust at his face before he could make his way to the door of the courtroom.

"Is there going to be a plea?" Ralph Penza wanted to know.

"We hear your client's been offered some kind of a deal," Magee Hickey said, hoping for some word of confirmation or denial. "Is that true?"

"Is he going to take it?"

"Are you going to trial?"

Dean smiled at all the attention but could think of nothing better to say than "We'll have to see." Not exactly the kind of stuff to get him on the six o'clock news, he knew, but at least he'd avoided the sinister "No comment." But if the media appreciated the distinction, their disappointed faces failed to register it.

Things were a little calmer inside the courtroom, but not much. The rows were rapidly filling up, with many of the seats occupied by uniformed police officers displaying an abundance of braids and stripes. The brass had turned out in force to make a strong show of support, ostensibly for their fallen leader. But Dean had his doubts that they were there out of some heartfelt loyalty to Commissioner Wilson; he strongly suspected that their presence had a much darker motivation to it, more like intimidation, with Joey and Dean himself as the objects. He made a mental note to object to their presence if they ever got far enough to pick a jury. He shuddered at the thought that he might actually have to go through with the trial.

Judge Rothwax entered from a side door, and the room fell silent. Dean hadn't been aware of the noise level until that moment. Elizabeth, the clerk, caught Dean's eye and seemed to be asking if he was ready to have the case called. He was about to signal her to wait for Walter Bingham to arrive when he felt Walter come up alongside him. He nodded to Elizabeth.

"What's it going to be, Dean?" Walter asked him in a whisper.

"I don't really know," Dean said. "I gave it my best shot. He seems to have the feeling somebody's been fucking with him. Though I can't imagine where he could be getting that idea from."

"You can tell him if he thinks he's being fucked with now, he doesn't know what fucking is."

There was a collective murmur from the audience as Joey Spadafino was led in. He walked slightly bent over and seemed to Dean to settle into his chair with difficulty. One of the six burly court officers surrounding him pushed Joey's chair all the way up forward, until its arms met the edge of the table, forming a wooden box of sorts that enclosed him, as though otherwise he might be tempted to make a break for it.

Judge Rothwax banged his gavel and Elizabeth called the case into the record. "Calendar number one, for trial, *People versus Joseph Spadafino.*" The lawyers stepped forward and gave their appearances to the court reporter.

"Come up on this, please," said Judge Rothwax. Dean and Bingham approached. As always, Dean was struck by Bingham's height; he could easily have fit into the NBA. The room grew quieter still, as spectators strained to catch some bit of the conversation at the bench.

"This case is on for trial," Rothwax said, keeping his voice low. "I understand there have been some plea discussions. Where do we stand?"

It was Bingham who responded. "Where we stand is, we've come to believe we may have some difficulty with certain technical aspects of our medical proof. There could be an issue as to the proximate cause of Commissioner Wilson's death. After a lot of soul-searching, we're offering the defendant a plea to petit larceny, with a sentence of time served. We're waiting to hear from him."

Rothwax turned to Dean. "Mr. Abernathy?"

"My client tells me he'd like a trial."

This seemed to shock even the usually unflappable Harold Rothwax. "Let me get this straight. Mr. Bingham recites some incomprehensible mumbo jumbo dealing with civil law issues that's supposed to appease me. But for whatever reason, he ends up offering Mr. Spadafino time served. No doubt he got the approval of supervisors in his office before he did that. What their thinking is, I can't begin to fathom. But so be it. And now, if I understand correctly, Mr. Spadafino, not to be outdone, exercises his own brilliant judgment and tops Mr. Bingham by saying, 'No, thank you, I'd prefer to do twenty-five to life.'"

"He didn't put it quite that way," Dean said, smiling. "But yes, essentially it goes something like that."

Rothwax shook his head and rolled his eyes in exaggerated disbelief. "All right," he said, "step back and we'll go on the record before all these reporters sue me for violating their constitutional right to make a living."

The lawyers walked back to their respective tables.

"Let the record reflect," Rothwax said in his stage voice, "that we've had a discussion at the bench, and during the course of that discussion, the People have conveyed a plea offer to the defendant, a very generous plea offer, I might add. The defendant is considering that offer. He shall have exactly twenty-four hours to do so. This case is adjourned to tomorrow morning. At that time the defendant will either accept the offer, or it will be withdrawn and we will begin the hearing and the trial in this case. Mr. Spadafino, you may go in now."

Back at his office, Dean forced himself to face the possibility, however ludicrous, that there was going to be a trial after all. He organized his file for the umpteenth time, checking in particular to see that the physical evidence he'd be needing was in order. It was all there: the blow-ups of Joey's signatures and the handwriting expert's report confirming the forgery, the toxicology and serology reports, the literature on dibenzepene, even the copies he'd kept of the original S. letters from Officer Santana. He removed these items from the file and inserted them in a separate manila envelope, which he sealed shut. On the outside of it he wrote the word AMMUNITION.

He prepared affirmations to give to other judges before whom he'd be expected to appear while the Spadafino trial was going on. He got out some letters and motions on other cases. He returned a few messages and paid some bills that were long overdue.

At some point it occurred to him to wonder why Judge Rothwax had given them the extra day before starting the trial. Everyone had been ready, after all, and the press had been champing at the bit. It wasn't like Rothwax to put something off for no reason.

Was he simply hoping that Joey would come around to his senses? Did he have some personal scheduling conflict? Or was there possibly some more complex motive to his action?

Dean smiled at the notion and dismissed it. There was enough of a conspiracy going on without involving the judge in it. Harold Rothwax was the last person in the world who'd make himself a party to something like this.

Nonetheless, before leaving for the day, he yielded to his rising level of paranoia. He picked up the envelope he'd marked AMMUNITION. He knew he wouldn't be needing it for several days, until after jury selection was completed and they were into the testimony itself. He looked around his office for a place to hide it. He settled for dropping it behind the couch that sat against the far wall. It'd been years since anyone had moved the couch. The notion that it *could* be moved had probably never even occurred to Martha the cleaning woman, who seemed to have enough trouble emptying wastebaskets and ashtrays.

Joey Spadafino has trouble falling asleep. The Hole's noisy with groans from other cells and the comings and goings of the CO's. Joey's ribs ache, and he's found he can only take little breaths without his insides hurting.

But it's more than that that's keeping him awake. In the past, every time he went to court, Joey's case has been put over for two or three weeks at a time, sometimes for as long as a month. It got so he felt like that would go on forever, that the trial date would always be pushed further and further away.

He once saw a TV documentary about animals they use to carry supplies through the jungle. They showed mules that would walk forward trying to get to a bag of oats, not realizing that the bag was attached to their own bodies by a long pole. Every step the mules took, the bag took a step too, so the mules never got to catch up with the oats. But they kept walking toward them anyway.

All this time Joey's felt like one of those mules, coming to court and getting a new date, only to have the date move away from him each time.

Only now it seems he's about to catch up to his oats, and the thought scares him. He tries to remind himself that he didn't kill anybody, that he didn't even rob anybody. He wonders if that'll be enough to save him, decides it will be only if it turns out that there's a God. Though Joey's never believed in God, he now says out loud, "Please, God, make 'em stop fuckin' with me. Lemme go home." He's able to say it out loud because the other noises drown out his voice. Otherwise, he would've had to say it to himself.

Joey wishes his father could be in court for him. He remembers a time, years ago, when he was a boy, before there was reefer and booze and drugs and hustling and jail, when his father took him to an airport to meet his uncle, who was flying in from Chicago or Indianapolis or somewhere else in Michigan, and Joey had seen pilots walking through the airport, in groups of two or three, in these terrific uniforms, with hats and medals and gold buttons and all kinds of stuff. They were all very tall and handsome, he remembers even now. And he had told his father then that that's what he wanted to be when he grew up: a jet pilot. And his father had laughed at him, had told him that Italians didn't pilot jet planes, they piloted garbage trucks. Joey had laughed, too, at the time, figuring it must have been a funny joke he wasn't old enough to get. He thinks about it now and isn't sure he gets it still, after all these years. He figures it's a pretty good bet he'll never even get to pilot a garbage truck, though.

TWENTY-SEVEN

The corrections officer who wakes Joey up Tuesday morning tells him to pack all his belongings to bring with him, because when he's finished in court at the end of the day he'll be going to the Tombs instead of coming back to Rikers.

"How come?" Joey asks.

"They've marked your card 'On Trial,'" the CO tells him. "Guess this is the big show for you, Spadafino."

Bringing all his belongings turns out to be relatively easy for Joey, since he has none, except for a toothbrush, a tube of toothpaste, a bar of soap, a washcloth, and a safety razor he's been issued.

Joey washes and brushes his teeth. He tries to smooth his hair, but it's messed up from the way he slept. He finds a plastic bag to put his toilet articles in. He's handcuffed and led to the bus for the trip to Manhattan. But when he goes to climb up the steps onto the bus, Joey suddenly feels lightheaded from the pain in his side, and he has to hold the sides of the door for a moment while his head clears.

"Yo, man, I don't need anotha muthafucking malingerer," the CO driver yells at him. Even though it's well before six in the morning, it's already close to eighty degrees, and dark sweat marks show at the armpits of the CO's blue jacket, part of the regulation winter uniform he's required to wear now since it's after Labor Day.

Joey doesn't know what a malingerer is, but he knows what muthafucking means, so he doesn't wait for an explanation. He manages to pull himself up the steps and says, "Sorry, I'm okay."

"Well, isn't that wonderful," says the CO, who removes one of a half-dozen pairs of handcuffs he wears clipped to his belt and handcuffs Joey's wrists to the bar that's part of the seatback in front of him. Because the CO's pissed off, he cuffs Joey too tightly, but Joey knows better than to complain: There's too tight, and there's much too tight.

The bus is only three-quarters full, but it turns out that's 'cause they have to make another stop. They follow the Brooklyn-Queens Expressway into Brooklyn, where they pick up three more inmates at Kings County Hospital. One of the three is a total psycho the COs call Luther, who screams and carries on the entire rest of the trip to Manhattan. As best as Joey can figure out, Luther thinks he's still in Vietnam, being driven back to the front lines, even though both of his legs have been blown off by a grenade. From time to time Joey sneaks a sideways glance at him—you don't want to let a guy like that catch you staring at him—but he can't see anything wrong with Luther's legs. As he's getting off the bus at 100 Centre Street, Joey asks one of the COs, not the driver, what's wrong with the guy's legs.

"Ain't nothin' wrong with his legs," the CO laughs. "Not only that, but he ain't never been in no Nam, neither. But the shrinks don't care—they says he's just fine. Certified his ass fit to stand trial. Lotta them shrinks they got at KCH, they'd certify a fuckin' radish fit to stand trial."

Joey's led up to the twelfth floor, where he's put in a holding pen with a dozen other prisoners. Luther is taken to a separate pen for observation cases, what the COs call obsos. They keep the obsos right next to the homos.

Dean spoke briefly with Joey in the pens, but Joey's resolve to go to trial had, if anything, only hardened. "They can carry me out in a fuckin' box for all I care, I ain't coppin' out," he said. "I ain't no obso, you know." Whatever that meant.

Back out in the courtroom, Dean told Judge Rothwax that there would be no plea. If the judge was surprised he didn't show it. "Be ready to call your first witness on the hearing at ten-thirty," he told Walter Bingham.

Joey's finally brought into court about eleven-fifteen. At first, the judge does a lot of talking, asking the two lawyers questions about the hearing that's about to begin. Dean's explained what the hearing's about, but now Joey can't seem to remember. He listens while the judge tells the people in the audience that any noise will result in ejection from the courtroom. It reminds Joey of being at a baseball game, where they announce that going onto the playing field or interfering with the ball in play will result in ejection. After repeating the word ejection *to himself several times it begins to sound, funny, and, despite the pain in his side, Joey smiles.*

"Is there something that strikes you as amusing about all this, Mr. Spadafino?" Joey suddenly hears the judge talking to him.

"No, sir," Joey says quickly, feeling like he's back in school and has been caught talking by the teacher. He promises himself not to smile anymore. He tries hard after that to pay attention, but the judge and the lawyers discuss things he knows nothing about, using words he often doesn't understand.

Finally, a uniformed police officer Joey doesn't recognize but who will say he was the first officer on the scene is led into the courtroom from a side door. He takes the witness stand, places his hand on a black book, and swears to tell the truth, the whole truth, and nothing but the truth. So help him, God.

The hearing has begun.

With no front-page story of a plea bargain, the press instead found themselves forced to sit through the far less exciting business of covering the pre-trial hearing, and many of them left as soon as the word spread that no deal had been worked out. Their numbers would continue to dwindle as the morning wore on, and those who remained would fidget impatiently for the hearing to end and the trial itself to begin.

As for Dean, he found he had to fight hard to concentrate;

his thoughts constantly wandered to Janet and her predicament. Part of his frustration was that he knew he couldn't win any part of the hearing. At issue was the legality of the police conduct in the way they'd arrested Joey and recovered the knife from him, whether they'd properly advised him of his rights before questioning him, and how they'd had any witnesses identify him after his arrest without being too suggestive.

Since the defense had no right to a jury to determine such issues, Judge Rothwax would be the one to rule on whether or not Joey's rights had been violated. And given the tendency of most judges—Rothwax included—to believe police officers (or at least publicly profess to), Dean knew that the outcome was a foregone conclusion.

But the hearing was important to Dean for another reason. It served as a preview of sorts for much of the trial testimony. At the outset of the hearing, the prosecution was obliged to turn over to the defense all written reports and statements of any witnesses it intended to call at the hearing. In a major case, this amounted to a large volume of material and often provided important trial ammunition for the defense.

Beyond that, the hearing gave Dean a firsthand look at some of the same witnesses who'd later be testifying at trial. He could size them up, test their reactions to different types of cross-examination, and risk asking them the "dangerous" questions he'd hesitate to ask at a trial with a jury present, where an adverse answer might do serious damage to the defense.

Finally, the presence of a court reporter at the hearing ensured that everything the witnesses said was taken down word-for-word. At trial, Dean would have the testimony in transcript form, ready to impeach any witness who contradicted his or her earlier answers.

So for Dean it should have been a no-lose situation, an unchecked fishing expedition into Bingham's proof, and a golden opportunity to create a record to fall back upon later. Instead, with his thoughts constantly drifting to Janet, he found he had to do his best just to maintain concentration, and the day seemed to drag on forever.

Joey spends all day in court, listening as each witness called to the stand is questioned first by Walter Bingham and then by Dean.

The first officer on the scene describes how he and his partner were in their patrol car when they got a radio run telling them about a robbery in progress. They drove to Bleecker Street and found a man lying on the sidewalk. He seemed to them to be dead, but they called for an ambulance anyway. Why, Joey wonders, do you call for an ambulance for a dead man? Doesn't that mean the cop is lying? But he figures maybe it's procedure. They talk a lot about procedure during the hearing.

The cop who arrested Joey testifies. He makes it sound like he was some sort of hero, chasing Joey on foot like in a movie scene.

"He's fulla shit," Joey whispers to Dean. "I practically ran into the guy's fucking arms." But Dean tells him it doesn't matter, don't worry about it. The cop talks about searching Joey and finding the money and the knife on him. Then he tells how one of the witnesses showed up and said that Joey was the guy he saw bending over the man on Bleecker Street.

Next comes one of the detectives who questioned Joey. Rasmussen. Joey remembers him well. He says he read Joey his rights before questioning him.

"He's lying," Joey tells Dean. "He waited till after I made the statement before he gave me my rights." But again Dean tells him it makes no difference. Joey wonders if anything makes any difference. He begins to worry that maybe Dean is one of them. Then he catches himself and tells himself to stop getting crazy. But he can't help it. So much has happened since that night, so much has gone wrong, Joey knows anything is possible.

The last witness is a cop who was told by the detectives to go look through a trash can on Seventh Avenue. He did, he says, and he found the money clip, right where Joey said it would be. At first Joey feels good about that, since it shows he was telling the truth. Then he thinks maybe he's being stupid. After all, if the cops are the ones saying it, it must be bad for him.

Joey's beginning to learn.

Dean was exhausted by the time they finished with the final witness at ten of five. Judge Rothwax mercifully broke for the day, announcing that he'd render his decision Wednesday afternoon, during his calendar day, with jury selection scheduled to begin first thing Thursday.

*　　*　　*

From court Joey's taken to what is officially called the Manhattan Detention Center at 125 White Street but is commonly known as the Tombs.

Attached to 100 Centre Street, the Tombs is the jail of choice for both the correction officers who work there and the inmates who reside there. It's far smaller than the complex of buildings that make up Rikers Island, and it is rarely the scene of a disturbance. Because it's literally connected to the courthouse, inmates in the Tombs with cases at 100 Centre Street don't have to be awakened at four-thirty in the morning for a long bus trip to Manhattan, and they don't get back to their cells late at night. Finally, because of its location, the Tombs can easily be reached by all types of transportation, making visiting far easier for family members.

Whereas corrections officers can evidently use their seniority to get assigned to the Tombs, inmates aren't selected on that basis. Instead, though there's no official policy, the single thing that counts most, at least to Joey's eye, seems to be the color of your skin. And Joey's skin is definitely the right color.

Although he's done nothing but sit in court all day, Joey's too tired and in too much pain to eat, and he asks to be excused from the chow line. He's placed on 4 North in a cell by himself. Although it's small, it's clean and actually has a bed with a mattress. Joey sits down on it, then lies down just to try it out. Within minutes he's asleep.

In his dream he's behind the wheel of a sleek silver garbage truck, his father sitting next to him, laughing. Joey feels younger, cleaner, less beat-up. They soar above the skyscrapers of Manhattan far below, heading over the clouds, out over the ocean. He turns to his father to tell him he was wrong, to show him he can fly after all, but his father's gone. Joey's all alone.

Dean hung around the courthouse until after six-thirty so he could get the transcript of the hearing testimony from the court reporters. He knew he could wait instead until the morning to pick it up, but he wanted to have it overnight to study, in case he'd missed anything important during his lapses of concentration.

So it was nearly seven when he got back to his office, exhausted, depressed, and worried more than ever about Janet. The front door was locked; evidently all of his suitemates had had the good sense to call it quits for the day. He found his keys and let himself in, noticing that whoever had been last to leave had neglected to double lock the outer door. He made his way to his corner office and flicked on the light switch.

"Hello, Dean."

Dean jumped and turned toward the voice. Sitting on his couch was Walter Bingham.

Dean's heart restarted itself. He forced himself to take a breath.

"Hello, Walter," he said, but his politeness masked a whole rush of thoughts. What was Bingham doing in his office? How long had be sitting here in the dark? How had he managed to get in in the first place? And what was going on *now?*

"Nice setup you've got here," Bingham said.

"Glad you approve," Dean said, taking off his jacket and draping it on a coat tree already overcrowded with several suits, a raincoat, and an assortment of ties and belts. "Something I can do for you?" He turned his back to Bingham without waiting for an answer and walked to his desk. He sat down behind it and started looking through the day's mail.

"Yeah," Bingham said. "You can listen to me for about five or ten minutes, if you don't mind. There are some things I think you should understand about all this."

"I'll listen," Dean said. "But I gotta tell you, I'm afraid I already got the speech from Bennett Childs. Or whatever his name really is."

"He was making *his* pitch out of fear. He and his friends are scared shitless. They've done some bad things in the name of what they originally perceived as a noble goal, and suddenly they find themselves staring into the mirror. What they see is everything coming apart, their careers and their whole lives in jeopardy. So they're strictly looking out for themselves at this point, and they're very desperate men. By the way, Child's real name is Barry Childress, and he's a deputy commissioner."

"Why are you telling me that?"

"Because to tell you the truth, I don't give a shit about him or any of the rest of his pals," Bingham said. "They stepped way over the line on this thing, and they had no right to do that."

"Who's Leo Silvestri?" Dean asked.

"His real name is Vincent Nomelini. He's a lieutenant assigned to the Organized Crime Strike Force."

"And Bobby McGrane?"

"Bobby is Detective Robert Gervaise. Earned his gold shield working four years as an undercover in Narcotics."

"They had me going for a while there," Dean admitted. "So what do you want from me, Walter?"

"I want you to think about keeping the lid on this whole business."

"Why should I do that?" Dean loosened his tie and swung his feet onto the desk.

"Certainly not to protect Childress and his people. They don't deserve your protection—or mine, for that matter."

"So why, then?"

"Because when it comes down to it," he said, "it happens to be the right thing to do."

Dean said nothing.

"As quietly and discreetly as I've been able to," Bingham said, "I've begun to review files in our office from the past ten years. So far, I've come up with a little over fourteen hundred cases where inmates currently serving life sentences for murder would have to be retried or released if the Brady File is made public. Of those, we could retry maybe a hundred, convict half of them if we're lucky. The remaining thirteen hundred and fifty hit the street. That's only the murderers, Dean, and that's just New York County, just Manhattan. There's got to be an equal number in Brooklyn and the Bronx. Throw in Queens and Staten Island and you've got to figure five thousand killers walk out the doors of the prisons and come back to the city to resume doing what they do best."

"Killing people."

"Right," said Bingham, rising to his feet. "Killing people. Forget the robbers and burglars and major drug dealers that are also going to get cut loose, the so-called quality-of-life criminals. Just imagine what adding five thousand murderers does to the city. And these aren't *suspected* murderers, or *accused* murderers. These are goddamn certified *convicted* murderers! I even came across a couple of your own clients."

"Who?" Dean asked.

"Remember David Billups?"

Dean nodded. David Billups had provided Dean with a first-hand introduction to the world of the serial killer. In the space of three and a half weeks Billups had murdered six people, starting with someone whom Billups had a "feeling" intended to rob him, and ending with gay men he would pick up while cruising Christopher Street in the West Village, because by that time Billups had discovered he was capable of killing and rather enjoyed it. The experience had all but converted Dean to a begrudging accepter of the death penalty, and shortly after hearing his client sentenced to prison for a term of one hundred and twenty-five years to life, Dean had readily admitted that Billups should at very least spend the remainder of his life locked in a cage.

"He'd walk?" Dean asked softly.

"Absolutely," Bingham said. "The search of his apartment was illegal. The cops went in before the warrant was signed. And their discovery of the sawed-off shotgun under the mattress was what led Billups to confess, remember? Throw out the shotgun and out goes the confession. The confession was the whole case; without it Mr. Billups goes home."

Dean swallowed hard.

"Johnny Casado?" he heard Bingham say.

Johnny Casado had been a Dominican hit man for a heroin and cocaine ring operating out of the Washington Heights section of upper Manhattan. Casado had been convicted after trial of shooting a rival drug dealer and sentenced to twenty-five years to life. At the time, he'd been suspected of at least fifteen other killings.

"Richard Spraigue?" Bingham was pacing pack and forth.

Spraigue and his brother had taken a young woman to the rooftop of a building in Harlem. She had been high on crack and had accompanied them on the promise of more to smoke. When the brothers were finished taking turns raping and sodomizing her in every orifice they could find, they threw her off the building to her death.

Dean fixed his gaze on the horizon, unable to meet Walter Bingham's eyes. "They'd go home?" he asked.

"They go home." Bingham nodded. "Turns out Casado asked for a lawyer at his lineup, and the detectives didn't bother to get him one. Spraigue was never read his rights before he confessed."

"Jesus," Dean muttered.

"That's three cases," Bingham reminded him, lowering himself into a chair across the desk from Dean. "Try to visualize five thousand."

Dean tried but found it impossible. The three specific instances from his own cases were overwhelming in their impact upon him; five thousand was just an abstract number that he couldn't begin to absorb in the same way, no matter how hard he tried. When he spoke finally, he was surprised by the crack in his own voice. "What am I supposed to do, Walter?"

"I don't know. For starters, maybe you oughta try to stop looking at this thing like a defense lawyer for a minute or two."

"But I *am* a defense lawyer."

"You're also a citizen, Dean."

They sat in silence for several minutes. Dean's thoughts whirled slightly out of control. "You want some coffee or something?" he asked Bingham, not even certain if there was any.

"No, thanks," Bingham said, standing again. "I gotta get going."

"What about Childs—or Childress—and his buddies? They walk free?" Dean asked.

"I'll have their jobs," Bingham said. "I'll see to it that everyone involved in Wilson's killing will be out of the department within six months. You've got my word."

"That's *it?*" he asked. "They murder the goddamn Commissioner, fry the brain of one innocent witness, and kidnap another, and run a decent cop into a truck, and all that happens to them is they get to *resign?*"

"Think about it, Dean. These guys are career cops, the ones who've made it almost to the top and the ones who are headed there. Their jobs are everything to them. It's like you or me getting our tickets pulled, suddenly being told we can't practice law ever again, anywhere. What would we do, go out and drive a fucking cab, for chrissakes? Only it's even worse with these guys. You've been on the Job, Dean. You know what it's like to be a cop. Your whole fucking life revolves around the Job. You've got no friends on the outside. Your closest buddies are your partner and your bottle. Your marriage sucks if you're lucky enough to still have one. Your own kids treat you like some kind of an ogre. Half these guys will eat their guns before a year is out. You'll see."

"You make them sound like victims."

"They are, in a way," Bingham said. "Try to remember they thought they were doing the right thing." He moved toward the door.

"I'll let you out," Dean said, starting to stand.

"No need."

"Yeah, I guess not." Dean forced a laugh. "Am I supposed to let you know, or what?"

"Just see that you do it, tomorrow or Thursday. Your man cops to the petit larceny, stealing less than five hundred dollars from a corpse. A fucking misdemeanor. Time served. Or"—and here Bingham took a deep breath and faced Dean square on—"I'll be ready to start picking a jury. 'Cause if we have to, we can slug it out, Dean, and throw open the Gates of Hell. It's your call."

Bingham had reached the doorway. Just before letting himself out, he stopped.

"And Dean?"

"Yeah?"

"Be careful."

It sounded more like genuine concern than threat.

TWENTY-EIGHT

Joey Spadafino's among a group of inmates awakened at five-thirty Wednesday morning. Despite groans from other inmates that it takes only thirty seconds to walk the length of the Bridge from the Tombs to the courthouse, it seems a Department of Corrections regulation requires that all inmates signed out to court must be up before six, whether they're coming by bus from Rikers Island or walking from the Tombs next door, and whether they're due in court first thing in the morning or not until the afternoon. "Equal opportunity for all," explains a corrections officer.

Around nine o'clock, Joey's led to the holding pen. Because Wednesday's Judge Rothwax's calendar day, the pen is jammed with inmates who'll be going into court to cop-out, get sentenced, or have their cases adjourned, and Joey does well to find a corner of the floor to sit in. Other inmates fill the benches; still others lie sleeping on the floor, obstacles to steer clear of. Accidentally brush your foot against one of them while trying to step over him to get to the toilet, and the guy's liable to jump up and attack you before he's even awake—Joey's seen it happen more than once. So he stays in his corner, holding his side to fight the pain and breathing through his mouth to avoid the stench. At one point he *counts thirty-seven men in the pen, which he figures is maybe twelve-by-twelve feet at most.*

Every time a lawyer comes to the bars, Joey looks up to see if it's Dean, but each time he's disappointed. He spends the entire morning waiting like this. At noon, he gets on a line and is handed two bologna sandwiches on white bread and a container of coffee. He gives away all of the bologna and two slices of the bread. He eats two slices of bread for lunch, slowly, and drinks the coffee. He's gotten to the point where he can drink anything the color of coffee.

On Wednesday afternoon, Judge Rothwax interrupted his calendar day to call the Spadafino case. With the parties in place and the press in attendance, the judge read his decision. It took less than fifteen minutes from start to finish, and denied all of the relief Dean had sought. None of the challenged evidence would be suppressed; all of it would be available to the prosecution at trial.

Next the judge took up the issue of to what extent Walter Bingham would be allowed to bring out Joey Spadafino's record if he was to take the stand. That decision went no better for the defense, as the judge ruled that Bingham could go into all of Spadafino's many convictions, except for one marijuana possession when Joey had been under eighteen and received Youthful Offender treatment.

Finally, a little after two, Joey hears his name called. He's brought into court and seated next to Dean, who tells him the judge is ready to render his decision in the hearing. "Render" sounds like a funny word for Dean to use. Joey has a cousin who once worked for a couple of months in a meat-processing plant on Fourteenth Street, way over on the West Side, who told him they used to render the fat they cut off the the meat by boiling it down in these huge vats he showed Joey. He lets his imagination wonder if that's what they're about to do to him now.

The judge reads a lot of stuff that Joey can't understand, except the part where he says he's not going to suppress any of the evidence.

"This is bad, huh?" he whispers to Dean.

"No," Dean whispers back. "I told you he'd do that. Don't worry about it."

Easy for him to say.

When the judge is finally finished reading, he talks to Dean and the DA about Joey's past record. They argue for a while, but Dean seems to lose this one, too. The judge rules that if Joey takes the stand at the trial the DA will be allowed to ask him about his past record. That's a fucked-up rule if ever there was one, thinks Joey. After all, he did his time for those things. They shouldn't have nuthin' to do with this case.

The case was adjourned to Thursday. "Make sure we have a panel of a hundred and fifty jurors," the judge told his clerk. "The first hundred should be here promptly at ten."

Dean comes upstairs to the pens after court to explain to Joey what'll happen next in the trial. Since the interview room is full, they have to talk through the bars of the pen, but Joey doesn't mind—most lawyers don't even come in to talk to their clients. Besides which, they've put Joey in the go-back pen (not too far from obsos and homos), since he's finished in court, and there's only a handful of other guys with him.

Joey notices that Dean's got both his hands around the bars, something inmates learn not to do the first time a CO walks by and slams a book or a clipboard as hard as he can against their knuckles. But he guesses it's different with lawyers, so he doesn't say anything about it. Anyway, Dean's on the same side of the bars as the COs, so he wonders why he was even thinking about it. Sometimes he thinks he's going fucking nuts with all this.

"So what's next?" he asks.

"You tell me," Dean says. "We're ready to start picking a jury tomorrow morning. It's up to you. I can still walk you out of here. You can't really want to go through with this."

"What're they offerin' you, man?" one of the other inmates asks. He's a big black guy, looks like an ugly Shaquille O'Neal.

When Joey doesn't answer, Dean answers for him. "Petit larceny and time served. Time served on a murder case."

"You for real?" Shaq asks in disbelief, his voice squeaking real high on real.

"I'm for real," Dean says.

"Take it, chump!" a Puerto Rican kid says.

"Jump on it, man!" someone else chimes in.

But Joey ignores them all. "I want a trial, man," he says. "Can't you unnastand that? These guys here, maybe they did their crimes. Me, I didn't—I'm innocent. I'm bein' framed by the po-lice. You know it, I know it, an' they know it. Am I right, or am I right?"

Dean nods and says, "You're right."

"So you guys shut the fuck up, hear?"

Nobody says anything more to Joey. Not even Shaq. The conversation is over.

Dean lay awake and listened to the sounds of the city at night, the tire noises and the beeping of horns and the noisy brakes of the garbage trucks that he imagined were elephants trumpeting in the jungle. A car alarm wailed somewhere off in the distance.

His thoughts wandered back to his conversation with Walter Bingham. Stop looking at this thing like a defense lawyer, Bingham had told him after bringing up three of Dean's own cases to prove his point. Bingham had stacked the deck, to be sure. The cases had been among the very worst Dean had ever handled: a serial killer, a hit man for drug dealers, and a rapist-murderer. Dean would be the first to agree that none of them should ever walk the streets again. Now Bingham was telling him that Dean held the power to keep them locked up where they were, or the power to turn them—and thousands just like them—loose on a helpless city.

Dean had never asked for that power. He'd asked only to practice his profession, to be permitted to represent a single client to the best of his ability. If he did that, no matter what the final result might be—win, lose, or draw—justice would be served. Or so they'd always taught him.

But now, all of a sudden, it seemed they'd changed the rules on him. It was no longer a simple matter of representing Joey Spadafino. They were telling him that more was at stake now, much more. And that along with the power that had been placed in his hands came a responsibility, a duty to exercise that power wisely, for the common good, lest a horrendous disaster occur.

Was that how the system worked? At some point was Dean really supposed to stop thinking like a defense lawyer who represented his client so zealously as to blind himself from all social considerations whatsoever, and start looking instead at the bigger picture? Did there finally come a moment when he was supposed to act just like the cop who bent the rules ever so slightly to make sure his arrest of a vicious felon stood up in court, or the judge who chose to overlook some minor technicality when dealing with a particularly horrible murderer? Was that what it meant to stop thinking like a defense lawyer?

But suppose Joey continued to insist on demanding a trial in spite of everything? Suppose he persisted in his "fuck you" attitude? What then? Was his right to a trial some ultimate, God-given thing? Or was is just something to be weighed against other things which might turn out to be more important? Was Joey's determination to have his day in court at the expense of everyone else just the stubborn act of one selfish brat? And if that's all it was, didn't Dean have the right to try to talk him out of it? Didn't he have the *duty* to do so?

He tried to picture Joey Spadafino, tried to imagine what Joey was doing at that particular moment, but he couldn't. Joey seemed small and far away and totally insignificant. Did it really matter what happened to him? When it came right down to it, was his life worth even a fraction of Janet's? Or a fraction of what Edward Wilson's life had been worth? Or Mr. Chang's or Officer Santana's? And how was Dean supposed to measure even those lives against the hundreds or thousands of future victims of the David Billupses and Johnny Casados and Richard Spraigues of the world? Who was he to say he might not have done the very same things as Silvestri and Childs and the rest of the cops had he found himself standing in their shoes?

While Dean lies awake tormented over dilemmas regarding conflicting sets of morality, on 4 North in the Tombs things are much simpler for Joey Spadafino, and—despite his pain—sleep comes easily for him.

TWENTY-NINE

Thursday came, and with it the beginning of jury selection in the case of the *People of the State of New York v. Joseph Spadafino.* Dean had given up trying to convince Joey to accept the plea offer; it seemed that Joey was turning it into a game of just how stubborn he could be. Instead, Dean had backed off, counting on the arrival of the jury panel to finally shake some sense into Joey. He knew from experience that many a defendant who'd been irrationally insisting upon a trial all along suddenly got cold feet the moment he was brought face to face with the panel. There was even a word for it, borrowed from the poker table: *folding.*

Maybe it was the opportunity for the defendant to look into the sea of faces of prospective jurors and to realize with sudden and sobering disappointment that too few were his color, or his age, or looked remotely like him, or seemed to be regarding him with anything approaching sympathy or understanding. Or maybe it was the simple awareness that after weeks and months of delays and postponements that had lulled him into a sense that there might never be a trial, here it was about to actually begin—the judge and the Assistant DA and the witnesses hadn't been bluffing all this time, after all.

But if Joey Spadafino was folding, he showed no sign of it.

The media was present again, but the front two rows were sufficient to contain their numbers. Apparently they'd somehow sensed that no deal had been worked out, that any hope of a quick headline story had given way to an acceptance that the next several days would be devoted to the more mundane business of listening to two lawyers competing to see who could put more people to sleep with his questions to the prospective jurors.

Dean tended to agree that the business of jury selection was not only excruciatingly boring, but largely unproductive the way most of his colleagues did it. His approach to the process was simple: He didn't much care what the jurors did in their spare time, or what magazines they read or TV shows they watched; he had no interest in knowing the schools they'd gone to or the neighborhoods they lived in. He left the gathering of such trivia to the judge and the prosecutor.

Instead, he framed his questions in such a way to tell the jurors as much as he could about the bad things they were going to hear about his client and his side of the case: a prior criminal record if the defendant was going to testify, or the very fact that he *wouldn't* be taking the stand if that were the case; a drug dependency; an incriminating statement he'd made to the police; or a weapon he'd had in his possession at the time of his arrest.

By bringing these things out in the open at the earliest possible opportunity, Dean hoped to lessen their dramatic impact. Also, by being the one to mention them first, he made it look like he was being open and honest and worthy of their trust. But there was yet another bit of psychology at work here, a more subtle motive. In telling them the bad news Joey's record, his history of drug abuse, the fact that he'd been arrested in possession of a knife just moments after the death of Commissioner Wilson and had freely admitted taking Wilson's money—while at the same time asking the jurors if they could promise to give him a fair trial in spite of those things (which they all hurriedly and earnestly assured him they could), Dean was actually soliciting their promises that they would, in effect, *ignore* those harmful things. In a sense, he was brainwashing them to disregard the very worst of the evidence against Joey!

So for Dean, this part of the trial took on great significance. At the same time, however, it was terribly repetitive and even more boring for him than for the jurors. While for them it was new, he'd done it a hundred times before.

So his thoughts kept wandering to Janet. Was her life really going to be the price of Joey's absurd insistance on going to trial? Dean found it hard to believe that the police would make good on their threat to kill her. But he couldn't get Bennett Childs's words out of his mind. "If the situation demands," Childs had told him, "we'll do whatever we have to do to contain this business." That was not a master of subtlety at work.

Jury selection proved even more tedious than Dean had anticipated. Almost all of the panel members admitted they'd read or heard something about Commissioner Wilson's death or seen TV footage of Joey Spadafino being led in handcuffs to the station house or standing in front of the judge at his arraignment. Many seemed to have legitimate doubts about their own ability to be fair to a homeless ex-con who seemed to have already confessed to just about everything he was accused of. Others used the publicity surrounding the case as a subterfuge to get excused so they could get back to their jobs or families.

By the one o'clock recess, only two jurors had been selected.

When Joey's led into court Thursday morning he finds the room almost empty. One entire side of the audience section is completely empty, as is half of the other side. He soon finds out why. At a signal given by the judge, the jurors are brought in. There must be close to a hundred of them, Joey figures. They fill the empty side of the room and the half-empty side, and even then some of them have to stand along the walls. Names get read from little slips of paper pulled out of a wooden thing, the way they pick numbers at Bingo Night at church, and the jurors whose names are called take seats in the jury box. By the time the jury box is filled, there are enough places in the courtroom for the other jurors to find seats.

The judge talks to the jurors for what seems like hours. Many of them say they can't be jurors on the case because it'll take too long, or because their mothers were mugged, or because they'd believe anything a cop would say or nothing a cop would say. Each time one of them gets excused, another name from the bingo thing is picked and the empty seat is filled with another juror. Then the judge has to ask that juror all the questions he missed. Sometimes that juror gets excused, too.

When the judge is finished asking questions, the DA takes over. He's very tall and very smooth, and Joey's afraid Dean may be overmatched. A couple of times the DA gets the jurors to laugh, and Joey worries that they're getting to like him too much.

Then it's Dean's turn. He's shorter than the DA and doesn't seem to have as many jokes, and Joey worries that the jury doesn't like him as much. But after a while Dean seems to loosen up a little and hit his stride, and the jurors seem to like him okay, too.

When Dean finishes he comes back to the table and goes over his notes with Joey. He's made a diagram of the jury box, with a little square for each juror, and he asks Joey how he feels about each one. Joey has ideas about a few of them. He doesn't like a couple of them who have relatives in the Police Department or who have been robbery victims themselves. He likes one black man who's out of work and a guy who talked about a bad experience he once had with the police. Also a young woman who doesn't seem afraid to look at him like most of them do.

But it turns out the DA knocks off all the people Joey wants. Dean knocks off the ones he and Joey don't like. When they're finished, it's pretty unbelievable, but only one juror's been picked. So they pick more names and start the whole thing all over again.

After a while Joey knows the judge's questions by heart, and the same for the DA's and Dean's. In order to stay awake he takes on of Dean's pens and begins drawing pictures on a piece of paper. He draws airplanes and rockets and a battleship. When Dean notices what he's doing he asks him to stop, saying he doesn't want the jury to think he's a jailhouse lawyer. Joey wonders what drawing a battleship has to do with being a jailhouse lawyer, but he stops.

At one o'clock they break for lunch. One more juror's been picked, making two. Joey spends the next hour and half sitting on the floor in the feeder pen alongside the courtroom. He's brought a cheese sandwich on white bread and a cup of something that's either strong tea or weak coffee, he isn't sure which. He drinks it anyway. Afterward he still isn't sure.

Joey's side still aches and it still hurts him to breathe, but he makes believe he's in a fight, resting between rounds. When the bell rings, he'll be ready to get up, whatever it takes.

*   *   *

For Dean, the first afternoon of jury selection went no more quickly than the first morning had. It seemed that a disproportionate number of panel members had relatives or friends who were members of the Police Department, and despite the protestations by many of them that they could be fair, Dean had his doubts.

By the end of the day he'd exhausted thirteen of his allotted twenty peremptory challenges, while Walter Bingham had used only nine. Five more jurors had been selected, bringing the number of sworn jurors to seven.

Judge Rothwax recessed until Friday morning, telling the lawyers he expected to complete the selection process then, after which they should be ready to make their opening statements.

Dean headed back to his office on the verge of despair. He had the sense that the process was absurdly irrelevant. Here he was, going through the motions of picking a jury, while Janet was locked up somewhere across the river in another state, her very life hanging in the balance. What difference did it make to her if some juror had an uncle who was a cop in Rochester?

To Joey Spadafino, the afternoon in court is a rerun of the morning session. The judge and the lawyers drone on. Names get picked from the Bingo wheel. Jurors come and go. Joey understands by this time that Dean and he can't pick the jurors they like, they can only keep off the ones they dislike. Dean tells him it works the same way for the DA, but somehow the system seems unfair to Joey. And stupid. This way, don't they end up with a jury nobody likes?

Since who gets picked doesn't seem to matter so much after all, Joey eventually loses interest and leaves the choices up to Dean. But without the jurors to worry about or his drawing to occupy him, Joey has nothing to do and finds he has a hard time staying awake. When he feels himself beginning to nod off at one point, he bites the inside of his cheek until he can taste his own blood. He knows it would be bad for the jury to see him asleep. They would figure he doesn't give a shit about his own murder trial. That would be even worse than them thinking he's a jailhouse lawyer, he bets.

By the end of the afternoon they've got some more jurors picked, but they've also used up the ones in the audience. The judge says they'll need to start with more in the morning and declares the court in recess.

Only when the last juror has left the courtroom do the court officers tell Joey to stand up so they can take him into the pens. Dean has explained to him that jurors aren't supposed to know he's in jail. Where the fuck do they think he is? If they're too stupid to know that, how are they supposed to figure out he didn't murder anybody?

It was close to eight by the time Dean turned off the lights and locked up his office. He wasn't particularly hungry, but he knew he should probably eat something—he'd had nothing all day. There was no food in his apartment—it had been days since he'd thought to shop for anything. So, against his better judgment, he stopped at a diner near his subway stop and found a seat at the counter. Somebody had once said the food was good, though he couldn't remember who it had been.

Nothing on the menu appealed to him. He looked around to see what other people were eating, but the fried chicken on his right seemed greasy, and the ham steak on his left looked truly scary. He spied a crayoned list of specials taped onto the mirror in front of him. OLD FASHIONED MEET LOAF PLATTER $4.99 caught his eye. Comfort food, he thought to himself, complete with down-home spelling. How wrong could he go?

Pretty wrong, it turned out.

Joey's dinner consists of old-fashioned macaroni and tomato sauce. It isn't good, like real food, but it's certainly better than what he was getting at Rikers Island.

The Tombs, Joey finds, is better than Rikers Island in almost all ways. Not only is the food better and the cells cleaner and less crowded, it seems the COs treat you better, too. The feature that most of the inmates like best is that it's easier for their "people" to get to than Rikers Island, so they get more visits. More visits means more comissary money, more fresh clothing, less isolation. Joey wonders if it's just a coincidence that there are so many white inmates in the Tombs compared to Rikers Island, which as far as he could tell was almost all black and Hispanic.

*   *   *

Dean lay awake with indigestion from meat loaf and gravy and mashed potatoes. He located CNN on his cable TV, and shortly after eleven he heard that "Opening statements are expected tomorrow in the trial of Joey Spadafino, the homeless man accused of the robbery murder of Edward Wilson. Mr. Wilson was New York City Police Commissioner at the time of his death early this year. Spadafino faces twenty-five years to life if convicted."

A mini-surge of adrenaline rippled through Dean's body. Added to his mounting concern for Janet and the edginess from the two cups of coffee he'd had with dinner, it made sleep impossible. But did nothing for his indigestion.

THIRTY

They were back in court Friday morning. Working on less than two hours' sleep, Dean struggled to stay awake while Judge Rothwax addressed a new panel of jurors. After that, Walter Bingham questioned them for a good forty-five minutes. By the time Dean's turn came, he had to request a ten-minute recess so he could go to the men's room and splash water on his face.

They picked the remaining five jurors by one o'clock. Judge Rothwax announced that he wanted six alternates. They broke for lunch, the judge reminding them that he wanted to proceed with opening statements that afternoon, as soon as the alternates had been selected.

Dean had known all along that his opening statement in this case would be absolutely crucial. Unlike some states that permit the defense to defer opening until the end of the prosecution's witnesses, New York procedure requires the defense attorney to make his opening immediately after the prosecution's or to waive it altogether, something Dean knew he couldn't afford to do in this case: He desperately needed to outline for the jury his contention that Joey was being framed to cover up the police conspiracy. Otherwise the jury would be at a complete loss, lacking the framework to understand where he was going with his cross-examinations of Bingham's witnesses and with his direct examinations of the witnesses Dean himself intended to call.

But how could Dean say what he needed to without playing his hand and thereby condemning Janet to death? That was the question for which he had no answer.

Which meant that for Dean a terrifying moment of truth was rapidly approaching.

It takes them till three-thirty to select the extras, and for the first time Joey gets to see the jury, his jury, all sitting together in the jury box.

Of the eighteen—Joey can't be sure which are the regular jurors and which are the extras—he counts eleven women and seven men. He doesn't know if that's good or bad, though Dean tells him women are generally more sympathetic. There are nine whites, five blacks, two Puerto Ricans or Dominicans (Joey isn't sure which), a Chinese or Korean guy, and a dothead from India or Pakistan or someplace like that. None of them look too smart to Joey, and he worries about that. How could they possibly understand in a few days what the real story is, when it took Dean, who's pretty smart, months to figure it out?

Judge Rothwax used the next twenty minutes or so to give them his preliminary instructions. Though the jurors seemed to listen intently, to Dean it was all a blur. It wasn't just that he'd heard the speech a hundred times before and knew it almost by heart; it was simply that his thoughts about Janet kept racing out of control, leaving room for nothing else. How could he decide between his duty to his client and her very life?

At some point Dean was aware that Judge Rothwax had finished and that Walter Bingham was addressing the jury. He tried his best to focus on Bingham's words, but it was a losing battle, and all that came through was gibberish. *I can't do this!* he wanted to shout. *It's not fair!*

The jurors come back in through a side door. Each time they sit in the jury box, they have to take the same seats. It reminds Joey of fourth-grade English class with Miss Sweeny.

This time the judge sounds like a referee going over the rules. Any minute, Joey expects him to start telling them about the three-knockdown rule and the mandatory eight-count. But instead it's all about presumptions and burdens and a lot of other stuff too confusing to understand. But the whole time the jurors look at the judge and nod up and down, pretending they get it, when Joey's sure they don't have a fucking clue.

These people don't know the first thing about the law, he realizes. Some of them said they'd never even been on a jury before. And now his life is in their hands.

It's very fucking scary, is all he can think.

The judge tells the jurors that the People give their opening statement first. Joey doesn't like the way the prosecution gets to be called "the People." It makes it seem like it's everybody in the world against him. Pretty unfair sides.

The DA gets up and clears his throat. He starts by reading his indictment, which says that Joey Spadafino murdered Edward Wilson and robbed him. Even though the judge has explained to the jurors that the indictment isn't supposed to count as evidence, the way the DA reads it makes it sound like it's all true, that Joey did all those things it says in there. It's like the game's over before it starts.

"This is a very simple case," the DA tells them next. "It's a case about a man who mugged somebody, robbed him. Only he picked the wrong man to rob. For one thing, the man he picked to rob turned out to be the Police Commissioner of the City of New York. For another thing, the man he picked to rob turned out to have a damaged heart. Unluckily for the robber, his victim had a fatal heart attack during the course of the robbery.

"The name of the victim was Edward Wilson. The name of the robber is Joey Spadafino. He sits right over there." And here the DA points directly at Joey, making a big deal of it, like they don't already know who he is. Fuck you, Joey thinks to himself, doing his best to stare right back at the DA in case anyone's noticing.

"We will produce the proceeds of the robbery, and demonstrate why they belonged to the victim and to no one else. We will produce the weapon used during the robbery. We will connect the defendant to that weapon by fingerprint evidence. We will prove the defendant's guilt not only beyond a reasonable doubt, but beyond any shadow of a doubt whatsoever." Here the DA pauses to take a sip of water from a paper cup. Joey knows he can't possibly *be thirsty after speaking for three minutes, that it's just for effect. He hopes the jurors know, but he doubts it. They seem to be eating up every word they hear. And the worst thing is, the DA makes it all sound like he knows it's true, when it's not, and when he wasn't even there in the first place.*

"Up until now you've heard me talk about robbery, but not murder. I'll be honest with you. I'm not going to be able to prove that the defendant intended to kill Commissioner Wilson. But the law is such that I don't have to. Judge Rothwax will explain to you at the end of the case exactly how felony murder works. Suffice it to say that I'm going to prove to you that the defendant intended to rob Commissioner Wilson, did rob him, and that Mr. Wilson suffered a fatal heart attack during the robbery. And that's all I have to prove in this case.

"After the evidence is completed, I'll be speaking to you again, and I'm confident that I'll be asking you to return a verdict of guilty on each and every count in the indictment. Thank you."

Joey does his best to look unconcerned as the DA sits down, but inside he feels like he's going to vomit.

Finally Dean, too, saw Bingham sit down. He was aware now that all eyes in the courtroom were on him, waiting for him to rise and begin his own statement. But all of the strength seemed to have gone out of his legs, and he felt absolutely powerless to push himself back from the table and rise to his feet.

"Mr. Abernathy," Judge Rothwax was asking him, "does the defense wish to make an opening statement?"

Dean fought to find his voice, but even as he spoke, it cracked. "May we approach the bench?" he managed to ask.

"Excuse me?" Rothwax stared at him.

"I need to approach, Your Honor." This time Dean mustered enough authority in his voice that the judge nodded.

Bingham fell into step with Dean and they walked forward together. "Do it, Dean," he heard Walter whisper menacingly to him. "Just fucking do it before it's too late."

"Is there some problem?" the judge asked once they'd reached him.

"Yes, there is," Dean said. "I can't do this."

"Excuse me?"

"I'm not ready to open."

"You—"

"Judge," Walter Bingham interrupted, "ordinarily I'd object. But it's after four-thirty on Friday afternoon. It's been a very long week for all of us. Under the circumstances, the People are willing to give Mr. Abernathy until Monday morning to resolve whatever problem he may have."

Still, Rothwax looked dubious. It wasn't like him to defer like this, even when the lawyers themselves were in agreement. But finally he nodded at Dean and said, "Only because I know you well enough to believe this must be something serious."

"It's pretty serious," Dean said.

They stepped back. Dean listened as the judge excused the jury for the weekend. He felt like he'd dodged a bullet with his name on it. He wondered if Janet would be as lucky when her turn came.

Joey sees the judge turn to Dean and ask him if he's ready to take his turn. Finally: This is the moment Joey's been living for all these months, for his lawyer to get up and tell everybody what really happened, how Joey's got nothing to do with the guy dying. But instead of saying yes, Dean's asking to have one of those secret huddles, "at the bench," they call it—they seem to have a lot of these secret huddles—and next the judge is telling the jury they'll have to wait till Monday morning to see if Dean's going to talk to them after all.

Joey's totally confused, confused and disappointed. He feels like Dean's selling him out. He's led back to the feeder pen, upstairs to the twelfth floor holding pen, back down to the third floor, and from there across the Bridge to the Tombs and his cell. He doesn't know what's going on now.

Teach him to trust a fuckin' free lawyer.

"Thanks," Dean said to Walter Bingham as they walked out of the courtroom and toward the elevators.

"It's not your thanks I need. It's your client's guilty plea."

"I honestly don't think I can get it, Walter."

"You've got no choice, Dean."

Some people had gathered nearby, so Bingham moved away from the elevators and opened a door to a staircase. Dean followed him, closing the door behind them.

"You've got to understand," Dean said. "I can't always control my clients."

"And I can't control these cops!" Bingham snapped.

"What's that supposed to mean?"

"You know fucking well what that means. They've got one card left to play, and I don't put it past them to play it."

"You really think they'd kill her?"

Bingham seemed to deliberately avoid Dean's stare. He said nothing.

"Maybe they already have." Until Dean heard himself say the words, that was one possibility that frankly hadn't occurred to him. But suddenly now it did. "I haven't heard from them—or her—for almost a week. How do I even know she's still alive?"

If Bingham knew, he wasn't saying.

The thought that Janet might already be dead consumed Dean all Friday night, and as exhausted as he was, he slept only fitfully, awaking several times from dreams in which he was either suffocating or drowning, always fighting for air and unable to breathe.

Joey's able to breathe as he lies on his bunk, though his insides still hurt. They've stopped giving him the Tylenol—it seems the doctor said he could have it for only five days. When Joey asks how come, they tell him something about being afraid he might abuse it.

If you've got money in here you can get heroin, cocaine, or crack. You can get reefer to smoke, booze to drink, glue to sniff, or mushrooms to eat. You can get dust or speed or acid. Got money, the word is there's one CO on the night shift'll even bring you paint thinner to inhale and fry your brains on.

And they're worried he's going to abuse fuckin' Tylenol!

Sometimes you have to hand it to these guys for dreaming up new and different ways to be assholes.

THIRTY-ONE

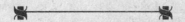

Dean spent Saturday morning in his apartment, alternately trying to absorb himself in the newspaper and mindlessly flicking the remote control on his television set. But Saturday's *Times* was only two thin sections, and he found himself reading the same paragraphs over and over without absorbing anything anyway. About all he could find to watch on television were cartoons and commercials, and some guy demonstrating spray paint for bald spots.

The phone rang shortly before noon. He toyed with the idea of not answering it, then picked it up on the fourth ring.

"I hear your lady friend had a pretty close call yesterday afternoon." It took Dean only a few words to recognize the voice of the man he knew as Leo Silvestri.

"How do I even know my lady friend's even alive?" Dean asked.

"Oh, she's alive," Leo assured him. "Take my word for it. She's doing just fine, so far. But she's depending on you. We're all depending on you. Only she's *really* depending on you, if you know what I mean."

"And suppose I don't want to take your word for it that she's okay? It's not like your track record's so great with me, you know."

"Still the wiseass, huh? Well," Leo said, "you think what you wanna think. We'll do what we gotta do." And there was a click, followed shortly by a dial tone.

Dean didn't know whether to feel intimidated or outraged. What balls these guys had! To call him and threaten him like that right over the phone required incredible arrogance. He wished he'd had a tape recorder hooked up to his phone. But of course Leo hadn't just been ballsy; he 'd also been smart enough to catch Dean by surprise, not giving him a chance to record his words.

Dean remembered once being advised by a client to keep a tape recorder hooked up to his phone at all times, just in case he ever needed to record a call without warning. Of course Dean had rejected the suggestion—it was simply too paranoid. Now he kicked himself for not having listened. He tried to think of the name of the client, but it eluded him. He could picture the guy's face, right down to the mustache that gave him a slick look. Yeah—he was the guy who'd given Dean a whole bunch of electronic stuff—Hotwire Harry Reynolds. Once he'd even presented Dean with a tape reocrder that was set up with an electronic impulse starter so that it would begin to record as soon as the phone rang or was picked up. "Even better than voice activated," he'd told Dean. "Those don't pick up till somebody starts talking." But of course Dean had had no use for any of the equipment. What other useless stuff had there been? A fancy radar detector. A caller-ID gadget for the phone. An electric—

He stopped right there.

The caller-ID thing. Couldn't that give him the number Leo had just called him from? Dean felt his heart race. Was it possible? Might this be the break he needed?

He went to his closet and fell to his knees. He began pawing through the clutter on the floor. A broken vacuum cleaner, a circular saw, a rusted toolbox, an electric drill set, a bicycle pump he'd given up for lost, a pair of paint-spattered work boots, and—finally—an old briefcase. He yanked it out by the handle, upsetting a gallon paint can in the process. Luckily, the paint had long ago dried into a solid glob.

He snapped open the briefcase and dumped its contents onto his sofa. A tiny tape recorder, a portable telephone, a radar detector, a few gadgets he didn't even recognize, a dozen batteries of different sizes and shapes.

And the caller-ID device.

It was nothing but a little digital screen with two cords attached to the back of it. One was a power cord with a plug, the other a telephone line. There was also a jack to accept an incoming phone line.

He carried it over to his phone. He unplugged the line that ran to his phone and inserted it in the jack of the device. Then he connected the phone line attached to the device to his phone. He'd never hooked it up before, but there didn't seem to be any other way to do it. He plugged the power cord into an outlet.

His heart pounded in anticipation. At first, nothing happened. Then the screen came to life. He held his breath as words formed in front of his eyes.

NO CALLS RECEIVED.

His elation evaporated into despair. Of course—he was too late. He'd missed Leo's number by not having had the device plugged in at the time the call came in.

Suddenly, the letters on the screen began changing.

HAVE A NICE DAY.

Then it went blank again.

And the blankness struck Dean as a perfect metaphor for the way things had been going lately.

Having given up on the newspaper, Dean spent the afternoon channel surfing. Cartoons and commercials had given way to a baseball game, an exhibition football game, a documentary about the depletion of the rain forest, and a panel discussion about the alarming decline of family values. They were all pretty uninspiring. Exhausted from his lack of sleep the past several nights, he stretched out on his couch and let his eyes close.

In his dream, Janet was strapped into a chair of some sort. People stood around. Dean made out the faces of Leo Silvestri, Bennett Childs, and Bobby McGrane. They all watched a large clock that sat on a metal table. Dean knew that time was running out, but the face of the clock was a blur to him. Try as he might, he couldn't focus on the hands to make out the time. Suddenly the alarm on the clock began ringing in long bursts, once, twice, three times, sounding just like a—

He sat up and fumbled for the phone. "Hello," he said, trying to sound awake.

"Dean?" It was a man's voice.

"Yuh."

"Lissen for yourself."

There was a pause. Then a woman's voice. "I'm okay, Dean." It was Janet. "They're going—" Then a click.

He gripped the phone desperately, as if to squeeze her voice back to life, but there was nothing but silence. Finally, a recording: "There appears to be a receiver off the hook. If you are trying to make a call, please hang up—"

He did as he was told.

Dean jumped to his feet and began pacing. Janet was alive! At least he knew that much. And she'd actually sounded okay. What was it she'd tried to tell him? "They're going—" He couldn't remember if there'd been any more.

Back and forth he paced, not even aware that his nervous energy compelled him to do so. Finally he realized how silly he must have looked, and he stopped himself by the doorway to his kitchen. From there he stared across the room at his phone, trying his hardest to will it into ringing again by sheer determination.

His eye caught an unfamiliar object sitting next to the phone where ordinarily there was nothing.

And he remembered.

Carefully, deliberately, as though if he rushed he might disturb it and spoil everything, he walked over to it and, holding his breath, dared look down at the little screen.

2015622939

He found a pen and, afraid the message might disappear while he tried to locate a piece of paper, copied the numbers onto the back of his hand.

He knew that 201 was an area code for northern New Jersey, including Hoboken. That gave him 201–562–2939.

It had worked.

Afraid to use his own phone or even another in the building, Dean threw on a shirt and hurried out the door. Downstairs, two

Clint Eastwood types who'd been waiting across the street followed him on foot around the corner but stayed outside when he entered a card store.

Using the public phone in the back of the store, Dean phoned Jimmy McDermott. He listened to ten rings before giving up. Then he remembered that Jimmy wore a beeper. He found the number in his address book and dialed it. He punched in the number on the coin phone and hung up. He prayed that he might find the investigator both near a phone and sober enough to dial it.

The phone rang, so loud it frightened him. He picked up the receiver. "Jimmy," he said, "Dean Abernathy. I've got that phone number in Hoboken. I'm pretty sure it's unlisted. Can you get an address for me?"

"You bet."

It took less than fifteen minutes for McDermott to call back with the information. By the time Dean returned to his building and waved good-bye to the two men who'd followed him, he was clutching a small piece of paper with a name and an address on it.

Ferguson, D.M.
Ferguson Enterprises
555 Dawson St.
Hoboken, NJ

Dean had no clue as to what kind of business Ferguson Enterprises was involved in, or if it was nothing but a front for the New York Police Department. But he didn't much care: He knew *he* was back in business.

Dean saved quarters in an old milk bottle, emptying it out whenever the discovery that he was out of clean clothes told him it was time for a trip to the laundry room. Now he raided the bottle, figuring his laundry would have to wait. His pockets heavy with change, he made a second run to the pay phone at the card store. As before, he had company on the way.

His first call was to his brother, Alan, who agreed to come over that evening. There were a few conditions, Dean explained: He had to come without his car ("No problem, I can never find a parking spot in your neighborhood, anyway"), be willing to stay the night and help Dean the following day as well ("I guess so"), and arrive in some sort of disguise that would hide the considerable resemblance he bore to Dean ("Are you out of your mind?"). The second call was to Dean's friend David Leung, who said he'd be home all day Sunday and be able to help Dean out as well.

Back at his apartment, Dean began gathering what he'd need. When he was satisfied, he stuffed it all into a small duffel bag. By late afternoon he'd done everything he could think of. He turned on a Yankee game and stretched out on the couch, a surefire recipe for a nap that he figured might come in handy later on.

The intercom buzzer woke Dean from a deep sleep, and the darkness of his apartment told him that it was night, which meant he'd been out for a couple of hours. He pulled himself up and groped his way to the kitchen, where he found the house phone.

"Yeah?" he said into it.

"Yeah, yourself. Let me in before the guys from Bellevue grab me with a net!"

Dean recognized his brother's voice and pressed the button to unlock the inner door downstairs. He opened the door to his apartment and waited.

Dean had learned to spot cross-dressers back in his Legal Aid days, when you could call them transvestites without risking an argument from a sociology major. That ability, along with the fact that he *knew* it was Alan standing in front of him in a blond wig, blue print dress, and heels, prevented Dean from being fooled now, but it was not enough to keep his lower jaw from dropping open in awe.

"Aren't you going to let me in, sailor?" Alan asked in a teasing, husky voice.

"No," Dean said, "I'm going to send you next door to Everett and Val's apartment. They'll take good care of you."

Alan ignored the comment and pushed past Dean and into the living room. He stepped out of his heels, pulled the wig off, and sat on Dean's sofa, knees spread very much like the truck driver he'd once been.

Dean locked the door. "That's *wild!*" he said. "You should've been a hooker."

"Thanks so much," Alan said. "Want to tell me what the hell's going on here?"

"Sure," said Dean, "but it's going to take some time. You up for a pizza?"

"Does the Pope shit in the woods?"

"Huh?"

"Never mind. I could never get those sayings straight. Sure, I could do pizza, if you're buying."

Dean found a flyer that had slid its way under his door one evening and tossed it to Alan, who read aloud from it. "Tulio's Pizza and Heroes. What kind of a name is *Tulio?* That's not Italian, is it?"

"What do you think it is?"

"Could be Greek. Could be Armenian. Could be goddamn *Portuguese* all we know. How you going to order pizza from a place that could be Portuguese?

"It's not Portuguese," Dean said. "What do you want?"

"Anything, I don't care. No anchovies. No olives."

Dean called and ordered a large pie with everything but anchovies and olives and garlic.

"Better tell them no octopus, too," Alan said. "They really could be Portuguese."

Dean ignored him.

"You got some clothes I could change into?" Alan asked.

"Yeah," Dean laughed, pointing to the bedroom. "Anything you like. But I kinda like you in the dress."

Over pizza, Dean brought Alan up to date on the late-breaking developments in the Spadafino case. They'd talked about the case before, but not since the business about the Brady File had surfaced.

Dean explained what he needed Alan to do. Although Alan had openly questioned Dean's sanity more than once during the course of the evening, he seemed to immediately grasp the seriousness of the situation. He listened attentively and didn't interrupt. He'd do whatever Dean wanted him to do, no questions asked.

"Get it?" Dean asked, when he was finished outlining his instructions.

"Got it."

"Good."

* * *

Rather than sleeping, they killed time by reminiscing. More than anyone else Dean knew, Alan was generally on the same page as Dean, and often on the very same line. They tended to view the rest of the world with the same blend of righteous indignation and bemused tolerance. Not that any of that was terribly surprising: In addition to their physical resemblance and the fact that they shared the same set of parents and many of their early experiences, they'd known each other for all of Alan's life and most of Dean's.

Sometime past midnight, Dean shaved. First his face, then his legs. Alan shook his head slowly as he watched. "Boy, Mom and Dad are going to have trouble adjusting to this," he said.

"Shut up," Dean said.

Around two in the morning they grew weary of talking, but not ready for sleep. Dean turned on the TV and flicked the dial before settling on *Mean Streets*, with Robert De Niro and Harvey Keitel looking like a couple of twenty-year-olds. The pulse of the rock 'n' roll score only added to their heightened levels of adrenaline as they imitated the Ronettes singing "Be My Baby." But Dean, having napped earlier in the day, figured there'd be plenty of time to sleep in a day or two.

THIRTY-TWO

Had anyone happened to be watching the front door of Dean's apartment building late that Saturday night and into the following Sunday—and indeed at one point there were no fewer than six men doing precisely that—he might have noted his observations much in the manner as they were entered in the surveillance log of Det. Robert Gervaise, aka Bobby McGrane. Portions of that log would later become important evidence in several different investigations, one of which was directed at the quality of performance of the surveillance field team itself.

0800	Units 1, 2, and 3 on duty outside subject Dean Abernathy's West End Ave premises. Advised by Central that subject is inside.
1136	White Female, possible prostitute, enters building.
0512	White Male recognized to be subject Abernathy exits premises & proceeds on foot to vehicle, 19?? blue Jeep. Enters vehicle.
0514	Subject Abernathy departs in vehicle. Unit 1 (Dets Grant and Snyder) follow in Dept.

Auto 2274. Unit 2 (P.O.s Lee and Ciccini) follow in Dept. Auto 13551.

0529   Unit 1 advises subject Abernathy entering Lincoln Tunnel to NJ. Units 1 and 2 continuing moving surveillance on subject.

0608   Unit 1 advises subject Abernathy has exited vehicle at 50 Rock Road, Upper Montclair, NJ, and entered premises.

0615   Central advises location is reported to be residence of subject Abernathy parents.

0530   Units 1 and 2 remain on subject Abernathy in Upper Montclair. Unit 3 (Dets Gervaise and Timmerman) remains on fixed surveillance at subject Abernathy's West End Ave residence. (Note overtime since no meal taken.)

0542   Unit 3 observes Hispanic male newspaper carrier arrive and enter building with newspapers.

0551   Newspaper carrier exists without papers. Central advises no need to follow.

0715   Possible tenant (MW) exists West End Ave premises. Central advises no need to follow.

0729   2nd possible tenant (MW) exists. Central advises no need to follow.

0808   3rd and 4th possible tenants (MW & FW) exit. Central advises no need to follow.

0848   FW exists. Unit 3 recognizes this FW to be same possible prostitute who entered Sat. night, now looking a little worse for the wear! Hails and enters cab. Central advises no need to follow.

The surveillance log entries would continue for another thirty hours, recording numerous arrivals and departures at the West End Avenue address. But during all that time, there would be no further notations indicating any sightings of Dean Abernathy, either by Units 1 and 2 at the Upper Montclair residence of his parents, or by Unit 3 at the West End Avenue apartment building. In fact, shortly before midnight Sunday, Units 1 and 2 would note that the last lights inside the Upper Montclair house had just been turned off, an observation that would prompt them to report proudly to Central that they had just "put the subject to bed."

"Good work, men," would come the appreciative reply. "Stay on the house all night just in case he makes a move."

"Ten-four, Central," Unit 1 would answer back. "Don't worry, we're right on top of Mister Bigshot Lawyer."

Mister Bigshot Lawyer settled into the backseat of the cab, adjusting his skirt to cover his legs. They itched and had tiny scabs where he'd nicked them the night before.

"Where to, *miss?*" the driver asked him. Apparently his disguise was not quite so effective up close.

"Just take me down to Thirtieth Street," Dean said, deciding there was no need to disguise his voice. He was reasonably confident that the cab hadn't been followed, but to be on the safe side he would get out and check before hailing another cab. Dean knew from his own observations that, several hours earlier, two cars containing two men each had pulled out and followed Alan in the Jeep. Dean's instructions to Alan had been to take his pursuers for a little ride to the Upper Montclair home of their parents. There a bit of pressure on a remote-control device would open the garage door and permit Alan to pull the Jeep inside, closing the door behind him and entering the house through an inside doorway. Once inside, Alan was to remain there for at least forty-eight hours, during which time, it was safe to say, his presence could be expected to continue to occupy the attention of at least four members of the surveillance team, while at the same time reducing the attention level of any members remaining outside Dean's apartment building to nearly zero.

"Wouldn't you do better on Forty-second?" the cabbie asked him.

"Excuse me?"

"Thirtieth Street's for straight hookers, sweetie. The drag queens usually stick to Times Square."

In the backseat of the second cab Dean changed outfits, from drag to jeans and sweatshirt. Twice the driver came perilously close to totaling the cab, so intent was he on watching Dean's transformation in his rearview mirror that he ran several red lights and almost rear-ended a Trailways bus. Somehow they managed to arrive at their destination, the Lower East Side apartment building where David Leung lived.

Upstairs, David ushered Dean into his apartment. Somewhat warily, he eyed the dress and heels bunched in Dean's arms and the heavy bag slung over his shoulder.

"And here I thought I knew you."

"Very cute," Dean said, unloading everything into a pile on the floor.

"Don't tell me. You've figured out some new and different way to get us both killed?"

"Something like that," Dean smiled.

"I'm afraid to ask."

"Good," Dean said, collapsing into the only chair in sight. "The less you know, the better."

Dean wrote out a shopping list for David, who read it over in amazement but left without asking questions. Dean flicked on David's television, but it was too late for the Sunday-morning panel shows, and not yet time for any sports events. Unless you counted golf or bowling, which Dean didn't. He settled for a cable news channel, in time to catch a summary of local events, including an item that testimony would be beginning Monday morning in the "Wilson case," where an "ex-con" was being tried for the mugging murder of the former New York City Police Commissioner.

He smiled at the reminder that it would never be the "Spadafino case." He guessed there was a lesson of sorts to be learned there. Want to become a celebrity murderer, you better pick unknown victims. Then you had a fighting chance to grab your little piece of immortality, to have your case remembered under your own name, like a Ted Bundy or a David Berkowitz or a Joel Rifkin. Make the mistake of picking a famous target and it would always be the Lindbergh kidnapping or the Martin Luther King assassination. In Joey Spadafino's case, it already seemed it would always be the Wilson murder.

It was late in the afternoon when David returned with the items Dean had sent him out for. David watched as Dean added them to those he had brought to the apartment, and seemed about ready to comment when Dean silenced him.

"Ask me no questions, I'll tell you no lies."

"Is there anything else I can do?" David asked.

"Yes, actually," Dean said. "About midnight tonight, you can drive me to Hoboken."

"Clams?"

"Not exactly."

David drove them through the Holland Tunnel to Hoboken. Then, with Dean wearing sunglasses and a bandanna tied over his head, they located Dawson Street and took a quick run past number 555. It was a nondescript seven-story redbrick office building in a commercial district. Dean noted that the building was centrally air-conditioned, with vents set into the brick work; that the mortar joints separating the bricks were slightly recessed; and that there were masonry ledges that extended out from the building line both above and below each window.

A soft rain began to fall shortly after one in the morning, just enough to cause David to turn on the windshield wipers. The black pavement turned shiny and reflected streaks of light, and the tires made a comforting hissing sound on it. For Dean the change in the weather was both good news and bad. The rain would make his job both more dangerous and less so: more so because of the poorer traction it would produce, and less so because of a phenomenon well known to every cat burglar who ever lived—people have a natural tendancy to avoid looking upward in rain.

It was just before two in the morning when David finally dropped Dean off at the corner of Dawson and Second Streets in Hoboken. Dean waited until David was out of sight before beginning the three-block walk that would take him back to 555 Dawson Street. He would have made a somewhat curious sight to anyone happening to notice him, in his red-and-gray suede ankle boots with their exaggerated black soles, toes, and sides, a duffel bag slung over one shoulder, and something looking remarkably like a long boat hook in his hand. Only there was no one around to notice him.

He reached Fifth Street, where the 500 numbers began. He spotted 555, the middle of a row of three seven-story buildings. Although there were hallway lights that dimly illuminated some of the stairwells, none of the windows was brightly enough lit to suggest any activity within. While 555 contained a number of large office windows, there was only a single vertical row of smaller frosted windows that would correspond to bathrooms. Dean stared at the one on the top floor for a few minutes. Then he circled around to the alley behind the buildings.

He crouched down and opened his duffel bag. He found his harness on top, and he stepped into it and fastened it. He placed his coiled rope over one shoulder and across his body; over that, and in the opposite direction, he slipped a sling containing lengths of webbing to which were fitted carabiners and various sizes of S-hooks. Taking the boat hook in one hand, he moved to one of the buildings adjacent to 555 to begin the climb of his life.

It had been raining lightly for several hours, and the first thing Dean did was to test the building wall. He placed the sole of one climbing shoe against it and tried to slide his foot up and down. The sole came free with moderate pressure, telling him that he could expect little help in the way of friction on his ascent.

He wanted to spend as little time as necessary at street level, so he quickly settled on a route that would lead him up between windows on one of the outer buildings.

He shoved the boat hook down his back, underneath the rope and sling, in order to free both of his hands for climbing. Then, using the ritualistic language of the climber as talisman rather than communication, he whispered the word *climbing* to himself and grasped the top edge of a brick above him.

The first dozen feet or so were easy enough. Dean took advantage of the masonry that surrounded the back doorway, using it for handholds while wedging the sides of his shoes into the joints that separated the rows of bricks. At fifteen feet he encountered his first problem. Standing on the cornice above the door, he was unable to find a handhold within reach that would permit him to continue higher. The nearest solid feature above him was a window ledge four or five feet higher, but it was far enough above him that it would require an all-out lunge and appeared to slope downward slightly, promising a poor handhold in the wet conditions. If he lunged for it and missed—or was lucky enough to grab it only to have his fingers slip off it—the result would be a fall all the way to the pavement below, since Dean was free-climbing, with no one belaying him to catch him in case of a fall.

Dean strained his eyes toward the window above him, squinting to keep the rain from obscuring his vision. He visually followed a line up from the lower corner of the glass until he saw what he was looking for, two-thirds of the way up the window frame: a restraining eye for a window washer's safety belt. Reaching behind him, he lifted the boat hook loose, got a good grip on its handle, and extended it upward toward his target. When the metal hook reached the eye, he probed it gently until he felt the hook drop into the opening. Then he tested the arrangement by applying some weight against it. He was careful not to use too much weight, knowing that the aluminum hook could easily straighten or the plastic handle slip off the pole. Instead, he held the boat hook in his right hand and used it tentatively, as an extension of his arm, while climbing toward the eye with his free left hand and both of his feet. As he neared the eye, he gradually slid his hand up higher on the pole, until he was able to release it altogether and place his hand over its hooked end, which was still safely threaded through the safety eye. He took a deep breath, the first one he'd been conscious of since starting from the bottom.

Once he was secured at the edge of the window ledge, Dean unhooked the boat hook, replaced it at his back, and free-climbed to the top of the window. There he repeated the process he'd used earlier, withdrawing the boat hook from behind him, hooking it to the safety eye of the next window above, and climbing to where his hook had found the safety eye.

So this was "buildering," thought Dean, remembering the first time he had heard the term and smiled at its clever derivation from the name "bouldering," given to the practice of scrambling over the largest of rocks. Its enthusiasts hailed it as the ultimate in urban climbing, while its critics faulted its repetitiveness: while Nature throws an always-varying series of challenges at those who tackle her heights, a building presents the same problem repeated over and over again, from bottom to top. But it was that very sameness that now enabled Dean to continue upward. Having once solved the problem, he found that the problem simply repeated itself at each window, and he realized that the headline grabbers who scaled tall buildings were less true climbers than competent problem solvers with an overdose of ambition and endurance.

As he continued upward, Dean pretended that he was climbing one of the World Trade Towers. He got into the rhythm of using the boat hook, storing it behind his back, climbing without it, and retrieving it once again when he needed it. And the climb to the top might have been an uninterrupted exercise in repetition had he not got careless.

Climbing accidents, Dean had once read, rarely occur at the crux move of an ascent. At such times the climber is fully concentrating on his craft and summoning all of his abilities, both mental and physical, to pull him through a perceived test of his outer limits. Instead, acccients almost invariably happen at that moment when the climber least expects them—when the very ease of the pitch has caused him to lower his guard and allow his thoughts to wander.

In Dean's case, it might have been his fantasy of scaling one of the Twin Towers. It might have been the relative ease with which he'd climbed from ground level to the second, third, and fourth floors, or the sense of automatic pilot that took over as he reached the fifth, sixth, and seventh. Whatever it was, when it struck, it struck loud and clear.

Standing on the top of the seventh-floor window, with only the overhang of the roof above him, Dean reached behind him for the boat hook, knowing it would be a simple matter to extend it upward, hook it over the edge of the roof itself, and climb the seven or eight feet above him to the top. He withdrew the boat hook, which he'd stored hook-upward on his back as before so it couldn't slide off his back. In clearing it from his back and bringing it alongside him, he rotated it downward, so that the hook portion ended up beneath him, as before. But whereas on each previous occasion Dean had been careful to swing the pole 180 degrees to get the hook end above him before pressing the shaft against the building and securing it there with one knee while he changed his grip on it, now he simply used the pressure of his hand against the building to hold the pole there while he rotated that same hand. In an unforgiving instant, the smooth shaft somehow eluded his grasp and slipped away from him.

There was a second or two of silence, followed by a clanging sound from the pavement below.

Dean froze in panic, his first fear being discovery from the noise. He knew he had no quick move he could make, a fact that resigned him to waiting motionless, sixty-five feet above street level, to see if anyone would come out to investigate. He decided to wait five to ten minutes, compromised on seven. He began counting slowly, silently, figuring he'd give it to four hundred. He thought the counting would serve to occupy him and eliminate any thoughts of falling, but it somehow failed to prevent him from shivering, which—he tried to rationalize—could easily be the result of either the wetness of his clothing or the fatigue brought on by the climb itself.

He counted off an extra minute to be sure no one was responding to the noise, and another minute after that for good measure. Then he told himself he was stalling and needed to get to work.

A climber stuck on a wall faces a dilemma. He knows it's a mistake to make a move beyond his capability. At the same time, the longer he stays put, the greater his fatigue becomes and he runs the risk of becoming so tired that he can no longer successfully accomplish a move he might have been able to do when first he found himself in trouble.

So Dean took stock of his situation. He knew he had two basic options. He could retreat to the windowsill and place an S-hook in the safety eye below him, attach himself to it by several lengths of webbing. That way, if he fell while trying to reach the roof, he'd be caught after a fall of twenty feet or so—if the contraption held. There were several problems with this choice, the first of which was the dangerous climb down to the windowsill, aggravated by the slippery condition of the west brick. After that, there was the unreliability of the safety eye: It was made to hold a stationary body at rest, not catch a falling one already hurtling by a thirty-two feet per second squared.

The only remaining option was to suck it up and go for it.

He looked up from his stance atop the seventh-floor window. The roof presented a classic overhang, maybe six feet above his head. He thought of Doug's Roof, a prototypical overhang route in the Gunks, and tried to remember whether it was a 5.10 or a 5.11. He remembered that wet conditions generally reduced a climber's ability by at least two full grade points. He looked to his left. Nothing. To his right. Was that a bit of movement in the dark? He blinked hard to clear the water from his eyes and peered into the blackness. There, perhaps eight or ten feet away, was a wire of some sort, a black cable or electric cord running up the side of the building and disappearing above the overhang.

And in that instant he knew that whatever it was, he had to go for it.

A traverse is often easier than an ascent, because the traverser, in moving laterally, doesn't defy gravity to the same extent as the ascender. But the traverser needs nonetheless to cling to the surface every bit as tenaciously as the ascender. With no rope to catch him or to permit him to pendulum back and forth in ever-increasing arcs, Dean knew he'd have to walk across the window cornice and somehow reach the next window over without falling.

"Here goes nothing," he muttered under his breath, and began the easy part. When he reached the far edge of the cornice, he faced the wall, dug his fingertips into the groove between two rows of brick, and did the same with the toes of his climbing shoes, making certain to place his feet high enough so that his rear end extended well out away from the wall.

The beginning climber has a natural tendency to want to flatten his body against the vertical surface as much as possible, in an attempt to adhere to it. But such a stance has precisely the opposite effect: His weight is directed straight downward to his feet, forcing him off the cliff. The knowledgeable climber instead assumes a crouched position, butt stuck way out behind him, so that his weight will be transferred at an angle to the vertical surface in front of him.

Thus positioned, Dean inched to his right, moving only one foot or one hand at any time, leaving him three points of contact with the brick. When he got close enough to reach the next cornice, he used his right foot to step on it. Then he walked across it to its right side, the side closest to the wire.

Still he couldn't reach the cable. But by unclipping from his sling a length of webbing with an S-hook attached to it, he was able to snag the wire on the third try and pull it to him.

He inspected the wire, more by touch than sight. It appeared to be a coaxial cable, the sort used by the television cable companies. It was plastic-coated and slick from the rain, but by looping it twice around his hand Dean was able to get a good grip on it. Then, after a barely audible *climbing*, he began walking up the brick to the overhang.

Coaxial cable is, at its best, not made to support weight. Moreover, the coaxial cable that had offered itself to Dean was old and rotten, having long ago been replaced by underground wiring as Hoboken became gentrified and yuppified. By the time it broke, Dean had reached the underside of the overhang. He had just grasped a rounded piece of rough concrete between the thumb and fingers of his left hand, and was in the process of pulling the entire weight of his body upward, sharing the burden equally between his grasp of the concrete with his left hand and his hold on the cable with his right, when the cable tore free. The result was a transfer of all of Dean's weight to the left-hand grip, accentuated by a sudden and violent swing of his body to the left. He felt his head bang into something hard, and he instantly knew his forehead was cut open, but somehow his fingers held, his arm fully extended, his feet kicking wildly beneath him. He let go of the useless cable in his right hand, and with nothing else within reach, used that hand to seize his own left wrist. The maneuver served to take no weight off Dean's fingers, but it did cause his body to rotate back toward the building, and he was able to plant first one, then both feet against the brick without slipping. Thus stabilized, he was able to loosen his right hand from his left wrist and grope desperately for a second handhold with it, up and out on the farthest extension of the overhang.

Some handholds, the learning climber is taught, are characterized in route descriptions as "minimal," a term one might use in referring to a hairline crack in a rock wall just good enough to contribute to holding the body in place, in conjunction with the efforts of the other hand and both feet; the shallow joints between the bricks afforded an example of just such a hold. Better handholds are classified anywhere from "fair" or "moderate" to "good" or "excellent," with their dependability increasing in direct proportion to the positive nature of the nomenclature. At the very top of the list is what climbers call the "bombproof" handhold, a term borrowed from the military lexicon to describe a hold so strong and secure that a climber would be justified in supporting his entire weight on it with a single hand, free to use his remaining hand and both feet in any way he wishes.

It was such a hold that Dean's right hand found on the overhang, and he knew it instantly. Despite the fact that he couldn't see it, the sheer pleasure of feeling it in his hand caused him to almost laugh out loud. With a whispered "Oh, yeah!" he grasped both hands around it and pulled his body out and away from the brick wall and up over the protrusion. With the rain meeting him like a welcoming party, Dean swung first one foot over and onto the roof, then the other, until he lay facedown at the very edge. Then, by lifting the upper portion of his body as though to begin a push-up, he worked his way away from the edge and toward the center of the rooftop. He kissed the wet asphalt surface, surprised at its warmth and salty taste, until he remembered his forehead. He wiped it with the back of his hand; it was wet and warm and stung to the touch, and he knew he was probably bleeding pretty freely.

But he had made it.

Knowing the rooftop was also the ceiling of the seventh floor, Dean realized he couldn't afford to make a sound. He stood up, got his bearings, and tiptoed to the airspace that separated the building he had climbed from the center building he needed to get to. He judged the gap to be about ten feet, a distance he knew he could clear with a running jump, but not without landing heavily—and therefore noisily—on the center roof. So he slipped his sling off one should and his rope off the other. Uncoiling thirty feet or rope, he fashioned a large, double-stranded lasso, using a mariner's square knot, which would permit the lasso to slip tight and then hold. For extra precaution, he fashioned a knot at the very tip of the rope so that the aptly named "bitter end" couldn't slip through the square knot.

He might have been good at knots, but he would have made one lousy cowboy, Dean decided. It took him a full dozen tosses—time enough for a whole herd to scatter—before the loop of his lasso found the small brick chimney that was his target. He pulled the doubled rope tight, replaced the unused portion over his shoulder, covered that with his sling, and moved to the edge of the roof. By wrapping the doubled rope around his back belay-style, he created a rappel system that would permit him to jump from his roof and land, not noisily on top of the center roof, but silently against the side of the center building.

He made the move almost flawlessly, rotating only slightly in midair, but managing nonetheless to break the impact with the soles of his shoes and the flex of his knees. Then, cheating a bit by using the rope as a climbing aid, he pulled himself up and onto the roof of the center building.

Dean untied his lasso and tiptoed to the front of the building, knowing that any sound could give him away. By leaning over the edge, he could just about make out the small frosted window beneath him and to his right.

He found another chimney, also brick, but more centrally located than the first. He uncoiled the full length of his rope, knowing he'd need its full length to fashion a double-stranded rappel that would reach the ground. Afraid to use his flashlight to locate the midpoint of the rope by sight, he instead placed the two ends together and, by running the two strands through a fist as one, eventually reached what had to be the midpoint. Marking that point by tying a short piece of webbing there, he repeated the process in reverse, this time working from the marked spot back to the ends. Satisfied, he knotted the ends together, providing a crude braking device in case he ran out of rope on the way down. Better to know it by being brought to a stop at a point close enough to the bottom to permit a careful drop the rest of the way than to unwittingly rappel beyond the rope, a sure prescription for a bone-crushing landing.

He knew it would be an easy matter to rappel down to the seventh floor. There would be a slight traverse to get to the correct window, but that would be simple enough to pendulum to. He had no idea how long it would take Janet to squeeze through the window—he knew it would have been physically impossible for him to do it with his larger frame, but she was considerably smaller, and he had no doubts about her determination to accomplish the impossible. The rest of the rappel down should take less than a minute, with the danger being a too-rapid descent due to the combination of Janet's additional weight and the reduction in friction that the wetness would have on the rope. Anticipating these problems, Dean had hooked up a figure eight as a braking device, and had brought along an old pair of ski gloves to protect his hands from burning on the rope on the way down. For this was going to be no slow, rope-protecting rappel: Dean knew the window could be alarmed, and they might have only seconds to get down and away.

He attached a carabiner with a brake-bar to the system, just in case they needed additional friction to slow them on the way down. But he couldn't engage the device yet. Too much friction in the system would prevent him from descending to the window.

He put on his gloves. Once again he worried about the possibility of an alarm. He hoped that the sheer narrowness of the window would have caused Janet's guards to deem it unnecessary. He cursed himself silently for not having looked for wires when he'd had a chance to inspect it from inside.

He lowered the knotted ends of the rope down the building toward the pavement below. He felt them go slack, the way a fisherman feels his line go slack when his sinker has reached the bottom of a lake. He had no way of knowing in the darkness if his knot had found the sidewalk or snagged on some obstacle above it. But he was reluctant to shake the rope, for fear of the noise it could make slapping against something. He tested the portion of the rope above him, eliminating any slack between himself and the chimney. He tried to think if he'd missed anything. He mopped his forehead with the back of his hand. It came away warm and slippery, and he knew he must still be bleeding.

He moved to the edge of the building, then stepped up onto an overhang identical to the one he had scaled before. He placed his empty duffel bag underneath the rope where it met the overhang, to protect the rope from abrasion. Leaning his full weight against the doubled rope in front of him and securely holding the portion that ran around his body tightly against his chest, he backed to the very edge of the overhang. Felt the moment of terror run through his body as he leaned back into a stance virtually perpendicular to the side of the building. Opened his arm away from his chest until the decrease in friction allowed the rope to begin slipping. And started walking down like a human fly.

As always, the fear vanished immediately. The figure eight supplied him all the friction he needed, and he lowered himself easily to the seventh floor. He located the only small window and tied himself fast to his rappel rope so that he would descend no farther.

He rapped on the window three times, trying his best to do it just hard enough to be heard inside, but nowhere else. He waited a bit. He realized the noise had probably been insufficient to wake Janet if she was asleep, but he was afraid to do it any louder. He rapped again, and again he waited. Still no sign of Janet. He checked his bearings. This was the only small window on the entire seventh floor; it had to be the right one. He rapped once more. Still nothing.

Moving on to Plan B, Dean reached into his pocket and withdrew a glass cutter, one of the items he'd put on David Leung's shopping list. He'd earlier tied a length of cord onto it, and now he clipped one end of that onto his belt so that he wouldn't lose it if he dropped it.

Back in his college days Dean had worked one summer for a picture-framing and matting store and had become fairly proficient with a glass cutter. It was a simple enough tool, a rigid metal handle that held a tiny wheel made of industrial-quality diamond. By running the wheel crisply and cleanly across the surface of glass, he'd learned how to score the glass so that subsequent pressure would cause it to break cleanly along the score line. The trick was that you had to score the glass properly on the first try. There was no margin of error, no such thing as a "do over," because you could never duplicate the score line exactly.

Of course, all that had been many years ago, and Dean had no idea if he still had his touch. He hoped it was like riding a bicycle. But even if it was, the score he needed to make now was a circular one, something he'd done no more than two or three times.

With a small ice pick, also courtesy of David Leung, Dean gouged a tiny indentation into the center of the windowpane. Next he unclipped the glass cutter and looped its cord over the shaft of the ice pick. The device he'd thus created crudely resembled the sort of a geometry compass a draftsman used to draw a circle. Keeping the cord taut and the glass cutter perpendicular to the window, Dean traced a 360-degree arc, all the while exerting even pressure against the glass. The tiny diamond wheel seemed to end up pretty much where it had begun, leaving a circle some seven or eight inches in diameter.

Dean pocketed his equipment, changing it for two large rubber suction cups. These were the items that had kept David out shopping until late the previous afternoon, until finally he'd located them as part of a toddler's toy set. Gently Dean now attached them to the glass, just inside the circle he'd scored. When he pressed them firmly against the already wet glass, they held tightly. Then, by alternately pulling on one while pushing on the other, he worked the circle of glass until it made a barely perceptible crunch and came free from the rest of the pane.

He moved his face to the hole he'd created in the window.

"Pssst," he hissed.

And waited.

Almost immediately, he heard movement inside. After a moment, Janet's face filled the hole.

"Window service," he said.

"What time is it?" she asked, rubbing her eyes.

"I risk my life to save you and all you want to know is what *time* it is?"

"Sorry," she said, smiling. "I was asleep."

"I know. Open the window," he told her. "And be careful, that round edge is razor sharp."

She pushed the window up. He handed her the circle of glass and she disappeared with it. She was back a moment later.

"My God," she whispered. "What happened to your head?"

"Shhh. I'm okay. But you're never going to fit through this."

And it was true. The opening was absurdly small, high enough now with the cut-out window pushed all the way up and out of the way, but perhaps only nine or ten inches wide. Dean fought off a feeling of panic that his effort had been for nothing: There was absolutely no way a person could fit through it. But she seemed ready to give it her best.

He watched helplessly as she tried, first one way and then another, to push herself through the impossibly narrow frame. First a shoulder would refuse to fit through, then an elbow wouldn't bend the proper way. Just when it seemed she might finally manage to squeeze her upper half through, her sweatshirt bunched up and she had to give up, twisting her body and pulling it back inside and out of sight.

When he next saw her, it was her head and one hand that emerged first. She pointed directly at Dean, then used her hand to cover her eyes, an unmistakable signal that Dean should close his. Then, without waiting for him to comply, she began squirming out of the window as before. This time, however, every inch of progress gradually revealed that she was totally naked and that in place of her clothing she had rubbed some sort of oily substance over the entire length of her body.

And it worked. Where before she had fought against the bulk and friction of her clothes, now Janet eased through the opening. As Dean lowered himself to catch her, she locked her arms around his neck and rotated herself to permit him to pull her hips through the window by pushing his feet against the building on either side. As she came free, he wrapped his own arms tightly around her back, while she scissored his body with her legs, both of them holding on as tightly as possible to avoid her slippng through his grasp. Face to face, Dean could see the fright in her eyes as he freed one hand to lower them on the rappel. Knowing he had to try to calm her to keep her from panicking, he could think of nothing to whisper to her but "I love you."

"Then please don't let me die," came her return whisper.

The effect of the rain on Janet's body seemed to make it even more slippery, but she held on with a death grip. They were halfway down when he whispered to her, "What *is* this stuff?"

"Soap."

But as slippery as Janet's body was, it was also light, and her grip never relaxed on the way down, enabling Dean to concentrate on controlling the descent on the rappel line. They touched bottom without running out of rope, and Janet released him.

Freeing himself from the rope, Dean grabbed Janet's hand and led her, still naked, across the street and into the shadow of a parked truck. There he removed his sling, pulled his filthy, soaked sweatshirt off, and handed it to Janet. She turned up her nose at it but put it on, smiling in gratitude that it was long enough to cover her. Then, motioning her to follow in the rain, he retraced his earlier route to rendezvous with David Leung and their getaway car.

The drive back into the city was something of a blur to Dean. He and Janet rode in the back, wrapped in old wool blankets from the trunk. David aimed the car through the early-morning rain, the windshield wipers slapping noisily. Dean woke from time to time, aware at one point that Janet was wrapping something around his forehead and looking at him with what seemed like concern. He shifted positions and slipped back into sleep. . . .

The hotel was a trifle too fancy for Dean's taste, and he wondered briefly how they were going to pay for it, but he was in no condition to argue. David went up to the front desk to register for them with fictitious names, then helped them up to their room on the second floor while an idle bellboy muttered something about "cheap tourists" and, looking at the blankets they were wrapped in, followed it up with "fucking Indians."

"Okay," David said to Dean once they were inside the room, "I'm outa here."

"Thanks, David," Dean said, and the two hugged tightly. When David stepped back he said, "Jesus, Dean, take a shower, willya?" Then he waved good-bye to Janet, who was still wrapped in her blanket and had curled herself up in an overstuffed chair.

Dean unzipped the overnight bag David had brought in from the trunk of his car. He found his toiletry kit, excused himself, and went into the bathroom to take David's advice.

He was startled by his reflection in the mirror. Even with his forehead wrapped in what appeared to be a torn strip of blanket, he looked positively frightening, like a crazed army commando who'd charged out of the pages of some comic book. Grime and blood smeared his cheeks. An ugly bruise had turned one side of his head an angry purple, flecked with patches of brighter red.

Gingerly, he peeled the strip from his forehead, wincing as it lifted pieces of dried blood off with it. Underneath was a four-inch gash worthy of a low-budget horror film, far too melodramatic to be real. In spite of himself, Dean found himself fascinated by it, and he studied it from several angles, even stepping back from the mirror at one point so he could admire it with the light hitting it better. Some secret part of him delighted in just how terrible it looked, a badge worthy of his heroism.

And in that moment, gloating at the bizarre reflection in front of him, he was suddenly struck by the enormous absurdity of what he'd done in the past several hours. He'd located the beautiful heroine held hostage in a secret castle in a foreign state, nearly fallen to his death while scaling a vertical wall to rescue her, then slid down with her naked body in his arms. Even as his knees suddenly went so weak that he had to grasp the sink in front of him with both hands for support, he began laughing at the sheer insanity of what he'd put himself—and Janet—through. And all for a worthless, homeless, two-bit, ex-con drug addict who was too goddamn stubborn or stupid or selfish or whatever to walk out the doors of the jail even after they'd been flung wide open.

"Are you okay in there?" It was Janet calling to him from the bedroom. Dean hadn't been aware he was laughing out loud.

"Yeah, I'm okay," Dean called back. But the face in the mirror kept grinning at him, and his wounds kept telling him it had really happened.

The warm water of the shower stung his forehead but felt good against his body, and the grime began to run toward the drain in visible streaks. He was surprised at the number of places where he ached to the touch, and at the incredible amount of dirt that still covered him. But when he reached for the soap, he discovered that there was none. None in the shower, none out on the sink. None of those tiny, cutely wrapped scented soaps with names like English Heather and Windsong and Marigold Bouquet that hotels always seemed to have an inexhaustible supply of.

"Janet?" he called out.

"Yes?"

"Is there any soap out there?"

He took her silence to mean that she was looking, and the delay following it as an indication of failure. But a moment later she was in the shower beside him, once again in her rappelling outfit.

"I figure I've got enough for both of us," she said, as her skin began to glisten and bubble up in the spray.

The next few minutes established Janet's clear superiority over all of those cutely wrapped soaps. She proved generous as she rubbed her body against Dean's, careful not to touch the worst of his wounds. She even created sufficient lather for them to shampoo each other's hair. For Dean, the effect proved far more than cleansing, as Janet was quick to notice. Looking down at one point, she laughed, "Oh sure! But where was that guy when I was looking for something extra to grab on to on the way down the rope?"

While Janet toweled off and announced that she was going inside to take the pick of his dry clothes, Dean stood at the mirror again, dabbing at his forehead. The bleeding, which had earlier stopped, had resumed from the shower water.

When he walked into the bedroom, a towel wrapped around his waist and tissues matted to his forehead, Janet was sitting on the bed, her back against the headboard, her knees drawn up against her chest. She was wearing a pair of Dean's jeans and a blue dress shirt of his, both of which were much too large for her. And she was crying softly.

Dean walked to the bed and sat down on the edge of it. He waited for her to speak.

"I need my baby," she said simply.

"Nicole's fine," Dean assured her. "I spoke to your sister—"

"I know," Janet sobbed. "But I need her *now*." And as though to prove her point, she lowered her knees to show Dean the front of his shirt, which she had completely wet through over the area of one breast. Her sobs mingled with laughs, and she finally allowed Dean to pull her to a standing position so together they could take Dean's shirt off her. Janet used only one hand because she needed the other to keep Dean's jeans from falling off her hips. As they both laughed, she gave up the battle for modesty, opting instead to pull Dean's towel off just as his jeans slipped to her ankles. They fell to the bed, facing each other on their knees. They touched first with fingertips, then with lips. As their kiss lingered and intensified, some ancient hormonal response seemed to send a quiver through the length of Janet's body and cause a sound deep in her throat. Dean felt his own chest dampen. He looked down in time to see the thinnest stream of bluish white spurt form Janet's nipple to his own body. It was surprisingly warm.

He looked back up and caught her eyes with his own. She didn't look away. "What does it taste like?" he asked her.

"It's sweet," she said. "Very sweet." And she touched her index finger to her nipple, then held the finger up to his lips for him to taste, and she was right. He felt himself grow hard again from the exquisiteness of the moment. He lowered his head and gently put his lips to her nipple and heard the same sound coming from her throat, now almost like an animal's purr. He felt the tiny stream of her milk spurt into his mouth, and he tasted its sweetness.

The sensation only made him harder still, and for a fleeting moment he was afraid his body might be doing something terrible by reacting, might be somehow violating Motherhood. But just as suddenly he felt her hands reach up between his legs and close so snugly and excrutiatingly around all of him that was there that he cried out, startling them both.

They made love hungrily, desperately, as though they were afraid they might never get another chance.

When finally they pulled apart, fighting for air, their bodies shiny with sweat, they didn't speak, listening instead to each other's breathing. It was Dean who finally spoke first.

"There's one thing I need to ask you," he said.

"Uh-oh," Janet said. "This sounds bad."

"No."

"Not bad?"

"Not bad," Dean assured her.

"Okay, go ahead," she said, pulling herself closer to him.

"Well, it's just that you've been separated from Nicole for like a week now, right?"

"Right." Janet nodded. She still seemed to be having difficulty breathing and speaking at the same time.

"Yet you still—" And here Dean ran out of words and touched the underside of one of Janet's breasts.

"I pumped."

"Excuse me?"

"Pumped." And by way of demonstrating, she cupped her hand around the same breast and pretended to squeeze it.

"Wow" was all that Dean could think of to say.

"You never heard of pumping?"

"Sure I've heard of pumping," Dean said. "I mean like tires and balloons. Rafts."

"Gas," Janet chimed in.

"Iron."

"So?"

"Well," Dean said, "I just never knew you could, ah pump—"

"Breasts, Dean. They're called breasts." But smiling gently at him.

"I knew that. Breasts."

"Ever hear of cows?" she asked him.

"Cows pump, too?"

"Dean?"

"Yes?"

"Shut up."

They made love again, but more slowly this time, more gently. Gone was the urgency, gone the groping. Now it was all soft and tender and easy. And when at last they fell asleep, it was wrapped in each other's arms.

THIRTY-THREE

The first light filtering through the curtains awakened Dean and summoned him back to the reality that it was Monday morning and only hours until he would be giving his opening statement.

They showered again, somewhat less eventfully than the first time. Afterward Janet tended to Dean's forehead, trying to make the scab look a bit less frightening.

"Now it's my turn to ask you a question," she said.

He was caught off guard by the seriousness in her voice, but he figured he owed her honest answers. "Go ahead," he said.

"How long have you been shaving your legs?"

"Never mind." He smiled.

Dean's blue shirt had dried, and Janet wore it tucked into his jeans, which she belted at the waist with his necktie. The overall impression she made was one of a street urchin dressed in grownup's clothing. They divided up the remainder of Dean's few things as best as they could. Janet promised to take a cab to a girl-friend's house, where she would hide out for a few more days until the trial played itself out one way or another. Dean would head to his office, where he kept a change of clothes he could slip into before going to court.

"You be careful," Janet whispered.

"I will be," he said, kissing the tip of her nose. "There's only one problem."

"What's that?"

"What am I going to use for soap?"

Dean arrived at his office around eight. He noticed that someone hadn't double locked the outer door again, and as he let himself in he couldn't help wondering if he'd find Walter Bingham waiting for him inside.

Bingham wasn't waiting, but a far nastier surprise was. Before he even reached the door to his room, Dean could see that the place had been trashed. Furniture was knocked over, file cabinets pulled open, drawers emptied and overturned on the floor. Books and papers were strewn about as though a tornado had ripped through the office, with his desk as ground zero. His clothes tree had been knocked over and the two suits that had been on it were ripped apart. This was no ordinary burglary, Dean knew immediately. Whoever had done it hadn't been content to just look for cash or stamps or whatever it was office burglars took; they'd gone on to vandalize and destroy everything in sight.

Dean righted his desk chair and sat down heavily. He cursed whichever of his suitemates had been in over the weekend and had left without remembering to double lock the outer door. Whoever it had been deserved this to a certain extent, perhaps, but Dean sure didn't.

And as he sat there trying to take some measure of satisfaction from the fact that the careless party had no doubt suffered as much as he had, a sudden chill came over him.

Slowly he stood up. He picked his way through the debris and out the door of his room. From the central corridor, he gently nudged open the door to the room next to his and peered inside. Everything was in place, every book in order. He went to the next door and opened it. Neat as a pin. A hollow feeling in his stomach told him he wasn't going to have to check any other rooms.

And just about then, he knew what had happened.

He walked back to his own room and looked at the couch. Instead of being flush against the wall, it had been pulled out a foot or so at one end. He went over to it and kneeled on it in order to reach down behind it. But even before he did so, he knew full well that he would find nothing there. Certainly no envelope marked AMMUNITION.

The elation that Dean had felt back at the hotel gave way to a sense of exhaustion and overwhelming depression. Only hours ago he'd been on top of the world. His rescue of Janet had freed him to go forward at Joey's trial, able to pull out all the stops without having to fear that the police would retaliate against Janet. But just when he thought he was home free, they'd managed to take everything away from him. For what chance did he have now of demonstrating the conspiracy without the physical evidence— the forged signatures, the dibenzepene findings, and the letters from Officer Santana?

First they'd tried to appeal to his conscience in order to avoid a trial. Then they'd kidnapped Janet, threatening to kill her. Next they'd made Joey and him an offer too good to refuse. And now, just when he'd finally managed to even the playing field, they'd broken into his office and stolen his evidence.

For the first time, Dean was aware how terribly his head ached.

Joey Spadafino's head doesn't ache, but his insides still do. He's led across the bridge a little before eight-thirty. He's been up most of the night. Not 'cause of the pain—he can live with that. More 'cause he's been thinking.

Miriam, one of the secretaries in Dean's suite, was the first to find him sitting in his room. By then it was after nine-thirty.

"My God! What happened?" she wanted to know, her stare alternating between his head and the chaos in which he sat.

"Earthquake."

She inspected his forehead. "Are you all right?"

"Yeah, I guess so."

"Aren't you supposed to be in court?"

"Yup."

"You can't go. You need to get to a hospital. Do you want me to call the court?" she asked. "Or go over and tell them you can't make it today?"

Dean thought of Judge Rothwax and how he'd already extended himself by allowing Dean the weekend before requiring him to make his opening statement. He knew his choice was between getting to court or a hospital emergency room. And court was closer.

"No," he said, "I'll be all right." Then, following her glance at the shorts and sneakers he still had on, he added, "I guess I need to find some clothes, though."

She went up front and returned a few minutes later with a suit that had been hanging in the storage closet. From the looks of its shiny fabric and narrow lapels, Dean guessed it had been there for a good ten years. No matter. It was all Miriam had been able to find, so it would have to do.

He found a pair of shoes and a belt that had withstood the attack. He was less lucky when it came to a shirt: the best he could find was a badly torn one.

Ten minutes later he stood in front of a full-length mirror on the back of his office door and assessed the situation. The suit hadn't turned out to be a suit after all. Instead it had proved to be a sport jacket and a pair of slacks that had nothing in common but the hanger they'd been sharing. The pants were corduroy, a faded purplish color and badly wrinkled, but at least they fit him. The jacket, a grayish green tweed, was a different story. Although he managed to get it on, it was clear it had once belonged to a jockey. The shoulders threatened to rip at any moment, the sleeves barely covered his elbows, and the front panels had no hope of ever meeting in the middle.

He'd selected his widest tie to cover the tear in his shirt. The former happened to be a red paisley, the latter blue denim. His black shoes looked okay, though his white sweat socks did set them off a bit harshly.

Then there was his raw, scabbed forehead and the large purple bruise on the side of his head.

"Pretty dapper, huh?" he said to his reflection.

It didn't smile back.

Joey Spadafino sits in the feeder pen alongside the courtroom, waiting for Dean to come to see him, as Dean always does right before they go into court. Joey's been thinking. Maybe he's wrong to go through with the trial after all. He's had the whole weekend to think about it, and what he's been thinking is that maybe he's being stupid. Maybe he should take the time served after all. At

*least he's reached the point where he'd like to talk it over one
more time with Dean.*

But Dean doesn't show up.

*Finally, about quarter after ten, they bring Joey into court
and sit him down. The judge is there and the DA, but no Dean.
He tries to ask a court officer what's going on, but no one'll tell
him anything.*

*About ten minutes go by. Then the judge looks at the clock
and says in an angry voice, "Let the record reflect it is now ten-
thirty. Bring in the jury."*

*When the jurors enter, it takes a few seconds for them to no-
tice that Dean isn't there. As soon as they realize, they start whispering among themselves like little children.*

"Goodmorning, jurors," says the judge.

They say good morning back to him. Like school.

*"Apparently we're going to be delayed for a little while" is
all he tells them.*

It was almost a quarter to eleven by the time Dean got to the courthouse, making him more than an hour late, ordinarily a surefire
prescription for a contempt citation from Harold Rothwax, who'd
been known to throw lawyers in jail for far lesser transgressions.
While Dean figured that his physical appearance alone would go a
long way to explain things, what bothered him most was that he
was back to square one. While the reason was different, without
his physical evidence he was in no better position to make his
opening than he had been Friday afternoon. What was he going to
tell Judge Rothwax this time? That he couldn't go forward because his head ached? He could imagine the judge's sarcastic response, reserved for just such occasions: "I can assure you,
Counselor, that your headache is a matter of lasting indifference
to me."

What he hadn't figured on was that by the time he entered
the courtroom, everyone—including the jury—would be present
and waiting for him. Apparently Judge Rothwax had decided to
dramatize Dean's lateness by forcing everyone to sit in their
places pending his arrival.

As Dean came through the door, every head in the courtroom—and it was packed to standing capacity—swiveled to look

at him. He hesitated for a second, then started to make his way up the aisle, his hands hanging empty at his sides, his head bloody and bruised, wearing an outfit that could charitably be described as uncoordinated and ill-fitting hand-me-downs. He was aware of an audible, collective gasp.

Still he walked forward, up to the rail that separated the audience section from the lawyers' well. Every pair of eyes followed him. At the far end of the room Judge Rothwax peered at him over rimless reading glasses from the bench. A television camera with a red light on top of it followed his progress. On both sides of the aisle, Dean's peripheral vision spotted familiar faces: There were the men he still thought of as Leo Silvestri, Bennett Childs, and Bobby McGrane, and several others he recognized from those who'd been following him for the past week or so. Up at the prosecutor's table, Walter Bingham had swung around and was shaking his head slowly from side to side. Even Joey Spadafino had turned in his seat at the defense table, his mouth hanging open in disbelief.

Joey sits in his chair waiting, trying to figure out what's going on, angry that they're not telling him. But that's the way it works, he knows. He's come to realize that of all the people in the courtroom, he's the one who matters least—he's just the defendant.

Just then there's a noise from the back of the courtroom, way behind Joey. Next thing, everybody's looking back there. Joey tries to turn in his chair, but the court officers keep his chair pushed up so close to the table it's hard for him to see what's going on. There's some kind of a commotion at the doorway, he can tell, and people in the courtroom start whispering, so it sounds like the whole room is buzzing. He hears the judge banging his wooden hammer, but no one seems to be paying attention. What Joey sees finally is someone coming up the aisle, a man with a big bandage on his forehead, wearing a suit that looks like he slept in it for a week. The man continues up the aisle, getting within arm's length of Joey before he realizes it's Dean.

At the rail, a court officer unhooked the chain for Dean and admitted him to the well. He was aware that Judge Rothwax was saying something to him, because he could see the judge's mouth moving and his hand gesturing Dean to come forward. But for some reason he couldn't hear what the judge was saying. There was too much noise—some sort of a commotion behind Dean. He turned to see what was happening.

What he sees is someone trying to rush up the center aisle, and others—he can make out Leo Silvestri and Bobby McGrane among them—are moving to restrain the person, trying to hold him back. But just when it seems they've got him tackled, he breaks free. Only Dean can see now it isn't a he at all—it's a woman, a dark-haired Hispanic woman, who slips through them and runs all the way to the chain before it stops her in her tracks, her momentum doubling her over at the waist. As Judge Rothwax bangs his gavel on the bench, the woman's pursuers catch up to her. Assisted by court officers, they grab at her flailing arms in an effort to subdue her, but at the last moment she cries out *"Mira! Mira!"* and flings something in Dean's direction. Reflexively, he raises his hands, as though to shield himself, but whatever it is comes directly at him, and he ends up catching it, feeling a heavy paper package landing in his hands.

"It's a bomb!" somebody yells, and Dean hears screaming.

"Look out!" someone else shouts. There is bedlam.

A court officer rushes over to Dean and reaches for the package, and Dean extends it toward him with both hands, his eyes riveted on it, absolutely certain it's going to blow up in his hands any second—

And sees the letter S pasted on it.

Just as the officer grabs for it, Dean pulls it slightly to one side so that the officer grabs nothing but air. Dean runs his hands over the package and makes out the shape of a thick book of some sort. Other people reach him, but he twists around in such a way as to place his body between them and the package. And begins to tear it open as quickly as he can.

He's right, of course. It's a book, a large black book, totally blank on the outside. Everyone around him stops. Somebody calls out that it's okay, it isn't a bomb. Eventually, the hysteria begins to subside, and the banging of Judge Rothwax's gavel can be heard again. The room gradually quiets down.

A single sheet of paper has slipped from the package to the floor, and Dean stoops to retrieve it. It is a letter, printed in a childish hand. Balanced on one knee, he reads it to himself.

Dear Mr. Lawyer,
  My husband give this to me when he is still alive.
He said if ever any thing happen to him I give it to the
mans lawyer.

                                        Marisol Santana

He opens the book to the first page, and sees only three words,

THE BRADY FILE

before his eyes fill with tears and the words blur. For a moment he
feels so lightheaded that he has to place one palm on the floor for
extra balance. The other hand he uses to tuck his prize under his
arm like a running back would protect a football. Then, slowly, he
rises to his feet. He is the hero who's recovered the fumble in the
closing seconds to save the victory. He extends his free hand as if
to straight-arm away anyone who would get too close to him. For
this is the game ball, and it's his alone.

Those who are closest to him react by backing away from
him warily, all the while staring at him as though he's gone completely mad. Order eventually returns to the room. The woman
has been removed, everyone else returns to their seats, and quiet
is restored.

This time Dean is able to hear what Judge Rothwax is asking
him.

"Mr. Abernathy, would you like a recess before we resume?
Under the circumstances—"

"No," he says. "That won't be necessary."

"Do you wish to make an opening statement on behalf of the
defendant?"

"Yes, I do." He rises, clutching the book in both hands. He
makes his way to the podium that faces the jury box. He clears his
throat, and takes a deep breath. And tells himself that he can do
this, that he's done it a hundred times before.

"This case," he begins, his voice cracking at first, "is much
more than a murder case. It involves not merely one death, but
several. Not just a single death that appears to have occurred during some botched-up mugging attempt, but an entire series of
cold, calculated, premeditated murders." His voice grows
stronger. "For this case is about a conspiracy, a conspiracy that

reaches into the very highest levels of the New York Police Department."

He pauses to let that sink in. There is silence in the room—absolute, stone-cold silence.

"You see, Edward Wilson didn't die as the result of being mugged by Joey Spadafino or anybody else. He died because of a book. The name of the book is *The Brady File*. The authors of the book are police officers. It is a book that is at once so true and so powerful and so dangerous that ultimately the police officers who wrote it felt it necessary to murder people in order to try to prevent its publication. One of the people they murdered was Edward Wilson. He was their own leader, and your own Police Commissioner.

"And this," he says, holding it aloft, both arms extended full-length above his head, "this is the book."

He walks to the rail and looks out into the audience. "Now for some strange reason—I'm sure I don't know why—many of the officers who wrote the book and murdered Commissioner Wilson are seated right here in this courtroom at this very moment."

Almost as if on cue, they begin to rise, trying their best to cover their faces and make themselves invisible as they work their way toward the aisles: first Bennett Childs, then Leo Silvestri, then Bobby McGrane, followed by a half-dozen others. As they step into the aisles and hurry for the door, a single reporter rises tentatively from the first row and moves to follow them. He's joined by a second, and a third . . .

EPILOGUE

The actual trial in the case of the *People of the State of New York v. Joseph Spadafino* lasted only three days. Upon the motion of Assistant District Attorney Walter Bingham, a mistrial was declared. Since the defendant had by that time been officially placed in jeopardy, any retrial would have been prohibited by the double-jeopardy clause of the constitutions of both the United States and the State of New York, and Spadafino walked out of the courtroom a free man.

Of the twenty-two New York Police Department members who were arrested during the following weeks by federal agents operating under the direction of the United States Attorney for the Southern District of New York, thirteen were indicted. Inspector Barry Childress, also known as Bennett Childs, served the longest of the prison sentences handed out, just over eleven years. Five others received prison terms ranging from six months to seven years. True to Walter Bingham's prediction, there were two suicides. Lieutenant Vincent Nomelini, aka Leo Silvestri, blew off the top of his head with a blast from a shotgun inserted in his mouth, and Det. Richard Rasmussen was killed when his personal vehicle crashed into an overpass abutment the night before his trial was scheduled to start. The speedometer on his car had stuck at 114 miles per hour. Detective Robert Gervaise, aka Bobby Mc-Grane, fled to Ireland and has not been apprehended to this date.

The Spadafino case was the last trial for Dean Abernathy. He spent six weeks recovering from the injuries he had sustained while rescuing Janet Killian.

Dean, Janet, and Nicole entered the Federal Witness Protection Program run by the United States Marshal Service and remained in it for close to two years. Today the three of them live together under new names at an undisclosed location somewhere in the southwestern United States, where Dean writes and teaches, and where Janet has resumed her nursing career.

Walter Bingham was rewarded for his role in prosecuting the conspirators by being appointed a New York City Criminal Court Judge. Despite Bingham's worst fears, the prison doors were never thrown open to the likes of David Billups, Johnny Casado, and Richard Spraigue. The New York Court of Appeals ruled that while the Brady File revealed improprieties in many cases, no prisoners whose cases had already been reviewed on appeal could avail themselves of material contained in the file. While the ruling seemed to fly in the face of several decades of precedent and surprised many in legal circles, most observers breathed a collective sigh of relief. Some accused the court of playing politics, and several appeals were taken to the United States Supreme Court, which, in the end, declined to consider the cases on the grounds that it was a matter of interpretation of state law better left for the state courts to decide.

Joey Spadafino lived in New Jersey with his mother for the first several months of his freedom. Gradually, he became restless and began spending less time with her and more on the streets of New York City. Nineteen months to the day of his release, he was shot and killed in a minor drug deal on Fourteenth Street.